'We've got a long w

Jane. *'I've waited so lc*

feel as happy and as cc

knife: we mustn't forget that.'

* * *

When the police cautiously entered the office Jennifer was sitting on the floor with Gerald Lomax's body cradled in her arms, weeping uncontrollably. She looked up and, her voice broken by sobs, said, 'He's dead. Stabbed. Please help me.'

As they separated her from the dead man the photograph of Emily that Lomax always kept on his desk fell between them. It was encrusted with blood.

A Mind to Kill

Andrea Hart

A MIND TO KILL
A CORGI BOOK: 0 552 14622 6

First publication in Great Britain

PRINTING HISTORY
Corgi edition published 1998

All the characters in this book are fictitious, and any resemblance to actual persons, living or dead, is purely coincidental.

Set in 10/12 pt Sabon by
Deltatype Ltd, Birkenhead, Merseyside

Corgi Books are published by Transworld Publishers Ltd,
61–63 Uxbridge Road, London W5 5SA,
in Australia by Transworld Publishers (Australia) Pty Ltd,
15–25 Helles Avenue, Moorebank, NSW 2170
and in New Zealand by Transworld Publishers (NZ) Ltd,
3 William Pickering Drive, Albany, Auckland.

Reproduced, printed and bound in Great Britain by
Cox & Wyman Ltd, Reading, Berks.

To John Poulter, for
many things. And to
Julie, too.

Chapter One

Jennifer had never imagined in her wildest dreams that she could be this happy.

It went way beyond happiness. It wouldn't have made sense to anyone if she'd tried to put it into words, because there weren't words to express properly how she felt. The best she could do to describe it, and only to herself, was as a total completeness. Everything was complete. Her perfect life and her perfect marriage to a perfect husband and the most beautiful, most perfect baby in the world, all absolutely and totally complete. And secure, as if there was a wall between her and everyone else to keep out anything bad, as high and as protective as the wall encircling the mansion she'd just left.

Jennifer sometimes became frightened, like she was unsettled by the reflection now, although it was something else she never tried to explain to anyone, not wanting to be laughed at.

Her fear was that she – anyone – didn't have the right to be as lucky as she was, so secure, so sure of everything and everybody. Of herself.

That feeling was easier to rationalize than the overwhelming happiness. It was, she knew, a guilt she'd never ever be able to lose absolutely. She'd read all the newspaper reports and gone through everything with Gerald – so many times he'd grown angry and wouldn't talk about it any more – before finally accepting there was nothing to reproach herself for. So it wasn't that. It was the even earlier unease.

It had been there from the very start of the affair, the first night even, long before she'd ever fallen in love with Gerald and realized that it wasn't simply an affair after all. The moment, in fact, she'd decided she'd been stupid to become involved with a married man and that everything was going to end in the mess it had.

Not, of course, the tragedy that had actually occurred. And from which she'd emerged unscathed and uncriticized to her own very special, locked-away happiness. A happiness she still found hard to believe she deserved. Soon after the tragedy she had considered seeking psychiatric help, unable to accept Gerald's assurances by themselves, anxious for an unbiased, unemotional opinion.

But she hadn't. And now Jennifer was glad. She'd never found it easy – virtually impossible in fact – to talk about personal, intimate things even to people close to her; even to Gerald. The thought of exposing herself to a stranger, mentally stripping herself naked, had stopped her then and now it made her physically shudder just to think about it as she came to the turn off to the kindergarten.

Jennifer had to wait because of the traffic congestion on the London road, smiling at another thought. She guessed a psychiatrist would judge how she chose to lead a lot of her life now as that of someone seeking atonement. She had immersed herself in charities and contributed substantially to every appeal and fund-raising approach made to her. The charity thought reminded her that for the rest of the month – maybe longer – she probably wouldn't be able to collect Emily so regularly. Virtually everything was set up for the AIDS ball at Grosvenor House but Jennifer gave minute attention to every detail of anything she did or organized, seeking confirmation of confirmation, a habit she'd developed as the leading trader in Gerald's company before their marriage. Now she didn't trade any more – another lingering although very secret regret – she'd transferred her never-lose determination to another activity, to the benefit of people not as fortunate as herself. And there was still one item, the most important, not absolutely guaranteed. A lot of the intended success of the ball depended upon final confirmation of the Royal promise to attend. She'd give it another day or two before approaching the palace again.

What she did so well wasn't atonement, Jennifer knew. She had nothing to atone for. When her other commitments allowed she collected Emily herself, instead of delegating to the nanny, because she adored the child and wanted her always to feel as safe as she did. She contributed to fund-raising because Gerald could more than afford it and she organized charity events superbly well because it was a practical and worthwhile way of occupying her mind as well as passing on just a little of the good fortune she'd never believed it possible to have.

Jennifer managed the turn at last, hurrying the final few hundred metres when she saw some children already being bundled into cars.

Miss Singleton formed a physical barrier at the kindergarten entrance, not releasing any child until she recognized the parent or the nanny. The teacher beckoned Emily forward at Jennifer's arrival and announced, 'She's been a very clever girl today.'

Emily proudly held up the postcard of a cow and Jennifer entered into the solemnity of the moment, taking her time to read the handwritten declaration on the back that it had been awarded to Emily Lomax for recognizing the letter C.

'Wonderful!' Jennifer enthused. 'I'm very proud of you.'

'Will Daddy be?'

'I know he will.' They began to return to the car, Emily automatically reaching up for Jennifer's hand, waving with the other to various children who called to her.

'I've got a card in my bag. Sally's having a party next week. Can I go?'

'Of course.'

'She's four, like me.'

'But you were four three months ago.'

'Does that matter?'

Jennifer laughed. 'No.'

'She wants a dog. A real one.'

Jennifer carefully secured the child into the rear-facing safety seat, brushing the bundle of curls from her forehead and kissing her. 'Maybe if she's a good girl she'll get one.'

'She doesn't know what C means yet.'

'Perhaps she will by the time her birthday comes.'

'Why must I look backwards! I can't see you like this.'

'This way's safer.'

'No-one else in my class has to sit like this.'

'If there's an accident, you won't get hurt.' Although the gap was sufficient Jennifer waited until an approaching van passed before pulling out.

'Is there going to be an accident?'

'No.'

'Never?'

'Never,' promised Jennifer.

'Why can't I sit the other way then?'

Jennifer smiled. 'I think you're going to be a lawyer when you grow up.'

'What's a lawyer?'

'A very clever person.'

'Cleverer than Daddy?'

'No-one's cleverer than Daddy.'

'What are we doing after lunch?'

'What would you like to do?'

'Go to Marwell zoo and see the animals.'

'Then that's what we'll do.'

Jennifer was late triggering the remote control as she came off the London road and had to wait for the high security gates to open fully before she could start up the drive. It was several moments before the square Georgian house became visible, through the trees.

Annabelle was waiting, just inside the entrance.

'I've got a prize,' announced Emily, producing the postcard. 'For knowing what C is.'

'What is it?' asked the nanny.

'Cow,' declared the child.

'Well done!' praised the girl.

'We're going to Marwell this afternoon as a reward,' said Jennifer, as they walked down the corridor towards the rear kitchen.

'*We've got a long way to go. We'd better hurry,*' said Jane. '*I've waited so long, almost seven years, for you to feel as happy and as content as this. Oh, don't forget the knife: we mustn't forget that.*'

Chapter Two

The office had gained architectural awards and the City nickname of The Goldfish Bowl, to which Gerald Lomax, proud of their aggressive commodity record, added 'for piranha fish.' Built literally on the rubble of one of the IRA's worst City bombings that totally destroyed the original building in which Jennifer had worked, it was a glass-walled expanse bare except for banks of computer stations. Lomax's office was suspended above it against an inner wall, the side overlooking the trading floor also glassed from carpet to ceiling. So was the corridor from the elevator to Lomax's eyrie.

The goldfish bowl self-consciousness had long ago vanished so no-one on the trading floor noticed Jennifer emerge from the lift. Three did look up, curiously, at the noise she made tapping her knuckles against the glass as she walked towards her husband's room. Her left hand was buried deeply into her large, shoulder-strapped handbag.

Lomax raised his head, surprised, as she entered. 'Darling, I didn't . . .' he began.

'MURDERING BASTARD!'

The first, sweeping slash opened the left side of Gerald Lomax's face, from ear to chin. He threw himself backwards so hard his chair overturned, crashing into the see-through wall, but every trader below was already staring, transfixed, attracted by the screaming accusation.

'Jennifer . . . for God's sake . . . !'

Lomax was on his hands and knees when she stabbed him twice, in the back. He clawed upwards, levering against the desk, and she stabbed him through the hand, actually embedding the knife in the wood and Lomax punched her in the side of the face, splitting her lip, as she wrestled the blade free, then grabbed out for it as she did so to drive it upwards into her free hand.

'Jen . . .' For a moment they clung together, in a frenzied dance, but he was already weak from the cuts and stabs and she was easily able to get the knife back. The next slash was across his nose, almost severing it. Lomax hit the wall again, although remaining upright, but his eyes were flooded by the slashing blow and he couldn't see to protect himself any more.

'Don't, Jen . . . stop . . .'

She drove the knife into his stomach so forcefully the blade went completely through his body and hit the glass, twisting it out of her hand. Lomax actually pulled it from himself and struck wildly at her, hitting her in the arm, but she jerked it from his grasp again. This time she held it dagger-like, stabbing again and again, driving him back initially against the glass and then on to the ground. As he lay there, helpless, she stabbed and slashed more, her head thrown back as she laughed, hysterically.

Blood gouted from Lomax, spurting over the glass before dribbling down in wavering streaks. Finally, leaving the knife protruding from his back, Jennifer lurched exhausted to her feet and stood legs spread-eagled to overlook the trading floor, her outstretched hands pressed against the pane, more blood trickling down from her own wounds. For a moment she remained there, panting, before throwing her head back to laugh, over and over, lips tight against her teeth in a triumphant grimace.

When the police cautiously entered the office Jennifer was sitting on the floor with Gerald Lomax's body cradled in her arms, weeping uncontrollably. She looked up and, her voice broken by sobs, said, 'He's dead. Stabbed. Please help me.'

As they separated her from the dead man the photograph of Emily that Lomax always kept on his desk fell from between them. It was encrusted with blood.

Chapter Three

John Bentley liked murder but decided almost at once there wasn't going to be any personal benefit from this one. There would automatically be some publicity from Gerald Lomax being a millionaire City high-flyer and Bentley was ready to bet a mistress with big tits would emerge within forty-eight hours but it wasn't like the other twelve he'd solved without a single failure to justify the promotion to Detective Superintendent at the age of thirty-nine and the legend he worked so aggressively to maintain.

If there was anything at all remarkable about this one it was that it was virtually over before it began, an open and shut domestic stabbing in full view of sixteen credible witnesses.

The only thing to do was organize the routine, find the motive when he found the mistress and hope she had a pretty face as well as big tits for the photographers. It would still count as a success on his record, which was all that really mattered.

The ambulance paramedic, leaving his partner applying the emergency dressings to Jennifer's arm and hands, crossed towards Bentley. Gesturing down to the blood on his jacket the man said, 'She's badly cut. Needs suturing.

And she's in pretty deep shock.' He rubbed at the bloodstains. 'It's a bastard getting this stuff off.'

Bentley looked towards the vacant-eyed woman. 'Wouldn't believe she was capable of it, would you?'

'She did a pretty good job. The poor sod is cut and stabbed to buggery. Whatever he did, it upset her.'

A young pathologist whom Bentley didn't know was bent over the body, mumbling into a hand-held tape recorder

'It'll be sex. Classic syndrome,' predicted Bentley. He turned to two policewomen in the outer corridor. 'Go with her in the ambulance. I'll come later.'

Jennifer allowed herself to be laid on the stretcher trolley and Bentley stood aside for her to be wheeled past him. Her eyes were closed but there was a faint smile on her face.

'Call us when the body's ready to be moved,' said the ambulanceman as they went by.

Bentley nodded, staying to the side of the room for the overalled forensic team to enter. He recognized Anthony Billington at the head of the group: he'd worked with the obese man on three of the previous murders.

'All fairly straightforward?' said the scientist.

'Looks that way,' agreed Bentley.

'Shouldn't take us long.'

'Let's get everything, just the same.'

'We always do,' said Billington, curtly.

'I know,' placated Bentley. Fucking prima donna, he thought. The room was becoming crowded, so he went into the outer corridor. From there he looked down into the trading room. Malcolm Rodgers, his inspector, had everyone seated at their terminal stations, giving statements to attentive constables. It really was straightforward. If it hadn't been part of the routine there wouldn't have been any reason for his even being there.

The pathologist scuffed out of the office and immediately began stripping off his protective suit. He smiled at Bentley and said, 'Hewitt, Felix Hewitt.'

They shook hands. Bentley was a gaunt, tall man who towered over the medical examiner.

'Multiple stab wounds and extensive lacerations,' said the pathologist. 'I won't know until after the post-mortem, obviously, but I'd say at least five would have been fatal. Quite a concentration around the heart area, as if she was specifically hitting him there. That and the face. A lot of cuts there, like she was determined to disfigure him.'

'Hell hath no fury,' said Bentley.

'I haven't got much on, so I can let you have a report by tomorrow.'

'That'll be fine.'

Rodgers emerged from the lift for which the doctor was waiting to descend. Looking down towards the trading floor Rodgers said, 'First time I've known sixteen statements all saying the same thing in virtually the same words. This is going to be the easiest ever.' The two had worked on eight of the previous murders and spent a lot of time together socially. Their wives liked each other.

'No question about it,' agreed Bentley.

'It'll be another woman.'

'Guaranteed.'

'Flat here in London, country house in Hampshire where the little wife lives most of the time with the baby. While the cat's away, the mice play.'

'Wonder what the mistress will be like?'

'Classy,' guessed Rodgers. 'Lomax was loaded. He could afford the best.' He looked needlessly at a notebook. 'This is the second wife. Name's Jennifer. Worked in the firm to begin with. Brilliant, from what they said down there. First wife, Jane, died of an overdose.'

Bentley turned hopefully from looking down at the trading floor. 'Anything suspicious?'

The inspector shook his head. 'She was a diabetic. It was an insulin imbalance, according to what they're saying.'

'Was Lomax having an affair with this one while the first wife was alive?'

'For almost a year, apparently.'

'So he made a habit of it?'

'Seems that way: lucky bugger.'

From the doorway Billington said, 'We're through with the body. Can we get it out of the way?'

A uniformed policeman further along the corridor looked enquiringly at Bentley, who nodded and said, 'Please.' The policeman, glad of something to do, began talking into his radio.

'She said anything?' asked Rodgers.

'She's in shock, according to the paramedic. She'll know who the other woman is. We might as well go and find out.'

Both men were keen rugby fans and on the drive along the Embankment the conversation was about that Saturday's international between England and Wales. Both had tickets. Rodgers, whose mother had been born in Swansea, offered a £5 bet on Wales, which Bentley took. They gambled between each other a lot. Bentley usually won.

'If this had been a difficult one it could have buggered Saturday up,' suggested Rodgers, putting their Scotland Yard identification on the dashboard as he parked in a consultant's reserved space.

Jennifer was in a single ward. One of the policewomen outside the room rose at their approach and said, 'They did the stitching under local anaesthetic. And the doctor insists there's no shock. They're happy for her to be interviewed.'

The second policewoman made room for them as Bentley and Rodgers entered the tiny ward.

Bentley formally identified himself and Rodgers and then said, 'You're Jennifer Lomax?'

'Yes.'

'You know why we're here?'

'Gerald,' said the woman.

Hurriedly, anxious for everything to be kept in its proper routine sequence, Bentley recited the official caution before she could say anything more.

As he did so Jennifer frowned towards him, head curiously to one side.

'Have you got anything to say?' demanded Bentley.

'It wasn't me,' said Jennifer. 'It was Jane.'

Chapter Four

'*Trapped you, bitch!*' There was a laugh.

'Go away! Leave me alone.' Terror jarred through her. What had she done? It didn't make sense: nothing made sense. She didn't understand. She didn't know.

'*Of course you know!*'

'Go away!'

'*I will if I choose to. But won't if I don't. And there's nothing you can do about it! I can do whatever I like with you. You're mine.*'

'Why?' This wasn't happening: couldn't be happening. It was a dream, a horrible dream. A nightmare.

'*You know bloody well why.*'

'I don't. Honestly, I don't.' Jennifer squeezed her eyes shut, wanting to close everything out. Wanting most of all to close out the memory of Gerald's slashed and bloodied body.

'*Look at them. They all think you're mad. That's what everyone is going to think.*'

Jennifer did look, forcing herself, at the small ward window through which the two detectives she had refused to talk to without a solicitor being present were frowning in at her. And then at the two policewomen actually in the room with her. As she did so the elder, a sergeant, came forward and said, 'What's the problem, Mrs Lomax?'

'*See!*'

The tone that echoed in Jennifer's head, in the Southern drawl she had forgotten, was triumphant. To the policewoman Jennifer said, 'Nothing. I'm all right. Thank you.'

'*You're not. You're possessed. But no-one is going to believe you because there's no such thing as ghosts or possession, is there?*'

She could beat her, Jennifer decided: had to beat her, for Christ's sake! If Jane was in her mind then she could read her mind – had already shown she could – so she didn't have to speak: it was just appearing to talk to herself that would make people think she was mentally deranged.

'*Of course I know what you're thinking but that won't do. I told you, you're trapped: mine to do with what I want. And I will do what I want with you. So you'll say the words for people to hear and they'll decide you're insane.*'

'Why?' implored Jennifer, aloud and unable to stop herself. She'd spoken! No! No! No!

'*You murdered me, you and Gerald. Bastards!*'

The accusation ended in a scream and Jennifer physically winced at the sound in her head. 'I didn't! We didn't! It was an accident! You did it yourself: an accidental overdose.'

'*LIAR!*'

It was a roar this time and Jennifer winced again and the woman sergeant came forward once more. 'Mrs Lomax?'

'I'm all right, really.' Both hands and her left arm were

heavily bandaged; a saline drip needle was strapped to her right hand. To gesture, which she did slightly, genuinely hurt. 'The anaesthetic is wearing off.'

'Do you want me to call a nurse? Or a doctor?'

'It's not that bad.'

'*You can't begin to believe how bad it's going to get.*'

Jennifer remained tight lipped. She had to think! Work it out. But she couldn't think without Jane – the voice – knowing what those thoughts were.

'*Don't sit there like a little child, all puckered up. You've got to learn there's nothing you can do to stop me.*'

'I'll find a way,' said Jennifer, falling back against the supporting pillows, feeling the strength drain from herself. Don't give up! Couldn't give up!

'*Of course you can't give up. That's going to be part of the fun. My fun. Maybe you'll even go genuinely mad, trying to beat me.*'

'I will beat you,' insisted Jennifer.

'*I know you'll try. Wasn't that what attracted Gerald in the first place, the Jennifer Stone implacable determination to win in all things . . . even husband stealing!*'

'We'll see who's the stronger.' She needed help. But who?

'*Indeed we will!*'

Jennifer was drawn again to the ward window by the arrival of more people.

'*And here is your solicitor,*' announced Jane.

It was.

There were, in fact, two. Geoffrey Johnson, who led their way into the ward, was the family lawyer, a plump, usually smiling man who smoked oddly shaped and carved pipes and drove a vintage Bentley. That evening he wasn't smiling. Momentarily he stood beside the bed, twitching towards a handshake he didn't complete when he saw her bandages. Equally unsure of how to greet Jennifer, he instead at once introduced the other man as Humphrey Perry.

'Criminal law isn't my field,' he apologized. 'Humphrey's our senior partner on the crime side.'

Perry was a tall, doleful-faced man with a hedge of black hair encircling a polished bald, egg-domed head. Unlike Johnson, whose suit was muted check, Perry wore a lawyer's uniform of black striped trousers with black jacket and waistcoat, complete with a looped gold watch-chain. As he pulled forward the chair just vacated by the woman police sergeant, now outside talking to the two detectives, Jennifer saw that Perry had very long, skeletal fingers. At the end of the introduction he moved his head in acknowledgement but didn't immediately speak. He didn't smile, either.

'*They're frightened of you.*'

'Shut up!' No! Shouldn't have spoken; given a reply.

'What?' frowned Perry. He had a deep, sonorous voice.

'I wasn't talking to you,' said Jennifer. Then, 'Oh God!' She hesitated. In a rush she blurted, 'You are going to think I am mad but I am not. I know people saw me kill Gerald but it wasn't me. It was Jane. She's possessed me.'

Johnson coughed and looked down at the floor. Perry remained expressionless, taking a large legal notepad from a very scuffed briefcase. He said, 'Who's Jane?'

'Lomax's first wife,' mumbled Johnson, still head bent. 'She was diabetic. Died of an insulin overdose six years ago.'

Knowing she was blushing, fighting against the absurd impulse to giggle, Jennifer said, 'She says I murdered her.

That we both did, Gerald and I. Which we didn't. It's ridiculous.'

Perry spent several moments ensuring the lead from a silver propelling pencil protruded to precisely the length he wanted. 'And Jane talks to you?'

Jennifer slumped back against the pillows again, closing her eyes against reality because this couldn't be real. 'I told you you'd think I was mad.'

'*They do! They do!*'

'She says you do,' said Jennifer, dully, feeling a wash of exhaustion.

'She's talking to you now?' persisted Perry.

'Yes.'

'How?'

'In my head.'

'You hear a voice?'

'Oh, dear God!' wailed Jennifer, desperately, realizing how it was all sounding to the two men. 'Help me! Please help me!'

'I will, Mrs Lomax. I truly will. But you must tell me what happened. What you can remember.'

'I can remember everything.' She had to concentrate; be rational with this rational, expressionless man.

'Good. So tell me. From the very beginning. From the time you got up this morning.'

Jennifer didn't speak immediately, then became horrifyingly aware that she was sitting with her head to one side as if trying to hear something being said to her. She straightened, abruptly, conscious that both men had noticed. As strongly and as positively as she was able she said, 'Gerald wasn't at home last night. He stayed here in London at the flat. But he called this morning to talk to me and to Emily. He always did when he didn't come home. I drove Emily to playschool and then arranged tonight's supper with our housekeeper; Gerald was coming home tonight. It was lamb. Welsh. Gerald liked lamb . . .' There was a sudden surge of emotion, choking her. She coughed, scrubbing a bandaged hand across her eyes. 'He's dead . . . Gerald's dead . . .'

Johnson looked wildly around the room, as if seeking help. Perry remained unmoving, one immaculate leg crossed over the other, notebook balanced on his knee. It was Perry who spoke. 'Do you want a doctor?'

Jennifer shook her head, not replying.

'You discussed dinner, with the housekeeper?' encouraged Perry.

Jagged-voiced, Jennifer said, 'Playschool ends at noon. I went to collect Emily. I usually do, unless I'm here in London, with Gerald. I was a little late. Emily had got a prize for learning her letters. I promised to take her to the zoo as a reward . . .' She trailed away, her shoulders beginning to heave again.

'Did you?' pressed Perry, not wanting a break.

Jennifer shook her head but didn't answer. She felt lost, falling into darkness, her stomach hollowed.

'Why not?'

'Jane told me to get a knife.'

'And?'

'To come to London.'

'Do you remember doing that?'

'Yes. But it wasn't as if I was driving.'

'What was it like?'

'As if I was a passenger.'

'Was Jane talking to you during the drive?'

'No.'

'What happened when you got to your husband's office?'

'I'm not sure.'

'You said you could remember everything.'

'I thought I could.'

'Tell me as much as you can.'

'We parked the car . . .'

'. . . We?' interrupted Perry.

'Yes,' repeated Jennifer, distantly. 'We parked the car. I remember going into the building. Getting into the lift. Then I was covered in blood. Bleeding myself. And Gerald was dead.'

'You don't remember the killing?'

'No.' Just the blood, blood all over Gerald. He was dead: wonderful, darling Gerald was dead.

'Or doing it?'

It took longer this time for Jennifer to stop crying. She sobbed into the bandaged hand – hurting herself with the tug of the saline needle trying to bring her other hand up to her face – managing to mumble a protest only when she heard Johnson say to the other lawyer that he thought they should call someone. 'I'm all right. I want to go on.'

'You don't remember doing it?' repeated the criminal lawyer, relentlessly.

'No.'

'Nothing at all?'

'No.'

'You were bleeding yourself,' prompted Perry.

'There were policemen. And ambulancemen. They put me on a stretcher and brought me here.'

'*Very good!*'

Jennifer whimpered, suddenly jerking back as if pulling away from something.

'What?' demanded Perry.

'She's mocking me again.'

'Again?'

'She's been doing it, ever since I got here.'

'*Tell-tale tit, your tongue will split and all the little puppy dogs will get a little bit.*'

'When was the first time you heard Jane's voice?' asked the lawyer.

'Today.'

'Never, ever, before?'

'No.' She *was* mad! Had to be. This couldn't be happening to any sane person. None of it. If she closed her eyes really tightly it would all go away. No, Jennifer corrected. Not a dream. A nightmare. Real. Horribly, terrifyingly real.

'Are you under any medical care, Mrs Lomax? Before your admission here, I mean.'

'No,' said Jennifer, tightly, knowing the question had to be asked but resenting it.

'I could check, obviously: will have to, in fact.'

'I want you to,' said Jennifer, hurriedly. 'I want you to check with everybody you can to know that I have never in my life suffered any psychiatric illness and that Gerald and I were idyllically happy.'

'I will, Mrs Lomax.'

'Good!' said Jennifer, in brief defiance. It slipped at once. 'You think I'm mad, don't you?'

'No. And if I am going to represent you and brief counsel on your behalf I shall never lie to you,' lied the lawyer.

'Not mad but a liar, about hearing voices!'

'I was setting out my position,' avoided the man.

'So what's your answer to my question?'

'I think you are suffering a mental illness, yes.'

'*I've won! I've won!*'

'I am not mentally deranged!' Wouldn't give in: couldn't give in.

'Will you agree to a psychiatric examination?'

'I demand a psychiatric examination.'

Perry retracted his pencil point with the care with which he had exposed it and closed the notebook. As he did so, Jennifer saw he had apparently made several pages of notes.

The lawyer said, 'I don't want any statement made to the police: I'll tell them that. You will be arraigned before a magistrate, initially for the formality of a remand, in custody. There will be no question of bail, so I won't bother to apply for it. In the circumstances, I will ask for that remand to be in a prison hospital wing when you're fit enough to leave here. Magistrates cannot try a case like this.'

'*I want you to suffer the whole process!*'

'I don't give a damn what you want,' said Jennifer. To Perry she explained, 'Jane says she wants me to suffer everything.'

The lawyer nodded, showing no surprise. 'You wish me to engage counsel?'

'The best you can get.'

'Is there anything else I can do?'

'What's happening to Emily?' How could she have forgotten Emily until now!

Instead of replying, Perry looked sideways to the other solicitor. Johnson said, 'She's being well looked after by the nanny.'

'I want to see her.'

'At the moment that's not possible. Maybe even not advisable,' refused Perry.

'When?'

'I don't know,' admitted the bald-headed man, maintaining the promise of honesty. 'Maybe not for quite a long time.'

* * *

In the corridor outside John Bentley accepted with a philosophical shrug the lawyer's refusal to allow a statement, sure he knew a way to get around it. Beside his superior, Malcolm Rodgers gestured to the policewomen re-entering the ward and said, 'According to them all she does is talk to herself. Madder than a March hare.'

'Or a bloody sight cleverer than one,' challenged Bentley.

'Meaning?' queried Perry.

'Voices in her head! Possessed by the first wife, seeking revenge! Come on! You ever seen a better performance for a plea of diminished responsibility?' demanded Bentley

'No,' conceded the lawyer. 'But why kill him in the first place?'

'When I find the woman Lomax was screwing I'll tell you,' promised the detective. In the few hours since seeing Jennifer Lomax hunched beside the blood-soaked body of her husband Bentley had changed his mind about this being a case with no personal benefit. His intuition, which he usually followed, told him otherwise. It wasn't intuition that convinced him Lomax had a mistress, though. That was good old hard-assed experience. All he had to do was shake the trees and he knew how to do that, too.

Back inside the tiny ward, Jane said, '*Just think what it's going to be like, shut up in an asylum with genuinely mad people for the rest of your life.*'

'Stop it!' screamed Jennifer.

'*And that's the way to get there.*'

Chapter Five

The role of chamberlain was created in medieval European courts, establishing the most important functionary in any royal household. A chamberlain was the buffer, and passport, to any king or queen. With his promoting approval, eager courtiers were guaranteed title, fame and wealth. By his obstructing disapproval, anxious fortune-hunters were forever doomed to oblivion and poverty.

Today there are few European royal courts and those chamberlains that remain do so largely in power-empty office from which they emerge bewigged, gartered and plumed for ceremonial occasions, in between which they shuffle back to memories of bygone ages and absolute authority rivalling that of the monarchs their predecessors served.

England is one of those few European countries in which a monarchy and the office of chamberlain still exist, one more of doubtful ceremonial value than the other. There are, however, four other very active courts in which operate chamberlains whose sacrosanct judgement is absolute and whose unwritten laws are as unchallengeable as their interpretation of enshrined British legislation.

They are the Inns of Court and the chamberlains of their members disdain any title loftier than clerk. They need nothing higher than that, which every sensible barrister knows. Those that don't, learn fast enough. Or leave for other professions.

Bert (as christened, not Bertram) Feltham was the chief clerk of the Temple chambers of Sir Richard Proudfoot, QC, a fiefdom he ran with a ruthlessness that had been enviously likened by lesser chief clerks in other chambers to that of the principles by which the Borgias operated and Machiavelli would have admired. He submitted briefs to his barristers before formal acceptance, as protocol required, but every one of the chamber's eight Queen's Counsel – including Proudfoot himself – knew Feltham had vetted the case and personally selected to whom it would be presented in advance of the first discussion. And there was never any discussion about anything whatsoever that Feltham considered unsuitable. He selected his submitting solicitors with the care with which he accepted their cases. It was a network that had developed over twenty years and worked after so long more by instinct than by legal formalities. Those honoured with Feltham's ex-directory home telephone number knew automatically what might be 'something for Bert'. Those that didn't have the knack only had the office number and Feltham rarely accepted their calls.

Humphrey Perry had the home number and he rang it that night from the car phone, before leaving the hospital grounds.

'You can't be serious!' protested Feltham. He had asthma and wheezed.

'Wouldn't you like to hear about it?'

There was a long pause. 'You know I don't like wasting my time. And this is wasting my time.'

Perry felt a bubble of uncertainty, despite being in

what he considered an assured bargaining position. 'You have to eat lunch somewhere.'

'I'm on a diet.'

'Smoked salmon and Puligny Montrachet. El Vino. Tomorrow, twelve-thirty, before it gets crowded.'

'I'm not going to take it.'

'Let's just have lunch then. It's been a while.'

'Don't be late.'

Perry arrived early to secure a basement table in the corner; the wine was already open when Feltham entered precisely at half past twelve. He was a man in need of a diet: case discussion usually began over lunch. His face had the reddening of blood pressure, too. It was an inverted snobbery – some even said Feltham's personal joke – to reject the dark-suited uniform of law in the way he dressed. Today the brass-buttoned sports jacket was brown and black striped, with fawn trousers. The shirt collar was button down. There were perfunctory handshakes. Perry poured the wine.

As he did so he said, 'You did well with the Hallett case.' There was a ritual that had to be performed, but today there was reason additional to the expected flattery.

'It was predictable we'd win.' The case of Peregrine Hallett was the most recent *cause célèbre*: Sir Richard Proudfoot himself had defended the society financier with minor royal friends against a charge of share-rigging a company take-over, exposed a flaw in the 1987 Banking Act that now needed Parliamentary legislation to correct, and gained Hallett an acquittal with costs and a public apology from the trial judge.

'Not to most.' It would have been Feltham who'd judged the potential from the beginning.

'All good for the chamber,' wheezed Feltham, reciting the inviolable credo. He did order smoked salmon, although a double portion, with a salad he soaked in dressing and a side order of new potatoes.

'How's the diet going?'

'Slowly. There was a lot of press coverage about your business in the papers this morning.'

'Attractive woman, isn't she?' Although there was no need for him to diet, Perry limited himself to a single order of smoked salmon, without extras.

'I'm not interested, Humphrey.'

'She's the beautiful wife of a millionaire commodity trader.'

'Whom, according to what you told me last night and what I read this morning, she killed because she's a menopausal paranoid schizophrenic obeying the voice of his first wife.'

'I didn't say she was menopausal. She isn't.'

'The rest is more than sufficient.' Feltham added more dressing to what salad remained.

'You know John Bentley?'

Feltham nodded. 'Headline hunter.'

'Good copper though. Best murder track record in the Met.'

'This isn't going to be one he's proud of.'

'He thinks there's another woman. And that the voice in the head is all bullshit, a prepared-in-advance defence.'

Feltham looked disappointedly at his empty plate. 'It doesn't matter which way you present it, Jennifer Lomax murdered her husband in front of sixteen people. She's *guilty*. I'm not into formal pleas of mitigation and you know it. I'm surprised you called me, I really am.' He nodded to cheese and port, vintage Warre in preference to the Dow.

'She wants the best.'

'She wants a miracle. Why are you trying so hard?'

'Lomax's American parent put all their European business through our corporate division.'

Feltham nodded. 'I sympathize. And understand. And I'd do it as a favour, if it were possible. But look at it objectively, from my point of view. Even if the voice in her head is bullshit, we couldn't win! I don't take cases that are lost before they begin. I wouldn't put this to any of my seniors. They trust me. They'd think I was the one who'd gone mad.'

'You did do well with Hallett.'

Feltham looked steadily across the table for several moments. 'We've already talked about that.'

'There's an Exchange inquiry going on, into some copper dealings Lomax fronted for some Far East dealers.'

'How did it go wrong?'

'A Tokyo dealer got over-extended. Went on buying to cover his losses, with money he didn't have. Persuaded the finance minister in Bolivia to use government money for a private portfolio they asked Lomax to set up.'

'Was Lomax part of it?'

'No.'

'Sure?'

'Absolutely.'

'But it'll go to court here?'

'Inevitably.'

'How long?'

'I'd say it'll run for three months. Maybe four. Some Lichtenstein royalty were conned. And a Hollywood producer.'

'High profile as well as a good earner?'

'Guaranteed.'

Feltham sighed. 'So we've got a problem.'

'One that can surely be resolved.'

'My seniors trust me,' repeated Feltham. 'It's a matter of integrity.'

'I understand,' said Perry, who did and saw nothing hypocritical or even odd in Feltham's remark. 'What about Jeremy Hall?'

Feltham smiled. 'You stay on top of things.'

'We both do,' said Perry, smiling back. Jeremy Hall was the newest arrival at Sir Richard Proudfoot's chambers, the first barrister in ten years whose acceptance hadn't been subject to Feltham's veto. Hall was Proudfoot's nephew.

'He's under my care.'

'Aren't all your people?'

'Special care.' Feltham gestured for a second port.

'At its worst, she's mad,' said Perry. 'She herself is demanding a psychiatric examination so we'll know soon enough. At its best, it's a cleverly planned murder. All right, so it's guilty, whichever. But the money's guaranteed and if there is another woman he'll be able to push the spurned wife defence. And she *is* beautiful, so the publicity to the chambers is as assured as the fee. It wouldn't hurt just occasionally to be on the side of the underdog, would it?'

'She cut him to pieces, according to this morning's papers!'

'Temporary insanity. All part of the same mitigation.'

'I'm still not totally happy.'

'I'm not saying it's perfect.'

'How much prelim work would be involved in the copper case?'

'Two months, minimum.'

'And the case would run for four?'

'At least. It'll be very worthwhile.'

'I'd have to explain the Lomax brief to Sir Richard.'

'Of course.'

'He was very pleased at the way the Hallett thing turned out.'

'I've heard the Lord Chancellor was impressed.'

'Sir Richard would make a good judge,' agreed Feltham, smiling in acknowledgement of Perry's preparation. 'I'd be sorry to lose him, of course.'

'Of course,' agreed Perry. 'The chamber accepting an obvious guilty plea wouldn't go against the consideration, would it? The contrary, in fact.'

Feltham smiled again. 'Good point, well made.'

'Are we agreed then?'

'I think so. I'm sorry if I was brusque at the beginning.'

Perry shook his head in dismissal. 'What's Hall like?'

'Young. A little brash. Good pass marks. Not a bad court presence. It'll improve when I've trained him up. Special case, as I said. Father was a Name at Lloyds: family was wiped out by the insurance crash. The old man killed himself. Sir Richard let Hall into the chambers literally as an act of charity: he didn't have any money to go anywhere else.'

'Riches to rags?' smiled the bald-headed man.

'Something like that,' said Feltham, unimpressed by the attempted joke. 'When's the remand hearing?'

'This afternoon, at the hospital.'

'You want him to be there?'

Perry gave another dismissive gesture. 'It'll only be a formality.'

'Properly handled, there will be some mileage in it for the chambers, won't there?'

'I'll look after him,' promised Perry.

'It's been a good lunch. Thank you.'

'Best of luck with the diet.'

'Thanks.' Feltham rose but remained standing at the table. 'Unwinnable cases are a bastard, aren't they?'

'An absolute bastard,' agreed Perry.

'All sixteen?' queried Rodgers.

'Until I get the name,' insisted Bentley. 'The place *is* a fucking goldfish bowl. Someone will know who he was screwing, like they knew he was popping Jennifer while his first wife was alive.'

'When do you want to start?'

'Directly after the magistrate's hearing. It'll be up and down, five minutes at the most.'

'You want me to warn Lomax's office?'

'No,' said Bentley. 'Let's surprise them.'

Chapter Six

Jennifer was totally exhausted, eyes sunk into black-ringed hollows, skin so numb it tingled and was sensitive to touch, as if it had been burned. It was a constant effort in the daylight to retain the consciousness she'd wanted so desperately to lose during the night but hadn't been able to. Because of the drip it hurt to reach up with her right hand and the bandages on her left made it difficult to knuckle the drooping tiredness away even to see around her. The hospital doctor, Peter Lloyd, had refused to give her the stimulant she'd asked for, saying it would counteract the painkillers she was having. He'd done so standing well back from the bed when Jane had made her call the man an awkward bastard. It had been Lloyd, whom she thought looked too young to be a doctor, who'd given her the time of the magistrate's arrival and she'd tried, before Humphrey Perry came, to tidy herself with a brush and make-up but she couldn't control the shake any more. Her lipstick had smudged, unevenly, and she'd had to stop where her lip was swollen and split and the liner was a mistake on eyes already too dark. The tears, when she'd cried from frustration as well as grief, had made the mascara run and she hadn't been able to clean properly the marks from her face and knew she looked dirty and unwashed.

'She wouldn't let me sleep. Not at all. She kept on at me all night,' Jennifer announced, as the solicitor came into her room. She saw one of the two departing policewomen shaking her head.

'Do what I like, do what I like!'

'It's all right.' Perry didn't think he'd shown any reaction but supposed there must have been something. He felt a twitch of pity, despite what she'd done: mentally sick people weren't responsible for their actions, however horrifying.

'It's not! I look like a mad woman.'

'You sure do, honey.'

Perry didn't think he would have recognized the gaunt, cadaverous-faced woman lying on the bed in front of him as the svelte, sophisticated person photographed and named as Jennifer Lomax in that morning's newspapers. If she continued to look like this it would contribute to the only plea it was possible to enter. 'It'll only last a few minutes today.'

'I've got to stop her! You've got to help me stop her.'

'You can't! Neither can he!'

'I will,' promised Perry, emptily. He'd probably be back in the office in time to call the psychiatrists he'd employed in the past. Mason was good. So was Denning. He'd use both. And anyone else they suggested. Get it over as quickly as possible. Bert Feltham was right: unwinnable cases were a bastard.

'What have you done already?' demanded Jennifer. She gripped the edge of the sheet and then covered one hand with the other to stop the trembling. It didn't.

'We're going to use Sir Richard Proudfoot's chambers. They're the best.'

'Is he a QC?'

Perry hesitated, with a choice of reply to a question he hadn't wanted. 'Proudfoot is, yes.'

Jennifer caught the qualification. 'He is going to represent me, isn't he? Proudfoot himself?' She felt her eyes closing, despite herself, and stretched her face to keep them open, distorting her features and making her broken lip hurt.

'His junior, at first. Jeremy Hall,' avoided the solicitor. Was she consciously pulling faces at him? Fleetingly he wondered if it was safe to have the policewomen out of the ward. There didn't seem to be anything in the room she could use as a weapon.

'But it will be Proudfoot, at the trial?'

'There's some way to go before we get that far.'

'*Can't you see he's lying, you stupid bitch!*'

Jennifer moved to speak but stopped, trying to assemble the words first, straightening against the pillows. 'I am not pleading guilty. I am not guilty. And I am not mad. And I want the best, not a junior.'

'You've got the best, believe me.' It was going to become very tiresome before it was all over. Hall was going to earn the chambers' copper brief.

'How old is Jeremy Hall?'

'I don't know.'

'How long has be belonged to the chambers?'

Perry shifted, uncomfortably. 'They're the best because they only take the best.'

'I want a QC. The most foremost criminal barrister there is.'

'*He's going through the motions! That's all any of them are going to do.*'

'Things have to go in sequence, in a proper order,' recited Perry. 'We've got to have this committal hearing and the proper medical and clinical examinations and then pre-trial discussions, before we even get into a proper court. You must trust me. I won't let you down. But I think it would be advisable to give Geoffrey Johnson your power of attorney to make sure everything goes smoothly while you're . . . you're indisposed. I've brought the authorizing document for you to sign.'

'He doesn't give a fuck. All he wants is the money. Ask him what he's going to charge.'

Jennifer didn't, momentarily pleased she was able to resist. Instead she remained looking at the man, feeling the despair as well as the frustration and exhaustion. There was nothing she could do! She was helpless! She tried to bite her lip, gnawing back the whimper, forgetting the split.

'That's exactly what you are, helpless!'

'Jane says I'm helpless.'

Perry sighed at the new face she was pulling but glad the delusion had taken over. 'You're not. You know you're not. Your lip's bleeding.'

'Listen to the lying bugger!'

'What about Emily?' Jennifer was pleased again, excited that she'd managed to change the subject without Jane's intervention. She ran her tongue over the cut.

'We told you last night she's all right. That the nanny is looking after her.' Perry hadn't bothered to check and made another reminder note to see if Geoffrey Johnson had done so. It was more Johnson's responsibility as the family lawyer. He had to tell the man about the power of attorney, too.

'I want Emily told that I love her. That I can't come home at the moment but that I love her and will see her soon.'

'How, exactly, do you think you're going to see her soon!'

'I'll ensure she's told that.'

Jennifer felt another dip of despair. She had no-one, she abruptly realized. No mother, no father: not alive any more. Gerald and Emily were her life: had been her life. No-one else. What about Rebecca? Rebecca was a friend. She'd help. Had to help. Stupid not to have thought of Rebecca before: been allowed to think of Rebecca before, she qualified. Abruptly she pulled herself upright, aware she'd had her head to one side again, listening. Had to stop that: stop looking mad. 'There's a trader at Gerald's company. We're friends. Rebecca Nicholls. I want her to come here. She can see Emily for me.'

Perry made a note of the name with his carefully pointed propelling pencil. 'I'm going to oppose any transfer from here, today. The doctors don't want it. But you'll need clothes. Perhaps I can ask . . .' He paused. 'Is it Miss or Mrs Nicholls?'

'Miss.' Where was Jane? Why wasn't she jeering, mocking?

'. . . Perhaps I can ask Miss Nicholls to do that for you, if she will.'

'She will,' said Jennifer, confidently. Incredible she hadn't thought of Rebecca before. Although perhaps it wasn't. But now she had. So it was all right. Rebecca wouldn't treat her as if she was mad. Rebecca even believed in clairvoyants: went to fortune tellers.

There was movement from the door and people entered as a group. Ahead of those Jennifer recognized, Bentley and Rodgers and the policewomen, there was a tightly costumed, open-faced woman with rigidly permed grey hair. Slightly behind her was a distracted, disordered man who appeared to have difficulty with two files he was trying to carry in addition to a briefcase. A second man also carried a briefcase and was supervising the policewomen manoeuvring ahead of them two tables like the one that fitted over Jennifer's bed for meals she had so far been unable to eat. A nurse and a doctor, at the very rear, carried chairs.

The room became almost impossibly overcrowded. From the rear Dr Lloyd said, 'We could all move to somewhere larger if you like.'

The grey-haired woman looked at Perry and said, 'I'm happy, if you are. It's not going to take long, is it?' The voice was the strident one of someone accustomed to being obeyed. In an apparent afterthought she turned to the distracted man and said, 'Do you mind?'

'It's going to be brief, as far as I am concerned,' agreed Perry.

The other man said, 'Strictly formal.' He put his files and briefcase down on one of the hospital tables and looked at Jennifer curiously for several moments before fumbling with his papers.

Perry edged around the bed to put himself beside the other man. They nodded to each other before introducing themselves by name to the woman: the distracted man's name was Norman Burden. Despite the formality, both men seemed to know her anyway but for the benefit of the unidentified court clerk at the edge of her table the woman named herself as Gillian Heathcote. In the same breath she said briskly, 'Right! Let's get on with it, shall we?'

Burden immediately called Bentley, who made a movement as if coming forward but in fact didn't, because there was no room. He recited the memorized oath and then, unprompted, said that at three-thirty the previous afternoon he had responded to a 999 call to the commodity trading offices of Enco-Corps Inc. in Leadenhall Street. There, in a third-floor office, he had found the body of an American, Gerald James Lomax.

'There were extensive injuries. There were at least fifteen stab wounds, as well as a number of deep cuts – slash wounds – to the face, neck and body. There had been a considerable loss of blood and the office, which I ascertained to be that of Lomax, was heavily bloodstained. Mrs Lomax, who was also bleeding extensively from knife injuries, was slumped on the floor, against an internal window. In my opinion she was close to unconsciousness. She was removed to this hospital, where I saw her at six forty-five last evening. At seven-thirty I formally charged Mrs Lomax with the murder of her husband . . .' Bentley paused, looking expectantly towards Burden.

Prompted, the prosecuting solicitor said, 'There are a number of other enquiries to be made before this matter can be proceeded with and I would formally ask, madam, for a remand in custody. I have no objection to that remand initially being here, in this hospital. I understand from the doctor he considers Mrs Lomax should remain under observation for several more days . . .'

It was as if she didn't exist, thought Jennifer, outraged. They were talking about her and across her but no-one was even looking at her!

'Mr Perry?' invited the magistrate.

'I have no objection to that course, madam. At a later date, in view of Mrs Lomax's injuries and other matters that need consideration, I would ask for any further remands to be in a hospital wing of a prison—'

'What about my objections!' Everyone looked at Jennifer as if for the first time, visibly stunned by the outburst. Before there was any other reaction, Jennifer said, 'I am not guilty! I want everyone to know that.'

'Mr Perry?' demanded the woman.

'*Tell the bitch to shut up and let you speak!*'

'Shut up! Let me speak . . .' blurted Jennifer. Then, 'No! Oh no! Damn! Damn! Damn!'

'*Caught you. Forgot I was here, didn't you?*'

'Now, now,' soothed the doctor, almost unseen.

'Don't patronize me as if I were mad! None of you!'

'I apologize,' said Perry, hurriedly. 'As I said, there are other matters to be pursued . . . medical and specialist examinations—'

'I said don't patronize me,' Jennifer screamed at her lawyer. Then, still shouting, to Bentley, 'Tell them what I said when you charged me!'

'Mrs Lomax . . . please . . .' tried Perry.

'Tell them!' yelled Jennifer.

'Go ahead,' said Gillian Heathcote, nodding to the detective.

'*The frumpy cow is patronizing you worst of all!*'

'Don't patro—' started Jennifer, then stopped.

'*Say it!*'

'She says you're patronizing me worst of all.'

'She says?' demanded the magistrate, bewildered.

'When I charged Mrs Lomax she said she hadn't killed her husband. That it was Jane . . .' Bentley paused, in a rare moment of embarrassment. 'Jane Lomax was the first wife of the murdered man.'

Gillian Heathcote smiled, bleakly, turning to Perry. 'I understand.'

'I want everyone to understand,' said Jennifer, her voice cracked from shouting. She came forward on her pillows, wincing as the drip needle bit into her arm. She couldn't support herself and at once fell back against the pillows, aware the magistrate had instinctively retreated at the movement. Jennifer tried to prevent it but she couldn't stop the crying. 'I didn't kill him. I loved him!'

'I think we can bring this quickly to an end,' said the

magistrate, anxiously. 'I agree to a formal remand, for seven days . . .' She remained half standing, looking at Perry again. '. . . I fully understand your problems but I think you should do all you can at future hearings to keep your client under some sort of control.'

'*God, this is fun. This really is so much fun!*'

Jeremy Hall came hesitantly into his uncle's rooms, momentarily stopping completely when he saw Bert Feltham comfortably seated beside Sir Richard's desk. Proudfoot himself was framed against the window overlooking the Inner Temple and the manicured grass leading down towards the Thames.

'Come in, come in,' encouraged the older barrister. 'Interesting case to discuss.'

'The Lomax killing,' said Feltham, uninvited. 'You read about it in the papers?'

'Briefly,' said Hall. He was a big man, the height accentuated by a build developed at Cambridge where he'd gained a rowing Blue: anxious that it wouldn't turn to fat he tried to scull as many weekends as possible. He appeared far too big for the chair towards which Proudfoot gestured him.

'It's going to be a high-profile case. Get your name in the papers,' encouraged the older man. He was tall, too, the greying hair swept back but worn comparatively long to fashion into two distinct wings, on either side of his head. He affected a slow, measured delivery when he spoke, either in court or out. That afternoon's stance was a favourite, too: hands clasped behind his back, winged head slightly forward, a lecturing pose.

'From the papers it looked like a simple domestic,' said Hall. After only nine months in chambers he wasn't in a position to argue against any brief but there wasn't any reason unquestionably to accept whatever he was presented with. There was still some lingering regret at having had to join his uncle's practice in the first place, instead of being able to make his way independently in a rival chambers, although he reassured himself there was even less reason to let pride outweigh the practical reality of earning a decent living after working so bloody hard for so bloody long getting a Double First as well as his rowing Blue and the pass marks he had in the Bar examinations. That and the fact he'd had no alternative. As his mother had told him at his father's funeral, beggars couldn't be choosers. He didn't enjoy being a beggar.

'It'll be a guilty, to manslaughter,' said Feltham, confidently. 'Diminished responsibility.'

'So it comes down to a plea of mitigation,' said Hall. 'What's that going to be?'

'Humphrey Perry's instructing. Arranging the usual psychiatric things.'

'Short, sharp but extremely profitable,' said Proudfoot, from the window. 'It won't do the chambers – or you – any harm. In fact I'm anxious for you to do it. We've had a long run of wins. Wrong for a practice to appear only to take the ones they're sure of. And this won't be a loss. It'll be a brilliant plea . . .' He smiled. '. . . Which I know it will be, for a sad, sick woman.'

Proudfoot finished what he was saying at an open cabinet and, as he leaned forward to accept the sherry his uncle offered, Hall was suddenly curious why such a case had to be pressed upon him over sherry by the chamber's head, even if it was his uncle. According to office lore, Feltham would have already accepted the brief anyway. Still unwilling to accept a *fait accompli*, Hall said, 'I'll be by myself?'

'Absolutely,' confirmed Proudfoot.

To Feltham, Hall said, 'She's mad? No other reason or motive?'

'Police haven't finished yet, but there doesn't seem to be any doubt. Cut her husband to pieces in front of sixteen people and then stood there laughing. I've fixed a meeting for you with Perry for tomorrow.'

So much for the pretence of discussion before acceptance, thought Hall. Pointedly – confident he could do it *because* Proudfoot was his uncle – Hall said, 'There's nothing else to it, is there?'

'Nothing else?' said Proudfoot. 'I don't understand the question.'

'It seems almost . . .' Hall paused. 'Almost too mundane: too small compared to most of the things we do.'

'I've explained my thinking on that,' said Proudfoot.

'I understand,' capitulated Hall, detecting the older man's irritation. He was being railroaded, Hall realized.

'Eleven tomorrow morning OK, here in chambers?' said Feltham, who already knew it would be because he maintained the appointment diaries and knew Hall's was hungrily empty.

'Fine,' agreed Hall.

'A well publicized murder's the best fast track for a reputation,' confided the chief clerk. 'This could be a good beginning.'

'It'll be my first murder,' admitted Hall.

'But not the last, if you handle this one right.'

As Proudfoot served him his second whisky, after Hall had left the room, Feltham said, 'That was a sharp question, about a hidden agenda.'

'His ability was more important than his relationship to me,' insisted Proudfoot. 'He's damned clever.' The man added to his own glass, disdaining the earlier sherry.

'Perry wouldn't do anything underhand about the copper thing, would he?'

Feltham shook his head, smiling. 'There isn't a solicitor in London who'd try to cheat me. Certainly not one who'd get half a chance to do it a second time. It's more than their job's worth.'

'That's good to hear,' said Proudfoot. 'We're not wasting our time on a tuppenny murder for nothing.'

Patricia Boxall didn't really want the relationship to end but knew it was inevitable. So, she suspected, did Jeremy. If it came down to a straight comparison Jeremy had more going for him than Alexander: he was adventurous in bed and made her laugh a lot. But she wanted more than Chinese take-aways and Spanish plonk in front of the television watching videos of old Oxford and Cambridge boat races. Alexander had an independent income and belonged to all the good clubs. She had been just two tables away from Mick Jagger the night before last.

'That was a hell of a race,' Hall said.

'You showed me before.'

'We were drunk for a week after that.'

Patricia wondered who'd paid. 'Must have been fun.'

'I got a case today. The murder that's in all the papers.'

'She's mad, isn't she?'

'Seems that way.'

'What can you do?'

'Enter a sympathy plea.'

'Any money in it?'

'Not a lot, I wouldn't think. It won't last long.'

'Why do it then?'

'I haven't been offered anything else,' admitted Hall. 'And I don't like having to watch old videos of boat races because I'm broke, any more than you do.'

'Let's go to bed then.'

'Well!' said John Bentley, triumphantly.

'No-one's admitted anything yet,' cautioned Rodgers.

'Wait,' cautioned Bentley. 'Just you wait.'

'How long?'

'An hour.'

'Five pounds says it'll take more than one session.'

'You're on.'

Chapter Seven

Rebecca Nicholls was slim and blond and enjoyed the effect she had upon men, particularly upon those to whom she was clearly unavailable, as she was to this overconfident policeman who'd emphasized his rank and held the handshake too long and dressed like an upmarket car salesman. In other circumstances she might have amused herself with this encounter but this afternoon these most definitely weren't the circumstances. Not that she was nervous. She could handle it. But she wished there hadn't been the feeling of uncertainty. She wasn't an uncertain person.

Rebecca allowed the open admiration of her legs when she crossed them, otherwise sitting demurely with her hands in her lap in the secretary's side office, inwardly steeling herself against looking in the direction of Lomax's adjoining room. Plastic sheeting had been draped completely over the outsides of the vast windows, hiding everything, but she didn't need any reminder of the scene inside that still needed the police release to be cleaned.

She hoped she didn't break down, although there was a perfectly understandable reason if she did, having witnessed a murder and now being questioned about it for a second time. Like it was perfectly understandable for her to have shivered when she'd entered, so close to the unseen horror. They shouldn't have done this here, in the building itself. If they had to do it at all it should have been somewhere outside, a police station even.

'I'm sorry to trouble you again.' Bentley, who prided himself on his adjustable interrogation technique, was sure he knew just how to handle this haughty bitch. Nice legs though, all the way up to her ass: good tits, too.

'I've already told your sergeant what I saw.'

'Inspector,' corrected Bentley, nodding sideways to the other man. 'Rodgers is an inspector, not a sergeant.'

Rebecca sighed. 'Inspector then.'

'I'm just filling in the gaps: trying to fit things together,' said Bentley, the tone still apologetic.

'What is it you want to know?' demanded Rebecca, impatiently.

'You're very busy, of course?'

'Of course. But I want to help if I can. Although I don't see how.'

Bentley appeared to study Rebecca's initial statement, open before him. 'You've been at Enco-Corps now for . . . ?'

'Ten years,' Rebecca supplied, when the pause stretched.

'. . . Quite so, ten years.' Bentley smiled up. 'You're American?'

'I transferred from the New York office six years ago. I've already told your inspector this, as well.' Bentley – *Detective Superintendent* Bentley – was thick, all mouth and trousers: it wasn't going to be too difficult at all.

'Indeed you have. Did you know Gerald Lomax in New York, before he came here?'

Rebecca hesitated. 'Not before he transferred here to run the operation, no.'

'But you did know him?'

'We met during his home visits.'

'Home visits meaning when he went back to New York?'

'Is this important?' There was another sigh.

Bentley regarded her blank faced. 'What, Ms Nicholls?'

'I don't see what relevance there might be upon his murder in how and when I met Gerald.' She shouldn't have made the challenge.

'Gerald?'

'What?' Smart-assed fucking car salesman.

'Is that what you called him, Gerald? He was your boss.'

Rebecca uncrossed her legs, knowing she was in control. 'You ever been to America, *Superintendent*?' It was silly using his sort of emphasis on the rank but she couldn't help it.

'Wonderful country.'

'But you haven't noticed that in America people call each other by their given names?'

Bentley smiled, contentedly. 'Slipped my mind. But hasn't how and when you met Gerald any relevance, Miss Nicholls?' She wouldn't be haughty in bed: probably went like a steam train.

'I've told you, I can't see any.'

'Everything is relevant in a murder investigation, Ms Nicholls.'

Rebecca was disconcerted by the way the man kept stressing the 'Ms'. 'I would have hardly thought what happened here yesterday requires much investigation: we've all told you what we saw.' She shivered again.

'Like I said, I'm just fitting the parts together.'

Rebecca breathed out again, heavily. 'I've worked for Enco-Corps for a total of ten years. Quite obviously I would meet Gerald Lomax during his trips to New York. He was a colleague.' The bastard was groping: maybe guessing – maybe someone down below had an inclination – but that's all there was. All there could have been. They were waiting for her to admit something and there was no way she was going to do that.

'Gerald Lomax came to London nine years ago?'

'I'm not sure of the precise date.'

'You're not?' queried Bentley, appearing surprised.

'I told you I wasn't.'

Bentley paused, looking down at the scattered papers on the desk in front of him. 'Gerald Lomax was transferred from New York?'

'I believe so.'

'You're not sure of that, either?'

'No.'

'You worked for Enco-Corps for ten years and Gerald Lomax was only transferred nine years ago. Surely there was a year's overlap in New York, when you would have worked together?'

Rebecca smiled, stretching the indulgent pause as long as possible. Patiently, speaking slowly as if for someone who needed simple words to understand simple things, she said, 'I joined Enco-Corps in their Paris office. I worked there for two years before going to New York. By which time Gerald Lomax had been moved here. I worked in New York for two years before coming to London. Does that fit your parts together?'

Bentley made an expansive gesture with spread-apart hands. 'Perfectly. So you met first during his visits to New York?'

'That's what I said.'

'A business colleague?'

'What else?' Rebecca's growing confidence dipped.

'There weren't any social occasions?'

She shrugged. 'There may have been situations in New York that could be described as social. Business receptions, things like that.'

'May have been? None that you can specifically remember?'

'No.'

'What about Mrs Lomax?'

'What about her?'

'Do you know Mrs Lomax?'

Rebecca gestured behind her, to the trading area below. 'We worked on the floor together before she married Gerald.'

'So you knew her as a business colleague, like you knew Mr Lomax?'

'We were friends.'

'*Were?*'

'Are. We don't – haven't – seen as much of each other since she had Emily and moved to the country.'

'You're Emily's godmother, aren't you?'

'Who told you that?' demanded the woman, actually turning to stare down at the working floor.

Bentley made a vague gesture. 'Someone said it, in one of the statements. You are, aren't you?'

'Yes.'

'So you know Mrs Lomax very well?'

'I suppose so, yes.'

'You sound reluctant?'

'It depends upon what you mean by very well.'

'What do you mean by very well, Ms Nicholls?'

Damn the 'Ms'. Rebecca said, 'We really haven't seen as much of each other in the last couple of years . . . longer maybe . . . as we once did. That's what I mean. That we've kind of drifted apart.'

'You were much closer when she worked here? When she lived in London?'

'Yes.'

'Did you know of her affair with Gerald Lomax, when she worked here?'

'That's an impertinent question!'

Bentley smiled. 'That's what policeman do, Ms Nicholls. Ask impertinent questions. Did you?'

'Yes.'

'Because you were close friends? Or because in these working surroundings . . .' Bentley gestured to the open-plan, all-glass working area. '. . . it's difficult to hide anything?'

'As a friend, first. Then it became pretty much common knowledge.'

'How did you feel about it?'

'Feel about it?'

'Gerald Lomax was a married man.'

'It was their business, not mine.'

'You didn't have any moral feeling?'

'I said it was their business!'

'Why did Jennifer Lomax kill her husband?'

Rebecca didn't have to feign the surprise at the abrupt, hard demand. 'I haven't the slightest idea! How on earth should I know?'

'She'd found out, hadn't she? About you and Gerald?'

Rebecca didn't speak. From the warmth she knew she was colouring. 'There was nothing to find out about Gerald and me.'

'It's difficult to hide anything in a place like this,' reminded Bentley.

There was no proof. The bastards down below might have guessed but they didn't know – she and Gerald had been far more discreet than he had been with Jennifer – so they didn't know and no-one could prove anything. 'I had no relationship with Gerald Lomax.' Rebecca was pleased at the steadiness in her voice.

'It's a nice flat, isn't it?'

'What?'

'Gerald's, here in London. A nice flat?'

'I've only been there once. At a party for Emily. But yes, it is a nice flat.' She shouldn't have qualified the visit.

'When would that have been?'

'It must be more than a year ago.' What was he getting at? They'd always been discreet there, too.

'Not weeks ago? Or just days?'

'No.'

'The security would have influenced Lomax's choice, I suppose,' said Bentley, conversationally. He loved questioning people who despised him: thought they were cleverer. 'Very American.'

Rebecca felt emptied by uncertainty. 'I don't understand.'

'You're on the CCTV recording, Ms Nicholls. We've got you several times. It's a long loop but it doesn't go back years.'

Rebecca Nicholls sat motionless, without expression, for several moments, before she began to sob. There were no tears.

Bentley and Rodgers afterwards agreed that it was always the same: once the dam broke you got washed away in the confessional flood water until in the end you had to say something positive to get them to stop telling you the sexual fetishes of their grandmother's pet hamster.

Rebecca Nicholls admitted the affair had begun a month before Emily had been born and gave dates and hotels where she and Gerald Lomax had travelled together on overseas business trips, in addition to her accompanying him on the three-times-a-year updating and assessment returns to New York.

'But Jennifer never knew.'

'You want me to pull down those screens and tell me that again?' demanded Bentley. He had what he wanted. He didn't have to go around in circles any more. This was the part when she learned he wasn't the dickhead she'd thought him to be but the hardest bastard she'd ever met and that he'd been playing with her – enjoying himself – all the time.

'Are you going to charge me with anything?'

'Fucking a married man isn't a crime. Not in this country at least.'

'What then?' She showed no outrage at the dismissive obscenity. He'd won. She supposed it was a spoil of victory to humiliate her.

'Bring a proper prosecution against Jennifer Lomax.'

'She didn't kill Gerry because of me.'

'Sure.' It was going to be a good case after all. Fuckable woman, eternal triangle, jealousy, revenge, all the ingredients. Plus a bloody clever – convincing almost – load of bollocks about hearing voices telling Jennifer what to do. Bentley was conscious of Rodgers looking at his watch beside him. He gave an imperceptible nod in return.

'Gerry was going to tell her. Get a divorce.'

'Did he?' pounced Rodgers, sharing the questioning now.

'No! He said he'd tell me before he did. But he didn't say anything. So he hadn't told her.'

It was wrong, reflected Bentley, to believe it was only men who had their brains between their legs. 'So you tell me, Ms Nicholls, why you think Jennifer Lomax came in here yesterday and tried to turn her husband into hamburger?' The Americanism for an American had come to him after he'd begun speaking and he was proud of it.

'I wasn't responsible for his death.' Real tears began, at last.

'If it hadn't been you it would have been someone else,' said Rodgers. It was well past conclusion time.

'We loved each other. We were going to get married.'

'And live happily ever after?' said Bentley.

'Yes! Jennifer was a mistake. Like Jane had been a mistake.'

Jesus, thought Bentley. 'It's a bastard, the search for eternal happiness. Maybe he's found it now.'

'What's going to happen to me?'

'You'll be called, as a witness.'

'I won't testify.'

'Don't tell me what you are or are not going to do, Ms Nicholls,' warned Bentley, savouring the attitude Rebecca had attempted towards him at the beginning. 'If you try to be stupid you'll be subpoenaed. And if you refuse in court you'll be jailed for contempt, among all those tongue-licking dykes. And if you try to leave the country I'll apply for an international arrest warrant, which won't achieve much but it'll guarantee your name and photograph all over every newspaper you can think of and everyone can make up their own mind whether you were responsible or not.'

'Bastard!'

'Believe it.'

'I'll lose my job.'

'You probably will,' agreed Rodgers. It had just gone past the floodgates time.

Bentley thought the same. 'Thank you for your help.'

'I don't want to go back downstairs. Not this afternoon.'

'Go home then,' said Bentley.

'Isn't there any other way?' pleaded the woman, tentatively.

Not even on your back with your legs splayed, thought Bentley. 'A man has been murdered, horribly. My only interest is in seeing that justice is done.'

'She has to know? Jennifer, I mean?'

'She already does, doesn't she?' Bentley pointed out.

'I suppose so. Gerald should have told me.'

'Gerald should have done a lot of things he didn't.'

'And not done a lot of the things that he did,' picked up Rodgers, as the door closed behind the girl. He stood, looking down critically at the other man. 'What the hell were you trying to do to me, about seeing that justice is done!'

They both laughed.

Bentley said, 'Lomax must have had a dick like a donkey.'

'And used it like one,' agreed Rodgers. 'You took a hell of a chance about a security camera. We don't even know if there is one.'

'She wouldn't have known either. She was too arrogant.' He grinned. 'Just like one of those television films, wasn't it?'

'Lucky,' insisted Rodgers.

'But I was right about another woman, wasn't I!'

'You took longer than an hour to prove it,' argued Rodgers.

Ceremoniously Bentley took a five-pound note from his wallet and handed it to the other man.

'You could have done it under the hour,' said Rodgers, accepting the bet.

'I can't stand superior cows like that: I enjoyed myself,

bringing her down. That was worth five pounds. Can you imagine those legs locked around your neck?'

Rodgers offered the money back. 'You were right, about the case itself.'

Bentley took his money back. 'Wrapped and parcelled. We've got the classic woman-scorned scenario.'

'What's the voice in her head going to tell her now?'

'That she tried but lost,' said Bentley. 'It's a fucking nuisance we've got to go through things properly.'

'That was part of it, wasn't it?' realized Rodgers. 'Refusing any statement until she had a solicitor.'

'Jennifer Lomax is a very cunning killer,' judged Bentley. 'We've got ourselves another good one here, Malcolm. It'll run.'

For the second night in succession, Bert Feltham got a call at home from Humphrey Perry.

'Things look very different,' announced Perry. 'There was another woman. It looks as if Jennifer Lomax found out.'

'She's faking the voice in her head?' It still inevitably had to be a guilty plea but it could turn out better. No-one liked insanity.

'Bentley wants to interview her tomorrow at the hospital. Your man's got to be there with me, obviously.'

'What time?'

'Ten.'

'There could be more mileage in this than we thought.'

'Isn't that why I have your home number?'

Perry was being wise after the event but Feltham didn't challenge him.

Chapter Eight

Jennifer – Jennifer Stone as she then was – had been Enco-Corps' leading London trader during her last two years with the firm: it had been one of Lomax's early jokes that he'd fallen in love with her professionally long before he'd been attracted in any other way.

All traders have to 'know' markets, to be able to assess margins and percentages but the very best additionally can 'feel', to judge instinctively when a price has peaked and is about to fall or whether it has the buoyancy of a few more points or a commodity can go up a few more cents to attain that extra eighth or quarter per cent that turns a good position into a spectacular one. Jennifer could 'know' and 'feel' and had the added ability of a gambler able photographically to memorize every card played in a poker game: indeed, it was a soon abandoned party trick for her mentally to add and multiply and subtract complicated equations faster than people could compete on pocket calculators.

All of which still only made up part of the legend of Jennifer Stone. It was completed by an awesome determination to be the best – to overcome any opposition or obstacle – in any trading deal upon which she embarked. It was another of Gerald Lomax's remarks that he'd had Jennifer in mind when he attached 'for piranha fish' to the description of the totally glassed office as a goldfish bowl.

The combination of abilities and attitudes made Jennifer special and without conceit or arrogance she knew it, like she knew she definitely wasn't mad. To allow herself to think that would be the final abandonment, giving Jane the ultimate victory. And she'd never do that.

It had been good – fulfilling – to have an unusual, unique mind: to be different. Living as she'd lived after her marriage had never been quite enough. She'd never admitted it but she'd felt wasted, unused, when she'd finally accepted it would be untenable for her to remain on a trading floor controlled by her husband or work on another in competition against him.

Now she didn't have that special mind any more. It had been stolen from her – invaded – and when she forced herself beyond the horror of Gerald's killing and the numbing ebb and flow of exhaustion and the terrifying, unbelievable unreality of what was happening to her – ghosts didn't exist! spiritual possession was nonsense! – Jennifer's overwhelming feeling was of outrage, of being mentally raped.

She'd lost Gerald, whom she'd adored. She wasn't going to lose anything more. She was going to defeat Jane – stop whatever it was being done to her – whatever it took, whatever she had to do to achieve it. She'd never lost anything upon which she'd set her mind in the past and she wasn't going to lose now.

It took a long time for Jennifer to get to that conclusion. Jane was constantly with her every unsteady step of every weary thought, knowing each thought as it came, jeering and gloating over every one to goad Jennifer into the furious, even shouted, responses that were met with sighs and headshakes from the successive, guarding policewomen.

But Jennifer learned in the persistently interrupted, disjointed process.

It was unconscious at first, an impression rather than a proper awareness. Her bone-aching exhaustion triggered it, at Jane's mockery of how grotesque she would look after the second utterly sleepless night she intended to impose: that and the physical sensation of numbness which Jennifer had imagined to be all part of the same fatigue. Until, that is, she made a different connection. The tingling, like the tingle of knocking the humerus in her elbow, seemed to precede by the merest fraction of a second the sound of Jane in her head. When there was no voice – a momentary gap in the possession – there was no numbness. It wasn't a positive experiment – Jennifer then hadn't learned enough.

In the evening of the second day, confronted with the agony of not sleeping again, Jennifer very positively experimented, waiting for a moment of normality when the nurses were fixing another drip before blurting, 'Please give me something very strong tonight to make me sleep.'

The feeling at once suffused her. '*No!*'

Jennifer's jaw hurt in her determination not to speak.

'*No! You don't want it!*'

'There was a note from the night staff yesterday that you didn't sleep,' agreed one of the nurses. 'You were . . . distressed.'

'Please,' gritted Jennifer, through clamped teeth, careless of the pain from her lip. 'I need something . . . so tired . . . very tired . . .'

Jennifer's skin was on fire, worse than ever before.

'You all right?' said the second nurse. 'You're very red.'

'Just want to sleep.' If she said anything about Jane they would dismiss her wanting a sedative as part of the madness: not give her anything.

'*Say it!*'

Jennifer stayed rigid faced.

'*Say it, damn you!*'

'I'll see what I can do,' promised the first nurse. 'It should be all right.'

Jennifer's shaking, which the nurses and the policewomen had become accustomed to, was from the physical effort of hanging on – of staying silent – until the nurses left the room. As soon as the door closed behind them Jennifer said, 'Beat you.' She spoke very quietly, her head sunk on her chest. The nearest policewoman looked, aware of the mutter but not hearing the words.

'*You won't, not again.*'

'We'll see.' Jennifer was euphoric, wanting to laugh.

'*Laugh then.*'

Jennifer tightened her mouth again. 'Another mistake. Warned me against it.' Jennifer tried but couldn't stop the moan at the screech of anger that pounded agonizingly through her head. 'Beat you,' she managed. 'Beat you again.'

'*You can't drug me out. They can't drug me out.*'

'Why are you so frightened then? So angry?'

There was another echoing scream, as loud as before.

'So angry, Jane? Lost control, haven't you? Lost control to me.' She wasn't going to laugh aloud but she was still buoyant at the excitement of fighting back.

'*Not going to do you any good though, is it? Still won't be able to convince anyone you're not mad. Still the rest of your life in a mental asylum.*'

Jennifer shook her head. 'I'll find a way, like I found this way.'

Jennifer brought her head up at the arrival of two new policewomen for the night-shift change-over.

'Anything?' asked the newly-arriving sergeant, ignoring Jennifer.

The departing sergeant said, 'Spent all afternoon mumbling to herself. Totally off her head.'

'Listen to them!'

'I'm not off my head!' shouted Jennifer.

None of the women bothered to look at her.

'Jennifer Stone's
A stupid drone
So much off her head
Might as well be dead.'

'Shitty poetry,' dismissed Jennifer.

'I thought it was funny.'

Jennifer went to speak but quickly stopped, halted by the entry of the nurse who'd changed the saline drip. Now she carried a kidney bowl covered by a cloth.

'I'll over-ride it!'

'The doctor says it's OK. That you need to get some sleep.'

'Waste of time!'

'Please,' said Jennifer, offering her free arm, sighing at the prick of the needle going into her arm. 'Thank you. Thank you so very much.'

Jennifer never fully lost consciousness. It was like the sort of half-asleep awareness she'd sometimes had when she knew she was dreaming and stayed like a spectator, refusing properly to wake up. Except this wasn't a dream but the distant, frenzied voice of Jane trying to get through the sedation, becoming even more hysterical when Jennifer refused, as she'd refused with the real dreams.

It was still early, although daylight, when she did surrender. But Jane wasn't inside her head. Jennifer remained lying as she was, waiting but there was nothing and hurriedly Jennifer began thinking of the day ahead, seizing the respite. Humphrey Perry hadn't given a time but she expected him to come that morning. With the barrister, he'd said. Jeremy Hall. Nice enough name. But not a QC. It probably wasn't etiquette to make the protest direct to the man but she would. Bypass Perry completely and if he didn't like it engage another solicitor. She couldn't be bothered with niceties as desperate as she was. She'd still do her best not to offend Hall, of course. Make it clear she wanted to retain him as well but insist her defence be headed by the most experienced person. Proudfoot himself, in fact.

She hoped Perry would have already contacted Rebecca. Would they let Rebecca come personally, here to the hospital? No reason why they shouldn't. It would be better if she could talk to Rebecca direct, rather than relay messages through Perry. She needed to talk to someone besides police and lawyers: needed a friend. Her only friend. She had to make a list, in her head, of the clothes she wanted brought in. Suits, she supposed, for the court appearances when she was discharged from here and from the hospital wing of whatever prison she was sent to. And for the psychiatrists' meetings. Important she talk to Perry about that today: get things set up immediately. To be declared sane – not totally off her head – and stop being regarded by everyone like the bearded woman in a sideshow. Except, she supposed, that when everybody at last believed her she'd be considered even more of an oddity.

A lot to think about: think about and get under way. End the whole terrible nightmare. It was good, being able to think like this. Think clearly, logically, as she'd always been able to think: to have her mind back. When would it start again, the chanting and the mockery? A distracting question: not important. What was important was getting everything she had to do established in her head. Not to forget anything. Good to feel better. And she did feel better. Not fully rested, because she hadn't rested fully. But enough. Sufficient to be able to work things out as she was working them out now. She wasn't shaking, either. Her hands and arms were throbbing from the cuts but not badly. Wouldn't need painkillers. Just another sedative, that night. Knew how to get it now. How to beat Jane.

The numbness warned her. '*No you don't.*'

'I had a wonderful night's sleep.'

'*You heard me.*'

'Not a sound.'

'*Liar.*'

'She's awake. At it again.'

Jennifer shuffled herself upright at the policewoman's voice. The day-shift sergeant was at the door, looking enquiringly at the yawning pair getting up stiffly from the easy chairs in which they had spent the night. The new arrivals positioned themselves with their backs to Jennifer, so that she didn't hear the muffled exchanges, but she was conscious of the looks from all of them. For the first time they didn't appear patronizing. One smiled and nodded at something one of the others said.

'What?' demanded Jennifer.

'Superintendent Bentley is coming to see you this morning,' announced the day sergeant.

'What about?'

Instead of replying the woman said, 'How is the voice?'

'Jane's started.'

'Sure,' said the sergeant and smiled sideways at the other newly-arrived policewoman, who smiled back.

'What is it?' insisted Jennifer, exasperated.

'You'll have to wait for the superintendent.'

'*I'm as curious as you are!*'

'Stop it!'

The policewoman remained smiling. The sergeant said, 'That damned voice again?'

'You know it is!'

'Do I?'

'*They're taking the piss out of you, Jennifer.*'

Jennifer fought back a response, grateful for the entry of the nurse with washing water and the repeated announcement that the police were coming to see her. 'And your lawyer. He asked me to tell you.'

When she began her make-up Jennifer realized her hands were shaking again, although not as badly as the previous morning. Today there were no smudged lines and the swelling on her lip had gone down enough to complete the colouring. She managed her hair more successfully than the previous day, too. Her eyes were still ringed, although not as darkly as before. She was glad there was no sensation to warn her of Jane, easily able without interruption to call to mind everything she wanted to tell Humphrey Perry.

She actually smiled when the shiny domed solicitor came into the ward, ahead of another man who politely held the door for the policewomen to leave. Perry remained expressionless introducing Jeremy Hall, who did smile back although very briefly.

'The police are coming to see me,' announced Jennifer, at once.

'We know,' said Perry. 'That's why we're here. To talk to you first.'

'There are things I want to sort out with you—' Jennifer began, but Perry cut across her.

'. . . We want to establish something at once, Mrs Lomax.'

'*They don't give a fuck about what you want.*' Jennifer's skin began to burn.

'I want, in fact, to hear your story,' said Hall.

The voice was very deep, more resonant than the solicitor's – an actor's voice, almost – and it was not until she concentrated fully upon the man that Jennifer realized how big he was, broad as well as tall. She decided, surprised, that he reminded her of Gerald. Younger maybe, but only by a few years. Same blue eyes and the direct, talking-only-to-you concentration. She could even find a similarity in the voice, although Gerald's hadn't been so deep. It registered mostly with her in the self-assured, unhurried way in which Hall actually spoke, a person confident of his own ability. Unlike everyone else he wasn't frightened of her, expecting her without warning to do something violent. Not that he would have had any cause to worry, as obviously fit as he was. A sportsman, she guessed. What sport? An active, energetic one to have a build like that. Rugby maybe.

The two men took the chairs vacated by the policewomen.

'*Why don't you try to compare the size of their dicks?*'

Jennifer jumped but managed to hold back from replying. The effort made the shake worsen, momentarily. 'Hear what, exactly?'

'It was this voice that made you go to London?' coaxed Hall.

'Jane, yes.'

'You couldn't stop yourself?'

'It wasn't me. It was Jane, using my body.'

'Your husband hadn't been home the previous night?'

'No. He stayed away two or three nights a week, on average. But he was always home at weekends. That was the arrangement.'

'Was there any other arrangement, Mrs Lomax?' intruded Perry.

'They're out to trick you!'

'Jane says you're trying to trick me.'

Perry sighed, audibly. The other man didn't. Perry said, 'You didn't answer my question.'

'I didn't understand it.'

'Were there any difficulties in your marriage?' demanded Hall, directly.

'*What have we got here?*' Jane's voice was excited.

'I still don't understand,' insisted Jennifer. A feeling began, a faint nausea, deep in her stomach.

Perry sighed again, more loudly. 'Were you and your husband happily married? Or did he spend two or three nights away from home for other reasons?'

'No!' said Jennifer, as forcefully as she could. 'Gerald was not having an affair.'

'*You sure? I'm not!*'

Jennifer shook her head but didn't speak.

'I am going to do my best to defend you against a charge of murder, Mrs Lomax—' said Hall.

'That's one of the things I want to discuss with you—'

'Please hear your counsel out,' broke in Perry, again. 'We have to get things clear in our mind before the police interview.'

'*See! Don't give a fuck.*'

'Make your point,' demanded Jennifer, to the younger man. She wouldn't be bullied.

'*You will be.*'

'If I am going to do that, defend you, you have to be completely honest with me.'

Jennifer succeeded with a half smile. 'I know it's bizarre. Preposterous. But I am possessed by Gerald's first wife, Jane. She thinks Gerald and I conspired in her murder. Which, of course, we didn't. The inquest verdict was that she died from an inexplicable overdose of insulin.'

'You did! You did!'

Hall refused to respond to Perry's look. Instead he stayed upon Jennifer and said, 'You know full well that is not a viable defence. It is, as you say, preposterous. Unless, of course, you expect a lesser charge to which we can plead diminished responsibility. Which would result in a custodial care sentence, with reviews until you could be declared recovered. And then released back into the community . . .' He paused. 'Released after a comparatively limited term of imprisonment.'

The heat Jennifer felt was more from anger than from Jane's presence. Her first impulse was to shout at the man but she stifled the urge. Instead, calmly, she said, 'How much opportunity have you had to discuss this case with Mr Perry?'

'Not a great deal,' conceded Hall. It had, in fact, been less than two hours and that included their conversation on the way to the hospital in the car. It was proving more difficult than he'd expected to get rid of this voice-in-the-head nonsense but she'd obviously prepared it for a long time so he supposed he had to expect some resistance.

'What has he told you about how I intend to plead.'

'Not guilty.'

'Not guilty to murder. And not guilty to any lesser charge,' Jennifer insisted.

'It's no good. He doesn't believe you.'

'Yes,' accepted the barrister.

'What has Mr Perry told you about psychiatrists?'

'That you wish to undergo psychiatric examination and assessment.'

Jennifer let her anger go at last. 'So what the hell's all this about diminished responsibility and short sentences! I will plead not guilty to a charge of murder – and only to a charge of murder, nothing less – and be declared sane and be found not guilty.'

'Mrs Lomax,' said Perry, patiently. 'That is not an option. No court – no judge – will accept it. Any of it.'

'Make them!'

Hall had been sitting almost languidly, one leg triangled over the other: as always the chair appeared too small. Now he put both feet firmly on the ground and leant towards her to emphasize what he intended to say. 'There are other circumstances in which a charge of murder could be proceeded with—'

'Then why are we having this discussion!' demanded Jennifer, uncaring how often she interrupted.

'You expect to be declared sane?' said Hall.

'I am sane!' She was irritated by Perry sitting there, taking notes with that ridiculous silver pencil.

'If you were declared sane – and a court accepted that opinion from psychiatrists – there would be prosecution evidence from sixteen witnesses of your having stabbed your husband to death. The mandatory sentence for murder is life imprisonment. In the circumstances of this case I have to warn you a judge's recommendation could be for that term to be a minimum of twenty years.'

'*Got you, one way or another.*'

'Why should I want to murder a husband I adored?' pleaded Jennifer.

'Here comes the man who believes he knows?' said Perry, as Bentley came forcefully into the ward.

'It's time for us to have a proper conversation, Mrs Lomax,' declared the murder squad detective, confidently.

The tiny room became as crowded as it had been for the magistrate's hearing. Hospital tables were moved in again, one almost completely occupied by recording equipment.

By apparent prearrangement Malcolm Rodgers became its operator, plugging leads into the mains supply and quietly mouthing into the microphone to test sound levels. Satisfied, he transferred the microphone to the table already positioned over Jennifer's bed.

'What's going on?' demanded Jennifer.

'*I can hardly wait.*'

'Shut up!' said Jennifer, forgetting herself.

The heavily breathing Perry breathed out again, looking at Hall before saying, 'We have agreed to a formal police interview, in our presence.'

'Without discussion with me?' Jennifer was aware of Rodgers hurriedly identifying the tape, her by name and the place and date at which it was being made.

'Is there any reason for you to refuse?' demanded Bentley, at once.

'*You're like some experiment, under their microscope.*'

The need to concentrate – an awareness of challenges she refused to anticipate despite the lingering nausea – made it easier to ignore the voice, like turning down a volume.

'My last legal advice was against making any statement,' she reminded, stiffly, looking at Perry as she spoke.

'This isn't a statement,' insisted Bentley. 'It is an interview, to further our enquiries.'

Jennifer looked to her two lawyers for help. When neither spoke she said, 'But able, according to your official caution, to be presented in any prosecution against me.'

'I will permit nothing that will endanger your defence,' promised Hall.

'*Ask him how many times he's defended in a murder case!*' demanded Jane.

Jennifer reminded herself she hadn't needed any specific reason to insist upon a senior practising, top-of-his-profession barrister to replace Jeremy Hall but if she had this could have provided it. It wouldn't stop with Hall and she didn't give a damn about offence, either. She'd get rid of him and the stick-thin idiot with a head like an egg to whom the length of a pencil lead seemed so important.

'*Who do you know who's better?*'

'It could still be produced in court?' persisted Jennifer. They were treating her like an idiot – like a mad woman – and she wouldn't allow that. Wasn't mad, wasn't mad, wasn't mad.

'Yes,' agreed the detective.

'I assure you—' began Hall.

'I'm not impressed by your assurances,' snapped Jennifer. 'Which we'll discuss after this meeting. I want a nurse . . . a doctor . . . someone independent from all this.'

'Mrs Lomax—' tried Perry.

'Get someone or get out!'

'*They'll think it's the madness coming out.*'

The assembled men regarded her solemnly, doing nothing.

'You,' isolated Jennifer, pointing to Perry with her unrestricted hand. 'Go and get someone.'

Rodgers snapped off the recording as the solicitor left the room. Hall said, 'This really is most unnecessary, whatever it is you want.'

Jennifer looked at him but refused to speak. There was some awkward foot scuffing from everyone except Bentley, who came close to overemphasizing the leg-stretched, arms-folded, seen-it-all-before condescension.

Within minutes, less maybe, Rodgers returned with Peter Lloyd. Jennifer guessed the physician would have been given an explanation from the detective inspector but before anything further could be said she gestured with the unencumbered arm and said, 'Turn the tape back on: give a time and the circumstances.'

'This really isn't . . .' persisted Hall. He wasn't sure of himself, not in control any more, and appeared disorientated.

'Do it!'

Rodgers did, formally re-establishing the interview. He did so looking uncertainly towards Bentley for guidance but before the senior detective could say anything Jennifer said to the doctor, 'I want you to listen, to everything that's said. I'll call you to court to testify on my behalf, if this tape is tampered with: to swear to everything that's going to be said.'

'*He'll think it's paranoia: all part of your hearing-voices paranoia.*'

'I really have more important—' started the doctor.

'No you don't! It's my life you're trying to save, although not medically. Listen . . . !' Jennifer turned directly to address the microphone in front of her. 'The making of this tape is being independently witnessed by Dr Peter Lloyd, of St Thomas's hospital . . .'

'Very impressive, Jennifer,' said Bentley. 'You sure you can keep it up?'

'Keep what up?'

'Voices in the head, telling you what to do.' It wouldn't be difficult breaking this arrogant bitch down, any more than it had been to beat Lomax's replacement fuck. Hall would probably cut him off, before he got a full confession but it wouldn't matter. He'd have enough. Sometimes things were almost too easy.

'I don't choose to continue with this interview, despite the agreement of my lawyers. Who will not be my lawyers after today,' announced Jennifer, talking directly into the microphone once more.

'*Go on! I didn't expect it to be as good as this.*'

'You're right to be scared, Jennifer. I'm on to you. Know what your plan was,' smiled Bentley.

'I didn't say you could call me Jennifer.'

She was breaking, Bentley recognized: trying to hide behind pomposity. 'Hurt like hell, didn't it, finding out about Gerald and Rebecca?'

'*Woweeeee!!!*'

Jennifer had assuaged the guilt of her affair with Gerald – and the never-quite-lost feeling after Jane's death – by knowing, positively, really *knowing*, not simply convincing herself, that her marriage to Gerald was invulnerable: complete, unendangered, absolutely and totally invulnerable. Which it had been, she determined, fighting back: *had* to be. It was a trick, a cheap trick to get her to admit something, anything, that wasn't true. Wouldn't work. Whatever they wanted – expected – it wouldn't work. To Hall she said, 'Why are you allowing this! Stop it!'

'*I don't want it to stop. Gerald was screwing your best friend, Jennifer! And you didn't even know it, any more than I knew he was screwing you. Oh this is wonderful! Perfectly wonderful.*' The hysterical laughter echoed in Jennifer's head.

Before Hall could speak, Bentley went on, 'That's it, isn't it, Jennifer? You found out your husband was having an affair with Rebecca Nicholls and worked out a perfect defence for a minimal sentence so that you could kill him in front of her. That's why you stood at the window, covered in his blood, laughing down at her. You wanted her to see, didn't you . . . ?'

'NO!' The denial wailed from Jennifer as she snatched her hands up, to cover her ears, to stop hearing the words. The drip rattled against its frame and she felt the needle tear out of her uninjured arm and then the warmth of the blood. 'Stop it! Go away! You're lying: all of you lying.' She slumped back against the pillows, the room misting in front of her, her bruised lips moving but forming no words.

'This can't go on!' protested Lloyd.

'No,' said Hall. 'It can't. I've allowed more than I should have done. It has to stop now.'

Bentley wheeled upon the lawyer, only just stopping himself from telling the man to go to hell. The bitch had got away with it by faking the collapse, like she was trying to get away with murder by faking insanity.

'*Get up. Say something.*'

Jennifer didn't hear the words. Lloyd pushed through to Jennifer's bedside, more fully opening the half-lidded eyes. 'She's not properly conscious. And she isn't faking it . . .' He became aware the tape was still operating. 'I am formally warning you this woman's health would be seriously endangered by attempting to continue this interview, which she isn't mentally capable of responding to anyway.'

Rodgers wasn't quick enough stopping the tape to prevent it registering Bentley's hand-slap of frustration against the table top.

It didn't, however, record Jeremy Hall saying to Humphrey Perry, 'We made a mistake. A very bad mistake.'

Chapter Nine

It was a room of angry people and a lot of confusion, the ward sister's office into which Lloyd herded them as nurses came running to his call. He had forbidden the re-entry of any policewomen – insisting they witnessed Jennifer's recovery through the corridor window – adding to Bentley's fury.

'The doctor said it was a genuine collapse,' said Hall. It *had* been a bad mistake to allow the interview: getting the doctor's agreement wasn't sufficient excuse. He should have insisted upon more time, properly to prepare the woman: protect her. And done that better – protected her better – before the police arrival. Someone with more experience wouldn't have let any of it happen.

'Rubbish!' rejected Bentley. 'The collapse is a fake, like hearing voices is a fake. I've got the motive, like I knew I would. It's murder, pure and simple and premeditated. I won't have any prosecution accepting diminished responsibility or an unfit-to-plead attempt.'

'It's not up to you what the prosecution will or will not accept,' reminded Hall, refusing to be bullied. No-one was sitting. Instead they stood either side of the small room, like opposing combatants, which Hall supposed they were. Like David and Goliath. It was hardly a good analogy, he realized: Goliath lost.

The detective's face tightened at the correction. Formally – but with difficulty – Bentley said, 'I'm going to conduct this investigation as a culpable homicide, with no extenuating circumstances like mental illness. And that will be how my report is submitted to the Crown Prosecution Service.'

'That's what we'd expect you to do,' said Humphrey Perry. The solicitor's irritation was personal. It was virtually inevitable that what had occurred would leak back to Feltham and he'd promised the man he'd keep an eye on Jeremy Hall to make sure something precisely like this didn't happen. It would be best if he actually told the man himself, to get his side of the story in first.

'There'll be no further interviews with my client,' announced Hall.

'*Is* she your client?' demanded Bentley, belligerently. 'Sounded to me as if you were going to be fired.'

'Until I am, properly, I represent Mrs Lomax,' insisted Hall. 'And while I do I won't allow a repetition of what took place in there.'

Cocky young bastard out to make a name for himself, judged Bentley. He was going to have his work cut out doing it with this case and Bentley decided he'd be buggered if he'd do anything to help. 'You actually believe all her nonsense?'

'From the beginning Mrs Lomax appeared genuinely unwell to me.'

'You heard the voice?' mocked Rodgers, who'd worked with Bentley long enough to gauge his superior's mood and knew that at that moment Bentley was as furious as hell.

'I got sufficient indication of a mentally distressed woman.'

'Which you'll get a lot of tame psychiatrists to swear to, in court.'

'It's Mrs Lomax's own wish to be psychiatrically examined,' said Hall.

'And we'll match you, trick-cyclist for trick-cyclist, to say that she's sane,' insisted Bentley.

Hall allowed himself to become angry at his own mistakes but had a barrister's control against letting it happen professionally at the attitudes of others. Bentley was the sort of overconfident person easy to handle in court, someone quickly coaxed into ill-considered response. 'Perhaps it won't be necessary. I thought you knew Mrs Lomax *wants* to be diagnosed sane.'

'That's the cleverest bloody part of what she's doing, isn't it?' said Rodgers. 'Playing mad but saying she doesn't want to be.'

Hall decided to experiment, to see how easy it would be to manipulate Bentley. 'I've told you I won't allow the interview to continue. There's no real point in your staying here any longer, is there?'

Who the fuck did this cocky little bugger just out of school think he was talking to? Red faced, Bentley said, 'I'll decide when and how to leave enquiries.'

'Of course,' said Hall, mildly. 'I was just trying to save you wasting time.'

'I'll make up my own mind when I'm doing that, too.' Bentley caught the smirk on Perry's face and realized, too late, what was going on. They'd see who had the last laugh, he promised himself, vindictively. The bloody woman thought she was making a fool out of him and these two smarmy sods thought they were making a fool out of him – actually laughing! – but before it was all over they'd learn who the real fools were.

'We'll set up the examinations as soon as we get the go-ahead from the doctor,' Hall said to Perry. 'You have names?'

'Several,' assured the solicitor, aware of the renewed irritation from the two detectives at apparently being ignored. It might have been unintentional but if it wasn't Jeremy Hall appeared to have mastered a useful court-room technique.

'We'll use several,' decided the younger man. 'And I want each totally independent, not one responding to the opinion of another . . .' Appearing to remember Bentley, Hall said, 'How soon will you submit to the Crown Prosecution?'

'When I'm ready,' said Bentley, petulantly.

Hall turned pointedly and dismissively from the man. To Perry again he said, 'Officially inform them we're acting. We'll need the earliest evidence exchange of everything she said and did immediately after arrest, for the psychiatrists to assess as well.'

Lloyd's arrival added another angry man to the room. 'I don't consider Mrs Lomax sufficiently well to be interviewed further,' he declared, looking challengingly between the police and the lawyers.

'I've already decided it won't be continued,' said Hall.

'When will it be possible?' demanded Rodgers.

'I don't know. Several days,' said Lloyd.

'And only in our presence,' added Hall. 'In fact I think we'll review whether or not it will be continued at all, in the light of medical evidence . . .' To Lloyd he said, 'Mrs Lomax's collapse was genuine, not feigned?'

The doctor appeared surprised at the question. 'Unquestionably genuine. I don't even understand the question.'

'I've had a lot of people collapse on me when they

didn't have answers to the questions I was asking,' exaggerated Bentley.

Lloyd sighed, impatiently. 'Mrs Lomax was medically unconscious. She remains extremely disorientated.'

'We'll require a statement from you to that effect,' said Rodgers.

'Which I'll be pleased to provide, including the cause of the distress that preceded Mrs Lomax's collapse,' came back Lloyd, irritably. He was very aware he had given the medical permission for the questioning and he, too, now accepted it had been wrong. He'd been on duty for fifty-six hours and thought the British National Health Service and all hospital trusts were a total fucking disaster and wished he was allowed to tell someone.

'I want to know the moment she's well enough for me to see her again,' insisted Bentley, moving towards the door. It had been an absolute bloody shambles and he'd been made to look a prick, not once but several times. He wasn't sure if Rodgers was loyal enough not to spread stories.

He'd spoken to the doctor but it was Perry who replied, 'We'll let you know as soon as we are told. And decide, upon expert professional advice, whether it should be resumed at all.'

In their car Perry said, 'Why did you antagonize Bentley like that?'

'To see how easy it's going to be in court,' admitted Hall. 'And it's going to be very easy indeed.'

Perry nodded, impressed. Guardedly he said, 'Maybe it wasn't a good idea to have allowed the questioning?'

'We had medical agreement,' reminded the barrister. 'The doctor who gave it is prepared to testify the collapse was genuine. *And* to criticize police aggression. Which a jury will be able to judge for themselves when they see how quickly Bentley loses his temper.'

Perry gave another gesture of approval. 'You thinking of going along the sympathy road: wronged wife temporarily driven beyond control by a cheating husband?'

'I'm keeping an open mind but it's a strong possibility,' admitted Hall. 'We'd need to get as many women as possible on the jury, during selection.'

'I'd recommend that anyway,' said Perry.

'And let's get started right away with psychiatrists. I really don't want any committee decisions – that's important – but I want them all singing to the same tune when it comes to giving their evidence in court. So we'll discard any that don't concur for one that does.'

Perry didn't think the younger man was going to need as much hand-holding as he had first thought.

Jennifer's first conscious impression was of fog, fog in her head so that she couldn't think clearly, get her thoughts together. Or cotton wool: head stuffed with cotton wool, so that everything felt thick. At once there was noise, a lot of noise of a lot of people, enjoying themselves, laughing and shouting too loudly like people laugh and shout at a party after drinking too much. But the fog began to lift and it wasn't a lot of people. Just one. One that she knew, just as she knew, abruptly, where she was and what she had been accused of doing and why the bored policewomen were slumped in their chairs, ignoring her for their newspapers and magazines. And knew, worst of all, most terrible of all, what the detective had said about Gerald and the woman she'd thought to be her friend. Wasn't true: couldn't be true. Gerald had . . .

'*Of course it's true!*'

'No!'

'Gerald didn't love you.'

'He did.'

'Didn't love anyone, except himself. And fucking. Fucking anything that moved.'

'Not true.'

'She's back,' said the woman police constable, looking over her newspaper to her sergeant. 'Should we tell someone?'

'Suppose we'd better.'

The younger woman started to move towards the summons button but the sergeant said, 'I'll walk down to the nurse's station. It'll be something to do.'

The sound in Jennifer's head was of cackling, near hysterical laughter. *'This makes it all the better. Brilliant. Fucking your best friend. Think they planned to kill you, too? Murder you, like you murdered me? Might have been a problem, though. Couldn't go on killing wives he didn't want, could he? Might not have got away with it twice.'*

'Don't want to listen.'

'Oh, you're going to have to listen Jennifer. Listen to all of it. Hear what a shit he was. What a shit Rebecca was.'

Emily! Who was going to see Emily for her? Tell Emily her mummy loved her . . . ?

'Why not still ask Rebecca? She was fucking your husband so she might as well go on keeping it in the family. She'd have probably had the brat anyway, after Gerald had divorced you. Don't forget how clever he was, getting whatever he wanted. All he wanted was a brat, not you. You were a breeding animal, like a sow.'

'Stop!'

'Mrs Lomax?'

Jennifer became conscious of Lloyd beside her bed.

Conscious, too, that there was something sticking to her ribs and that thick leads connected her to a machine on one side but that the drip, although the bottle still hung from its hook, wasn't in her arm any more. But there was a fresh dressing on what had been her uninjured arm almost as large as the one on the other arm. It hurt.

Seeing the frightened head swivel the doctor said, 'You tore your arm rather badly, where the needle was inserted. I'm not sure you need it any more anyway . . .'

'What's the machine for?'

'Heart monitor.'

'*Broken-hearted Jennifer. See it on the machine!*'

Jennifer fought against a response and won. 'Have they gone?'

'Yes. I'm sorry. I shouldn't have allowed it.'

'You heard what the policeman said?'

'Yes.'

'Wasn't true.'

'*Don't be stupid.*'

'I don't know anything about that,' refused Lloyd, uncomfortably. He wished another doctor had been covering emergency when she'd been admitted.

'He wouldn't have done that. Not Gerald.'

'Mrs Lomax, I can't help you with any of that. I have to care for you medically.'

'You don't believe I'm mad, do you?'

'That's not my field. I'm concerned with your physical recovery.' To cover himself he should have a hospital psychiatrist examine her: make a report. Should have done that before agreeing to the police interview.

'*Course he thinks you're mad.*'

'Mrs Lomax?' intruded the woman police sergeant. 'Do you feel well enough now to talk to my superiors again?'

Jennifer flinched back on the bed and Lloyd wheeled towards the uniformed woman. '*I* have spoken to your superiors and told them there won't be any more interviews until I authorize it . . . *if* I authorize it. Nor are either of you to attempt to question her. If you do I shall insist upon your remaining outside of this room. Do you understand?'

The grey-haired woman retreated to her chair, face blazing.

'Thank you,' said Jennifer. 'Are you my friend?'

Lloyd blinked at the question. 'I'm your doctor.'

'*You haven't got any friends, Jennifer. No-one. And I'm going to leave you, too. I don't want anything to get in the way of your realizing how totally alone and helpless you are.*'

She *was* alone, Jennifer accepted. Totally. Clever of Jane to leave her, to think herself deeper into abandoned despair: to make mistakes like it had been a mistake to forget the numbness of Jane's presence . . . There was an abrupt contradiction. No it wasn't! Not clever at all. Alone she was able to think clearly – even the fog had gone – like she'd thought clearly before. Made decisions. What decisions were there to make now? The most important: the one never to forget. Wouldn't give up. Never had. Never would. And not just for herself. Because there *was* someone. Emily. If she gave up she would be giving up Emily. Which was unthinkable. By herself she had to fight – find a way out – and make a life with Emily. Just the two of them. The only thing that mattered now. Herself and Emily. She could do it. Had to do it. There was no alternative. What about the other decisions she'd made, earlier? Still the same. And in the same sequence. Couldn't plan anything about herself and

Emily until she'd proven herself innocent. More difficult, now. There had been a motive. A reason everyone would understand: oldest story in the book. Hadn't Gerald loved her, ever? All lies? Not all. It couldn't have been all lies. Just sex then with Rebecca? She'd never thought Rebecca sexy. The opposite, in fact. Icy. Couldn't remember their ever discussing men, talking about men sexually. Only remembered one man, an American broker. Wesley or Weston. Something like that. Flown over a few times, after Rebecca's transfer from New York. Spent one weekend with them in Hampshire. Never laughed and wanted to talk metal futures all the time. What was wrong with the sex she and Gerald had? Nothing, she hadn't thought. He'd liked sex, certainly. But so had she. Wanted it, whenever he had. Integral part of successful, ambitious people, a strong sex drive. Did whatever he wanted, like he'd done whatever she'd wanted. Maybe she should have known he'd need sex when they weren't together. Why hadn't he used hookers! It wouldn't have been so bad if he'd done that. Could have understood it: accepted it even. It wouldn't have meant anything. A business transaction. That was the pain, not that he'd slept with someone else but that it had been someone she knew, believed to be a friend. Humiliating. The office would have known. Inevitable that they would. Laughed at her: about her. Gerald not getting enough at home, has to look elsewhere. He wouldn't have wanted a divorce. Wouldn't have wrecked their perfect life. Wouldn't have hurt and bewildered Emily: wouldn't have hurt and bewildered her. Just sex, that's all it had been. Her own fault, for not realizing the risk. For being too complacent. Too late now. Gerald – Gerald who'd loved her but had an affair – was dead. Her life with him was dead, too. Had to start again. Rationalize it, accept it had happened and move on. Move on to her and Emily. Needed to get a lot of obstacles out of the way first. Jane most of all. Big mistake for Jane to have left: to have given her time. Couldn't let her realize it. Had to pretend to despair: to be devastated. Wouldn't be difficult. She had been humiliated: cheated. Gerald was a bastard, even if it was a casual affair. Not a problem to despise Rebecca. Bastard and a bitch. Easy enough to think like that. Had to be alert, for the tingling sensation: be even more alert for the gaps, when she could say things without Jane being able to interrupt.

Why had Gerald done it? Why hadn't she been enough for him?

'She's crying,' said the police constable.

'She's got every reason to,' said the sergeant. 'They always do when they get caught out.'

'Why's Mummy had to go away?'

'Mummies have to, sometimes,' said Annabelle.

'When will she be back?'

'I'm not sure yet. Eat up.'

'I don't want to eat up.'

'And I don't want you to be a rude girl.'

'Don't care.'

'No story tonight then.'

'Don't want a story. Want my mummy.'

Chapter Ten

Jennifer timed the sedative demand with the care of the previous night and resisted Jane's frenetic wake-up attempts even longer than before and felt better upon awakening than she had the previous day.

'Told you I'd find a way.' She didn't care any more about the sighed reaction from the attendant policewomen.

'It won't help you.'

'You can't control me all the time, can you?'

'*Whenever I want.*' Without her being able to stop it happening both of Jennifer's arms rose and in unison fell heavily back upon the bed. The police sergeant moved towards the door.

'I'll stop that happening, too.'

'*You're my puppet, Jennifer. Jump, puppet: jump puppet.*' Jennifer managed to stop her arms jerking to the chant that time.

'I can resist,' insisted Jennifer, excited by the discovery.

'Not enough to stop me doing exactly what I want with you. And whenever I want to do it.'

'Mistake, Jane! You've just admitted I'm right.'

For several moments Jennifer's head cleared. Then, from a long way off, there began a distant sound that grew louder by the second, like an onrushing, siren-wailing train. Except it wasn't a siren but a manic scream that rose and rose until Jennifer thought her head would explode, the pain so bad she screamed aloud herself. With her arm no longer tethered she tried to clamp both hands against her head, to close out the mind-splitting cacophony but couldn't because it wasn't coming from outside and her whole body convulsed with the vibration of the noise. The agony was so bad it was a long time before she became aware of restraining hands – an arm even encompassing her – and only then when the pain at last receded, as the sound passed. It was Peter Lloyd with his arm around her, a placating nurse on her other side. Both policewomen were at the foot of the bed, eyes bulged.

'Pissed yourself, Jennifer. Dirty girl!'

She had. She was, in fact, soaked, sweat glueing the hospital smock to her, hair lank rats' tails. 'She screamed. I thought my head was going to burst. I've made a mess.'

'It doesn't matter: we can clean you up,' assured Lloyd. Still with an arm around her, he squeezed her shoulder in added reassurance. He wouldn't argue against the hospital board's decision about the psychiatric examination. He hoped to Christ her lawyers agreed. The board's problem, not his: his was avoiding any fall-out from what had happened yesterday. The Social Services business was her lawyer's, too. Make sure the wounds didn't become infected: that's all he had to do. Then pass the problem on. It was still difficult to believe she could have done what she did. But then he'd never before treated – even seen – a murderer.

'She wants to prove how helpless I am.'

'And I did, didn't I!'

'We're going to do some tests today,' said Lloyd, pressing on, refusing any diversion.

'What tests? Ask him what tests?'

Jennifer managed to prevent herself, seizing a victory. 'To prove I'm sane?'

'Part of it.'

'I want to do that right away.' At the nurse's pressure she held out her least bandaged arm for a blood pressure cuff to be attached.

'*What tests?*' repeated Jane's voice, insistently.

'We must be medically sure you're recovered enough for a psychiatric examination,' explained Lloyd, unwittingly answering the question. 'Your heart monitor has been stable throughout the night. That's why we disconnected it.'

Until that moment Jennifer had been unaware the adhesive pads and their attaching leads had gone.

'*You're not . . .*' started Jane but the nurse was already releasing the cuff.

'Fine,' guaranteed the woman to Lloyd.

'Because of the . . .' started the doctor, then stopped. Determinedly he started again. 'Because you're officially facing a criminal charge, we've approached your lawyers. Invited them to participate . . .'

'With a psychiatrist?'

'Not from the hospital: our tests are to be strictly medical. Neurological. We'll take blood, faeces and urine samples and I also want to do a spinal tap now.'

Jennifer curled herself up in a ball, as the man instructed, but continued talking over her shoulder. 'Are they bringing a psychiatrist?' She'd intended dismissing Perry and Hall without the concrete assurance of a QC, she remembered. Not important, this early. The absolute essential – the essential upon which everything hinged – was to be declared sane. The insistence upon a senior barrister could wait.

'The Lord Chief Justice himself can't save you! You're lost. Can't prevent yourself being lost.'

'Call them,' ordered Jennifer, straightening herself as she was told and lying flat, without a pillow, to prevent any headache or nausea after the lumbar puncture. 'Tell them I want a psychiatrist, as well: that I won't have a neurological examination unless I have a psychiatric one.'

Precisely what the hospital board wanted, accepted Lloyd: the responsibility – and any unforeseen repercussions – that of the woman's advisors, the hospital's accountability tightly limited to scientifically provable and universally acknowledged medical criteria. 'That's your definite wish?'

'That's my positive instruction. Tell them that I demand it. And that I want it today.' There was a sudden rush of confidence, a feeling of being in charge. She had other feelings – other impressions – but refused to let herself think of them.

'What?'

'Not things for you to know,' refused Jennifer, embarking on another experiment.

'I beg your pardon?' frowned the doctor.

'I wasn't talking to you,' smiled Jennifer, apologetically.

Lloyd gestured for the nurse to leave with him. 'I'll call your solicitor.'

'Think it!'

'Make me!'

The numbness worsened, into a burn, but Jennifer easily resisted. 'I'm finding weaknesses about you all the time, aren't I, Jane? My mind was always better than other people's. I'm going to prove it.'

'And I'm going to enjoy taking that arrogance from you, like I'm going to take everything else from you.'

* * *

It wasn't Jennifer's demand but Julian Mason's insistence that a neurological screening was necessary that persuaded Jeremy Hall to change his mind about a joint examination. It wasn't, explained Mason, a shared discipline but a complimentary one. Hall was as impressed by the man as he was by the argument. Julian Mason was a past President of the Royal College of Psychiatrists, a senior lecturer at Essex University and the author of two acknowledged reference books on forensic psychiatry. Hall also liked that the man didn't *look* an absent-minded, long-haired psychiatrist, baggy jacketed, shapelessly trousered and meerschaum-piped. Mason wore a crew cut, jeans and an Essex university T-shirt under an unzipped cotton blouson: Hall hoped he had a different outfit for court. What Hall appreciated most of all was the absence of any condescension at their meeting in his cramped rooms overlooking the car park at the rear of the chambers, identifying him as the most junior member of the practice.

Mason listened intently to the facts of the murder, not interrupting until Hall linked schizophrenia with the voice in Jennifer's head. At once the man raised a halting hand, 'You're the lawyer. *I'm* the psychiatrist. I'll make the diagnosis.'

'Bentley thinks she's faking.'

'People try.'

'How difficult is it for you to tell?'

'Sometimes impossible. Sometimes easy.' Seeing the reaction on Hall's face the other man grinned and said, 'It's very difficult to fake genuine mental illness. People who try usually make lots of mistakes.'

'Her husband was having an affair,' reminded Hall. 'Could she have gone temporarily insane at discovering it?'

'There's no insanity as temporary as that. You're talking of enormous, hostile rage.'

'But she would have known what she was doing, no matter how enraged?'

'In my opinion, yes. You'll probably find others who disagree, if that's the way you want to go.'

'I want to defend her, to the best of my ability.'

'That's refreshing,' said Mason, in what could have been the first reference to Hall's inexperience.

'Let's hope I can do it.'

'I'm sure Mrs Lomax hopes the same.'

They rose at the announcement of Humphrey Perry's arrival with the car. Perry and Mason greeted each other with the familiarity of long association and Hall remained silent for most of the journey while the other two men brought each other up to date with personal happenings. Mason, it emerged, was a bachelor but Perry had six children, all boys but none in law. Both the youngest two had dropped out of university, one ironically from Essex. Mason said he didn't know the boy but that Perry wasn't to worry unduly: a lot of kids rebelled at the educational grind at university level and most returned after a year out.

From the greeting Mason also appeared to know the neurologist waiting for them at the hospital. George Fosdyke was a fussy, quick-speaking man with a wet handshake who made a specific point of quoting a psychology as well as a medical degree when he was introduced to Hall. The man's stiff white coat glistened from starch and his baldness was practically identical to that of Humphrey Perry, who stood slightly apart during the initial meeting. Hall thought the solicitor and the neurologist looked as if they had come off the same assembly line.

'How is she?' he asked Lloyd.

'Had quite a trauma this morning,' said the doctor. 'She became very distressed at what she described as a terrible noise she thought was going to make her head burst. But no collapse, like yesterday. Heart and blood pressure are quite normal.'

'All the other tests done?' interrupted Fosdyke.

'I did the spinal tap myself.'

As they walked towards the elevators Mason said, 'Is she mobile?'

'She hasn't been, so far,' said Lloyd. 'But she's not on any intravenous treatment any longer and she's off the heart monitor, so there's no reason why she couldn't be.'

'You're going to do a brain scan?' Mason asked the neurologist, expectantly.

'Of course,' said Fosdyke.

'You any objection to her walking to the scanner?'

'Good idea,' agreed Fosdyke.

It was Fosdyke who slowed first, bringing the group to a halt at the sight of Bentley and Rodgers outside the guarded ward: the woman police sergeant was with them. Lloyd said, 'I didn't know they were here. I gave no permission to resume the interview.'

Hall eased his way through the group to confront the detectives. 'This is a medical and psychiatric examination.'

'So she's well enough to be interviewed.'

'Not by you. My client declines to talk to you.'

'This is obstruction.' Bentley felt his temper slipping and made a conscious effort to stop it happening.

'It's her right. And my advice . . .' It needed Hall's professional control to avoid his annoyance at Bentley's presence becoming obvious and abruptly he determined to end the interference. Careless of the effect he knew it would have upon the other man he said, 'We'd appreciate no more irritations like this. There will be no further police interviews with my client . . .' He indicated the uncertain policewoman who had obviously warned Bentley of the examination from overhearing the arrangements being made. '. . . Nor will I accept the introduction in any later court hearing of anything my client says or does . . .'

Bentley moved to speak but Hall refused the objection, anticipating it. '. . . Your initial caution does not extend to remarks or actions overheard by police escorts, which you well know. Or should know. If you didn't, you've been officially told now. I want your policewomen *outside* my client's ward from this moment. If you ignore what I have just said . . . any of it . . . I shall complain through a judge in chambers to your Commander. Is there anything about which I've left you unsure, Superintendent Bentley?'

It was possible to gauge the detective's heartbeat from the throbbing of the protruding vein in his red-mottled forehead and for several moments the man was beyond speech. At last he managed, 'I will report this to my superiors.'

Hall didn't have to force the smile at the ludicrously ineffective response. 'I'd strongly urge you to do that.' He gestured through the window to the constable still inside the room. 'Please call her out.'

Rodgers did so, at a nod from the senior detective. As she emerged Hall said, 'Please make it clear they are to remain outside from now on.'

Rodgers did that, too. As Bentley stumped off down the corridor, trailed by his inspector, Julian Mason said, 'What was that all about?'

'An over-inflated sense of importance,' said Hall, hoping Bentley was still close enough to hear.

Inside the ward Jane said, '*Look, they're here. Let's really see how stupid we can make you, shall we?*'

Jennifer tried to clench the sheet on either side of her, wanting something physically to hold on to, but totally against her will her fingers wouldn't grip, splaying out helplessly instead.

'*It's no good, Jennifer. No good at all.*'

It wasn't. As the group entered her arms flapped up and down, in unison again but slapping harder against the bed, and Jane said, '*Now you're not a puppet, you're a penguin. Tell them you're a penguin.*'

Jennifer bit her lips between her teeth to prevent the words, holding her breath, but she couldn't stop a meaningless sound growling in her throat.

'What's the voice tell you to say?' asked Mason, conversationally. 'Let's hear it.'

Jennifer's breath came out in a rush. 'That I'm a penguin. Oh dear God, this is ridiculous!'

'I'm the one who's got to decide if it's ridiculous or not. That's why I'm here.' Mason pulled up the chairs abandoned by the police sergeant. Fosdyke took the other. Both ignored the lawyers, who pulled back against the wall furthest from the bed. Peter Lloyd remained at the foot of the bed. Hall was conscious of the two policewomen side by side looking through the window from the corridor.

'You're the psychiatrist,' smiled Jennifer. 'God, am I glad to see you! What's your name?'

Mason told her and introduced Fosdyke as well. Jennifer extended her hand, but as Mason went to accept the gesture her hand began rotating, as if challenging him to catch it. Mason laughed, although not nervously. So did the neurologist. He didn't sound nervous either.

'It's not funny!' protested Jennifer.

'You could laugh at her.'

'*No, you fucking well can't!*'

'Does it hurt, in your head, when you hear the voice?' demanded Fosdyke.

'Only when she screams. She did that this morning.'

'Why?'

'I said I could resist her.'

'Can you?' came in Mason.

'Sometimes.'

'How?'

'She'll know, if I tell you.'

'Don't tell me then,' agreed Mason.

'Tell him!'

'No!'

'What's she saying?' prompted the psychiatrist.

'She wants me to tell you how I do it.'

'Don't. Let's resist her.'

The screaming started, not as loud as before but still agonizing. Jennifer said, 'Oh no,' and felt herself begin to shake. She tried to get her hands up to her ears but couldn't move her arms. It stopped more quickly than before and she hadn't wet herself.

'She screamed again?' said Fosdyke.

Jennifer nodded, not immediately able to talk. When she could she said, 'Stop it!'

'You talking to Jane?' demanded Mason.

'You! Both of you. You're patronizing me. Pretending you believe me but you don't, do you? Because it's not possible to be possessed, is it?'

'I don't know,' admitted Mason. 'I've never heard of a proven case.'

'So why are you pretending to believe me?'

'Don't you want me to?'

'*I haven't really got to try, have I? They've made their minds up already.*'

'Jane says you've already made your minds up that I'm mad.'

'I haven't,' denied Mason.

'Neither have I,' said Fosdyke.

'*They're liars.*'

'Help me!' pleaded Jennifer, looking between the two men. 'For God's sake, help me!'

'How do you want to be helped?' asked Mason.

'Get her out of my head! Find a way to prove that I am sane and didn't kill Gerald.'

'I'm not sure I can do that,' admitted the psychiatrist. 'But I'll try. And for me to do that you'll have to help me.'

'Anything. Whatever.'

'*Why not open your legs? You're good at that.*'

'Tell me everything she says.'

'Everything?'

'Yes.'

'*Fuck him. Don't!*'

'She says fuck you. And that I should help you by opening my legs.'

Mason showed no reaction. Neither did the neurologist. Mason said, 'She tried to stop you repeating everything?'

'Yes.'

'So you defied her?'

'*He's a cunt.*'

'She says you're a cunt.'

Again neither Mason nor Fosdyke gave any reaction to the obscenities. Instead, suddenly, Mason said, 'You were having an affair with Gerald Lomax when his wife was still alive, weren't you?'

'*Whore, whore, whore.*'

Jennifer didn't reply at once. 'She's calling me a whore.' Then, 'Yes, we were having an affair.'

'You feel guilty about that?'

'*Of course she didn't. Mad whore.*'

'Yes,' said Jennifer. 'Jane says I didn't but I did.'

'Before his wife died? Or after?'

'Before and after.'

'*Liar.*'

'Did she know it was going on?'

'No, she didn't. And she called me a liar.'

'*No, I bloody well didn't know, you cheating whore!*'

'Were you going to tell her?'

'I wasn't. Gerald wanted to. She's calling me a cheating whore.'

'Why didn't he?'

'I asked him not to. I didn't want to be the person to break up a marriage.'

'*Lying whore!*'

'She says I'm a lying whore.'

'Are you lying?' asked Mason.

'No.'

'What did Gerald say?'

'That he didn't want things to go on as they were. That he didn't love Jane and wanted the marriage to end.'

'*LIAR!*' The voice roared, making Jennifer wince. Only slightly quieter, Jane said, '*Happy with me. Loved me until you came along.*'

'What does the voice say?' anticipated Mason.

'That I'm lying. That Gerald was happy with her until the affair started.'

'You think that's true?'

'Gerald said it wasn't.'

'You thought everything was all right between you and Gerald, didn't you?' pressed Mason.

'You want me to talk about Rebecca?'

'Do you want to?'

'Answer *me*!' demanded Jennifer, angrily. 'Why do you respond to every question I ask with another question? Can't you think for yourself?'

'*They got a crap psychiatrist, Jennifer. Because they're*

just going through the motions. You don't even know if he's qualified: from the way he's dressed, he could be a hospital porter.'

'Are you?'

'Am I what?'

'A qualified . . .' began Jennifer, before stopping. 'She says you're a crap psychiatrist. Could even be a hospital porter.'

Mason laughed. 'We're really upsetting her, aren't we?'

All the gauze-thin confidence that she could confront Jane had gone. Once more Jennifer felt totally lost, as if she was being sucked towards a whirlpool that would drag her down into a vortex from which she'd never escape.

'*That's it, honey. That's how it's going to be. Suffocating. Drowning. Like this . . .*'

It became difficult for Jennifer to breathe: it was as if someone had their arms wrapped around her, squeezing the air from her and not letting her inhale any more. She began to pant, noisily.

'You're panicking,' said the psychiatrist, calmly. 'Don't do that . . .' He felt out, enclosing her hand in both of his. 'Breathe with me, slowly now . . .' He began to space his words. 'In and out, in and out, in and out . . .'

Gradually – too gradually – the band around Jennifer's chest began to ease. 'That was awful. Frightened me.'

'You're all right now.'

'She could kill me, couldn't she? Make me kill myself?'

'*Good thought, honey. I'll keep it in mind . . .*' There was the cackling laugh. '*Your mind, my mind, somebody's mind. Thanks for the idea.*'

'I thought you said you could resist her?'

'Not when she makes me move my . . .' She stopped as first her left leg, then her right, kicked up under the bed covering. 'Shit! shit! shit . . . !'

'You stopped telling me what Jane's saying?'

'She said making me kill myself was a good idea. And that suffocating, as if I was drowning, was how she was going to make me feel. It was what it seemed like, when I couldn't breathe.'

'You can now.'

'Yes.'

'So how else do you feel?' demanded Mason, quickly.

'How do you think I feel?'

'Don't answer my question with another question.'

Despite herself – despite everything – Jennifer smiled at having her earlier protest thrown back at her. 'Frustrated! Impotent!' Then she repeated, 'How else do you expect me to feel?'

'Very different from that.'

'*What's he mean?*'

'She wants to know what you mean?'

'If she's so clever, tell her to work it out for herself.'

'*Tell me!*' It was a shout, loud enough to make Jennifer grimace yet again.

'Don't tell her!' Jennifer used the ploy she'd learned, uttering the words before the thought came in time for Jane to intercept.

'I'm not going to.'

'*Bastard!*'

'She's angry. Called you a bastard.'

'Good.' Then, quickly, 'You didn't know about Rebecca?'

'No.'

'Do you believe it?'

'I want to hear Rebecca say it.'

'Don't you believe the police?'

'I want to be in a room . . . somewhere . . . where she has to say it in front of me.'

'Why?'

'I thought she was my friend. Wouldn't do a thing like that to me.'

'Have you got a lot of friends?'

'No.'

'Does that worry you?'

'It didn't, until now.'

'Why does it worry you now?'

'I need someone to help me. Clothes. And there's Emily.'

Both lawyers stirred against the wall. Mason and Fosdyke ignored them.

'Tell me about Emily,' suggested Mason.

Jennifer smiled, distantly. 'She's our life, Gerald's and mine. He wanted a baby so much.'

'*Liar. Made me take the pill.*'

'She says I'm a liar. That he made her take the pill.'

'Do you know if that's true, about the pill?'

'Jane was a severe diabetic: that's what she died of, an insulin overdose. I know Gerald was warned that medically it would have been dangerous for Jane to become pregnant.'

'*Murderers.*'

'She's calling me a murderer. That's what she says: that Gerald and I murdered her, so we could be together.'

'Did you?'

'Of course we didn't. It's an absurd thing to say.'

'Gerald didn't ask you to take the pill?'

'I told you, he wanted a baby very much.'

'But there's only Emily?'

'I just didn't become pregnant, afterwards. I had tests: we both did. There was no reason why it didn't happen. It just didn't.'

'Will you hate Rebecca, if she admits the affair in front of you?'

'I don't know.'

'Will you hate Gerald?'

'I couldn't hate Gerald. Ever.'

'Not even if it's true?'

'It wouldn't have been love. Just sex.'

'Wouldn't you hate her, just the same?'

'I don't think so.'

'Why not?' The psychiatrist had come forward on his chair, jabbing the questions at her.

'If he needed another woman it would have meant I was inadequate, wouldn't it? That I'd failed. It would have been my fault.'

'*That you weren't such a good fuck, after all.*'

'She says I'd realize I wasn't such a good fuck after all.'

'Were you?'

Jennifer felt herself colour. 'I thought we had a more than satisfactory sex life,' she forced herself to say.

'You're embarrassed?'

'Of course I'm embarrassed.'

'Do you swear?'

'Swear?' frowned Jennifer.

'*Fuck, fuck, fuck.*'

'She's saying fuck all the time.'

'Do you? Use the word, I mean.'

'Yes,' admitted Jennifer at once.

'So you're not offended by it?'

'No. Are you?'

'No.'

'Tell me what you thought about driving up from the country.'

'I don't remember much about that. It was as if I was a passenger.'

'What about when you got to Gerald's office?'

Jennifer shook her head. 'I don't properly remember

that. I mean I do, but not as if I was part of it. It was as if I was looking on.'

Fosdyke stirred, a signal. 'What illnesses did you have, as a child?'

Jennifer frowned. 'The usual, I suppose.'

'I want to know, specifically.'

'I'm not sure, specifically. Is it important?'

'Very. Can we find out from your family?'

'I don't have a family. My mother died twelve years ago: my father four years later. I don't have any brothers or sisters.'

'No aunt or uncle who could help?'

'Both my parents were only children, like I was.'

'We could try a trace through the family doctor,' offered Peter Lloyd, from the bottom of the bed. 'We've got his name on the case notes.'

'Do that, will you? Now,' said the neurologist, without turning to the doctor, who hesitated and then eased his way past the silent lawyers.

'What about accidents?' persisted Fosdyke.

'*Being born.*'

'She says my being born was an accident,' Jennifer told Mason, who nodded but didn't say anything.

'What's the proper answer,' prompted Fosdyke.

'No.'

'No broken legs? Arms?'

'No.'

'What about head injuries?'

'*I've convinced them. You haven't any idea how insane you sound.*'

'She says you're convinced I'm insane . . . that I sound insane.'

For the neurologist's benefit, Mason said, 'What about a head injury, at any time?'

'No. Never.'

'How about your pregnancy?'

'Perfectly straightforward . . . wonderful . . . no problems at all.'

'The birth itself?'

'The gynaecologist said it was the easiest he'd ever known.'

Fosdyke turned invitingly to Mason, who shook his head. To the lawyers the neurologist said, 'I'm going to carry out a physical examination. Excuse us.'

Hall and Perry filed obediently into the corridor to the hostile glares from the two policewomen. The barrister continued walking until he was beyond their hearing before turning to the solicitor. 'Well?'

'I don't know a court that would put up with it,' said Perry, flatly.

'I don't think I do, either.'

'I'm frightened what the reaction might be to what I've got to tell her about Emily,' said Perry. 'Maybe I should wait until tomorrow?'

Hall shook his head, forcefully. 'Not in the circumstances. Make sure Lloyd's with you.'

'What about you?' asked the solicitor, seeking as much support as possible.

Hall looked sceptically at the older man. 'All right.'

Peter Lloyd emerged from the elevator at the far end of the corridor. When he reached them Lloyd said, 'The family doctor is faxing what medical records there are. Which aren't very much. We went through it on the phone: she's never had a day's illness in her life.'

'Until now,' said Perry, as the doctor moved on to the ward. 'And now she's making up for all the lost years.'

Inside the tiny room Jennifer lay on top of the bed as Fosdyke went through the neurological routine. Her toes contracted when a pencil tip was drawn across the soles of her feet and with her eyes closed she correctly isolated every point at which he lightly touched a pin against unbandaged parts of her arms and legs. Still with her eyes closed she correctly brought her finger-tip unfalteringly to the tip of her nose and resisted his pressure when he pushed against her raised legs. He repeated the test more gently against her injured arms but she was still able to respond.

'If you can't prevent it, don't worry, but I don't want to hear anything the voice says in your head,' warned Fosdyke. 'I just want your answers to my questions.'

'Jane isn't here,' broke in Jennifer.

'How do you know?'

'There's no tingling, burning sensation.'

'Why didn't you tell us about that earlier?' demanded the neurologist.

'I didn't want her to know. That's how I'm warned she's with me: how I can beat her.'

'When were you born?' demanded the neurologist, briskly.

'June eighth, nineteen sixty-six.'

'So you're thirty-three?'

'Thirty-two.'

'What's your name?'

'What?' frowned Jennifer.

'Answer me.'

'Jennifer Lomax.'

'What was it before you were married?'

'Stone. Jennifer Stone.'

'Where were you married?'

'Caxton Hall.'

'When?'

'January fifteen, nineteen ninety-three.'

'What time?'

'Two o'clock.'

'Your degree's economics?'

'And mathematics. I took an additional module.'

'Where?'

'Oxford.'

'What was it?'

'Double First.' Before either man could speak further, Jennifer said, 'Why is this important?'

'That's for us to decide,' said Fosdyke. 'Do you know what a brain scan is?'

'Like an X-ray, of my head.'

'*They won't see me!*'

'She's back. Says you won't see her.'

'I'm not looking for her.'

'*What's he want?*'

'She wants to know what you want.'

'It's nothing to do with her.'

'*Tell me!*'

'She's demanding to know.'

'She isn't going to,' said Fosdyke. 'Do you think you could walk to the scanner? It's one floor below.'

Jennifer looked to Lloyd, who said, 'Do you feel up to it?'

'Of course.'

Lloyd helped Jennifer into a shapeless hospital dressing gown, over the smock that had been changed after she'd wet herself. Jennifer looked down at herself, then smiled wanly up to Mason. 'Not actually haute couture, is it?'

'That worry you?' asked the psychiatrist.

Jennifer remained smiling, although sadly. 'I was going to ask Rebecca to bring some of my own stuff in. That's ironic, isn't it?'

The two policewomen straightened into something like attention when Jennifer came out into the corridor, hands clasping the dressing gown around her. They quickly fell into step behind the specialists, who walked either side of Jennifer. It wasn't until they shouldered into the elevator that Jennifer realized Hall and Perry had joined them. No-one spoke. Jennifer remained tensed for Jane, who never came. The lawyers and the policewomen stood separately outside the scanner room.

Sure he was beyond their hearing, Perry said, 'You sure it was a good idea to antagonize Bentley quite so much?'

'It was a good idea to close down any further interviews.' Hall nodded towards the uniformed women. 'And insist they remain outside. From now on the prosecution is going to be kept strictly within the rules of exchange and disclosure.'

'Does that matter, considering the case they've got?'

Hall smiled at the solicitor. 'If they've got enough then they've got enough.'

It was almost an hour before Jennifer and the doctors left the scanner room. In the tiny outside vestibule Fosdyke said to Lloyd, 'We've got all the samples?'

'The spinal tap was with pathology an hour ago,' said Lloyd.

'Then I'm finished.' He looked at Mason, who said, 'I've got enough, for the moment.'

'For a preliminary finding?' demanded Hall.

Jennifer felt the onset of numbness and blurted, 'Not in front of me: I don't want her to know!'

'*Bitch!*'

'Too quick for you,' said Jennifer.

'She back?' asked Mason.

'Called me a bitch.'

'I'll need an hour, to go through the tests, apart from my own,' said Fosdyke.

'I'd like to think about it too, before we talk. Let's make

it an hour, shall we?' suggested Mason.

'My rooms,' offered Fosdyke.

'We've got some other business to go through,' said Hall. He looked at Peter Lloyd. 'And I'd appreciate your being with us.'

No-one spoke during the walk to the upper corridor. Immediately inside the ward again Jennifer said to Perry: 'Can you arrange for me to get my own clothes in here? Have someone call Annabelle and go down to fetch them . . . ?' She smiled, as the uninterrupted thought came to her. 'Would it be possible for me to see Emily?'

There was a moment's silence between the two lawyers. Perry said, 'That's the other business we have to go through, Mrs Lomax. Social Services want to get involved with care provisions for Emily.'

'NO!' screamed Jennifer.

'*Everything destroyed completely,*' mocked the voice. '*I'll leave you all by yourself to think what it's going to be like to lose Emily for ever.*'

Chapter Eleven

'She can't be taken away! She's all I have now.' There was no sensation of Jane and Jennifer forced herself to remain icily calm after the initial outburst. Panic or hysteria wouldn't save Emily. And saving Emily – keeping Emily – was abruptly the most important consideration. The only consideration. It was still difficult to sit on the side of the bed and not do more, speak louder, to make them understand. Dr Lloyd was beside her, still holding the wrist he'd snatched up to check her pulse rate at the screamed protest.

'Is she all right?' demanded Hall, worriedly.

'Pulse is OK,' nodded Lloyd.

'Don't talk across me!' demanded Jennifer. 'I'm perfectly under control: Jane isn't here. I said Emily isn't being taken away from me. You've got to stop it. Stop it now.'

'Is there no family, on either side, who could become legal guardians in your . . .' Perry hesitated. '. . . in your absence?'

The question unnecessarily reminded Jennifer once more of how totally alone she was and momentarily she couldn't reply. Swallowing she said, 'No. No-one.'

'What about Gerald's family?'

'There isn't one. He was an only child, no uncles and no aunts. And his parents are dead.'

'The local authorities do have a legal responsibility, although I am surprised they're exercising it so quickly,' warned the solicitor, cautiously. He ignored the now vacant chairs. So did Hall. The doctor remained where he was, beside Jennifer on the bed, although he released her wrist.

'Emily hasn't been abandoned. Left.' Jennifer became aware of the two policewomen staring through the window. 'Must they look in like that? I'm like a bloody freak show.'

'They're not being allowed in here any more, so I'm afraid you've got to put up with it,' said the barrister. He should have anticipated the effect upon her of the official approach about the child but hadn't. But then neither had Perry. At least there'd been the forethought to get Geoffrey Johnson the woman's power of attorney.

Jennifer made an impatient dismissive gesture. 'Emily can't be taken away from me! I won't let that happen.'

Hall breathed in, heavily. 'I won't hold out any false hope. Legally she can be, if you're convicted.'

'I've not been convicted, not yet,' seized Jennifer. 'I'm still innocent, aren't I?'

'Yes,' conceded Perry and Hall regretted the doubt in the man's voice.

'Then they can't do anything. Emily is being cared for by a certificated nanny, in a mansion for Christ's sake. She's the best looked after child in England.'

'That's probably right, at the moment,' agreed Hall. 'You want us legally to oppose any move by the authorities?'

'Of course I do!' said Jennifer, with fresh impatience. 'I

want you to do every conceivable thing to block whatever they try to do. I don't care what it is or how much it costs. Just do it.' There was a sudden empty feeling of helplessness. 'Please . . .' She half reached out, towards the barrister, before stopping, embarrassed at the unthinking movement. She was glad the man hadn't instinctively responded.

'We could prove adequate care provision with an onsite visit: attend ourselves,' Perry suggested. Halfway through he remembered Jennifer's dislike of being ignored and turned away from Hall to include her as he spoke.

'Arrange it,' said Jennifer, eagerly.

'This nanny . . . ?' Hall let the question trail.

'. . . Annabelle,' prompted Jennifer.

'. . . Annabelle is definitely certificated?'

'Norland trained,' assured Jennifer. 'She's been with us since Emily was born . . . Emily adores her . . .'

'There's no question of her not continuing in the job?' pressed Perry, careless of the grammar.

'Of course not! Why should there be!'

'We'd better establish that positively, before any meeting with the authorities,' said Hall. He didn't have any real doubt from the woman's behaviour with the psychiatrist and the neurologist that she was suffering some mental abnormality. How much worse might it get if the child was officially put into care? He probably could, technically, prevent the child being taken until after a court verdict but it didn't amount to anything more than postponing the inevitable. He really didn't intend offering false hope but there was nothing to be achieved, apart perhaps from a worse collapse, from being too honest with her. A doubt began to flicker. It was curious that all talk of voices in her head ended at the threat of losing her daughter. Hall stopped the reflection, positively: wrong to risk preconceived impressions before hearing the professional opinion of the two specialists. Worth mentioning to them, though.

'You'll do it all today: stop the process before it begins?' demanded Jennifer, urgently.

'Before doing that I think it's important to get things clear between us,' said Perry. 'During the interview with the police I got the feeling you were dissatisfied with your legal representation . . .'

Hall frowned. It was something that had to be clarified and Perry was the person who had to do it but he wished the timing could have been different. His look towards the bed was for a reaction but for the first time he properly focused on the woman herself. Almost unconsciously his initial impression had been that Jennifer Lomax really had looked like a mad woman, lank-haired, bedraggled and distraught. But today the eyes weren't black ringed any more, the blond hair had a semblance of a style and what little make-up she'd bothered with wasn't smudged: the swelling had gone down and the cut lip was scarcely noticeable. She was, in fact, looking more like the woman whose photograph was yet again blazoned over that day's newspapers, although the head-tilted, almost arrogant confidence of the pictures wasn't evident in the woman at whom he was looking. But then it would have been impossible to appear elegant in the hospital smock and towelling robe.

Jennifer returned Jeremy Hall's attention, although not appraisingly but honestly. He was a very broad-shouldered man and she liked the way he looked directly at her, not avoiding her eyes as if he was embarrassed or afraid of her. The blue striped suit was beginning to shine at the elbows and she guessed the shirt was on its second wearing. It looked like a family crest on the signet ring.

She really didn't want to do what she had to: she simply didn't have a choice. Maintaining the calm – enjoying being able to feel it without the Southern drawl voice echoing in her head – she said, 'I am not mad but I could easily be made so by the nightmare I'm living in, right now . . .' A smile came, briefly. 'Except that I am not going to let it happen. But for me to survive, in any court, I need the very best criminal lawyer it is possible to get. Which means someone with murder trial experience. Someone, in fact, whose very reputation is going to make a court listen: to believe him because he believes me. I'm not trying to be offensive or doubt you. But I'm fighting, literally, for my sanity and my freedom and now I'm fighting for my child. I can't concern myself with hurt feelings . . .' Jennifer straggled to a stop, not sure how further to explain herself.

'I can assure you, Mrs Lomax . . .' began Perry but Hall broke across the solicitor's stood-to-attention formality.

'No, let me. I am not offended by anything you've said, today or prior to today. We are still very much in the preliminary stages of your case. We've talked about that. Like we've talked about my being a junior counsel. Which is the capacity in which I will act, to the best of my ability. No leader – that's what we call a QC, heading a case – becomes involved now. Don't be offended for your part, but what we are doing now is the nuts and bolts of a defence preparation. Which is the function of a junior counsel.' He found it virtually impossible to believe a woman who had just expressed herself so logically and reasonably was the same person who a few hours earlier had been ranting and raving obscenities.

'So there will be a QC with previous experience of murder trials?' insisted Jennifer.

Just as pedantically Hall said, 'There are eight QCs in my chambers. I will ask the most experienced, in murder, to represent you.'

Jennifer did not speak for several moments. 'Thank you. I trust you.'

For even longer Humphrey Perry remained staring at the barrister before turning to Jennifer. Still stiffly formal he said, 'So you wish to retain our services?'

'Yes,' said Jennifer, although speaking to Hall. Then, briskly, she went on, 'You will personally go down, for the onsite visit with the authorities?'

'Yes.'

'When I am taken from here, to the hospital wing of a prison, will I be allowed to wear my own clothes?'

'Yes,' guaranteed Hall.

'The Hampshire visit will have to be arranged, beforehand. I want Annabelle to sort out some clothes for me. Tell her to use her own judgement. I want suits . . . nightwear and a dressing gown, obviously. Underwear. And toiletries and make-up.'

'I'll see it's arranged,' promised the barrister.

There was a silence but it was obvious there was something more Jennifer wanted to say.

'What?' prompted Hall.

Turning to the doctor, Jennifer said, 'When will you give medical permission for me to be transferred to a prison hospital?'

Lloyd hesitated. 'Two or three days. You're very much better, medically.'

Jennifer ignored the qualification, although it registered. To Hall she said, 'I'm not convicted. I can have visitors. I want Emily brought here, to this proper hospital to see me. I don't want her brought into a prison.'

'I will try to arrange it,' promised Hall.

Perry strode intentionally fast to their assessment from the psychiatrist and neurologist, to distance them from the doctor who lingered to speak to a nurse. Perry said, 'That was totally outrageous! No senior in your chambers will take over this and you know it!'

'They will, if my uncle decides they should.'

'And why should he do that?'

'To keep his part of whatever deal you arranged with Bert Feltham for us to act in the first place. I need your help, Humphrey, not your condescension. And I need you to understand that I'm not stupid.' Hall stopped at the elevator, turning to face the man. 'We'll get on much better if we have that understanding, OK?'

'It's an indefensible case,' protested Perry, unthinkingly.

'Then whatever you promised Sir Richard must be mega,' said Hall.

Chapter Twelve

Neither Mason nor Fosdyke was talking when the other three men entered the neurologist's rooms. Both were lounged with polystyrene cups balanced on their chests, Fosdyke behind his desk tilted far enough back in a much-used round-back chair to gaze up at the ceiling, Mason with his feet propped on some unrecognizable carved protrusion from the front of the equally much-used desk. The surprise didn't finish with desk and chairs. In total contrast to Fosdyke's over-starched, pristine appearance it was a cluttered, disorganized room of half-open drawers and sagged cabinets. On top of one paint-chipped cabinet a neglected, unidentifiable plant had withered into the vague shape of a sacrificial cross. The only cleared space on the paper-littered desk was around three photograph frames: close by a tower was slowly rising from previously much-fingered polystyrene cups placed one inside the other.

Fosdyke brought himself up at their arrival, gesturing towards three straight-back chairs obviously newly installed in an uncertain, formal line opposite Mason. Opposing combatants again, thought Hall.

Fosdyke said, 'Waiting Room issue, I'm afraid . . .' He raised his coffee container. 'Like this: can you believe cleaners and patients steal anything else! God knows what for! But I grind the coffee myself. Colombian . . .' There was another gesture, to a table near the window where a full pot stood on its hotplate. '. . . Help yourselves.'

Lloyd continued straight on to the coffee. Perry hesitated, then followed. Hall sat down, looking around the room. Perhaps, he thought, the mess was a camouflage against further larceny. The idle reflection was short lived. A few hundred yards away there was a mentally ill murderer who'd cut another human being – her husband – to pieces and this meeting to help her began with an apology about hospital furniture and coffee cups. Wrong, Hall corrected himself, at once. They were doing a job, all of them performing different expertise from different perspectives. But as proper, dispassionate professionals, not allowing the distraction or influence of personal involvement. My first murder, he reminded himself: their attitude was right, his was wrong.

Still at the machine the solicitor turned and said, 'You sure?'

'Black, no sugar,' accepted Hall. He hoped Perry hadn't imagined he'd waited to be served. He was sorry taking it within seconds of Perry giving him the container: it was too hot to hold without a handle, and he hurriedly placed it on the floor. The returning Lloyd repositioned his chair more towards the doctors before he sat down. Combatants, Hall thought again.

'Well?' invited Perry. 'What's the verdict?'

'Limited, from my side,' said Mason, lowering his feet to the floor. 'So let's start with medically provable findings.'

On cue Fosdyke came further upright, too, assembling a few sheets of paper and some X-ray plates before him. As he did so the psychiatrist said, 'Remember, as far as I am concerned, this isn't a verdict. It's a very preliminary impression.'

Fosdyke coughed. 'Quite obviously mental problems –

insanity even – can be brought on by physical factors or illness. We know now, from symptoms still recorded in the archives, that George III wasn't mad: he suffered from porphyria, which we'd control by pills today . . .' He was playing with his notes but Hall didn't think the neurologist needed them.

'As well as for organic reasons, apparent mental illness can be caused by head or brain malformation or injury,' continued Fosdyke, looking up. 'A difficult birth, the use of forceps or Caesarian section, things like that can result in cerebral anoxia, damage the temporal lobes and bring about epileptic dysfunction in later life . . . cortical atrophy even . . .'

Perry stirred, smiling sideways to Hall. 'This could be better than any defence we've thought of so far . . . !'

'If I could find any of it, which I can't,' stopped Fosdyke, immediately puncturing the expectation. He made an inclusive gesture towards Lloyd. 'As a part of my assessment, we've carried out faeces, urine and blood tests. Earlier today there was even a lumbar drain, to examine spinal fluid for any cranial bleed or infection. In nothing we have done have we found the slightest evidence whatsoever of any medical conditions or illness from which Mrs Lomax might be suffering: most certainly nothing that would reflect upon or cause the mental collapse she appears to have undergone—'

'What about physical damage or malformation?' pressed Hall, reluctant to lose an acceptable defence avenue.

'She responded a hundred per cent normally to every sensory test I carried out in the ward,' refused Fosdyke. 'In the examination room I even extended the scan, beyond the brain, to include the upper part of the body. There is absolutely no brain abnormality or malformation to account for Mrs Lomax's behaviour. Neither is there in the upper body: anything that could be interrupting the oxygen or blood supply to the brain, for instance . . .'

'. . . In short?' invited Hall.

Fosdyke lifted the plates and printouts from the scan and said, 'In short, Jennifer Lomax is, *physically* and *neurologically*, probably the fittest thirty-two-year-old woman I've ever examined in my life. Actuarilly, she'll live to be a hundred.'

Hall finally picked up his cooled coffee. It was excellent, despite its container. 'There's no other test left you could carry out?'

The neurologist shook his head. 'I'm sorry.'

'So am I,' said the barrister, with feeling.

Beside him Perry said to Julian Mason, 'Which means our hope comes back to you.'

'I'm not sure you're going to be any better pleased,' said the psychiatrist. He got up, refilled his cup and stayed slightly propped against the window in an attitude reminding Hall of how his tutor had sometimes tried to explain particularly esoteric points of law. The recollection prompted a reminder of its own, which he put aside until he'd heard Mason out.

'You can't have found *nothing*,' challenged Perry in irritation.

Mason smiled, unoffended. 'The problem may be that I've found too much but that I need even more.'

Hall detected a move of fresh irritation beside him and quickly said, 'Perhaps you should talk us through it.'

The psychiatrist paused, preparing himself but unencumbered by any notes. 'You've got to understand from the outset that one session, like we had today, was always going to be totally inadequate. I'll need more – probably a lot more – if I'm ever going to be of any practical use to you or to a court.'

'Of course we accept that,' said Hall. 'What we're looking for today is a *suggested* way to go forward.'

Mason nodded, extending the gesture towards the neurologist. 'George was looking for a pathological cause for Mrs Lomax's condition. And didn't find one. On face value Mrs Lomax is showing some of the classic symptoms of schizophrenia. There are no pathological tests for schizophrenia. It's decided upon by the psychiatrist from visual and behavioural perception. For which they observe the symptoms devised by a German psychiatrist named Schneider: technically it's called the Schneider Present State Examination. Mrs Lomax's most obvious symptom is Second Person Auditory Hallucination: people – in this case one person – are talking to her. Equally obvious is Delusion of Thought Insertion: Jane can think for Jennifer, is aware of Jennifer's thoughts . . . is inside her head, listening.'

Mason paused to sip his coffee and Hall waited, far from impatient at the lecture. Rather, he wanted a lecture: whatever defence they decided upon, he was going to need the phrases and the methodology. To be able to use and understand them.

'There are some other schizophrenic indicators,' resumed the psychiatrist. 'The apparent uncontrolled movement of her arms and legs. Not having many friends is schizoid. Using obscenities is another . . . the actual murder would come under the heading of dyssocial personality disorder . . .'

Humphrey Perry didn't have Hall's patience. 'So she's genuinely mentally ill? Not properly aware of what she's doing so we can suggest she's suffering diminished responsibility or is unfit to plead?'

'No,' said the psychiatrist, shortly.

'No!'

'I've treated and diagnosed dozens of schizophrenics: a lot of paranoid schizophrenics who've killed. And I've never before encountered anyone like Jennifer Lomax.'

'So she's faking it?' persisted Perry, easily able to dance to a different rhythm.

'I don't think that, either.'

There was a sharp sideways look from Lloyd. The neurologist gave no reaction and Hall presumed the two specialists had fully discussed everything before their arrival. He had to remember the absence of the voice, as well as raise the query from the long ago Cambridge debate. He said, 'Until this moment I've understood everything you've said. Now you're losing me.'

'What was the first thing that interested her when we met, knowing I was a psychiatrist?' demanded Mason.

Perry shook his head.

'Your name,' recalled Hall.

'Exactly. And she smiled. A schizophrenic wouldn't have been interested in my name. Nor have smiled, to *fit* the circumstances of the introduction. Facial reaction is usually dysfunctional, out of context or keeping with the moment: she frowned in the right places at the right time and she smiled in the right places at the right time.' Mason seemed surprised his polystyrene container was empty and added to it. 'Mouthing obscenities is a common manifestation. But being embarrassed by them isn't. When she told me Jane had called her a good fuck and I asked her if she was, she visibly blushed, discomfited, although she admits to using the word herself. The context of everything she did and said is vitally important. And everything she did and said *fitted*, as if there was a person none of us was aware of, taking part in the discussion . . .'

Perry sighed, too heavily, and Mason grinned at him.

'You think I'm enjoying saying this . . . even considering possession . . . !

'Faked!' dismissed the solicitor.

'Then answer me this!' demanded Mason, coming forward with the challenge that reminded Hall again of his Cambridge tutor when he'd laid a trap for an inattentive student. 'If you were faking a mental illness and were confronted by two supposed experts . . .' He waved his hand towards the neurologist. '. . . Like George and I, what would be absolutely vital for you to know . . . !'

Once again, uncomfortably, Perry shook his head.

'Whether we believed you or not,' supplied Fosdyke, re-entering the conversation and confirming Hall's guess of a rehearsal. 'When we came out of the scanner Peter and I said we had sufficient and Hall asked if it was enough for a preliminary finding—'

'—And Jennifer stopped either of us replying,' came in Mason. 'She actually said "Not in front of me: I don't want her to know" and claimed the voice called her a bitch for not letting us speak, even if we'd intended to.'

'All part of a damned clever act,' suggested Perry.

'I've never encountered a schizophrenic that clever that quickly: they're cunning but not conventionally or logically so,' insisted Mason. 'We need to know a lot more about her personal history – a hugely lot more, in fact – but we do know from the newspapers she was a highly intelligent trader in Lomax's office before they got married. Some papers are calling her a genius. So OK, let's go along with your disbelief that she's genuinely ill: that she's faking it. If she's faking it, why is her only concern to be declared sane! That doesn't make any sense. Mentally ill she has a defence, a sympathetic sentence. Sane and she's a calculating murderer looking at life.'

'Could the voice be her own invention, without her realizing it?' suggested Perry. 'Her guilt that Jane died after she'd started the affair: imposing her own punishment upon herself?'

Mason smiled at the lay effort. 'A very outside possibility. There would have been symptoms before that would have shown up on her medical records, I would have thought.'

'So would I,' agreed Fosdyke.

'What other contradictory features are there?' intruded Hall.

'People who are mentally ill don't argue as forcefully or as logically as she did: they shout and scream but again out of context. She argued logically. Schizophrenics don't complain of feeling frustrated or impotent at their condition. She does,' recited Mason. 'The meeting today was disjointed, on our part . . .' Once more he gestured towards the neurologist. '. . . In fact the closest we came to a structured Schneider clinical interview was when George asked her the personal questions . . .'

'During which I intentionally miscalculated how old she was, after she told me her date of birth,' Fosdyke pointed out.

'She corrected him at once,' reminded Mason. 'That wouldn't have been important to anyone suffering a schizophrenic dysfunction.'

'That all?' queried Hall, anxious now to get to his own points.

The psychiatrist shook his head. 'There are appearance exceptions – there's even a clinical description for it – but predominantly mentally ill people don't bother about how they dress: they're usually a mess, with no attempt at colour co-ordination. Her appearance upset Jennifer: she was embarrassed at looking like she did, in a hospital gown and robe that somebody else would have worn before her and didn't fit her anyway . . .' He paused, needing more coffee. 'And I've got a problem about the uncontrollable limb movements. That's why I wanted her to *walk* to the scanner, even before I knew there was going to be sudden arm or leg movements. If she was faking, she would have performed something as we walked down the corridor for the scan. She didn't . . .'

'And I've never got a genuinely mentally ill person into a scanner unless they've been catatonic or sedated,' said Fosdyke. 'They're invariably terrified of being put into what looks like a claustrophobic tunnel. We actually hesitated, to test her out. She asked us what we were waiting for.'

There was an abrupt, empty silence in the room. The concentration settled upon Hall, who stood up and used the coffee machine as Mason had to become the centre of everyone's attention. By letting him do so – instead of hurrying condescendingly to fill the vacuum – Perry had deferred to him, establishing the proper solicitor-barrister relationship. Hall hoped it wasn't an isolated concession: he didn't enjoy the idea of being manipulated by Perry and Feltham, as he was sure he was being manipulated. Perry hadn't even bothered to argue against the accusation when confronted with it.

Hall said, 'I'm still confused but I'd like to get some things clear in my mind. After an initial examination you can't say she's suffering a mental illness, nor can you say she's faking one?'

'No, I can't,' agreed Mason.

'A person – a very clever person, like Jennifer Lomax – could have learned of schizophrenic symptoms, even know what Schneider guidance is, by reading a psychiatric text book?'

'Yes,' agreed Mason.

'And there's no pathological reason for how she's behaving?'

'None,' agreed Fosdyke.

'I haven't read up on it yet, but I remember a discussion when I was a law student about—'

'Multiple Personality Disorder?' anticipated the psychiatrist, smiling once more at a lay question.

'Wouldn't that come within the range of schizophrenia?' agreed Hall, wishing he hadn't been interrupted.

'It's an American favourite,' said Mason, still smiling although not patronizingly. 'It goes all the way back to 1957 and the film *The Three Faces of Eve*. Joanne Woodward won an Oscar playing a woman in whose body three separate personalities existed, a housewife, a good-time girl, a sophisticated woman . . .'

'I'm not interested in Hollywood films,' dismissed Hall, aware of Humphrey Perry's vague smirk.

'The American Psychological Association is,' offered Mason. 'It has published accepted Papers that the condition affects up to five hundred thousand Americans, practically all women. In nineteen-eighty it was accepted as an official psychiatric diagnosis, even though at that time only two hundred cases recognized as genuine were on record . . . in nineteen-ninety a man in Wisconsin was charged with rape for having sexual intercourse with a consenting twenty-six-year old who became a six-year-old child during the act: at the beginning of the trial each of the twenty-one personalities occupying the woman had to be sworn in separately . . .'

'Could what Mrs Lomax appears to be suffering be Multiple Personality Disorder?' Hall saw that his instructing solicitor wasn't smirking any more.

'In America, probably,' conceded Mason. 'It's not a

diagnosis accepted here, as far as I know, although there are widely known case histories. I've actually heard *The Three Faces of Eve* discussed among professionals as if it was a clinically diagnosed and proven case, not a movie.'

'It's never been offered as a defence in an English court, to my knowledge,' said Perry.

'Nor mine,' said the psychiatrist. 'You're going to get other opinions as well as mine, of course?'

'Of course,' agreed Perry, happy to be back on solid, legal procedural ground.

'Then use an American psychiatrist who's familiar with the syndrome.'

'We will,' accepted Hall, at once. 'But you want more sessions?'

'Very much so. I'd particularly like to examine her under hypnosis, if she'd agree to it.'

'Can people lie under hypnosis?' demanded Hall, recognizing a new opportunity.

'They're less inclined to. There are some people who can't *be* hypnotized.'

'If she were – if she agreed and was a suitable subject – would you be able to decide whether or not she was faking the voice?' asked Hall.

'I might get a better indication than I've got so far,' offered the psychiatrist, guardedly.

'I think she's undergone enough examinations, of every sort, for one day,' came in Lloyd, protectively.

'I agree,' said Mason, at once.

'There's something you don't know,' Hall said, remembering. It only took him minutes to explain the local authority approach about Emily's care but before he reached what he thought might be important Mason broke in to demand how she'd reacted.

'Outrage at the very beginning,' recounted Hall. 'Then

calmly, logically. She's instructed us to oppose it. But there was something I thought might be important. There was no second voice. She was quite rational, throughout.'

'Did she explain that?' frowned Mason.

'No. Perhaps you should have been there?'

The psychiatrist shook his head. 'It'll be a starting point tomorrow. With the hypnosis.'

'If she agrees,' cautioned Lloyd.

Jennifer did, at once, fifteen minutes later. Still without any physical sensation of Jane's presence she asked, too, for the sedation to keep the voice away during the night.

'Don't you want to hear about the preliminary findings?' asked Mason, experimentally.

'No!' refused Jennifer, anxiously and at once.

'He said what?' demanded Feltham. They were in El Vino again, because Jeremy Hall had insisted on returning to chambers and Perry hadn't wanted obviously to meet the chief clerk there. And Feltham was annoyed because he didn't like being around this late. Lunch was his time.

'Words to the effect that he knew there was a hidden agenda and that to keep whatever else was on offer he'd get a leader – Sir Richard himself, he hinted – for the Lomax case.'

'Cheeky bugger! What did you say?' One advantage of not having to return to the office to work was that he could drink claret instead of lighter white wines. The St Emilion was excellent.

'Nothing.'

'Didn't you even deny it?'

'I dismissed it. Said the case was indefensible.'

'How *is* it shaping up?'

'Bloody nightmare. Hall is taking it all so seriously, as if there is a worthwhile plea to enter. And he's far more confident than I thought he might be at our first meeting. Had me call the Hampshire Social Security people from the car, on our way back, and then dictated a list of instructions as long as my arm before we got here. His last insistence was that I go down to Hampshire with him tomorrow. When I asked him how he expected me to do that as well as everything else he said he had every confidence in me.'

Feltham nodded to another claret. 'Judges don't like cocky young beginners. You want me to have a word in his ear?'

'No,' said Perry. 'Just wanted to keep you up to date with things.'

'How is she?'

'Totally mad.'

'No leader from my chambers is going to appear in court and talk about ghostly murderers,' decided Feltham, positively. 'I don't give a damn whether Jeremy bloody Hall is a nephew of Sir Richard's or not. He'll do as he's told, like they all do.'

In Jennifer's hospital room, less than two miles away, the sedative began to take affect. The last thing of which Jennifer was aware was Jane's distant voice. '*You can't begin to guess the plans I've got, Jennifer. It's much more fun than I thought it might be.*'

'I'm sorry.'

'So am I,' said Patricia Boxall, beside him in the darkness.

'I'll be all right later,' promised Hall.

Was it still too late to leave: call Alexander from the car? Probably. It had been close to midnight before they'd got back from the poxy Italian restaurant with its stale spaghetti and acid wine. 'Wake me,' she said, turning away from him. If the sex was over then so was everything else.

Chapter Thirteen

The traffic was heavier than they anticipated but they still arrived almost an hour ahead of the appointment with the council and care officials. When they turned into the driveway and stopped for the gate to be opened after identifying themselves through the speaker grill, two men with cameras and another with a tape recorder ran from an unseen car parked opposite. There were momentarily blinding flashes and the man with the tape recorder said, 'May I ask . . .' before the gates opened and Perry accelerated through.

'Bastards!' exclaimed the solicitor. 'Frightened the hell out of me!'

'Weren't you told of this, when you spoke to the house?' Hall asked Johnson.

'Annabelle said she'd been bothered but didn't tell me there were ambushes outside the gate,' said the family solicitor.

Alerted by the gate telephone Annabelle Parkes was at the open door by the time they reached the square, creeper-clad mansion. The nanny was a plump, round-faced girl who wore her hair short and disdained any make-up. The impression, even for someone who could only have been in her twenties, was motherly, which Hall decided was an advantage. There was a firm, no-nonsense handshake but no smile. Coffee was already set out in the drawing room at the front of the house, overlooking the terraced lawns and the distant coppice which hid the gate. It was a room of heavy velvet drapes and brocaded furniture which Hall guessed to be Regency. It could, he supposed, have been Georgian in keeping with the period of the house. Some looked similar to the antiques his father had sold, trying to stave off the Lloyd's bankruptcy. There were a lot of photographs, the majority of Jennifer with Lomax, with Emily completing the family in several. They were smiling and laughing in virtually all of them, apart from two posed studio portraits. The one of Jennifer reminded Hall of the picture that most of the newspapers had used. She was more than simply beautiful, he decided. The head-tilted confidence he'd earlier recognized made her intriguing, too. Meeting her in any other circumstances would have made him curious to discover just how intelligent she was.

As she poured coffee Annabelle said, 'I've kept Emily home from kindergarten. I didn't know if they – if you – would want to see her. She's upstairs in the nursery, playing. You said you wanted to talk before the others arrived? And I've packed clothes. Quite a lot, to give Mrs Lomax a choice. She takes a lot of trouble about how she dresses.'

'Mrs Lomax is resisting Emily being taken into care,' announced Johnson. 'We can do that, certainly until after any trial. But it's very necessary that we know if you're prepared to remain here, looking after the child.'

'That's what I'm employed to do,' said the girl, stiffly.

'And are happy to continue doing so?' pressed Perry.

'Absolutely.'

'That's good to know,' said Hall. 'I'm surprised this approach came from the council so quickly.'

'I'm probably responsible,' confessed the girl. 'Ever since

it happened we've been besieged by newspapers and television people: they even got over the perimeter wall and came up to the house through the tradesmen's entrance when we wouldn't let them through the main gate. I complained to the police: said I had a child here that I wanted protecting . . .'

Hall sighed, nodding. 'Yes, you probably are. We were confronted by some of them at the gate.'

'I wish I'd been given some indication,' complained Johnson.

'I'm sorry if it was the wrong thing to do.'

'It wasn't,' said Perry.

'In fact,' reassured Hall, 'it might even make things easier.'

The girl went to a bureau near the window, returning with several envelopes. Handing them to Johnson, whose authority she already knew, Annabelle said, 'They put these in the postbox at the gate, too: offering money for photographs and for interviews. I thought you'd want them. And there's some other mail, as well. I've kept it all for you.'

Johnson accepted the package, moving away from them to go through it.

Hall checked his watch, deciding there was sufficient time. 'Describe Mrs Lomax to me,' he demanded, suddenly.

Annabelle frowned. 'I don't . . .' she started. Then, 'Of course, I'm sorry. A wonderful woman. We got on very well together.'

Perry had frowned, too. Then his face cleared and hurriedly he got out a pad and the silver pencil. 'Did she and Mr Lomax ever fight?'

The girl shook her head. 'That's the strangest part, about what's happened. I've never known them argue, ever . . .'

She smiled for the first time. 'Almost unnatural, we used to say.'

'We?' queried Hall.

'There's a housekeeper who also cooks and a daily lady and a gardener. And there's another man who comes in to help the gardener . . .' She gestured behind her. 'There's a lot of ground.'

'Mr Lomax stayed in London during the week?' coaxed Perry.

'Rarely more than two nights. And when he was away he always telephoned. As I say, they were devoted to each other.'

'Did Mrs Lomax ever talk to you about someone named Rebecca?' asked Hall.

There was another frown. 'I think she's a friend of Mrs Lomax. Came here a long time ago.'

'But Mrs Lomax didn't mention her more recently?'

'In what way?'

'Just talk about her,' shrugged the barrister, refusing to lead.

'No.'

'What about illness? Was Mrs Lomax ever ill?'

'Hardly ever caught a cold.'

Hall searched for a way to ask the most important question without doing so directly. 'Did she ever complain about headaches?'

The girl shook her head. 'Not that I can ever remember.'

'Anything about her head at all?'

'Has she gone mad?' demanded the forthright girl.

'It seems there's an illness,' said Perry.

'Will she get better?'

'She's been examined by specialists,' said Hall. 'You didn't answer my question.'

'She never complained about anything to do with her head.'

'Or behave strangely.'

Annabelle hesitated. 'Only the day it happened.'

'Tell me about it.'

'There's hardly anything to tell, really. She went to collect Emily from playschool: she usually did. They came home excited because Emily had learned a letter of the alphabet and Mrs Lomax said they were going to the zoo. There's a zoological park nearby. We went into the kitchen and then almost at once Mrs Lomax walked out.'

'Did she say anything?'

'Nothing.'

'Was she walking normally?'

'I suppose so. I was sitting Emily up. I was scarcely aware of Mrs Lomax leaving.'

'You didn't see her take a knife?'

Annabelle shuddered, slightly. 'No. I didn't even know she'd left the house. I thought she'd forgotten something in the car or gone to the bathroom or something. It wasn't until I went looking for her, when our lunch was ready, that I saw the car had gone.'

A woman in a black dress that also looked like a uniform appeared at the door and said, 'I've let the people from the council in the gate.'

'Mrs Jenkins, the housekeeper,' identified Annabelle. 'Can she help you at all?'

'I don't think so,' said Hall. 'Thank you.'

From the bureau by the window, Johnson said, 'It's difficult to believe, isn't it?'

'What?' asked Perry.

The other solicitor waved several letters. 'All from the charities Jennifer worked for and supported . . .' He looked down at the topmost one. '"In view of recent circumstances we will, of course, have to ask you to stand down from the committee",' he quoted. 'Charity certainly seems in short supply, doesn't it?'

There were two cars carrying a total of five people, two of them women, one of the men in the uniform of a police inspector, that drew up outside. Annabelle met them at the door as she'd greeted Hall and Perry. The housekeeper directly followed the group into the drawing room with more coffee, which Annabelle distributed while everyone else exchanged cards.

'I hope this preliminary meeting is useful,' declared the county solicitor, Stewart Baxter. 'You'll agree our concern about the child is justified?'

'No,' said Hall. 'I won't.'

The man blinked. 'In the circumstances—'

'The only circumstances that need concern you is the welfare and safety of a four-year-old child,' broke in Hall. 'Emily Lomax is being cared for by a certificated nanny, living in a house with a full-time staff. It is her mother's wish that she remains so . . .' he looked towards the two women, a doctor named Maureen Snare and social worker Victoria Pryke. '. . . Emily is here, for you to see and speak to, if you wish.'

'The local police were summoned to protect her,' said the social worker.

'Quite properly so,' agreed Hall. 'But not to protect *her*: to remove from the estate trespassing journalists who could have terrorized a child as young as Emily . . .' He crossed demandingly to Johnson, hand outstretched for the appropriate letters. 'These followed, when the journalists were expelled. And will be produced by me when I protest to the Press Complaints Commission. As I will protest about those blockading the gate and by whom you were doubtless confronted . . .' The pause was perfectly timed. 'I sincerely hope none of you co-operated to provide a headline about Emily being taken into care. Because she isn't. And if any such stories appear I shall officially complain to your authorities and not only demand a full and public retraction but an explanation for why people in your position commented upon a matter that has *sub judice* implications . . .' The second pause was as well timed as the first. '. . . But as you were accompanied by an inspector from the local force to which the press complaint was initially made it is, I'm sure, unnecessary for me to have that concern.'

Humphrey Perry guessed immediately there had been co-operation at the gate from the look that passed between Victoria Pryke, the fair-haired man described as a member of the same division named Eric Pringle and the hot-faced police inspector, Paul Hughes. It was a passing realization. Perry was far more interested in Jeremy Hall. On this showing he wasn't by any means the cheeky bugger of the previous night's judgement: he was an extremely aggressive advocate who appeared to possess another essential weapon in a lawyer's armoury, the ability to seize a weakness and hammer it into defeat.

'This isn't at all the sort of meeting I'd hoped it would be,' said Baxter. He was a large, self-satisfied man accustomed to deference and was disorientated at not getting it now.

'How, then, can we help you?' smiled Hall.

'We have to take into account the fact of Mrs Lomax's arrest. And the reasons for it,' insisted Baxter. He was red faced too, although from irritation, not guilt, at what had happened at the gate.

Hall made much of examining the exchanged cards before coming up to the man. 'You're a lawyer?'

'You know I am!'

'I accept that criminal law may not be your field, but we can surely agree the principle of innocence until the proof of guilt?'

'Yes,' said the man, tightly.

'Then aren't you acting prematurely?'

'Our only concern is Emily's welfare,' persisted Victoria Pryke, a prim, cardigan-and-pearls woman.

'Then we're all on common ground,' said Hall. 'You've seen the circumstances in which Emily is living . . .' He gestured towards Annabelle. 'And you've met the nanny in whose care she is: I'm sure Ms Parkes will be only too pleased to show you her certificated qualifications and diplomas . . .'

He hadn't expected it but Annabelle returned at once to the bureau in which she'd kept the media offers and came back with several documents, offering them generally to the group. Victoria Pryke took them, passing them one by one to the doctor who in turn offered them to Baxter.

'You have a nursing qualification?' queried Maureen Snare, looking up.

'Specifically in paediatrics,' elaborated Annabelle, triumphantly.

'. . . and we'd be pleased to assure you of Emily's care and well being in any other way we can,' finished Hall, finally.

'We'd like to see Emily herself,' said the fair-haired social worker.

As Annabelle left the room Baxter said, 'This is obviously a matter that will have to be considered after Mrs Lomax's trial.'

'*After*,' stressed Hall. 'At which time it will be most vigorously opposed by me, for the same reasons you've been made aware of today.'

Emily was holding Annabelle's hand when they entered

but confronted with a room full of strangers she took her hand away and wrapped her arm around Annabelle's leg. The nanny put a comforting hand around the child's shoulders. Emily was wearing jeans and a Thomas the Tank Engine T-shirt. Her hair, bubbled in curls at the front, was plaited at the back, secured by ribbon with the same cartoon motif.

Both the woman social worker and the doctor hunched down, to Emily's level.

'Hello,' said the social worker.

'Hello.'

'How are you?' asked the doctor.

'All right.' At Annabelle's touch against her shoulder, Emily added, 'Thank you,' and looked up apologetically at her nanny.

'That's why we've come to see you,' said the doctor. 'To see that you're all right.'

Again the child frowned up at Annabelle. 'Why?'

'That's our job,' said Victoria Pryke.

The child stood, regarding the council group steadily.

'Do you like it here?' asked the social worker.

Emily's face crumpled although more in bewilderment than at the hint of tears. 'I live here!'

'With Annabelle?' persisted the woman.

There was a smile. 'She's my friend.'

'Like your mummy is your friend?' persisted the social worker.

Emily's bewilderment became more obvious. 'My mummy is my mummy! But she's not very well. My daddy's away.'

'I won't let this continue indefinitely,' warned Hall.

'Are you Mummy and Daddy's friends?' asked the child, unexpectedly.

'No,' admitted Victoria Pryke. 'We want to be your

friends. To make sure you're all right while they're away.'

'Annabelle does that,' said Emily and Hall decided every lawyer should be blessed with witnesses like the child.

'Do you want a more specific answer than that!' he demanded.

'No,' said the doctor, straightening.

The other woman briefly remained crouched, then she stood. 'No,' she agreed.

As Annabelle led the child from the room Victoria Pryke said, 'There was no way we could prevent our photographs being taken at the gate. It was done before we knew what was happening.'

'We were approached by a man with a tape recorder. We didn't speak into it,' said Perry, seizing the opportunity to enter the conversation. 'Focusing publicity upon a child would be the last thing you'd welcome, as a social worker, wouldn't it?'

The woman was the first to leave the room, ahead of the rest of the group. The three lawyers stood at the window, watching the departing cars. Perry said, 'You mean it, about complaining to their departments?'

'Of course, if the reason for their being here is published. It would be monstrous if Emily were brought into it because some bloody social worker wanted her picture in the papers.'

They turned, at Annabelle's re-entry.

'They've gone?' she said, surprised.

'It's over, at least until after the trial,' promised Johnson.

'She'll be found guilty, won't she?' demanded the girl, forthright again.

'There could be mitigating circumstances,' said Hall.

'But she'll go to jail?'

'Probably a special one, for treatment.'

'Broadmoor!'

'There are others.'

'Poor Mrs Lomax.'

'What have you told Emily, about her mother not being here?' asked Perry.

'Just that she'd had to go away, at first. Then I said she's ill and needs special doctors. And that her daddy's away, working. He often was.'

Hall nodded. 'She wants to see Emily. Before she's transferred from a proper hospital. You'll have actually been telling the truth.'

Annabelle frowned. 'Is it . . . ?'

'. . . Safe? There'll be doctors there. But it would be quite safe anyway.'

'Will she frighten Emily? With her illness, I mean?'

'She might appear odd. Say things she wouldn't ordinarily say.'

'Is there any way I can explain it to Emily in advance, so she won't be frightened?'

Hall shrugged, helplessly. 'You could say it's the medicine she's taking.'

'When?'

'Tomorrow,' said Johnson. 'I'll collect you by car.'

Annabelle nodded. 'Use the tradesmen's gate. They don't watch that so much.'

There was a remote control beam in the drive which automatically opened the main gate when it was broken by departing vehicles, lessening the need to slow, but at Hall's insistence the surprised Perry stopped the car as soon as they emerged. There were three cars and a television van outside now. At once men disgorged from all of them: a television strobe burst on before the running cameraman got to them. The man with the tape recorder who'd been there when they arrived said, 'Can we have your name, as Mrs Lomax's lawyer? Is Emily being taken into care?'

'There were some offers we'd like to consider,' said Hall. 'Can you give me some cards?'

There was a confetti of pasteboard as identification was thrust through the open window at him.

'What can you tell us?' demanded the man with the recorder.

'That there will be a complaint to the Press Complaints Commission about everyone whose card I have here, as well as their organizations, for harassment and totally unwarranted intrusion. I will also complain in open court, at an appropriate time, and invite comment from a judge.'

As Perry swept the car out on to the London road Hall said, 'We'll be back in London by early afternoon. You'll be able to file the complaints today, won't you?'

'Yes,' said the solicitor, tightly.

'Don't forget the authorities here, either. We know now that they gave interviews.'

'We won't forget,' promised Perry.

'Perhaps you'd drop me off at the hospital, on your way past?'

'Relax. Don't fight against me . . .'

'I'll fight him. He won't be able to do it!'

'. . . Just listen to me, nothing else. No-one else. There's a lot to talk about. To get you well.' Mason's voice was even, monotone. He'd unstrapped his plain-faced wrist-watch and was holding it towards her: it moved back and forth very slightly.

'Can you see the numbers?'

'Don't look!'

'Yes, I can see them.'

'What's before twelve?'

'Don't play games!'

'Eleven.' It was hard, so very hard. Jennifer tried to make rigid her entire body, to hold it stiff so there couldn't be any movement she didn't want: to keep her lips stiff, too, so that only her words would come out, not Jane's.

'What's after?'

'One.'

'Stop it!'

'Eleven to one, one to eleven, eleven to one, one to eleven,' incanted Mason, like a mantra. 'Like a clock, back and forth, back and forth.'

Fosdyke and Lloyd stood motionless against the wall by the window. Hall intentionally stood half obscuring the window, the only unrehearsed part. He felt uncomfortable: intrusive. Was Mason right that strong-minded people were more easily hypnotized than the weak-willed; the mentally ill? He supposed the psychiatrist had to be. That was his job.

'Shut up! Don't listen.'

'Count the numbers to me the right way: your right way . . .'

'. . . One, two . . .' picked up Jennifer. 'Three . . . four . . .'

'Stop. Don't do it!'

'. . . five, six . . .' Jennifer's voice faded.

'Good,' said Mason, soothingly. 'Very good . . . five . . . ?'

'. . . six . . .'

'No!' Jennifer's legs jerked, but not as fiercely as before, little more than an exaggerated twitch.

Hall thought she looked so much better, in her own clothes, into which she'd insisted upon changing the moment he'd entered with the suitcases. Jeans and a sweater, her legs actually crossed at the ankle as she lay back on the bed.

'No need to do that,' warned Mason. 'You can stop jerking your body about. You're in control, not Jane. And you can close your eyes if they feel heavy. That's it. Relax . . .'

The next leg twitch was hardly noticeable.

'There . . .' Unhurriedly, Mason restrapped the watch. 'You know you're not asleep, dreaming, don't you?'

'Yes.'

'That we've got a lot to talk about?'

'Yes.'

'Do you want to talk to me, Jennifer?'

'Yes.'

'So you won't lie to me?'

'No.'

'Promise?'

'I promise.'

'What's the most important oath you could swear on, to keep that promise?'

Jennifer's brow furrowed. 'Emily's life.'

'Will you promise on Emily's life to tell me the truth, all the time?'

'Yes.'

'What about Gerald's life?'

'Gerald's dead.'

'How did he die?'

'Stabbed. Cut.'

'Who stabbed and cut him?'

'Jane.'

'*Wake up! Don't listen.*'

'Don't want to listen.'

'Yes you do, Jennifer. Is Jane telling you not to listen?'

'Yes.'

'*Listen to me. Not to him.*'

'Let's stop her, Jennifer. Drive her out.'

'*Can't!*'

'Can't.'

'Yes, we can. I want you to do what I tell you. I want you to stop hearing the voice.'

'*Can't!*'

'She won't stop.'

'Go away, Jane! We don't want you!' said Mason. He didn't raise his voice.

Hall was suffused with a feeling of unreality: this sounded more insane than when Jennifer was spouting the words supposedly from someone else.

'*You can't stop me!*'

'Can't stop her.'

'Let's put her in another room then. Close the door. Think of Jane in another room, with the door closed. A very thick door, closing out the sound. Go on, close the door. Can you do that, close the door?'

'Yes.'

'*No!*'

'Shut her out, Jennifer. It's easy to shut her out, from another room . . . the door's very thick . . .'

'*No!*'

'Yes.'

'Have you closed her out?'

'Yes.'

'She's not so loud now, is she? Put in another room, like a naughty child.'

'*Who the fuck's he calling a naughty child?*'

'No, not so loud now.'

'Hardly hear her at all?'

'*Listen to me!*' There was a vague leg movement.

'Hardly hear her.'

'That's good: that's very good. Easy to ignore her now. We've shut her out. Do you want her shut out?'

'Yes.'

'Gone completely?'

'Yes.'

'*Never get rid of me!*' The sound started.

'She's talking, but not loudly.'

'Is she real? Is Jane real in your head, Jennifer?'

'Yes. She's trying to scream but it doesn't hurt.'

'So we can talk now, without her?'

'Yes.'

'What's that going to be like?'

'Wonderful.'

'Do you hate Jane?'

'No.'

'What then?'

'Just want her to go away.'

'*Won't go away. Ever! You've got to wake up, in a minute. You'll be mine again then.*'

'Tell me how much you loved Gerald?'

'Totally.'

'And he loved you?'

'Totally.'

'Who's Rebecca?'

'Rebecca Nicholls. Works with Gerald.'

'Is she your friend?'

'*Fucked Gerald. Fucked Gerald.*'

'Not now.'

'You thought she was?'

'Yes.'

'Why isn't she your friend any more?'

'Had an affair, with Gerald.'

'Did you know they were having an affair?'

'No.'

'Never suspected it?'

'No.'

'The police think you did.'

'Not true.'

'Is Jane true? Or did you make her up?'

'She's true. Here, now.'

'But in another room?'

'Still hear her.'

'Do you know what a Cyclothymic Personality Disorder is, Jennifer?'

'No.'

'I'd really like you to tell me. I want to know.'

'Don't know.'

'What's a Paranoid Personality Disorder?'

'Don't know.'

'You sure you don't know?'

'Yes.'

'Can you tell me what an Anankastic Personality Disorder is?'

'No.'

'You sure you can't. I'd really like you to, if you can.'

'I can't.'

'*Trying to trick you. Don't answer him.*'

Without turning to the men ranged behind him Mason raised his hand in a don't-interrupt, warding-off gesture. He continued it to take a pen from the inside from his shirt pocket. 'Can you see this pen?'

'Yes.'

'It's very hot. Very hot indeed. Do you believe me?' It was a cheap ballpoint, plastic cased.

'Yes.'

'I'm going to put it against your arm . . .'

Lloyd started forward but Fosdyke snatched out,

stopping the protest. It was difficult for Hall to hold back. He was sweating, his back clammy, his hands wet. Jennifer winced, jerking away. Almost at once a perfectly round red burn mark formed on the arm in which the drip had been, before she tore it out.

'Does your arm hurt?'

'It burns.'

'I want to do some tests. Is that OK?'

'Yes.'

'I'm going to ask you some questions again. And every time I do, before you answer, I'm going to put the hot pen on your arm. If you tell a lie, it will burn. But if you tell the truth, it won't. Do you agree to that?'

'Yes.'

'Define a Cyclothymic Personality Disorder?' asked Mason, putting the harmless pen to Jennifer's arm.

'I can't.'

Hall tensed forward. No mark appeared.

'Trick! Music-hall trick!'

'Define a Paranoid Personality Disorder.' The pen casing went down.

'I can't.'

No blister formed.

'Define an Anankastic Personality Disorder.' The pen descended.

'I can't.'

Jennifer's skin remained unmarked.

'Does it still hurt where I first put the pen?'

'Yes.'

'I'm going to put it there again. It's going to take all the pain away. And the mark will go.'

Hall felt an unnerved sensation at the back of his neck as he saw Mason place the pen on the angry mark. Almost at once the red began to fade.

'There won't be a mark,' promised Mason. 'All the pain's gone, hasn't it?'

'Yes.'

Hall was conscious of a relaxation from the two doctors alongside him. He didn't look at them and they didn't look at him.

In front of him Mason was asking Jennifer, 'Do you like the cinema?'

'Yes.'

'Did you go, with Gerald?'

'Sometimes.'

'Did you ever see a film called *The Three Faces of Eve*?'

'No.'

'You sure?'

'Yes.'

'What's a Multiple Personality Disorder?'

'Don't know.'

Mason learned forward with the pen again, putting it against Jennifer's arm, and repeated the question. The skin remained smooth and even.

'You're aware people are trying to help you?'

'Yes.'

'So it's very important to tell them the truth.'

'Yes.'

'So I want you to tell me the truth. Remember, it's very important.'

'Yes.'

'Did you kill Gerald because he was having an affair with Rebecca?'

'Didn't kill Gerald. Jane killed Gerald.'

'Would you have killed him, if you'd known?'

'No!'

'Why not? You'd have been humiliated, wouldn't you?'

'Yes, but I couldn't have killed him. That's not right.'

'*Killed me, you bitch!*'

'What would you have done?'

'Asked him to stop. Asked him what was wrong.'

'You'd have wanted your marriage to go on?'

'Yes.'

'Do you love Gerald?'

'Yes.'

'Even though he was having an affair with Rebecca?'

'Just sex.'

'Was it just sex with you and Gerald, when your affair began?'

'Yes.'

'You didn't love him at first?'

'No.'

'Did he love you?'

'No.'

'Who fell in love with whom first?'

'Me with Gerald, I suppose.'

'What did you do?'

'Said I wanted it to end.'

'*Liar! Let me in, Jennifer. I want to talk to you. Let me in to talk to you.*'

'She wants to talk to me.'

'I don't want to talk to her. I want to talk just to you. Why did you want to end your affair, if you loved him? I don't understand.'

'He was married to Jane.'

'*Let me in!*'

'Why was that important?'

'Didn't want the marriage to break up.'

'Why did you sleep with him in the first place?'

'He was attractive. I wanted to.'

From where he stood Hall could see sweat glueing Mason's shirt to his back. The man held a handkerchief to wipe his face. Jennifer appeared quite relaxed, eyes half closed, legs still crossed at the ankles. He couldn't make out any discolouration on her arm where the burn had been, minutes earlier.

'It wasn't wrong then?'

'No.'

'Only when it became serious?'

'Yes.'

'*Liar, liar, liar!*'

'Why?'

'Because it was serious. A threat.'

'Not to you.'

'Jane wasn't well.'

'*Spare me, do!*'

'Her dying made it easy, though?'

'Yes.'

'Did you think that might happen?'

'How could I?'

'By killing her.'

'We didn't kill her.'

'*You did! You fixed the dose.*'

'Do you believe in ghosts?'

'No.'

'Why not?'

'It's ridiculous. Ghost's don't exist.'

'Jane's in your head: possessing you?'

'Yes.'

'Ghosts must exist, if Jane's possessing you.'

'I know. But they can't. I won't accept it. I'm frightened.'

'*I've scarcely begun yet.*'

'What are you most frightened of?'

'People not believing me.'

'Would it send you mad, if they didn't?'

'She won't send me mad. She says she will but she

won't. I'll beat her. Beat everyone as a trader.'

'*Oh, yes, I will!*'

'How are you going to beat her?'

'I don't know.' Tears began slowly to make a path down Jennifer's cheeks, although there was no sound. She scrubbed a bandaged hand across her face.

Fosdyke moved, at last, reaching forward and patting Mason's shoulder. The psychiatrist nodded, again without turning.

'I want to go backwards now, back to when you were young. A baby even.'

All Hall's voyeuristic discomfort went, forgotten, to frowned disbelief. Jennifer relived Emily's birth ('No pain. She's coming. Beautiful: so beautiful.') and Jane's death ('Sorry. I'm so very sorry.') and her first day arrival at Enco-Corps ('I'm going to be the best here. Top the trading commissions. Make a million.') and the sadness of the Randolph celebration meal after her Oxford graduation ('I know Mummy would be as proud as you are, Daddy.') The voice change, from adult gradually to baby talk, was imperceptible and it wasn't until they went through teenage into puberty into childhood that Hall became conscious of it. It took him almost as long to realize the purpose of the regression, when the frequent medical questions registered and he realized the exercise was not for the psychiatrist's benefit but for Fosdyke's, a search for pathological causes for whatever it was Jennifer was suffering. None emerged.

It was late into the afternoon and Mason's shirt was black with perspiration before he finally stretched up from the bed and for the first time Jeremy Hall became conscious of the odour of too many people being for too long in a small room. He became conscious, too, that he was contributing to it.

'When I clap my hands you'll become aware not just of me but of other people,' said Mason. 'And from now on you're to help your barrister, Jeremy Hall, as much as you've helped me. Will you do that?'

'Yes,' said Jennifer.

'And I want you to help everyone else like me: doctors like me. There will be a lot who want to talk to you. Is that all right?'

'Yes.'

'And if I want to talk to you again like this, we'll count the numbers on the watch. Will you do that for me, whenever I ask you?'

'Yes,' promised Jennifer. She blinked, opening her eyes more fully, at the sound of Mason's hands coming together. 'Did I help?' she demanded at once.

'Absolutely,' said Mason. 'Thank you.'

Minutes later, back in the neurologist's convenient rooms, Mason helped himself to the ever-ready coffee, looked around the assembled men and said, 'She hasn't learned how to fake her condition from text books. I've no doubt whatsoever that Jennifer Lomax is as sane as any of us in this room. Maybe more so. Just as I've no doubt whatsoever that Jennifer Lomax isn't inventing the voice in her head. It's there!'

'So I've got the first case of ghostly possession in British criminal history?' demanded Hall.

'I don't know what you've got,' replied Mason, ignoring the intended cynicism. 'But I've got a Paper that's going to turn psychiatry on its head, worldwide.'

'You sure?' demanded John Bentley, in frustrated disappointment.

'I've gone through every line of the inquest evidence *and* talked not just to the investigating officer but the coroner's officer as well,' assured Rodgers. 'Jane Lomax died from an accidental overdose of insulin. There's nothing we could use to reopen the case.'

'Fuck,' said Bentley, viciously. 'I would have just loved sticking Jennifer bloody Lomax with a second murder. Can you imagine the bombshell that would have been?'

'Easily,' said Rodgers, who feared the other detective was endangering professional objectivity through personal pique. 'But we'll have to make do with what we've got.'

'And what have we got?'

'Everything wrapped up and tied in ribbon,' said the inspector. 'We're ready to go. Fastest case ever.'

'Don't rush the submission to the Crown Prosecution. Let them go around in a few more circles.'

'Until we submit the evidence they won't be able to brief psychiatrists,' reminded Rodgers. 'They'll need to do that.'

'A week,' decided Bentley. 'We'll wait a week.'

'We're going to see Mummy in hospital?'

'Would you like that?'

'What's wrong with her?'

'Her head hurts. The doctors are making her better.'

'Is she going to die?'

'No, darling. Of course not.'

Chapter Fourteen

Until Perry's hurried call Jeremy Hall had not intended being at the hospital for Emily's visit. It had nothing to do with the eventual trial and although that trial, his first murder, was of great professional importance he'd already recognized, objectively, that he was spending too much time personally involved in situations with Jennifer Lomax which more properly should have been handled by the solicitor at that moment talking far too quickly to him on the telephone. Quite apart from offending the man himself, trickled into the gossip mill that filled to overflowing the Inns of Court trough it could – and, he was sure, would – be represented as his nervous inability to delegate anything through fear of failure. Which, even further apart, would be compounded by his having – apparently – willingly accepted a totally indefensible brief the outcome of which could only be failure anyway. So why was he bothering?

Perry's call abruptly changed the intention. According to Geoffrey Johnson's mobile phone alarm from the car bringing an excited Emily and the nanny to London, he'd been seen entering the tradesmen's entrance to the mansion to collect them and emerged to confront at least three, maybe more, media cars. He was now heading a cavalcade towards London: one vehicle had already drawn level at a traffic light and attempted photographs, through the window.

Perry confirmed, indignant at the question, that he'd filed the Press Commission complaint at their own ambush and individually warned the editors of every journalist whose card had been thrust through their window not just of that protest but also of the intention to complain to a trial judge, once one was appointed.

'Add this to the Commission complaint, by fax, today,' instructed Hall, coolly. 'Also fax all the editors you wrote to yesterday that we intend raising with a judge in chambers, today, the danger of their representatives perverting the course of justice . . .'

'. . . How the hell . . . ?' Perry tried to argue.

'. . . Annabelle Parkes will be called as a witness for the defence,' said Hall, patiently. 'She's received letters, which we have and can produce before a judge, offering her money to talk to the press in advance of giving evidence in court. Financial inducement could influence the veracity of anything she might give. The fact that we know it wouldn't doesn't affect my submission, agreed?'

'Agreed,' conceded the solicitor, at once. 'Don't forget we haven't been appointed a trial judge yet.'

'I haven't forgotten that,' said Hall. 'Make a point of it. Repeat the warning to the editors whose names and media organizations we have to the Press Association, ensuring its distribution to every media outlet. In the individual letters and the news agency release, also say we are applying for a chambers judge to extend the precincts of any court in which Mrs Lomax might eventually appear to the house in Hampshire, Emily's kindergarten and St Thomas's Hospital and every residence or place of work of witnesses – particularly medical and professional witnesses – likely to be called by the defence. Therefore any media intrusion would constitute contempt of court—'

Perry's intake of breath was sufficiently loud to interrupt the instructions. 'You'll never get all that,' the man insisted. 'It's unheard of.'

'I don't expect to get all of it,' admitted Hall. 'And I know it's unheard of. Which is why it'll frighten the bastards off. And I will get the house and Emily's school and maybe St Thomas's, which is all I really want.' He hesitated. 'Did Johnson tell you where he was, when he called?'

'Guildford.'

'Call him on another line – I'll hold – and tell him I don't want him to get to the hospital for at least another hour.'

Perry put down the phone unquestioningly. Hall heard a mumble of conversation but not what was said. The solicitor returned very quickly. 'He doesn't think he can do it under that time anyway. The traffic's bad.'

'Good,' said Hall, briskly. 'Separately fax the police station local to the hospital. Warn of a serious risk of a potential murder trial being endangered by an attempt to pervert the course of justice. Ask for a police presence to prevent that happening, to be in place at the hospital within the next hour. Make sure a copy of that request goes to every editor and to the judge in chambers.' He paused again. 'Anything I've overlooked?'

'Hardly.'

'Any thought?'

'You're going to alienate every newspaper you've ever heard of.'

'What's that got to do with it?'

'A lot, if you're thinking about your career.'

'I'm not. I'm thinking of a client and her four-year-old daughter.'

There was a moment's silence. 'In whose name are these letters to be sent.'

Hall matched the length of the silence. 'Mine.' He allowed another gap. 'You want me to tell Feltham or do you want to do it?'

'Are you making a point with that question?' asked Perry, frigid-voiced.

'Just ensuring that everything is conducted in the proper manner,' said Hall, easily.

'Officially, it's my function.'

'Then let's do everything officially, shall we?'

'Are you going to the hospital?'

'I am now.'

'Do you want me to come?'

'You'll hardly have time, if you're to do all this. I can manage.'

'I'm sure you can,' said Perry, attempting a small point of his own.

Jeremy Hall didn't hurry, knowing there was no need. The traffic was already almost completely blocked over Westminster Bridge and along both directions of the Embankment by the time he got there. He paid the taxi off and walked the last three hundred yards to the hospital. There were at least six uniformed officers controlling the exit and entrance, commanded by a superintendent inside the perimeter. The traffic jam caused by their checking every entering vehicle and person was compounded by two police vans, in which other officers were visible, and three motor-cycles. A constable immediately announced his arrival over a radio when Hall identified himself and the superintendent hurried from a plainclothes group with whom he had been talking.

'You Jeremy Hall?'

'Yes.'

'Are you sure this is necessary?' He was a large man, imposing in his uniform. He was perspiring, despite the wind off the river.

'I didn't catch your name?'

The man faltered. 'Hopkins. I asked you if this is necessary.'

Hall extended his hand. There was more uncertainty before the policeman took it. Hall said, 'If I hadn't thought it necessary, superintendent, I wouldn't have asked for it to be done.'

Hopkins gestured back towards the group. 'There are lawyers from four newspapers there. One from television. And executives. They say it's ridiculous.'

Hall looked towards the group. He didn't recognize any of them. Those he guessed to be lawyers were older than he was. 'It'll be discussed before a judge in chambers. I'm content for him to decide if it's ridiculous or not, aren't you?'

The policeman coloured slightly. 'Have you a time of arrival?'

Hall looked at his watch. 'Maybe in the next fifteen minutes. Apparently the traffic's bad. It's an old Bentley. Green.'

'If you know the route we could intercept, with a police escort.'

The attitude appeared to have changed abruptly, thought Hall. 'I don't. Perhaps it wouldn't be a good idea: I don't want to frighten the child any more than she has been, already.'

As he continued on towards the hospital he saw Lloyd

and Mason hovering just inside the glassed entrance. He went to go by the group outside but five detached themselves, blocking his path.

'You Hall?' demanded a bulge-bellied man.

'Yes.'

'What on earth's this all about?'

'Press intrusion sums it up, I think.'

'Not a crime,' insisted another of the group.

'Perverting the course of justice is. So's contempt of court.'

'Let's be reasonable,' smiled the first man. 'This is absurd. Way over the top.'

'I agree that pursuing a four-year-old child and a potential witness to whom a bribe has already been offered is way over the top,' said Hall. 'I'm confident a judge will agree with me this afternoon.'

'Overenthusiasm,' dismissed a third lawyer. 'A mistake. But it doesn't need to be handled like this. We'll cool our people down and that will be the end of it. Judges get irritated if their time is wasted: chamber hearings are for emergencies, don't you know.'

Hall surveyed the men ranged in front of him, wondering if the physical barrier they formed was prearranged or accidental. 'I do know, very well. And I'm quite prepared to confront a judge's irritation. I hope you all are, too.' As he shouldered his way through he heard a voice say, 'Arrogant young bastard!'

Another voice sneered, 'Out to make a name for himself.'

The two doctors were waiting for him, directly beyond the door. Mason said, 'What the hell's going on?'

Hall told them, very briefly. Mason's face cleared by the time Hall finished speaking. The psychiatrist said, 'Very forceful!'

'Very necessary,' said Hall. He was aware of Lloyd's attention shifting over his shoulder and turned to see the arrival of Geoffrey Johnson, with Emily and the nanny. More police had come out of the waiting vans and were lined along the entrance, listing the numbers and taking driver details of the cars indicating their intention to turn into the hospital behind the solicitor's Bentley. All the lawyers and the other men with whom they'd earlier been standing were there too. There was a lot of arm waving, particularly from the sweating superintendent. A solid police line formed across the entrance immediately after Johnson passed through. Abruptly the indicators of the following cars were cancelled.

A strained-faced Annabelle Parkes hesitated momentarily when she came through the doors, the relief palpable when she saw Hall, the only man she knew. Beside her Emily looked very frightened, not just clutching the girl's hand but pressing close to her leg as she had in the mansion. Her hair wasn't in plaits today but frothed around her head. She wore a red tartan dress with white bows. Her free hand clutched a much-held pink-eared white rabbit that wasn't white any more and a card already slightly bent.

It was Mason who went forward, ahead of Hall. The psychiatrist scooped down, ignoring Annabelle, and said to the child, 'Was that fun?'

Annabelle went to reply but stopped at the head shake from Hall.

'Not really,' said Emily, uncertainly.

'Grown up games aren't.'

'Was it a game?'

'A silly one.'

'I thought they were going to hurt us. They were shouting and taking pictures.'

'You remember Mr Hall?' asked the psychiatrist, nodding behind him.

Emily looked at the lawyer, a smile hovering. 'Yes.'

'He's told them to stop playing like that. They won't any more.'

'Won't they?' Annabelle asked.

'No,' said Hall.

'Thank God for that.'

Geoffrey Johnson entered from parking the car in time to hear the last part of the exchange. 'I've just spoken to Humphrey. The hearing's fixed for three. It's Jarvis.'

Sir Ivan Jarvis was the most cantakerously irascible judge on the Inner London circuit who deeply resented the mandatory retirement age and whose place upon that circuit, according to the rumour mill, was to be filled by Sir Richard Proudfoot. Jeremy Hall said, 'It should make for an interesting hearing.'

'You'll want me?' anticipated Johnson.

Hall nodded, looking at the nanny. 'You too, possibly. To swear the financial offer letters and what went on before.'

'What about Emily?'

At the mention of her name the alarmed child looked up and said, 'Where are you going?'

'Nowhere,' promised Annabelle. 'Nowhere without you.'

'I don't want you to go away!' Emily's lip quivered and her voice broke.

'No-one's going to leave you,' said Mason, quickly. 'You're not going to cry, are you?'

'Yes,' said the trembling child, truculently.

'What are you here for?' asked the psychiatrist, gently.

Emily looked up questioningly to Annabelle and then said, 'To see Mummy.'

'You don't want to cry when you see Mummy, do you?'

'No.'

'Let's not then.'

'Who are you?' demanded Emily, with abrupt child logic.

'I'm a doctor, trying to make your mummy better.'

'What's wrong with her?'

'She's not well.'

Hall was glad it was the psychiatrist and not him confronting the not-to-be-lied-to inquisition.

'Is she going to die?' demanded the child, with an equally bizarre lack of emotion.

'No,' said Mason. 'It's not an illness you can die from.'

'Is she coming home today?'

'Not today.'

'When?'

Mason straightened, no longer able to remain with his legs buckled at Emily's height. 'As soon as she's better.'

'I want her to come home again. And Daddy.'

'She has to get better first.'

'I've brought her a present,' declared Emily, proudly.

'What?'

'It's a secret.'

'Shall we go and give it to her?'

'With Annabelle?'

'Of course with Annabelle.'

'All right.' As she began to walk, Emily handed the comfort toy and the card up to Annabelle, who took both.

Hall wished the attention from a lot of people hadn't been so obvious as they made their way to the elevators but Emily did not appear aware of it. He led with Lloyd. 'How is she?'

'Excited. She's been ready a long time.'

'Any difficulties?'

Lloyd shook his head. 'Nothing at all since she woke up.'

'I wish Mummy could come home,' said Emily, as they got into the lift.

'She's missed you, too,' said Mason.

Could Jane have gone: not be there any more? It seemed impossible to imagine but then what had happened was impossible to imagine. Totally, utterly and completely beyond imagination or understanding. But it wasn't happening any more. Today Jane wasn't there. Hadn't been during the night, either, shouting and calling through the drugged fog to stop her sleeping. For the first time for days – nights – she'd slept without interruption and woken late but quite normally, without any chant in her head. Now she felt rested, fully recovered. Fully recovered and fully in control of herself, not sharing her mind or her reasoning with anyone else. Better: well again.

Jennifer was standing, waiting, when Emily came uncertainly into the room, holding tightly to Annabelle. Jennifer was glad because her throat filled and her eyes blurred and she couldn't think of the words that had been there, ready to say, just seconds before.

'Hello, darling.' It was a croak, like the funny voices they used when they played after school. She coughed and said, 'Hello darling' again, normally this time, and held out her arms.

Emily didn't move at first. Then her face opened into a smile and she cried out, 'Mummy!' and ran forward into Jennifer's arms.

Beside him Hall was conscious of Julian Mason tensing

and looked at the man, who didn't respond. Instead he remained fixed upon mother and child, head actually craned forward. Hall thought the transformation in Jennifer Lomax was remarkable. She'd obviously washed her hair and the perfection of the cut showed in the way it looped in a shining coil just short of her shoulders. The dress was too formal for the morning but he guessed she'd chosen it for its long sleeves, which only allowed a fraction of the bandages to show. She'd compensated with the make-up, just lip and eye line: probably, he thought, all she'd worn on the school runs. She wasn't actually crying but her eyes were wet, which he understood, and unclouded, which he thought was encouraging. She appeared, in fact, absolutely normal.

They clung together for a long time before Jennifer eased herself away but only far enough to be able to kiss the child. It wasn't until she looked over Emily's shoulder, towards Annabelle, that she became conscious how many people there were.

She said, 'Hello Annabelle. Thank you for bringing Emily,' and then, to Hall as a focus, 'I thought this was for me to see Emily!'

At once Johnson said, 'There's no reason for me to be here,' and retreated back out into the corridor. Peter Lloyd followed.

'I think I should stay,' said Hall, impromptu, his mind completely changed from the beginning of the day and Mason said he wanted to remain, too.

Jennifer sighed and for a moment Hall thought she was going to argue. Instead she shrugged, turning back to Annabelle, pulling Emily on to her lap in the chair as she did so. The conversation with Annabelle was stilted and self-conscious, Emily's presence a bar to any proper answer to Jennifer's litany of questions, ambiguously phrased again because of Emily.

Both were relieved when the child broke in, refusing to be ignored. Plucking at the bandage protruding from Jennifer's left sleeve and then feeling the dressing on her hand Emily said in sudden alarm, 'Did you have an accident?'

'Yes,' said Jennifer.

'Is that why you're here?'

'Yes.'

'And then you're coming home?'

Jennifer hesitated. 'When I'm quite better.'

'When will Daddy come home?'

Jennifer had to swallow, very hard. 'I don't know. He might have to be away for a long time.'

'Why?'

'Because.'

Mason remained tensed forward, oblivious to everything but the woman. Hall was just as intent, a doubt growing within him. Jennifer Lomax was entirely normal, a loving mother hugging a child from whom she'd been separated. So the hunched-forward man beside him had to be wrong. Jennifer Lomax had to be a clever enough woman – and they knew she was clever – to defeat hypnosis and fool an experienced psychiatrist she hadn't faked a voice in her head. *I've got a Paper that's going to turn psychiatry on its head, worldwide*, he remembered. Did Julian Mason *want* to believe it, to achieve some sort of academic notoriety?

'I love you, Mummy,' Emily was saying.

'I love you too, my darling.'

'I want you to come home.'

'I will, as soon as I can.' Jennifer had to cough, to clear her throat.

'I brought you a present,' announced Emily, proudly, slithering from Jennifer's lap to scurry across the room. Unasked, Annabelle offered the card. Emily returned with it behind her back until she reached the chair. With a conjuror's panache the child produced it and announced, 'I know M, for Mummy!'

Hall had a fleeting, sideways image of the letter and of a stick figure with crossed-eyes and spikey, sun-ray hair before Jennifer yelled, 'NO!'

Emily started back, crying out in immediate terror, as Jane roared, '*Brat! Filthy little brat. Kill little brats.*' Jennifer grabbed out, getting one hand around Emily's throat but not managing to link it with the other because of the dressing and because Emily tripped and actually fell backwards to get away from her mother. Jennifer started to rise from the chair, bellowing, strangling hands outstretched towards the cowering child but Annabelle got to her first, scooping her up and turning at the same time. Jennifer clenched her clawed hands into fists and began pummelling the nanny, trying to force her to the floor.

'*I want her! Give her back!*'

Hall was aware of Mason moving and of Lloyd bursting through the door, followed by the policewomen, but was unable to move himself, paralysed by what was happening. Lloyd got between Jennifer and the staggering nanny, taking the blows. Blood burst almost at once from his nose but he managed to grab one of her arms. It off-balanced Jennifer, who stumbled, giving the police sergeant time to grab the other arm. The constable wrapped her own arms around Jennifer's body, half lifting her from the floor. The bull-like bellowing continued and as soon as her feet came back on to the ground Jennifer began hauling the three clinging to her around the room, rocking to dislodge them. The side table overturned, spewing its contents, and the bed slewed across the room, scattering chairs.

Hall moved at last, seizing Annabelle, still shielding the child, and bustled them out of the room into the waiting arms of a white-faced Geoffrey Johnson. Hall turned back into the room but remained in front of the door, barring it. He at once realized that Jennifer was about to throw off the police sergeant so he grabbed that arm as well, conscious that the wounds had opened and that both Jennifer's arms were sticky with blood.

'Hold her! Just keep her steady!' demanded Mason, dancing around the struggling group to get in front of the woman.

With four people holding her Jennifer came briefly to a breathless pause. At once the psychiatrist was before her, hands out to hold her head. Jennifer reared away, trying to bite him, but missed.

'Eleven to one, one to eleven, eleven to one,' Mason chanted. 'Back and forth, back and forth, eleven to one, one to eleven.'

Jennifer was bulging eyed, nostrils flared, breath rasping into her. There was one desperate heave, which almost dislodged them, but then the panting eased and the sightless eyes receded.

'Can you hear me, Jennifer?' asked Mason, monotone.

'Yes.'

'Who was it who did that?'

'Jane. I tried to stop her, I said "No", but she came too quickly. She was waiting.'

'*Always waiting. Always here.*'

They were all shocked, Mason less than the others. Annabelle wasn't with them in the ward sister's office, because the trembling, breath-caught Emily refused to let go her hand from beside the bed that had been made available and Lloyd was delayed, re-stitching the burst open wounds before sedating Jennifer.

'I've had to tell the hospital management: we can't risk the danger to other patients,' announced Lloyd, when he finally entered. His white coat was blood splattered and he had cotton wool plugs in both nostrils. His nose was beginning to swell.

'There won't be any danger,' declared Mason.

'You can't still maintain that she's sane, after that,' demanded Hall. He was totally confused about the psychiatrist's professional opinion: at that moment he felt confused about everything.

'I'm prepared to argue it. And I'm prepared to bet others will be, too.'

'How much damage has been done to Emily?'

Mason made an uncertain gesture. 'Kids are resilient but that was pretty bad.'

'Pretty bad!' exclaimed Hall. 'It was bloody terrifying! She tried to strangle her own daughter: would have done, if she hadn't been stopped.'

'I've already asked for a child psychiatrist,' said Mason.

'And a paediatrician, too,' added Lloyd. He spoke adenoidally because of the plugs.

'It was a mistake as far as Emily was concerned, letting her come to the hospital,' admitted Mason.

'One that won't be repeated,' insisted Hall. 'I think it was a mistake for all of us.'

'Not for me it wasn't,' said Mason, honestly, and Hall thought again of the man's remark of having a sensational psychiatric Paper.

Chapter Fifteen

Jeremy Hall hadn't expected the gauntlet of cameramen through whom he had to pass for the hearing and did so unsure if their jostled presence was defiance or attempted intimidation. He didn't like the way they kept shouting, 'Here, Jeremy . . . this way, Jeremy,' as if he knew them. He walked staring straight ahead, refusing to look in any direction. Humphrey Perry was in the corridor, with Johnson. Both men looked isolated and uncomfortable, like stowaways stranded on a desert island. The newspaper group had at least doubled from that of the hospital forecourt that morning. There was a lot of noise and some laughter, a clublike camaraderie.

Perry said, 'I've heard what happened with the child. It sounds awful.'

'It was worse than awful.'

'Answering a lot of uncertainty, though.'

'Not according to Mason it hasn't.'

The concentration from further along the corridor was obvious. The laughter had seemed to increase at Hall's arrival. Perry said, 'You've thrown a bomb in the beehive here. And we couldn't have got a worse judge than Jarvis. He'll know whose chambers you're from.'

'Can't be helped.'

'I wish it could.'

'My tutors used to talk about the impartial objectivity of the law,' remembered Hall.

'Academics with no idea of the real world,' dismissed Perry, matching the cynicism. 'We've drawn a short straw, which is a problem.' The case was getting out of hand – out of his protective hands – and he was worried.

'A problem about which we can do nothing,' said Hall, realistically.

'You spoken to Feltham since you left chambers?'

'No.'

'Sir Richard wants a meeting, after this is over.'

'I want to ensure Emily is OK. And that she and Annabelle get back to the house safely.'

'I said Sir *Richard* wants a meeting,' repeated the solicitor, emphatically.

'I heard what you said. We'll have it not just after the hearing but after I'm happy about the child and the nanny.' He turned to Johnson. 'You'll take them back of course?' It was phrased as a question although it wasn't.

'Of course,' blinked the family lawyer, who had fervently decided during the journey from Hampshire how fortunate it was he hadn't chosen criminal law.

The judge's clerk came into the corridor, obviously startled at the number of people awaiting the hearing. Perry hurried off, to identify himself, momentarily disappearing into the mêlée that formed at once around the surprised court official. It seemed a long time before Perry re-emerged. He was clearly flustered, making jerky shrugging-off gestures as he returned along the corridor towards them.

'*The Times*, *Mail*, *Sun* and *Express* have engaged senior counsel. All QCs. Every organization is represented. God knows how many barristers. Bloody field day.'

'Which shows how worried they are,' pointed out Hall.

'Not as much as I am,' said Perry, with feeling.

'Thanks for that expression of confidence.'

'This is extreme.'

'So I've already been told.'

They did not have to gown up for a chambers hearing, able to enter immediately there was a general summons. Sir Ivan Jarvis appeared even more surprised than his clerk by the number of barristers before him. Jarvis was a tiny, wizened man whose smallness was less obvious in a robe and wig and from the elevated bench of a Crown court. Now, on the same level as everybody else, the man appeared almost to be crouching like an enquiring squirrel behind a table the size of a car park, his head twitching from face to face. There were several spare smiles at barristers he recognized from the press side, a total lack of expression in the direction of Hall.

Hall perfectly concealed his inexperience of hearings in chambers, letting Perry lead to their expected place, any hesitation doubly covered by the confusion of seating the hiss-voiced squabbling newspaper contingent, which the clerk attempted with the arm waving urgency of an end-of-term photographer trying to assemble a disorganized class for proud parents' end-of-term souvenir. The muttered disputes were heightened with sighed rearrangement and Jarvis said in a voice unexpectedly loud for such a small man, 'Get along, get along. This is a simple application, not a major trial.'

'He's in a bad mood,' whispered Perry, unnecessarily, from behind Hall.

It still took almost another five minutes for the media lawyers to be seated in their self-elected order of priority. Only at the very end of the chaotic process did Hall identify at the rear of the court the superintendent,

Hopkins. He'd half expected Bentley and Rodgers, who looked back at him stone-faced, but not the uniformed Hampshire Constabulary inspector who had been with the council officials for the onsite child care meeting. Hall twisted more fully, frowning to Perry who said, 'Hughes, remember? If he'd cleared the roads around the house like he should have done all this wouldn't have been necessary. So why shouldn't he be inconvenienced?'

'I'll call him,' agreed Hall, approvingly. 'And go and remind Bentley he's precluded from talking about anything that has happened at the hospital and what his policewomen witnessed.'

'Why?' demanded Perry, soft voiced.

'Just do it.'

Jarvis pawed some papers in front of him and said, 'Mr Hall?'

Jeremy Hall rose, bowing his head deferentially and said, 'I appear before you today, my lord, to press the application that has already been laid before you . . .'

'. . . from the chambers of Sir Richard Proudfoot?' halted the judge.

'That is so, my lord.'

'I don't believe I have had the pleasure of your appearing before me?'

'The pleasure, my lord, is mine.' I hope but very much doubt, he thought.

'An extreme application, Mr Hall?'

'Reflecting an extreme situation, my lord.'

'I hope you'll be able to satisfy me of that.'

'I'm confident I shall be able to.'

'We'll see.'

Behind him Hall heard the scuff of discomfort from Humphrey Perry.

From Hall's left there was a continuous undertone of

coughs and foot movement and paper shuffling. Jarvis looked towards it and said, 'A matter of some considerable importance then?'

'I would not have brought it before your lordship did I not consider it to be so.'

'That's encouraging to be told, Mr Hall. Hearings in chambers are not to be requested lightly.'

The movement sounds grew from the other side of the room. Hall didn't look in their direction. 'At the conclusion of this hearing, my lord, I am confident you will accept my invitation to find that the circumstances are anything but to be considered or judged lightly.'

'Then we must hope, Mr Hall, that we are both satisfied, myself more than you. Proceed.'

For the first time Hall looked sideways, to see smiles of satisfaction on the faces of several opposing lawyers. They were all relaxed, languidly sure of themselves. He had sketched prompt notes for himself but mentally adjusted with the benefit of the unexpected Hampshire police officer. Within minutes – seconds it seemed – of his trying to detail the press ambush which he and Perry had personally experienced Jarvis began what progressed into a persistent barrage of interceptions, initially with a totally unnecessary query about the time of day and length of their being inconvenienced. Every time Hall halted, without a choice but without any impatience either and far more importantly never once losing his way. During the brief pause it took the clerk to carry to Jarvis their officially written Press Commission complaint, along with the bundle of letters promising money for photographs and interviews, Perry muttered, 'He's against us. And they know it across the room. They know they've won.'

The judge's disconcerting disruptions continued when

Hall offered the Hampshire officer and Geoffrey Johnson as witnesses to the harassment.

The policeman totally misconstrued the constant challenges as criticism and conveyed the impression that the mansion siege had at times been beyond police control. Hall snatched his first opportunity. 'Yet you brought no action for breach of the peace.'

'No, sir,' admitted the inspector.

'Nor for obstruction?'

'No, sir.'

'Why not?'

'It was the opinion of my superior officers the case would not succeed in court.'

'Why not?'

Had suicide been an option at that moment, Hughes would have taken it. 'I do not know, sir. The power of the press, I assumed.'

'You yourself were subjected to harassment, were you not?'

The man desperately sought an escape and failed. 'Yes, sir.'

'Did the media surrounding the mansion show any respect for your uniform, officer?'

'No, sir,' admitted the miserable policeman.

'They were aware there would subsequently be a trial?'

'Of course,' frowned Hughes. 'That's why they were there, trying to obtain background material.'

'So they were showing no respect for a court, either?'

The man hesitated. 'No sir, I don't suppose they were.'

The policeman's report of wall-climbing and back entrance intrusion established a consecutive narrative with the solicitor's account of that day's sixty-mile car chase with cameramen leaning out of open windows whenever his car was momentarily brought to a standstill by lights or traffic congestion: twice, when traffic was slowed to a crawl on his way through Wandsworth, photographers had jogged alongside, taking pictures.

'What effect did this have upon the child?' prompted Hall, looking sideways at the other lawyers, none of whom were smiling any longer.

'She was extremely distressed,' said Johnson.

'And Ms Parkes.'

'She was also extremely upset. Her concern was for the child: Emily did not understand what was happening. She thought she was going to be hurt.'

'Were you nervous, Mr Johnson?'

'Very much so. There were several occasions when I feared there was going to be a serious accident.'

None of the press lawyers questioned either the policeman or the solicitor when invited.

By the time he reached the end of his application Jarvis's intrusion had virtually stopped. Hall concluded by insisting Annabelle Parkes would be called as a material defence witness at the trial of Jennifer Lomax, finally finishing, 'I ask your lordship to find there is a very real risk that justice will not be served if this behaviour is allowed to continue. I therefore seek the protection of your lordship on all the points set out before you in my application, which I repeat in the most humble manner I have not brought lightly nor wantonly.'

There were a total of eighteen newspaper, television and radio lawyers, each of whom addressed the judge separately but with very little variation. Those representing the organizations identified by the money offer letters and by the cards thrust upon Jeremy Hall set the tone. The behaviour described was reprehensible and apologies for any excess were sincerely made for each episode. Each lawyer individually undertook on behalf of his organization to guarantee that neither the Hampshire house, the kindergarten nor the hospital would be subjected to any further press interest or intrusion.

'I submit, however, that it is unnecessary legally to extend the precincts of any future court to include these named premises,' said the white-haired lawyer who'd first accosted Hall in the hospital grounds. 'It is my contention that the press of this country are more than capable of policing themselves. I would further ask your lordship to find that there was no risk of justice being interfered with, by the letters that have been produced, but which, incidently, Ms Parkes has not been called formally to swear to as having received. While questionable, such approaches are not uncommon in cases attracting great public interest. The newspaper I represent has made no such approach, nor will it. Once more, I contend the press is capable of establishing its own standards.'

There was a parade of agreement from lawyers that followed and those who hadn't initially given personal undertakings on behalf of their media outlets all asked to be heard again, to do so. Jarvis allowed them, never once interrupting.

For several moments Jarvis looked between Hall and the lawyers ranged against him. Jarvis did so with his fingers on the very edge of the table, almost as if he was hanging on to prevent himself disappearing beneath it. Then he said, 'I think the problems of this application, which I accept, Mr Hall, is quite properly brought, have been sufficiently aired. I am minded to accept the assurances of the learned counsel that such behaviour will not be repeated. And I am reluctant to extend on behalf of a judge not yet appointed the precincts of a court not yet convened: I am not aware, in fact, of a precedent. Would you, Mr Hall, be prepared to accept the verbal undertakings offered before me today, upon my making it clear that I would regard any transgression most unfavourably?'

Hall rose, slowly, wondering as he did so just how much he was endangering the career about which Perry was so constantly warning him. 'Before answering your question, my lord, I would seek to address you on a matter of legal precedent.'

It took him a total of fifteen minutes to list the ten most recent and most highly publicized cases in which trial judges had publicly condemned financial offers to witnesses, in advance of their giving evidence at prominent trials. He did so individually, each time having the clerk carry the identified case record to Jarvis, who risked being even further submerged behind the growing wall of case books.

'With the greatest respect, my lord, I would be reluctant to accept undertakings not supported by the strength of a legal finding by yourself. What I have complained of today is not the overenthusiasm or momentary lack of judgement that it has been presented to you as being . . .' He was conscious of Jarvis's face hardening into an affronted mask and of the total silence of every lawyer in the room at what each would consider upstart impudence. '. . . As you will see from the stated cases I have produced before you, every time complaints such as mine are made the argument is advanced that the press should be allowed to put its own house in order, to maintain its own standards and integrity. Which lasts only until the next time, when the same excuse is put forward, to yet another excess. There is a need for a precedent, a benchmark, and it needs to be established by someone of your lordship's stature and pre-eminence . . .'

'You've failed to cover an important point,' stopped the determined judge yet again. 'You have assured me Ms Parkes is to be an essential witness. Yet you've failed to bring her before me to satisfy me she was the recipient of these letters. Why?'

'If it is your lordship's wish then of course I shall make arrangements to have Ms Parkes brought here. She is, at the moment, at the hospital bedside of Emily Lomax . . .'

Jarvis leapt in at the hesitation, as Hall had prayed he would and which was why he'd paused. 'Hospital bedside?'

'I regret to inform your lordship that Emily Lomax was made so unwell by the events of the day that doctors at St Thomas's felt it necessary to put her under observation. I am, however, pleased to inform your lordship the problem is not serious: I expect the child to be released later today. But she is extremely dependent upon Ms Parkes: wishes the girl to be with her at all times. It is for that reason I did not insist upon her being here. But as I say, if it is your lordship's wish—'

'No, not at all,' broke in the judge. 'I'll take the evidence of the inspector and Mr Johnson as sufficiently supporting . . .'

'. . . As I was saying,' came back Hall, hurriedly. 'I am particularly grateful it is before you, my lord, that I make this application today . . .' The mask had begun to soften, he thought. '. . . If my newness to the Bar makes me precocious, then I ask your lordship's forgiveness and indulgence. I am so solely in the best interests not only of a client in need of defence but also of a four-year-old child who today had no-one to defend her and upon whose behalf I have made this submission to you.'

There was an ice-like chill in the room. Jarvis coughed, a bird-like sound. 'There is a complexion upon this episode that makes it an important one, with profound legal implications. I was unaware, until this moment, of the effect upon this tiny child and I am obliged to Mr Hall for bringing it to my attention. I am persuaded, therefore, by the eloquence of the presentation, to grant the application, although to limit the precinct extensions to the Hampshire home of Mrs Lomax and the child's kindergarten but not the hospital in which Mrs Lomax is currently undergoing treatment . . .' He looked directly at the press lawyers. 'In doing so, I would advise each of you to bring to the notice of your clients and your employers what has been said and ruled here today. Until the appointment of a trial judge, the precinct order is mine and I will deal most harshly with any transgression.'

As they left the room Perry said, 'Jesus, you took a risk talking of the child's collapse like that.'

'It wasn't a lie,' insisted Hall.

'It wasn't the truth, either.'

'As much of the truth as any of the others were offering.'

'Where the hell did you get all those stated cases of press complaints?'

'You weren't the only one working late last night. I was in the chamber library until midnight, preparing for any press complaint hearing. Came in handy, didn't it?'

Emily was in a playroom attached to a children's ward when Jeremy Hall returned to the hospital but ignoring the toys. She still clutched the much-hugged rabbit but her eyes never left Annabelle: when the nanny moved towards Hall as he entered Emily scurried alongside, grabbing up for the ever present hand. Julian Mason was there, with a slightly built, heavily bespectacled girl whom Hall assumed to be the child psychiatrist. He didn't think she was much older than the nanny.

'The press have been barred from the house,' he announced to Annabelle. 'And I don't think you'll have any problems going home. If you do, call me immediately.' He encompassed the other two in the room. 'Can Emily go home?'

'Whenever she wants. We just waited for you,' said Mason.

'You've got to put Ronnie Rabbit to bed, haven't you?' encouraged the bespectacled girl to Emily.

The child ignored her, gazing up at Hall instead. 'Why doesn't Mummy like me any more? Annabelle won't tell me.'

'Your mummy does like you,' said Hall, totally out of his depth and looking desperately at the others for help. 'She loves you: she told me.'

'She tried to hurt me, like the men.'

'I've told Emily it's the medicine her mummy's taking to make her better,' offered Annabelle.

'That's what it is,' seized Hall. 'She has to take the medicine to make her better. But it makes her do funny things, like today.'

'Will she do it again?'

'No.'

'She didn't want my drawing.'

'She did. She's got it now.'

'Will I see her again?'

'She's asleep now. Getting better.'

'Let's go home,' said Annabelle, briskly. 'It'll be late, by the time we get there. We'll come and see Mummy another day.'

'Will the men chase us, like before?'

'No,' promised Hall.

'Good,' said Emily, positively.

Hall and Mason walked Annabelle and the child to Johnson's waiting car. At the entrance Emily perceptibly held back, frowning through the glass. There was no traffic jam or obvious press pack.

'I'm sorry about today,' Hall told Annabelle.

'So am I,' said the girl. 'I suppose nobody could have guessed it would happen.'

Hall looked at Mason but said nothing, waiting until the Bentley eased from the hospital and turned immediately left towards the bridge. 'Is it going to affect the child?'

'Not permanently,' said Mason. 'It won't have helped Jennifer, though.'

'I'm not sure there is anything that will,' said the lawyer.

Everyone was assembled, waiting in Proudfoot's riverview office, when Jeremy Hall got back to chambers. The QC and Feltham were drinking whisky. There was a half-empty sherry glass on the table beside Perry. There was no immediate invitation to Hall.

Proudfoot said, 'I thought it was time we had an assessment.'

'The child is going to be OK. There's still a lot more tests to be carried out upon Mrs Lomax.'

'I meant legal assessment,' said Proudfoot, impatiently. He indicated Perry. 'We've heard what happened at the hearing.'

'We've got protection from the press, which was very necessary,' said Hall.

'Bentley's a headline hunter,' chipped in Feltham,

wheezily. 'He'll tell his press friends why the child collapsed and they'll tell their lawyers. Who'll make damned sure it gets back to Jarvis. He won't rescind his order but he'll make equally damned sure every judge on the circuit knows what you did. He'll think he's been made a fool of.'

'You didn't do yourself – or the chambers – any favours today,' said Proudfoot.

'It was right that the restrictions were imposed,' insisted Hall.

'You've alienated the press and the bench, in one go,' said Feltham, just as insistently.

'In the best interests of a client,' fought back Hall. He was tempted to help himself to sherry, uninvited, but decided against it.

'Aren't you losing perspective here?' asked Proudfoot. 'It's right that we've taken this case and it's right – a matter of professional integrity – that we defend it to the best of our ability. But at the end of the day, it comes down to mitigation. The plea for which, after what happened with the child, seems perfectly obvious.'

'Shouldn't the application have been made?' challenged Hall.

'I've no fault with the application,' accepted the chamber's leader. 'But the press undertaking would have achieved the same effect as the definite order and we – you – wouldn't have been exposed to judges' irritation.'

'Do you wish to transfer the brief?'

'No,' said Proudfoot, quickly. 'Just remember that if you'd like to discuss anything, my door's always open . . .' He made a general movement with his whisky glass towards the chief clerk. 'And I've never found Bert's advice unwelcome.'

But I don't want it, from either of you, thought Hall. 'Thank you, for your support and confidence.'

When he got home there was a message on his answering machine from Patricia Boxall that she couldn't make the following evening. She'd call. Hall felt relieved.

Chapter Sixteen

Jennifer gave up. On everything. On everyone. Even Jane. Particularly Jane. The voice was always there, mocking, goading, jeering. And Jennifer said words that weren't hers and swore when she wouldn't have sworn. She didn't argue any more: didn't try to win any mental battles. Didn't care.

Awake or asleep – even drugged sleep – there was a constant image blocking her mind more than Jane occupied it. Emily's face. Emily's face contorted in open-eyed terror, Emily's face broken in disbelieving fear as she twisted away, Emily's face blanking in horrified dread as she briefly lay, helplessly, on the floor. Emily's face, screaming. Always Emily's face, the face of an Emily knowing her mother wanted to kill her – would have killed her – until she'd been stopped. Only just stopped. Wouldn't have been without the hypnotic key implanted in her brain. Thank God. Except there wasn't a God. Couldn't be. What God would let this happen.

'That's right. Prayers – exorcism – won't help. You haven't got anyone. Not even Emily any more. Alone. Lost.'

Jennifer's lassitude was absolute. She wouldn't have washed unless she'd been washed or brushed her hair if it hadn't been brushed for her or dressed if she hadn't been dressed or undressed. Make-up wasn't considered. She made the very slightest effort with Mason, because he'd saved Emily, but didn't bother with the other psychiatrists or psychologists or neurologists who followed intermittently, with their questions and their tests, but not any more trying to prove her sanity because she wasn't sane: she'd known for every second what she was doing when she'd tried to get her hands around Emily's throat but hadn't been able to stop herself. Only a mad woman would have behaved like that. Sometimes mad, sometimes sane. But mad when Jane made her so. Couldn't win. Jane had won. So why bother? Lost, like Jane said. All gone. Everything gone.

Jennifer didn't try to stop herself, to stop Jane, during the examinations – several more hypnosis sessions and more brain scans and having her head connected to electrical sensors and three times being injected with a drug they'd identified by name but which she couldn't remember, any more than she could remember the names of all the experts who'd conducted all the tests. Or in front of the rigid-haired magistrate whom Jane called a menstrual cow and a menopausal mare and asked if she fucked pigs, to the woman's fury and who, at the second hearing, moved the remand to a women's prison. The hospital pressed for the transfer, citing the attack on Dr Lloyd as well as that upon the child and arguing their concern for other patients. Jennifer had heard the hospital lawyer's argument and agreed with it: Jane had told her to agree with it, shouting out.

Jennifer was only vaguely aware but totally disinterested that Jeremy Hall or Humphrey Perry didn't any longer come so regularly, although both attended the magistrate's hearings, as unconcerned as she was by their travelling with her in the ambulance to the prison. On the way Hall said she was going into the ward there, not the general prison, so it was nothing more than a change of hospitals.

'You'll be looked after there. Safe.'

'*He's lying again. Full of dykes. Tongues in your pussy. Dildo rape. You'll be popular. Fresh meat. Your pussy will be red raw. Bleed maybe. They won't care.*'

With the exception of the bars it did appear exactly like the hospital she'd left, even to the small separate room into which she was settled, at the far end of the general, ground-floor ward in which lay two women, one with both wrists heavily bandaged. The other called out something to Hall and Perry as they escorted Jennifer through the long room. Neither man reacted and Jennifer didn't hear but there was laughter from everyone else, two uniformed nurses and two trustees in prison drab. David Emerson, the white-coated prison doctor who was walking with them, called out, 'That's enough, girls.'

The woman who'd made the unheard remark said, 'There's never enough. That's how I stopped being an innocent virgin,' and there was fresh laughter.

A big-busted, broad-shouldered matron who hadn't been in her office at the ward entrance abruptly bustled into the private room after them and said, 'Right now, let's get you settled in, shall we, my love?' and at once began hanging Jennifer's belongings in the closet from a suitcase she opened without asking.

'Lovely clothes,' she said, admiringly.

'*Didn't take long, did it?*'

'No.'

'What?' frowned the matron.

'It's a psychiatric situation,' Emerson explained to her.

At Perry's gesture the doctor followed him out into the corridor, with Hall trailing uncertainly behind. The more experienced solicitor, to whom the remark about the clothes had registered, like the suitcase opening, said, 'You won't forget that Mrs Lomax is a remand prisoner, will you?'

'Mrs Lomax will get as good care here as she got in St Thomas's.'

'It's the particular type of that care to which I was referring,' said the solicitor, pointedly.

Hall looked quickly back into the ward, understanding. Jennifer was sitting docilely in the chair, oblivious to what the other woman was doing. The larger case was unpacked and she'd started on the smaller one, examining each article as she took it out, fingering the material and looking at the labels.

'I don't understand that remark,' Emerson was saying. He was a dark-skinned man with wiry hair and a rugby-flattened nose.

'Mrs Lomax's psychiatric symptoms are still being assessed but she's obviously traumatized,' said Hall. 'I don't want anything to occur that might worsen her condition.'

'I don't . . .' the doctor began to repeat and then stopped. For several moments he looked between the two lawyers. Then he said, 'I'll do my best.'

'I'd like better than your best, doctor. I'd like a guarantee,' said the barrister.

'I can't be in the ward twenty-four hours a day.'

'The answer, I would have thought, would be to have people here upon whom you can rely, when you're elsewhere,' said Perry.

'All I can do is my best,' insisted the man.

By the time they re-entered the private ward, which was actually bigger than the one in St Thomas's, all Jennifer's things were put away and the two suitcases stowed in a locker above the closet.

Perry said, 'Here's the inventory of her things. I'd like you to sign receipt.'

'That should have been done at admission, with her jewellery and money,' insisted the matron. Her identification plate read, Beryl Harrison.

'It was,' said the solicitor. 'I'd like you to counter-sign it. Her valuable personal items remain in reception. Her clothes are here.'

'There's no regulation,' persisted the woman.

'Is there a reason not to?' demanded Perry, mildly.

'There's no regulation,' said the woman, doggedly.

To the doctor Perry said, 'Perhaps you could take us past the governor, on our way out. We'll get it counter-signed there.'

The matron snatched the inventory from Perry and scrawled her name below that of the admissions clerk. 'Satisfied?'

'Perfectly. Thank you,' smiled Perry.

The wardress who had brought them to the hospital escorted the lawyers back to the entrance, leaving Emerson and the woman with Jennifer.

'*What happened to your nose? Get it smashed by some dyke?*'

Emerson looked up, startled, from the St Thomas's case notes when Jennifer repeated the questions, then gestured to the dossier for the benefit of the equally startled matron. 'Voices in her head.'

'Jane,' offered Jennifer, forcing herself to talk. 'It's Jane.'

'This isn't going to be easy,' predicted the matron.

'*I'm not going to make it easy.*'

'She says she isn't going to make it easy.'

'Maybe I won't bother with my own admission examination today,' said Emerson, indicating the dossier again.

'It's all comprehensively listed here. Tomorrow will be soon enough.'

'*Frightened I might attack you, fat nose!*'

'She thinks you're frightened.'

Emerson ignored Jennifer. 'There's a lot of medical notes,' he said, reading from the papers. 'Sedatives, mostly.'

'I always think medication's the best way to handle the difficult ones, if they're mad,' said the matron.

Jennifer stirred, to protest the madness, but then sat back in the chair, disinterested. Why bother?

'I got a warning from her lawyers.'

'The younger one looked pretty new to me.'

'The solicitor started it,' qualified the doctor. 'The young one came in at the end.'

'Been around the block,' dismissed the woman.

'I said we'd do our best.'

'Why don't they come and babysit if they're so worried?'

Jennifer was only distantly aware of the discussion, indifferent to whatever they were saying: if she just slightly closed her eyes she could picture Emily's face when she'd grabbed out for her throat, as if it was projected on to the blank wall opposite. Beautiful Emily, pretty Emily, terrified Emily. About-to-die Emily.

'There's a lot of money involved here,' cautioned Emerson, not looking up from the case notes in front of him. 'Expensive lawyers with big mouths. Could make trouble. We will do our best, won't we?'

'You treat the aches and pains, David. I'll run the ward.'

Emerson, who regretted allowing the domination in the first nervous months of his arrival but was resigned to the fact that it was too late to do anything about it now, said, 'I'll leave you to give the medication then?'

'Of course.'

'It's been given intravenously at St Thomas's.'

'Let me have the case notes. I'll look after everything.' She walked from Jennifer's room with the doctor, releasing in their necessarily correct order the three locks securing the reinforced door of the dispensary with the three separate keys attached to her waist belt. Jennifer hadn't moved when she returned.

'Just a little prick in your arm,' the woman said. 'And a little more than you've been getting at the other hospital, so you can properly relax after the upheaval of coming in here. You'd like that, dear, wouldn't you?'

As the needle bit into her arm Jennifer was curious that Jane hadn't made her arm move, to try to prevent being closed out, but it was the fleetest of passing thoughts, which didn't matter, like nothing mattered any more.

In the car taking them back towards the centre of London Hall said, 'You really think Jennifer is threatened?'

'The absolute archetype,' said Perry. 'Young, beautiful, wonderful body and rich: one way or another, with hardly an exception, everything that's been denied all the rest of them in there. There'll be a queue.'

Hall shuddered, 'To do what?'

'Everything you can imagine. Quite a lot you can't.'

'We've got to stop it!' said Hall, furiously.

'We can't: prisoners run prisons, not the staff,' said Perry, flatly. 'What we did was all we can do.'

'What about the governor?'

'I made it very clear to the governor Jennifer is a remand prisoner,' reminded Perry. 'He knew what I meant, just as the doctor knew.'

'Let's do it again, in a letter or something.'

'It would make her even more of a target,' insisted Perry.

'How much more?'

'Getting her face cut into more pieces than she cut her husband's.'

'When will it start?' asked Hall, dully.

'They won't wait,' predicted Perry.

They didn't.

The first trustee was a bottle-yellow blonde and slight, with no bust. Her fingernails were badly bitten. The one who came in behind her had mousey hair in a pony tail and a black and red confusion of tattoos on both arms. They were crude prison drawings, jabbed with a pin for ink to be rubbed into the wounds. FUCK was spelled out across the fingers of her left hand, HATE across the right, and high on her left cheek there was a drooped-wing bird.

'I'm Frances,' said the blonde. 'Fran.'

'Emma,' said the second one.

'*Hello. Say hello.*'

'Hello.'

'Are you frightened, in a place like this?' asked Emma.

'*A little. I'd like some friends. Say it!*'

'A little. I'd like some friends.'

'We'll be your friends. Look after you,' said Fran. 'You need looking after here.'

'*I'd like that. Say it!*'

'I'd like that.' Jennifer felt very relaxed: warm.

'That's why we've come,' said Fran. 'People helped you to dress and undress at the other hospital, when you couldn't be bothered, didn't they?'

Jennifer shook her head, not bothering. Very warm: warm and comfortable. Better than the other hospital.

'Can you be bothered now?' asked Emma.

Jennifer shrugged. Silly conversation. Not important. Nothing was important. Couldn't see Emily's face on the wall any longer. Glad about that.

'Would you like us to help you? Get you ready for bed?' suggested Emma. 'It's time you went to bed.'

Another shrug. All right where she was.

'Here,' said Emma. 'Let me help you.' She held her hands out, for Jennifer to grasp and when she did eased her out of the chair.

Emma was in front of her, Fran behind. Jennifer felt someone's hands on her breasts but it was very gentle, not unpleasant.

'Nice. Very nice,' said Fran.

'*Say nice. Go on, say it!*'

'Nice.'

'Do you like that?' said Emma, softly.

'*Yes. Say yes.*'

'Yes.'

'Time to undress,' said the woman in front of her. 'Put your hands on my shoulders, so we can help you.'

Obediently Jennifer felt out, putting her hands where she'd been told. The pony-tailed girl leaned forward, to make it easier, and kissed her very gently, on the cheek at first, then on the lips, parting Jennifer's lips with her tongue. It was hard, not soft, like a tongue should be soft, pushing and probing. Jennifer pulled back, turning her head. 'Don't.'

'It's nice,' said Emma.

'No,' said Jennifer. The hands from behind were squeezing her breasts and she shrugged, to loosen the grip. 'Don't. Hurts.'

'Nice if it hurts,' said Fran, mouth close to Jennifer's ear.

'Let's get these clothes off,' said Emma. 'They're in the way. Don't you think they're in the way?'

Jennifer felt the hands on her breasts loosen and lowered her head to see the buttons undone on her jacket. There seemed to be a lot of hands, hands in front and hands from behind, busy fingers, like spiders' legs. She thought it was funny and sniggered. The jacket came off, then the shirt. She felt the zip go at the back of her skirt and Fran pulled it down from behind, with the waist slip.

'Step out now. One step forward.'

Jennifer did as she was told, in bra and pants. The blond-haired girl came around from behind, standing with Emma. Both looked at her.

'Wonderful tits,' said Emma.

'Wonderful.'

'I want the tits.'

'I'm happy with the cunt.'

'You're beautiful, Jennifer. Very beautiful.'

'*Say you like it. Say it now! I like it.*'

'No.'

'Yes you are, darling,' said Emma, not able to understand.

'*I like it!*'

'No.'

'We think so.'

'*I like it!*' shouted the voice.

'I like it.'

Both women smiled, in front of her. 'We're all going to like it,' said Emma. 'We don't want that bra on any more, do we?'

Jennifer felt the straps go and looked down as her breasts dropped forward, very slightly. Beyond she saw Fran on her knees and felt her pants ease down over her hips. The girl didn't stand, but stayed kneeling, hands hard against Jennifer's buttocks bringing her crotch tight into the face. Jennifer felt something wet, against her clitoris, and wriggled, to try to stop it.

'Don't . . . please . . .'

'It's nice, darling. You know it's nice.' Emma's voice was

from behind, both her hands on Jennifer's breasts, kneading, pricking the nipples between her finger and thumb, hard soft, hard soft.

'Don't. You're hurting.'

'Lay down,' urged Emma. 'It will be better if you lie down. Here we go.'

Unprotesting, consciousness ebbing and flowing, Jennifer let herself be laid on the bed and was glad because she wanted to lie down. She felt her legs eased apart and looked down and saw only the top of a blond head between her legs and felt a lot more wetness, something stiff yet soft licking at her and something stiff inside her, working up and down, and she grew wet. Briefly, momentarily, the wetness stopped from outside although something inside still went up and down and Fran's head came up, so that Jennifer could see her smiling face and then it was gone again, back between her legs. She couldn't see the blond head any more because Emma was in the way now, bent over her breasts, gently biting and sucking and biting and sucking. It hurt but not badly and Jennifer didn't protest or try to close her legs because she was too tired and really couldn't feel any more. Jane was trying to say something but Jennifer couldn't properly hear. Maybe it wasn't words. Maybe it was just laughter.

'I want her cunt now.'

'Not yet.'

'We should have brought the cock.'

'Next time.'

'Let me have the cunt now.'

'She's tight, on two fingers.'

'Did she come?'

'Yes.'

'This is going to be wonderful, having her like this.'

'Let me have her cunt now!'

The two women hurriedly swopped. Neither spoke, engrossed in new things, new parts.

At last Fran said, 'This is fantastic.'

'Her ass is tight, too,' said Emma. 'Hardly get my finger in.'

'I don't want to share her, not yet.'

'We won't.' Emma rose, from between Jennifer's legs. Fran came down to the bottom of the bed and together they stood gazing down at the spread-eagled, unconscious woman.

'You've made her bleed,' said Fran.

'Probably her ass. She really was tight.'

'We'll bring the cock tomorrow.'

'That'll be fun.'

'I came,' said Fran.

'So did I.'

'But I want to come again. I want you to fuck me.'

'With the cock.'

'Yes.'

'That'd be good. Fun tonight as well as tomorrow.'

As they passed the matron's office they both chorused 'Goodnight' and Matron Harrison said 'Goodnight' back. She didn't have to go to the dispensary again, because she'd got what she wanted the first visit.

She stood for a long time gazing down at Jennifer's naked, leg-spread body, as the other two women had done. In a baby-soothing voice she said, 'What did they do to you, you poor little thing. You'll be all sore in the morning. But don't cry, little one, nursey will make it better. I'm going to rub it with nice, soft cream. That'll make it better. Nice and soft, take the pain away. There . . .'

The voice said, '*You don't know how you're going to suffer*,' but Jennifer didn't hear.

Chapter Seventeen

There was no alternative to a mental-illness defence. Jeremy Hall supposed he had known that from the beginning, despite Jennifer's insistence and the unexpectedly conflicting opinions from a lot of the professional experts – prosecution as well as defence – quite a few of whom still had tests and examinations they wanted to carry out or repeat but all of whose findings so far were going to make that defence a mountainously uphill struggle. He'd let them go through the motions, of course: all part of justice being seen to be done. But that's all it could be, recognized routines with fancy names like Schneider's First Rank Symptoms assessment to protect their judgement against contrary challenge and impressively to fill the invoice page when they submitted their exorbitant final bills.

Hall was most surprised of all – disappointed even – by Julian Mason's adamant refusal, after Jennifer's agreement, to have their final sessions with her under the influence of pentathol, the truth drug, to testify to a mental imbalance, despite having personally witnessed Jennifer's attack upon the child. Any small doubts that Hall had harboured – and they'd been very small indeed – had disappeared with that frenzied episode that to remember still made his skin crawl.

But Mason wasn't alone: just the only psychiatrist who'd had the personal experience. With the exception of Milton Smith, the London-based American psychiatrist who was prepared to give evidence of Multiple Personality Disorder, the independent and preliminary agreement of the other three defence psychiatrists was that although Jennifer showed some signs of schizophrenia by hearing a voice and the depressed regression into which she'd sunk after the attack on Emily, mental illness was too arguably uncertain for them to give a positive diagnosis. So arguable, in fact, that each had so far indicated they were coming down on the side of sanity.

Most bewildering of all was their unanimous finding, like that of Mason, that the coherent if sometimes obscene conversational logic of what Jennifer claimed to be Jane speaking – the prime indicator of schizophrenia – proved rather than disproved she wasn't suffering from the illness. Hall's problem of mounting any sort of defence acceptable to a court was compounded by each of the three prosecution psychiatrists, although again agreeing some mental disorientation, also being prepared to swear there was insufficient mental disturbance to amount to diminished responsibility. Which wasn't the end of Hall's problems. There'd been two separate neurological examinations, during which Jennifer had undergone electroencephalograms, in addition to all the other tests administered by George Fosdyke, including brain and upper body scans. Both had registered absolutely normal, showing no physical cause for Jennifer's condition.

Hall accepted that what little he had was all he could possibly expect for a very fragile and uncertain mitigation plea, apart from the outstanding psychiatric assessments which he didn't anticipate would do anything to help him and which shouldn't take longer than a week to complete.

Perry had made brilliant background preparation. Because of Jennifer's possession claim – the major thrust of his intended defence – the solicitor had gone beyond obtaining a complete transcript of the Jane Lomax inquest – discovering in doing so that Bentley had done the same in an effort to uncover a missed murder – by having a Washington lawyer provide a full medical and personal history of Gerald and Jane Lomax before their transfer to England. Perry had extended the lawyer's investigation to include a dossier on Rebecca Nicholls, which they'd had to make available to the prosecution under the rules of disclosure and which Hall was sure would be made into a major part of the case against Jennifer.

It appeared Lomax's affair with Rebecca had begun at least three years earlier – maybe even before that – and that during their return trips to New York they had occupied Rebecca's Manhattan apartment virtually as husband and wife. They'd continued to do that, in the London flat, during the nights Lomax spent in London while Jennifer remained in the country with Emily. When he'd given Hall the Rebecca Nicholls' file Perry had remarked that Lomax seemed quite a bastard and after reading it Hall agreed with the assessment. In view of her mental state he would have liked a lot of it kept from Jennifer but objectively realized it was a forlorn hope, providing as it did the vengeance grounds upon which the prosecution were making their case, which was founded on the incontestably concreted evidence of sixteen people witnessing the killing. And which was going to be supported, because of their doubt about mental illness, by at least half a dozen of the country's foremost mind doctors. By contrast – but he feared easily overwhelmed by the weight of evidence against her – the biography he had of Jennifer Lomax, née Stone, was of a Mensa-level woman who professionally had been relentless to succeed, which she had, and whose only known failing was to have embarked upon an affair with a married man whom she'd subsequently married and who, ever since, had lived a faultless, blameless, charity organizing life. He paused at the final thought: charities that couldn't now fast enough get rid of her, an embarrassing encumbrance.

The final acknowledgement of the obstacles he faced further unsettled Hall, who single-mindedly had set out on a Bar career to become even more respected and famous – but more importantly, richer – than his respected and famous uncle. Which required the same absolutely ruthless objectivity which his uncle possessed and of which irritatingly he knew himself at that precise moment to be a victim. But an absolute ruthlessness which he, personally, hadn't so far shown: if not his heart he'd most certainly worn his integrity on his sleeve. He'd wanted to do his best for Jennifer Lomax – was still determined to do his best for and by Jennifer Lomax – but he had to accept reality. And the reality was that he was defending a case as hopeless as he'd recognized it to be from the very first sherry-and-bullshit session with Sir Richard and the inhaler-puffing Bert Feltham, partners in cynical ruthlessness. Recognized but refused to recognize, he reminded himself, permitting no personal excuses. He'd been fooling himself: allowing himself to forget and minimize the horrific awfulness of her crime because he'd been too hungrily eager to make a career. Which he would – because he was determined – but not with this case. He'd given it a potential it didn't have. Had never had.

At once came another scathing personal examination. If he'd known it was an unwinnable case from the beginning – which he had – and known he was an inconsequential cog in some complicated higher chambers machination – which he also had – why did he have this incomplete feeling, this belief he couldn't shake off that there was something more that he should have done, should have recognized, but hadn't? Get-to-the-top-whatever ambition? Nothing to do with it. Something quite different, quite inexplicable. There was a gap, an empty place or a missing piece from a jig-saw with no missing pieces, a complete picture that didn't have to be assembled. He had all the parts: every statement, almost every scientific and forensic result, every reason, every motive, every witness. Himself a witness to the madness even. There couldn't be a gap, a piece that didn't fit. Inexperience, Hall decided. Easy to rationalize – to understand – if he stopped looking outside and looked inwardly instead at himself, which he was at last doing. His first murder. Newspaper coverage because Jennifer Lomax was beautiful and her cheating husband was a millionaire. The carnage of the crime. He'd *wanted* her to be not guilty. So he'd disregarded facts and common sense and more forensic evidence than any other murder case in the English criminal history of homicide about which he'd read about or studied or been officially lectured about.

It had all been absurd fantasy, the half-awake-at-night dream that indefensible though it appeared he was going to produce some incredible, last-minute proof of innocence – virtually impossible and almost certainly inadmissible under the rules of disclosure – and lead the beautiful, blond, smiling Jennifer Lomax to face the cameras and a life of innocent freedom. If he tried hard enough, he could probably have imagined the soaring music – lots of violins – that normally accompanied such soap-box endings.

Despite the self-honesty the overlooked feeling wouldn't go. It stayed nagging in his mind and he wondered if this was what Jane's voice in Jennifer's head was like until he realized *what* he was wondering – that he was accepting the very presence of a voice in Jennifer's head – and refused to let the speculation run.

His internal telephone buzzed, to warn him that Humphrey Perry was on his way up from that day's remand hearing, and Hall pushed the case notes aside.

'Before we begin,' Hall said, as the older man entered the room. 'I want to say that I think the preparation is magnificent. I'm in your debt. Thank you.'

Perry, whose opinion of the barrister had changed during the pre-trial weeks, actually flushed. 'I wish there was a possibility of it working out differently from how it will.'

'That's what I want to discuss,' said Hall. 'The way forward.'

'There was no change,' reported Perry. 'She's still wrapped in apathy.'

'Abject depression is a schizophrenic symptom.'

'I've read all the expert opinions: I commissioned them,' reminded Perry.

'What about outbursts?'

'Usual abuse, to Mrs Heathcote: asked her how many times a day she masturbated. And references again to Jennifer herself being assaulted in the prison hospital.'

'What about that, exactly?' pressed Hall.

'"Ask Jennifer who's fucking her,"' quoted the solicitor, literally.

'Did you?' asked Hall.

Perry nodded. 'After today's hearing. She said nothing was happening: that it was Jane, making her say it. And immediately afterwards said it *was* true but that Jane made her say that, too.'

Hall sighed, shaking his head. 'Mason says he thinks there's some abuse . . .' Hall rustled his hand through the dossiers in front of him. '. . . Not in his report. He telephoned.'

'He told me the same,' said Perry. 'That's why I made a point of seeing the governor again today. He assured me she's in the safest place, in the hospital. And that he's made the matron personally responsible.'

Hall sighed again. 'What about the election to go direct to a higher court, bypassing committal?'

Perry smiled, wryly. 'If I hadn't applied for it I think Mrs Heathcote would have suggested it herself. She seems to be the only person without the slightest doubt that Jennifer Lomax is stark, raving mad. I've sent her a note, thanking her for her forebearance. She's taken a lot of abuse.'

Hall tapped the files in front of him, reminded. 'Despite what all the experts say, it's got to be diminished responsibility?'

'That's all it was ever going to be.'

'And because of what the experts say – or rather won't say – we're going to have to introduce the episode with Emily,' insisted Hall. 'Bring it out when Lloyd and Annabelle Parkes are on the stand and call the two policewomen. You and Johnson, too.'

Perry shook his head, sadly. 'What a way to prove she's mentally unstable.'

'Can you think of a better way, so that I can avoid doing this?'

'It wasn't a criticism,' said Perry, quickly. 'It's the only thing you can do: the best of a bad job.'

'Did you tell her I'd need two or three sessions, before the trial?'

'Yes.'

'Anything about a QC?'

Perry shook his head. 'There hasn't been, for quite a while now. Like I said, her apathy is pretty complete.'

Hall moved the papers around again, although aimlessly. 'Your preparation is brilliant.'

'You said,' frowned Perry. 'Thank you.'

'So you know everything there is, in the files?'

The frown remained. 'Yes?'

'So what's missing?'

Perry stiffened, affronted. 'There's nothing missing!'

'I'm not suggesting you overlooked something: it's complete. It's me. Us. It's probably there, staring us in the face, but we can't see it. *I* can't see it.'

Perry looked curiously at the younger man. Hall's first case, he remembered. 'There's nothing I haven't pointed up that would help us,' he insisted.

'I'm sure you're right,' retreated Hall. 'Maybe I'm trying too hard.'

'Maybe you are,' agreed the solicitor.

It was only a short walk across the expansive car park to the back entrance to El Vino and Perry was at their regular corner table when Bert Feltham panted down the stairs. Perry waited for the man to recover his breath, pouring the Montrachet without speaking.

'All set?' demanded the chief clerk, finally. Today's outfit was a dove-grey suit, with a tie to match worn with a black shirt. He looked like a Mafia capo from Central Casting.

'As ready as we'll ever be. Medical experts are being a bloody nuisance, but that's not unusual. Won't come out positively to say she's mad.'

'Persuaded her to plead guilty?'

'Not yet. That's Jeremy's job. I've done all the other donkey work. Lomax was a bastard. Prosecution's got a good case for a woman scorned.'

Feltham ordered a double portion of potatoes with his beef, looking pointedly at the white wine.

'Margaux?' suggested Perry.

'Good choice,' accepted Feltham. 'How's Hall shaped up, overall?'

'Very well. I'm impressed, genuinely. Had a funny five minutes this morning, about something that we've overlooked but then he agreed himself that he was trying too hard and whatever he thought it was didn't exist. We've left the magistrates now. It's trial time.'

'When?'

'Soon as we get a date and a judge.'

'Think she'd be persuaded to plead?'

'She was pretty firm at the beginning but she's gone downhill a lot since. Shouldn't be a problem.'

'All done in a day?'

'Three at the most.'

'That'll help. He's behind with his chambers' rent.'

Perry gave a dismissive nod. 'We've got the summonses, on the copper affair.'

'I think we can accept that brief,' said Feltham, smiling broadly.

'We've brought a friend,' announced Fran. 'This is Harriet.'

The newcomer was black, with very short hair, and tall, towering over the other two prisoners. 'Hello.'

'And your other friend,' said Emma, holding up the dildo. 'You like this friend, don't you?'

'No, please,' said Jennifer. The injection hadn't worked, like it had on the other nights. She felt relaxed but she wasn't drifting off, to blot everything out.

'*Say fuck me!*'

'No.'

'You know you want it,' said Emma.

'*Say fuck me!*'

'Fuck me.'

'There, we knew you did.'

The black girl was undressing, at the foot of the bed, watching as the other two women, on either side, unbuttoned Jennifer's dress.

'Go away!'

'Is that what you like? Fighting?' said the black girl, leaning forward. Abruptly she slapped Jennifer, back-handed, across the face.

'Careful!' warned Emma. 'Don't mark her.'

The black girl drew back, strapping the dildo around her waist. When it hung like a penis between her legs she said, 'Look Jennifer, for you.'

'*Say it's nice.*'

'No.'

'*Nice. Say it.*'

'Nice.'

'It is, isn't it?' said Emma. 'But you were a naughty girl today, Jennifer. You said something about the fun we're having to the magistrates, didn't you?'

'No. It was Jane.'

'We know you did. Matron told us. And we told you what would happen if you did that, didn't we?'

The dress was totally open, leaving Jennifer in bra and pants. From the top pocket of her prison overalls Fran took a double-edged safety razor blade. One side was embedded between two pieces of wood, bound in place with twine.

'No!' whimpered Jennifer.

'*They're going to cut you!*' screamed Jane, excited.

With one quick, downward slash Fran brought the exposed part of the blade down between Jennifer's breasts, severing the strip between the two bra cups but missing her skin. Emma pulled both cups apart, briefly leaning forward to kiss Jennifer's nipples. The moment Emma's head lifted Fran lay the edge of the razor against Jennifer's right nipple. 'We'll cut them off,' she said. 'If you complain, we'll cut your tits off and then you won't be pretty any more.'

'*Say you don't care. That you'd like it.*'

For the first time in days, weeks, Jennifer bit her lips shut, refusing the words, the effort trembling through her.

'Excited!' said Harriet. 'Look, she's coming! Go on, cut her, just a little.'

'Too soon, yet,' refused Emma. She pointed to the prison-tattooed bird, on her left cheek. 'Would you like one of these, Jennifer? I'll give you one, when the court hearing's over.'

'I want her!' demanded Harriet.

Fran cut the pants away with the razor and Jennifer's legs were jerked apart, for them to be pulled clear. Emma and Fran stood either side, still holding Jennifer's legs wide, as the black girl climbed between them, the artificial penis erect in front of her. Jennifer tightly closed her eyes, refusing to look, but she couldn't avoid the feeling, when she was penetrated, not that time or when Emma followed or Fran, behind her.

'This is the suffering I promise, Jennifer. And it's going to go on and on and never stop.'

Jennifer was shivering and sobbing when the matron entered the enclosed, now empty ward. 'Here's nursey, darling: nursey with the lovely cream.'

Jennifer lay unresisting, eyes still tightly shut, needing the balm for the soreness scouring between her legs.

'That's not nice, is it darling. Shouldn't do that to you, should they?'

Jennifer didn't speak. Didn't open her eyes.

'Shall nursey make them stop?'

'No!'

Again Jennifer managed to hold the word back. 'What?' She opened her eyes.

'Nursey make them stop, shall she?'

'Yes.'

'But you'll have to help nursey.'

'How?'

'Sign the form I've got here. It says I can look after your cheque-book for you. That will be all right, won't it.'

'Why?'

'We'll pay them, not to come near you. You'd do that, wouldn't you? Pay them?'

'Yes. Oh God, yes.'

'No!'

Jennifer didn't say it.

'How much do you think? Three hundred pounds, I think, don't you?'

'Yes. Yes.'

'You make the cheque out to nursey and nursey will pay them not to come in any more.'

'Thank you. Oh, thank you.'

'*Bitch.*'

'Here's the authorization. And nursey will go on rubbing this lovely cream in, until the soreness goes. It's all right if nursey does it all the time, isn't it?'

'*Here goes your money, Jennifer. Cheaper to be fucked.*'

The following day Feltham appeared early at Jeremy Hall's door.

'We've been offered a provisional date, if we're ready.'

'We are. When?'

'Two weeks' time. The Monday. Simon Keflin-Brown QC is against you. Robert Morley's the junior.'

'Who's the judge.'

'Jarvis. Probably his last case.'

'Oh,' said Hall.

'When your luck's out it's out,' said Feltham, philosophically. 'And he wants pre-trial conferences.'

Chapter Eighteen

The only difference from their previous encounter appeared to be the greater number of files barricaded on Sir Ivan Jarvis's massive desk: the squirrel collected more nuts, the kernel of his case among them, thought Hall, as he followed Simon Keflin-Brown, QC, into the judge's rooms. Keflin-Brown led as if by divine right. He was an urbane, avuncular man who out of court affected broad-striped suits which the inevitably worn pastel-shaded Garrick tie rarely matched. In court, usually to the tolerance of judges to whom he was well known, Keflin-Brown performed tricks to impress and influence juries: he'd produced one in the corridor outside, immediately looking enquiringly beyond Hall to ask who his leader was and reacting with exaggerated, wide-eyed surprise when Hall said there wasn't one, which the man had well known all along.

'Thought the woman was rich?'

'She is. And she's satisfied,' said Hall. That still wasn't certain, he remembered. But he was happy with the retort.

'Should be an easy one, I suppose.'

It posed an equally easy retort – why had Keflin-Brown accepted such a mundane brief – but Hall didn't ask it: according to Feltham the QC only took on sure-fire winners if he had the opportunity and had jumped at the Jennifer Lomax prosecution. There was a smirk from Morley, whom Hall guessed to be only four or five years older than he was, although the man was thin-haired and paunchy and looked at least fifteen years his senior. Perry appeared disinterested in the exchange, a man privately admitting lost battles before a shot had been fired.

Jarvis greeted Keflin-Brown with a thin-lipped grimace that passed for a smile but which had gone by the time he got to Hall. The judge completely ignored the other barrister and Perry.

After the grimaced smile came the nod and after the nod the beginning of the required verbal minuet.

Jarvis said, 'Mr Keflin-Brown,' and the QC said, 'My Lord,' and then Jarvis said, 'Mr Hall,' who echoed, 'My Lord.'

Adept from long practice at the intricate steps, Keflin-Brown said, 'With my friend, Mr Robert Morley, I prosecute on behalf of the Crown, my Lord.'

'And you are in a position to proceed?'

'We are, my Lord.'

'Mr Hall?'

'We will be ready on the suggested date, my Lord.'

'Does being ready also mean you will be in a position to mount a satisfactory defence?' demanded the tiny man, pedantically.

Hall heard Perry shift behind him. On their way there the solicitor, with questionable Jewish cynicism, had said confronting Sir Ivan after the press complaint was going to be like facing Himmler with toothache. Hall said, 'It does mean that, my Lord.'

Jarvis briefly shifted some files, for no reason. Hall realized it was customary for the man to sit with his finger-tips on the table edge, which really did make him seem to be holding on to keep himself in view. The judge said, 'Something like twenty-five prosecution witnesses, Mr Keflin-Brown?'

'A total of twenty-eight, if all are called, my Lord,' said the QC.

'Indeed,' said Jarvis. 'Perhaps you can help us with that, Mr Hall?'

'My instructions are to enter a plea of not guilty, my Lord,' said Hall. The point and purpose of the meeting, he knew, aware of the concentration not just from the judge but from Keflin-Brown as well.

'Not guilty?' pressed Jarvis, ominously.

'Those are my instructions,' repeated Hall.

'I have had certain advice, in advance of this hearing,' said Jarvis. 'As you know, Mr Keflin-Brown . . .' the tight-lipped smile flickered and died. '. . . and as I am taking some pains to advise you, Mr Hall, I expect the correct propriety to be shown in my court, at all times . . .'

'I am obliged, my Lord,' said Hall, realizing too late that he had spoken prematurely, interrupting the old man before he'd finished.

There was a moment of glacial, eternity-stretched silence before Jarvis said, 'As I was intending to make clear I do not like the time in my court to be wasted. Nor do I like – indeed, I will not in any way tolerate – my court to be abused.'

This time Hall said nothing. Keflin-Brown said, 'Quite so, my Lord. I'm obliged.'

'Mr Hall?' prompted Jarvis.

'I'm obliged, my Lord.'

'It is important that your client is given every protection under the law available to her.'

'Which I shall do my best to provide, my Lord.'

'Were I for a moment to believe that wasn't being done, I would take steps to ensure any failure or omission be immediately rectified.'

Hall waited, to ensure the man had finished. 'Quite so, my Lord.'

'I understand certain medical evidence will feature strongly in this case?'

'That is so, my Lord.'

'With the benefit of evidence exchange, is the prosecution in a position to suggest a certain course of events, Mr Keflin-Brown?'

'If it is your Lordship's wish I could discuss certain matters with my learned friend,' accepted the QC, dancing to the judge's lead.

'Mr Hall?'

'My instructions are to enter a plea of not guilty to murder,' said Hall.

'I am not deaf, Mr Hall: I heard you the first time. And several times after that. Surely you are aware we are talking of a lesser charge to which a different plea could be considered in which the mercy of the court could be exercised!'

Hall felt the perspiration wet across his back and hoped it wouldn't show on his face. 'I regret to inform my Lord that my client resists in the strongest possible terms that course of action.'

There was another long pause, as glacial as the first.

'Mr Hall, there is a period of two weeks before the scheduled trial date,' said Jarvis. 'I would suggest that in that time you discuss with your client in the clearest possible manner the offer that has been intimated by Mr Keflin-Brown here today . . .' He looked enquiringly at his clerk. 'Is there a diary convenience, say, two days before trial?'

'Yes, my Lord,' said the man, not needing to look.

'Here,' declared the judge, patting his hand impatiently against the desk. 'Ten o'clock on the fourteenth. Is that acceptable to you both?'

'As my Lord wishes,' said the QC.

'Thank you, my Lord,' said Hall.

As they began to gather up their papers, Jarvis said, 'Mr Hall, I would have you remain, if you so please.'

For the first time the equanimity of Keflin-Brown faltered. He filed out after his junior with his pinkly bland face creased with curiosity. Perry was frowning, too.

Hall wondered if Jarvis intended the reminder of a headmaster's punishment in the way the man kept him standing, appearing suddenly engrossed in one of the files. Finally he looked up and said, 'Since our last meeting certain matters have come to my attention. I do not intend to dwell upon them, Mr Hall. But I want you to understand, without the remotest possibility of any misunderstanding between us, that I will not tolerate any future nonsense. I will not have the authority of my court put into question, nor will I have it humiliated by being turned into a music-hall. There will be no tricks. Have I made myself clear, Mr Hall?'

'Completely so, my Lord.'

'As I will, from now on, if there is any transgression.'

'I am obliged, my Lord.'

'I will see you before me, as arranged.'

'Thank you, my Lord.'

'You will be careful, won't you, Mr Hall?'

'Yes, my Lord.'

Keflin-Brown was poised directly beyond the entrance. He hurried forward, smiling, and said, 'Anything I should know about, Jeremy?'

'If it had been I'm sure Sir Ivan would have asked you to stay.'

The smile went. 'Do you think you can afford attitudes on your first murder?'

'No,' replied Hall, honestly. 'I'm not trying to create one.'

Disarmed, the other barrister said, 'He's a miserable old bugger. We'll have to be careful.'

'So everyone keeps telling me.' Hall hadn't intended the reply to sound as testy as it had.

'You'll let me know in advance, before we see the old bastard again?'

'If there's anything to let you know about.'

'Either way,' insisted Keflin-Brown. 'And if you'll take my advice you'll do your best to fix it the way he wants.'

Perry, who'd waited patiently and politely out of hearing, fell into step as Hall continued along the corridor, listening without interruption as they made their way from the building. Just before the exit he said, 'You're not going to be let off lightly.'

'I know,' said Hall.

'She's got to accept diminished responsibility.'

'She won't.'

'Then we're in serious trouble.'

'So's Jennifer Lomax.'

'That's what I mean.'

'Of course,' accepted Hall, knowing that wasn't what the solicitor had meant at all.

'It's called a temporary interruption,' announced the matron. She lounged back expansively in her chair, in control. 'I got a heavy hint, from the governor: it's time to ease off.'

'Who gives a fuck about the governor?' said Emma.

'We're going to.'

'What the fuck are you talking about?' demanded Fran, even more aggressively.

'We're going to leave her alone,' insisted the ward supervisor.

'Who says?' The voice was strident, that of a woman accustomed to hitting before she was hit.

'I did.'

'We got a problem here, Beryl?' demanded Fran, threateningly.

'Not unless you make it into one. Which you'd be stupid to do.'

'Bollocks,' said Harriet. 'We've got a brand new toy and I like playing with it. I haven't had enough yet.'

'We're leaving her alone, until after the trial,' insisted the matron. She was glad of her position of command, behind the desk: it made her appear more confident than she felt.

'Beryl, don't tell *us* what *we're* going to do. We tell *you* what we're going to do,' said the tattooed woman. 'We want to play.'

'While we've got the chance,' picked up Fran. 'She won't come back here, *after* the trial. She's off her head, full of voices. She'll be sent to some secure mental institution for other people to play with . . .' She puckered her lips, for the amusement of the others. 'It's not fair!'

The huge woman shook her head, smiling dismissively. 'You just can't think, can you?'

'What are you talking about now?' demanded Fran.

'She's got more than tits and a cunt for you to play with. She's got money.' Triumphantly the matron produced a sheaf of notes. 'I promised to keep you away if she paid me. And she did. Authorized me to withdraw her cheque-book from admissions . . .' The smile expanded. 'So now it's *ours*!'

All three women smiled back. 'How much?' demanded Emma.

'Hundred for you, hundred for me.'

'Ours gets split three ways, you get the lot,' challenged Harriet, at once.

'Because I'm officially in charge and I'm taking the risk giving her to you.'

'For which we paid you,' reminded Emma.

'And here there's lots more, more money than you've ever thought of. And we'll get it providing we're not greedy.'

'I want to fuck her again before she goes,' insisted Harriet, in reluctant agreement. 'Cut her a little. I like seeing blood run.'

'She might not be going after the trial,' lured the matron. 'Don't forget I've looked after her at the remand hearings here: seen the papers. The police think she's faking the voice. If the court agrees she's sane she'll come back here, for a time anyway. How's that sound?'

'Wonderful,' said Emma.

'Perfect,' agreed Fran.

'All right,' accepted the still reluctant Harriet. Then: 'If she comes back here permanently we could sell her on when we've finished and get even more money couldn't we? This could work out very well.'

'See!' exclaimed the matron, when she entered Jennifer's ward an hour later. 'They didn't come, did they?'

'Thank you.'

'*Now she's got you all to herself.*'

'Nursey's brought her cream.'

'I don't want you to do it, either.'

'Nursey likes doing it.'

'No.'

'*Open your stupid legs. Tell her you want it.*'

It was a personal test for Jennifer to stop herself and she succeeded.

'Don't make nursey angry.'

'*Open your legs!*'

'Would nursey like another sort of present?'

'What?'

Jennifer felt a sensation in her legs, a pressure to part them but she managed to resist it. 'Give me my cheque-book.'

'A girl at school said she saw Mummy's picture in the papers.'

'She must have been mistaken,' insisted Annabelle.

'She's going to bring it tomorrow to show me.'

'Which girl?' asked Annabelle, as casually as she felt able.

'Margaret Roberts.'

That night Margaret Robert's mother said she quite understood the telephone call and of course she'd destroy the newspaper. 'What's going to happen to poor little Emily?'

'I don't know,' admitted Annabelle.

'Such a lovely child.'

'Yes.'

'An absolute tragedy.'

'Yes.'

Chapter Nineteen

The repelling and physically real horror of lesbian rape – literally of being their beck-and-call sex slave – shattered Jennifer's previous near catatonic shock of what had come close to happening to Emily.

It would have been trite – too easy, too simple a metaphor – for Jennifer to have thought about awakening from nightmare upon nightmare. But the return of Jennifer's implacable determination to overcome everything and everybody was very much like coming to her senses after being too long asleep.

She positively refused to equate one nightmare against the other. Each, by itself, sickeningly revolting but with this new awakening she could separate them. Believed, even, that she could get them into some proportion.

It hadn't been her, Jennifer Lomax, who'd attacked Emily. It had been Jane, like it had been Jane who'd murdered Gerald. Using her body. Not her responsibility then. And she *had* been raped and sexually terrorized: drugged at the very beginning and afterwards threatened with disfigurement if she'd resisted. Not her responsibility either. So it would be immature – ridiculous – to feel guilt or shame for what had happened, like rape victims did. No woman invited rape, of any sort. And she certainly hadn't invited what had been inflicted on her.

But which wouldn't be inflicted again. Ever.

The grotesquely fat matron with the probing finger had shown her how to stop it and never in her life had Jennifer needed the same lesson taught twice: certainly not this lesson. The balance came at once. There *was* an equation here. Matching it was knowing of Jane's presence, which in her apathy she'd almost forgotten, opening her mind to the unseen presence like she'd opened her legs to the monsters that she had very definitely been able to see and feel.

Something else she'd recovered, with her waking-up determination. And why she felt safe now, without any tingling to warn her of Jane. It was difficult to be sure, because she hadn't kept any sort of count, but it seemed Jane hadn't occupied her so much in the last few days: almost as if the accept-anything, unopposing indifference had taken the pleasure from the taunting.

Jane was going to be surprised at the reversal. Upset, hopefully, at not anticipating it. Jennifer hoped so. It would represent a victory – a triumph over a presence, a thing, that believed itself able to control her every thought and every word and every action. It was exhausting – draining – to fight against mouthing the rudeness and the profanities but she'd learned how to do it, as she'd realized how to be sedated to keep Jane as far out of her head at night as possible.

Now she had to control her body movements, too. Gerald's murder should have been warning enough but hadn't been: Jennifer had been taken utterly by surprise at the total possession that had made her attack Emily. After that episode Jennifer knew she had to be alert at all and every time for a physical outburst that could ridicule her – worse, possibly harm people – in any situation with another human being.

But she could do it, like she'd always been able to do anything she set her mind upon. The confidence ran through her, a good feeling, despite the caution that immediately followed. She'd never imagined – how could anyone imagine? – confronting what she had to do now. She still couldn't imagine. Just knew she had to do it. Had to survive.

Would it become any clearer today how to do that? Perhaps, although she wasn't sure. Pre-trial conferences with counsel, Humphrey Perry had called it in his pencil-pointing way. What about the long ago insistence – not long ago in terms of time but certainly in terms of what had happened in between – upon being represented by a QC? Something else she'd let go, hadn't even thought about, after Emily. Was there still time? A question for Jeremy Hall, along with a lot more. She should have made a list, against the distraction of Jane appearing. Or should she? It would be a hell of a recovery if she was able to resist Jane's intrusion and words and body movement *and* conduct a rational conversation with the barrister. More than a hell of a recovery: it would be that all important proof – proof to herself more than to anyone else – of her sanity as well as of her strength to resist.

Even the scars, on her arms and hands, didn't depress Jennifer. The bribe-obedient matron ('nursey will be good if you're good to nursey,') had removed the stitches that morning and left the bandages off, allowing Jennifer properly to look for the first time. The right arm was worse, the wound deep and jagged, in a zig-zag from wrist to elbow. She'd have to wear long sleeves all the time, until she was able to get plastic surgery advice. Have the left arm and her hands done at the same time. She was ugly, like this. Emily would be frightened.

Abruptly the reflection dipped. Could Emily ever be more frightened than . . . Jennifer didn't allow the thought to finish. She could only try to think of so much: the most immediate things. Too soon yet – there was too much in the way – to plan how to build things with Emily: to make Emily love her again. She would, of course. Plan. And recover. She had to. Emily was all she had left. Her life, as soon as she got rid of everything else in the way. Soon, she thought, now there was a trial date. She was impatient to get it over with. There was movement from the main ward entrance and through the window of her separate room Jennifer saw Hall and Perry approaching.

'Good morning,' Jennifer said, brightly.

The vague numbness registered seconds before the voice in her head said, '*And good morning to you.*'

Jeremy Hall was surprised. It was almost three weeks since his last meeting with Jennifer Lomax. She'd been zombie-like then and according to Perry had remained so, apart from the shouted outbursts, at every remand hearing in between. Today she appeared more in control of herself – her hair and make-up immaculate, sharp-eyed, aware of everything around her – than at any time since the murder. Completely normal, in fact.

'It's good to see you,' she said, smiling.

'*Tell him how much of you the dykes have seen! And played with.*'

'You're looking much better,' said Hall, as much for Perry's benefit as well as for Jennifer's.

'*Show him your sore cunt!*'

Jennifer resisted for the second time: she hadn't fully decided what to do about the rape and sexual assault, satisfied enough for the moment that she could prevent it. 'She's being obscene.'

'It doesn't matter,' said Hall.

'It does!' contradicted Jennifer, at once. 'I'm fighting her: refusing to say what she's telling me to. And for that I feel very much better.'

'You stupid bitch. You really are mad to think you can resist me!'

Jennifer saw the strained look pass between the two men before Hall said, 'There's quite a lot we have to talk about, now that we have a trial date.'

'It's not going to be delayed?' demanded Jennifer, at once.

'No,' assured Perry. 'But we have to make a positive decision upon a defence.'

'There isn't one!'

'There is only one defence,' insisted Jennifer. 'Not guilty because I didn't do it.'

Hall sighed. 'Jennifer, I want you to listen very carefully. Sixteen people saw you do it. The evidence against you is overwhelming. Incontrovertible. And with Rebecca Nicholls the prosecution has a motive. You don't have a not guilty plea: it's pointless – ridiculous – persisting with it. All you have is a mitigating submission . . .' He paused. 'And I have been given guidance by the judge and the prosecution that they'll consider a lesser charge and consider psychiatric evidence—'

'No!' said Jennifer, too loudly. She saw the matron's head emerge questioningly from her office, at the far end of the long ward.

'You don't have an alternative, Jennifer,' insisted Hall, almost as loudly. He was suddenly aware of calling her by her christian name.

'What do the psychiatrists say?'

'Barking mad! The rest of your life among the loonies.'

'There's a conflict,' conceded Hall.

'No-one will definitely say I'm mad!' seized Jennifer, triumphantly.

'The American is prepared to testify to Multiple Personality Disorder,' said Perry. 'Everyone else talks of some indications of mental imbalance.'

'But they won't say I'm mad,' persisted Jennifer.

'*Of course they will. You've got a voice in your head.*'

'No,' admitted Hall.

'*Bastards!*'

It came with a roaring scream and Jennifer put her hands over her ears and kept her arms tightly against her sides, holding herself against giving in to the agony. Which she managed to do. Uneven voiced she said, 'She's very angry. Yelling.'

'Jennifer, you're not understanding the implications of what I'm saying,' said Hall, gently. 'Even though the experts disagree there's enough for a defence of temporary mental instability. There's supporting evidence to call with what happened with Emily—'

'WHAT!'

This time the matron hurried the length of the open ward, bustling through the door at the same time as knocking. 'What's going on? She mustn't be distressed.'

'Nothing. Please leave us,' said Perry.

'Perhaps I should—'

'Leave us!' said Hall, not looking at the woman.

'*Aren't I doing well! Trapped whichever way you turn!*'

In her anger it was easier for Jennifer to ignore the intrusion. Tight-lipped, she said, 'It was Jane who attacked Emily. Which you know. But I won't have Emily brought into it. Into any of it. Which is the strongest reason I have for *not* agreeing to your defence, quite apart from it not being true in the first place.'

'Jennifer, you're not making it easy for me. For yourself.'

'I'm not interested in making anything easy! If you won't accept my instructions, then you're fired.'

'If that's your wish then I will make the case file and notes available to you,' said Perry, at once.

Hall wished the relief hadn't been so obvious in the other man's hurried voice. 'You'll have great difficulty getting anyone else to represent you at this late stage. You'll probably end up defending yourself. It would inevitably mean a postponement of the trial.'

'*How long do you think Fran and Emma and Harriet with that sharp little razor blade can be bought off! And sticky-fingered nursey?*'

'You promised me a QC,' reminded Jennifer, no longer strident. She didn't want a postponement: to remain here for a moment longer than she had to. Jane was actually right. Bribery wouldn't work for ever.

'No QC in Mr Hall's chambers is prepared to lead in this case,' announced Perry, irritated that the young barrister hadn't accepted the escape that had been offered them.

'Help me,' said Jennifer softly.

'I want to,' said Hall urgently, matching her plea. 'But you're making it impossible . . .' He hesitated. She'd already suffered enormously – maybe in ways he didn't know – and he was nervous how she'd react if he consciously tried to frighten her further. But he couldn't think of another, kinder way. 'If you don't agree to plead guilty to a lesser charge and the case runs its full course you'll inevitably be found guilty. As a sane person, the murder was the calculated, premeditated action of a wife being cheated by her husband. You'd probably be sentenced to at least twenty years . . .' Hall paused again, remembering Julian Mason's belief of sexual abuse. '. . . You'd probably serve a minimum of twelve. Do you think you could survive twelve years in a place like this, as opposed to a custodial sentence in a secure hospital unit, where you'd be eligible for release probably much sooner on the advice of doctors?'

Jennifer was gouged by fear and Jane said, '*That's how you're going to feel for the rest of your life.*'

For the first time Jennifer responded. 'I won't!' Then, quickly although spacing the words through tight-together lips, she said, 'I – won't – give – in!'

'*I'm always going to be around when you do. And you will, over and over again.*'

Hall slumped back in his chair, defeated. Perry actually shrugged.

'I accept your instructions to plead not guilty to the charge of murder,' said Hall, momentarily as pedantic as his instructing solicitor.

Perry said, 'Don't forget Jarvis's religion.'

Hall nodded. 'All the clinical and medical tests have been completed but I want to suggest something further. You're possessed, correct?'

'You know I am.'

'We'd like you to undergo exorcism,' announced Perry.

'*Don't bother. It won't work!*'

'You mean by a priest or vicar?' queried Jennifer.

'Yes.'

'Who's Jarvis? And what's his religion got to do with it.'

Hall looked uncomfortable. 'He's the appointed trial judge. A very strong Anglican.'

'Who'd be impressed by the involvement of a minister?' recognized Jennifer.

'Yes,' admitted Hall.

'I didn't believe in any God before all this happened,' said Jennifer. 'I certainly don't after what I've gone through.'

'That's not really the point,' argued Perry.

'So I'd go through the motions of praying and whatever else is involved to score points with a judge!'

'Scoring points with a judge is what trials are all about,' said Hall, matching the older man's cynicism.

'If I don't believe it wouldn't work, would it? So Jane would still be there and I'd have achieved nothing.'

'You wouldn't know that until you'd tried,' said Perry.

Jennifer shook her head. 'I'm satisfied with none of the psychiatrists being prepared to say I'm mad.'

'She must be mad!' erupted Humphrey Perry, when they reached the courtyard outside the main prison gates. 'Only someone completely mad would have failed to see the only way out, with a plea to a lesser charge!'

'I know,' said the younger man, resigned.

'We had a chance to get out. Why didn't you take it?'

'I want to help her.'

'How the hell can you do that? She won't let herself be helped in the only way available.'

'I'll enter the plea she wants, go through whatever pantomime the voice in her head causes and let Jarvis instruct the jury to return a verdict of the lesser charge made obvious from her behaviour in court. That way she'll get the care she so obviously needs.'

Perry gazed across the car at the other man, acknowledging the ploy with an admiring nod but not immediately starting the engine. 'Jarvis doesn't want court time wasted on a full trial.'

'Bugger what Jarvis wants!' said Hall. 'Show me a

different way to achieve what has to be achieved, in the best interest of Jennifer Lomax, and I'll take it!'

'I wish I could,' said Perry, solemnly.

'So do I,' said Hall.

'Jarvis will feel—'

'I don't need to be told what Jarvis will feel,' stopped Hall. 'I know.'

The ponderous silence stretched interminably, Sir Ivan Jarvis staring fixedly at Hall, and even Simon Keflin-Brown, who normally would have found the temptation irresistible, didn't attempt any courtroom idiosyncracies. There were no coughs, no foot scuffing.

At last Jarvis said, 'Could it be that I failed to make myself clear?'

'You made yourself abundantly clear, my Lord,' said Hall. He'd wanted to cough but hadn't and the assurance croaked out.

'Then perhaps you haven't made yourself clear to your client?'

'I have, my Lord.'

'During how many conferences, since our last meeting?'

'Three, my Lord.'

'Logged meetings?'

'Yes, my Lord.'

'I am displeased, Mr Hall.'

'I have explained, in the clearest possible detail, the courses open to my client. She repeats her instruction that she pleads not guilty to the major charge, that of murder.'

To the prosecuting barrister the judge said, 'You have been apprised of this?'

'I have, my Lord: I'm obliged to my learned friend.'

Turning to his clerk Jarvis said, 'What's the calendar allowance?'

'Two weeks, my Lord,' said the man, as usual not needing to consult the diary.

Coming back to Hall, the man said, 'You will remember what I said about tricks, won't you?'

'I will, my Lord.'

'If you don't, I shall be very quick to remind you.'

In the corridor outside Keflin-Brown said, 'I don't envy you one moment of it. I'll do what I can to help. My case is proven before it starts, after all.'

'Thanks.'

'You did make three prison visits, didn't you?' pressed the older barrister.

'Yes.' Jennifer had remained as brightly alert as before and boasted about resisting the voice, which she appeared to be doing: certainly there hadn't been any unintelligible interruptions or swearing. She'd actually become angry when he'd pressed her to reconsider the plea, dismissing it and instead handing him a long list of clothes and accessories she wanted brought up from Hampshire for her court appearances.

'Good,' said Keflin-Brown. 'You know the old bugger will check, don't you? That's why he asked if they were logged.'

'You're joking!'

'There's nothing ever funny about Sir Ivan Jarvis. Which you're going to find out.'

He'd spent the two previous weekends engrossed in the case notes and been unsure if he could spare the time to come out on the river this Saturday. In the end he decided he needed the relaxation in anticipation of what the next fortnight might bring. But he was stiff, not concentrating sufficiently: at the beginning he frequently mis-oared and dug too deep to feather until he consciously forced himself to dismiss the case from his mind, to get the slide moving easily and build up the rhythm. Hall got it, finally, feeling the cramped tension ease from his back and shoulders, building up until the narrow boat was smoothly cleaving the water: as he thrust beneath Richmond Bridge a group of Japanese tourists leaned over the parapet to photograph him and Hall wondered how many times in the next two weeks his photograph was going to be taken. For what, he reflected, could be the obituary of a failed legal career.

It was inevitable that Jennifer would commit some outrage from the dock and just as inevitable that because of it Jarvis would intervene with instructions to the jury about diminished responsibility. And most inevitable of all that the old man would consider it the sort of trick against which he'd specifically warned, forcing as it would the court to make the decision Jennifer Lomax had failed to be persuaded to make for herself. Trick or not – and Hall didn't totally agree that it was – it would serve Jennifer Lomax's best interests. Which was his primary concern, as her counsel.

Jeremy Hall wished he could resolve the doubt in his mind that he was still in some way failing her. He abruptly decided to cut the row short and spend the rest of the afternoon and evening going yet again over notes and statements he'd already read so many times he knew them verbatim. His rowing concentration gone again, he missed his stroke altogether with his left blade, veering the boat abruptly sideways, and a group of people watching from Mortlake bridge laughed at him.

* * *

He finished reading everything and considered calling Patricia, who hadn't telephoned him since the can't-make-it message on the answering machine. Hall supposed he'd have to become accustomed to being laughed at in the coming weeks.

Chapter Twenty

Jennifer had a soaring, uplifting feeling of release being taken from prison, which she acknowledged at once was precisely what it was and what it should be: since the day of Gerald's death she *had* been imprisoned, first in the cell-like hospital room and then in an actual cell, although part of the prison hospital.

The escape wasn't total, however. There was, in fact, something new, a torture that hadn't been inflicted before. Jennifer hadn't been conscious of the voice when she'd emerged from her drugged sleep that morning, as she usually was, but when she became fully awake her body tingled with the numbness of Jane's presence. But there wasn't a taunting voice. Instead, at Jennifer's moment of awareness, there was a cough, the subdued sound of a watcher in the shadows. Which, she accepted, was the perfect description, except that this watcher wasn't in the shadows, waiting to pounce, but in her mind. But still waiting, she didn't know for what. Or when. Jennifer positively let the thought linger, challenging Jane to read it and react – to let Jane know she wasn't surprised or caught out by the change of torment – but still the voice didn't come. There were, though, the occasional coughs of a patient stalker.

Which Jennifer ignored, practically succeeding in submerging the occasional interruption beneath the growing euphoria at getting beyond four narrow, enclosing walls. For which she made meticulous preparation. A £100 cheque kept the insistent matron ('nursey will wash you: just lay back,') on the other side of the locked bathroom door and provided the dryer to get her hair in perfect shape. Because the mirrors were larger she made up in the bathroom, too. She did so discreetly, the lightest blusher, the minimum of mascara, a pale lipline, determined to look her absolute best. And most of all, for every minute of every day that the trial might take, to appear in control.

She decided she'd made a good clothes selection during that last plea-persuasion meeting with Jeremy Hall. For the opening day of the trial she chose the severe, although loosely tailored blue Dior suit and a plainly cut voile shirt to create the appearance she'd favoured when she'd worked at Enco-Corps, subtly feminine but more obviously no-nonsense businesslike. It was also, she remembered, how she'd usually dressed for the committee meetings of the charities and fund-raising groups that had so very quickly found her name an encumbrance. Jennifer returned to the larger bathroom mirror to survey the complete effect, glad the long sleeves completely hid the worst of the scars. She'd included gloves in her clothes request and considered wearing them, to cover the damage to her hands, but decided against it until she'd assessed the court.

Beryl Harrison was waiting directly outside the bathroom when Jennifer emerged. She said, 'You look lovely. Beautiful.' The reaching out was not really to feel the material but for some brief, physical contact. As Jennifer followed the escort along the corridors, towards the exit, she passed Emma and Fran, together as always. Emma told her to hurry back and Fran said, 'I like that outfit. That would look good on me. I'll have to try it on.'

Jennifer strained to see something, anything, of the streets along which the prison van moved but the windows were small and heavily tinted and hardly anything registered. One of the escorting wardresses, a motherly woman, said, 'Here it is then. Your big day.'

Jennifer smiled but said nothing. There was a cough in her head, a more positive throat-clearing than any before. Jennifer stiffened but nothing came.

The same wardress said, 'We're almost there. I'd sit back, if I were you.'

Jennifer did, although not knowing why. The van began to slow and then abruptly there was an eruption of blinding light through three of the windows.

'Cameramen,' explained the wardress. 'They shoot blind through the windows. It hardly ever works. Don't know why they do it. They won't have got you.'

After the virtual isolation of the past weeks, Jennifer found the sudden bustle and activity strangely disorientating. The yard beyond the shielding-off, high-gated entrance was jammed with police cars and vans and men and woman in police and prison officer uniform. The escorting wardresses formed up either side and walked her into the building. Almost directly inside was a reception office, where her arrival was officially listed in a ledger and a clerk signed a receipt which Jennifer realized was for her, as if she was a product or a package. Still unspeaking they led her on, nodding and occasionally greeting other officers and prison staff as they passed.

The cell at which they stopped was half-tiled. In its centre there was a scarred table with a tin ashtray in its middle. There was a chair either side and two more against the wall, below the barred window. There was no bed or obvious toilet, but there was a pervading smell of urine. The wardress who had remained silent until now said, 'Do you want to pee or anything? Once you're in court you'll be stuck, not able to go.'

'I don't think so. Thank you.'

'It's your last chance.'

'No.'

'If her brief hurries, we'll be able to get a cup of tea before we have to go up,' said the talkative wardress to the other. And then smiled as Jeremy Hall appeared at the door.

Hall was smiling, too. Humphrey Perry was directly behind. He was blank-faced.

'The suit's just right. Perfect.'

'Good.'

'How are you feeling?'

'OK.' The excitement of no longer being incarcerated was ebbing away, back in yet another cell.

'Not frightened?' asked Hall.

Jennifer didn't answer at once. 'I've never been in a court before but no, I don't think so.'

'There's quite a lot of ritual. Tradition. Don't pay any attention to it. But you must leave everything to me. Not try to address the court yourself.'

'I'll do my best not to let anything happen. She's doing something different. I know she's with me but she's not talking. Trying to upset me now by saying nothing. Just lurking.'

Perry, who'd brought up one of the spare chairs to sit beside the other lawyer, shifted but didn't speak. His chair grated, jarringly.

'How do you know she's with you?' asked Hall.

'I won't tell you, remember? She'll know if I tell you. Maybe do something to stop me knowing.' She wondered if that would get any reaction but there was no sound in her head.

Perry sighed.

Hall said, 'I forgot. If you want to say anything to me you can do it through Mr Perry. Write a note or ask him to come up to the dock. That's acceptable. For several days it'll just be the prosecution evidence.' And a lot more he didn't want to contemplate, he thought, fearfully.

'All right.'

'We've done well with jury selection.'

'What's that mean?'

'Ensured, as best we can, what might be the most favourable jury.'

Jennifer's frown deepened. 'I don't understand?'

'I challenged the men to the allowable limit and got them replaced by women.' He regretted now making the comment at all: the composition wouldn't have meant anything to her if he hadn't mentioned it.

'More sympathetic to me about Rebecca, you mean?'

'Yes.'

'That's not part of my defence.'

'It's the key to the prosecution, which I've got to do everything to confront.'

'Which I expect you to do very well.'

Hall half shrugged, looking around the bare room. 'You can have food brought in during the trial, if you'd like. I don't think what they provide here is much good.'

'I'm not very interested in eating. Maybe I'll think about it tomorrow. But thank you for the thought.' It seemed a long time since anyone had treated her with any kindness or personal consideration. She realized how much she'd missed it. Suddenly she demanded, 'Are you frightened?'

'No,' blinked Hall, startled. He was glad she hadn't asked if he was apprehensive, which he didn't consider the same thing, the most minimal element of fear and therefore hardly qualifying. And if she had he would have lied to retain her confidence. But he was apprehensive. Not of any one single danger but generally concerned, mostly about the unknown. Whatever happened it was going to be a parody of a proper trial until Jarvis intervened to stop it and Hall accepted he personally would be the object of every sort of criticism and outrage. And not only – just most immediately and directly – from Jarvis but at every other legal level. Realistically Jarvis's influence disappeared with the old man's retirement and Hall expected to retain his place in the Proudfoot chambers even after Sir Richard's elevation because he was the man's nephew. But it would be a long time, if ever, before a brief was offered to him by name. And even longer before Bert Feltham accepted one for him, named or not.

'I'm glad you're not frightened,' said Jennifer. 'And I appreciate what you've done for me.'

'I haven't done anything for you yet,' Hall reminded.

'What you're going to do for me,' Jennifer corrected.

'I have to go and robe,' said Hall, standing. 'Do you want to make yourself comfortable before the court?'

'No,' refused Jennifer again. 'And I want to apologize, for going on about a QC. I trust you.'

As they climbed the stairs to reach the robing room Perry said, 'Yet another amazing transformation. The voice has mysteriously gone away and you're the barrister she wants after all.'

'She'll change her mind soon enough when she sees how I'm going to let the trial go.'

'What mind?' dismissed the solicitor, allowing the contemptuous cynicism.

Hall shrugged but didn't bother with a reply. He was taking the only defence course open to him with Jennifer Lomax but he couldn't lose the feeling that he was in some way failing her.

Preoccupied as she was by space – or lack of it – Jennifer was surprised by the comparative smallness of the court. Her expected imagery came from films and television, invariably American, in which legal surroundings barely achieved their supposed officialdom from just the raised dais for the judge and the pen for the jury, but otherwise looked like church halls.

Where she was going to be tried didn't look anything like a church hall and scarcely appeared half the size of one. Jeremy Hall's word – tradition – came immediately into her still clear mind as Jennifer entered the dock and gazed around her, registering everything. The brass-railed dock that was to be her place for the duration of the trial dominated the floor of the court, only slightly lower in its elevated height to the carved, wood-canopied and Royal emblem-surmounted bench from which the judge would preside, from the huge and momentarily unoccupied red leather, button-backed throne.

In the well of the court, seemingly far below her, were the bewigged and raven-robed barristers – Jeremy Hall's wig was far whiter, his robe far newer than any around him – with their instructing junior counsel and solicitors in battle-ready formation behind: surrounded by so many artificial headpieces, Humphrey Perry's domed bald head stood out like a pebble in a stream. Facing them but directly below the judge's position was the robed and wigged court clerk with other officials and to their left a bespectacled, grey-haired woman at a stenograph.

The press gallery was behind her and already full, a flurry and buzz of attention erupting the moment Jennifer's head appeared above the rail. A girl in a jean suit and a bearded man at the very edge of the gallery immediately began sketching in large pads, heads jerking up and down like mechanical dolls as they tried to capture her likeness. The jury box was on the opposite side of the court to the press, tiered up on two levels. Remembering the downstairs cell conversation, she counted ten women and two men. They all concentrated upon her entry but with less noise than the press opposite. The public gallery was behind and above, far too high for her to see how many people were in it. From the noise she guessed it to be crowded. The seat towards which her two escorts gestured her was centred in the dock to micrometer exactness and appeared heavily padded until she sat down. The leather didn't give, remaining rock hard and Jennifer accepted it was going to be an uncomfortable experience physically as well as in a lot of other respects.

Down in his pit far below Hall turned unexpectedly, catching her eye. He smiled and nodded to her. She was unsure whether to respond but in the end nodded back, although she didn't smile. With the barrister facing in his direction, Perry leaned forward for a huddled conversation. Hall's smile died, his face at once serious. There were more jerky nods of agreement before he turned back to the still empty bench.

There was a cough inside Jennifer's head.

'The court will rise,' demanded the court clerk, loudly.

It did, in straggled unison. Jennifer had been ready,

aware of the clerk preparing to make the announcement, but the unintended movement surged through her as she rose. It would have brought her forward in a jump that might have spread-eagled her over the bar of the dock if she hadn't been ready for that, too. As it was she staggered forward and clutched out for the rail, needing to cling to it in the effort to suppress the uncoordinated vibrations that racked through her body, violent enough to have thrown her off her feet if she hadn't been holding on. She felt the wardresses at either arm, holding her, and saw the entering judge stop and stare red-faced towards her. His attention directed that of the lawyers, most of whom turned. The jury and media were already gazing at her in astonishment, several of the journalists scribbling hurriedly.

'Mr Hall!' demanded Jarvis, still standing. 'Is your client unwell?'

Beside her the chatty wardress from the prison van whispered, 'Come on love, don't bugger about. It won't help.'

Perry was already scurrying around to the edge of the dock, just able to get his chin over the edge. Having done so there was nothing for him to say. Lamely he said to the escorts, 'Is she going to be all right?'

The two women had prised Jennifer's hands free themselves to support her, still shaking, back to her chair. Having got her there they remained holding her up because Jarvis was still standing.

'It's all right,' hissed Jennifer, as the sensation subsided. 'Sorry.'

At a nod from the returning Perry, Hall said, 'I crave the court's indulgence, my Lord. A momentary incapacitation.'

'Which I hope does not recur,' said Jarvis, finally sitting.

As Jennifer was lowered on to the rock-hard seat the laughing started in her head, hysterical, and Jane said, '*How's that for openers! And they ain't seen nuthin' yet!*'

'Beat you. Stopped it happening,' mumbled Jennifer, softly, her head lowered to conceal the lip movement as she'd tried to conceal it in hospital from the guarding policewomen. She ached, painfully, from the effort of holding herself against the unintended movement.

'*Not enough. Everyone saw. Are still looking.*'

A lot still were, from the jury and the media, although the lawyers had turned to look in Jarvis's direction. Small though the court appeared to Jennifer, the judge was still dwarfed by his surroundings.

'The prisoner will stand,' declared the clerk and Jennifer was unable to prevent herself wincing.

Getting unsteadily to her feet again, Jennifer muttered, 'Help me,' to the wardresses, who closed in tightly. It was fortunate they did and that Jennifer additionally snatched out for the rail again. All feeling vanished instantly from her left leg. She swayed into the escort on that side, who grabbed her arm, taking her weight. It hurt where she'd been cut. As the clerk read out the formal murder charge, Jennifer felt the support disappearing from her other leg and knew the two women could not hold her entire weight. Suddenly the feeling came back. Then seeped away again. Then returned, causing Jennifer to bob up and down, despite the effort of the other two women to keep her stable. Through misted eyes Jennifer saw Hall on his feet, only vaguely aware of his returning a plea of not guilty on her behalf. The women virtually carried her back to the chair again. As they sat her down, one said, 'You sure you don't need a doctor?'

As quickly as it had gone, all the feeling – although still with the numbness of Jane's presence – rushed back and the voice said, '*Don't want any doctors, taking you back to hospital and spoiling things! Maybe I'll take a little rest. But then again, maybe I won't.*'

'I'm all right,' Jennifer said, to the enquiring woman. She felt physically drained, the ache in her arms and legs and body worse than after the first attack. Now the tension had gone her legs were shaking, although sufficiently below the wall of the dock for it not to be visible to anyone except the women now seated beside and slightly behind her.

As the older barrister rose ponderously to his feet and like the actor he was paused to get the attention of his audience, Jennifer forced herself to concentrate, knowing that her future, her everything, depended upon every word and every nuance that was going to be uttered or conveyed in the coming days.

There was a lot of what Jennifer supposed Hall had meant by ritual, the judge always addressed as my Lord and Keflin-Brown describing Hall as his learned friend and phrases like 'may it please the court' used as verbal commas and parentheses before Keflin-Brown turned to face the jury to outline the case he assured them he would prove beyond any reasonable doubt.

'Indeed,' he intoned, 'I will submit to you there have been few murders in the last hundred years – even longer – when the preponderance of guilt can be more strongly proved.'

'*You listening?*'

Jennifer jumped, startled, angry at herself for allowing one concentration to become greater than the other.

'*Yes, you did relax, didn't you? Got to stay on your toes, Jennifer. I'm going to destroy you: everything about you. The game is for you to try to stop me. Shall we do that? Winner takes all, you or me. Fight to the death.*'

Jennifer stiffened against any response. And succeeded.

'. . . You may feel, after having heard certain evidence that will be produced before you, that there is a clinical explanation for this horrendous crime,' Keflin-Brown was saying. 'Upon that, upon the law, you must at all times be guided by my Lord. But from the outset, you must know the prosecution's case. It is that Jennifer Lomax, before you in the dock . . .' The man performed his first obvious trick, turning to extend an unwavering, accusing finger in Jennifer's direction. '. . . is a calculating, premeditating murderess who killed her husband most horribly having discovered that he was having an affair with another woman, a woman, ladies and gentlemen of the jury, whom Jennifer Lomax once regarded as a friend . . . just as she believed her marriage and future with Gerald Lomax was untouchably secure . . .'

'*Don't worry, Jennifer. No-one will think you're that. A month from now we'll have you safely tucked up with all the Jesus Christs and Franklin D. Roosevelts and Napoleons and Catherine the Greats, just one big happy, crazy party.*'

Jennifer sat upright, arms straight by her side, anchoring herself by gripping the underside of the uncomfortable chair, thinking again how much the prosecutor was making her sound like the sign-here package that had been delivered that morning. Me! she thought, agonized. It's me! Me sitting here, holding on here: a person, a body. Jennifer Lomax. Me. Flesh and blood. A person with feelings. Not 'her'. Or 'the accused'. Or 'this woman'. Or 'a calculating, abandoned wife who decided upon the ultimate punishment for a deceiving husband'. Not true: hadn't known.

'*Tell them it's not fucking true, you lying bastard!*'

'Not fucking true, you lying bastard!' Jennifer was on

her feet before she could stop herself, the unpreventable shout reverberating around the court to the discernible echo of sharply indrawn breath. She said, 'No . . . I'm sorry . . . I didn't mean . . .' but her control was gone and the voice said, '*Don't let the short-assed judge stop you: tell him to stay under his fucking mushroom where the pixies belong*,' and as Jarvis opened his mouth to speak Jennifer stopped him by saying, 'Stay under your fucking . . .' before she managed to halt. Silence embalmed the courtroom, every eye upon her. Hall was swivelled, horrified. Perry was coming half bent, crablike, towards her. The interrupted Keflin-Brown struck a pose, head to one side, bewilderment sculpted into his face.

'Sit *down*!' said the solicitor, in a stage whisper heard by everyone.

But Jennifer didn't sit down, despite the wardresses plucking at her arms. At the dock rail she said, imploringly, 'I'm sorry! It wasn't me! It's never me! It's Jane.'

'Shut up and sit *down*!' said Perry, still loud.

'Mr Hall!' demanded the judge.

'I beg the court's indulgence, my Lord. A problem from which my client is suffering which I intend bringing to your Lordship's notice, during the course of this trial—'

'A problem this court does not wish to suffer,' cut off the tiny, irascible man. 'Do I need to remind you about turning this court into a music-hall?'

'No, my Lord.'

'Do you wish an adjournment, to advise your client how properly to behave in my court?'

'I do not think that will be necessary, my Lord.'

'Don't have me make it necessary, Mr Hall.' Jarvis raised his head, looking directly at Jennifer. 'Do what your legal advisors tell you, Mrs Lomax. Sit down. And do not interrupt the proceedings of this court again.'

As Jennifer once more was put back into her seat Jane said, '*The dwarf doesn't like you. No-one likes you. Not even Gerald liked you. All alone. Poor little Jennifer No-Friends.*'

'May I proceed, my Lord?' unnecessarily asked Keflin-Brown.

'I wish you would,' said Jarvis, grimly.

Keflin-Brown's opening had been broken at his background sketch, back to which he returned with a professional's skill. Jennifer Stone had been born to privilege and known no other life, the barrister resumed. She was the only daughter of an army Brigadier whose outstanding service as military attaché first in Washington and then in Moscow, at the very height of the Cold War, had culminated with his appointment as deputy chief of the Britain's Defence Staff and for a time permanent NATO representative.

'The accused travelled and lived in high places. She knew no other life. Such echelons *were* her life.'

Nothing in that life had been difficult for her, nothing barred to her. She was a natural linguist, fluent in German and French. The Oxford double degree in economics and mathematics had been gained with an appropriate Double First.

'Before you, ladies and gentlemen of the jury, sits a woman upon whom life has always smiled, the sun always shone . . .'

'*. . . And a murderess. Tell them you're a murderess!*'

Jennifer was clutching the underside of the chair and tensed as the words and the desire again to leap up surged through her. She kept her head tight against her chest and wrapped her feet around the chair legs, the effort shuddering through her. There was a stir from the press gallery and the jury looked. Hall jerked around, face creased. Keflin-Brown remained looking steadfastly at the jury, his only concession a hesitation measured with stop-watch accuracy.

'. . . Truly a beneficiary of the Gods,' the man picked up on the absolute edge of hyperbole. The transition from a brilliant academic student to an even more brilliant financial career was as flawlessly smooth as everything else that Jennifer Stone had ever undertaken in that flawless life.

'She became, ladies and gentlemen, a commodity trader, a vocation so far removed from the sort of mundane lives that you and I enjoy as to be difficult for us to comprehend. In previous centuries such people would have become swash-bucklers, pirates even. Today they are the sort of entrepreneurs who daily pledge millions, hundreds of millions, upon their ability to forecast and predict the value of commodities – metals, oil, grain, meat, money even, in fact every essential of life – in a month, three months, a year. It *is* a piratical existence, a hard, unrelenting, dog-eat-dog, give no quarter occupation. Those who follow it are hard, unrelenting, unforgiving people which as the facts of this case unfold you might well bear in mind, ladies and gentlemen of the jury . . .'

It was overly theatrical and flamboyant but at the same time true, thought Jennifer. That's exactly how she so nostalgically remembered Enco-Corps: price-assess before anyone else, better than anyone else, buy or sell before and better than anyone else, forgive and forget no-one else, no mercy, no excuses, no escapes, ready to kill to stop being killed . . .'

'*Kill to stop being killed.*'

Jennifer's mouth was open, the words formed. 'Kill' emerged although indistinctly and she managed to smother the rest in a choking cough. There was a what-did-she-say coming together of heads among the assembled journalists and another nervous, backwards glance from Jeremy Hall. Perry half rose, then lowered himself again. The judge remained poised longer, waiting.

It was another opportunity for Keflin-Brown to demonstrate his finely balanced timing. Jennifer Stone was such a person, the barrister picked up once more. In her first year at Enco-Corps she'd topped the in-house chart of successful trades, earned bigger profit-related commission than any other dealer and maintained that supremacy every year until she left.

'That departure was to marry Gerald Lomax, a millionaire vice President of Euro-Corps' American parent company and its head, here in Europe,' continued the prosecutor. 'It was a marriage that took place just six months after the death of Lomax's first wife, from what an inquest jury concluded to be an inadvertent overdose of insulin upon which, as a severe diabetic, she was dependent . . .'

Jennifer saw Jeremy Hall's sharp, sideways glance at the other barrister at the innuendo of the phrasing seconds before the voice burst through her head in a screaming, echoing tirade. '*Murdered. Killed me. The bastards killed me.*' And then, over and over, the same roaring chant, '*Murder, murder, murder, murder.*'

But Jennifer was prepared, more so than ever before, alerted by the first reference to Jane. She clung desperately to the chair edge, her body rigid, pulling the control into herself and with her chin tight against her chest hopefully to prevent anyone seeing the bizarre, eyes-shut, face-squeezed contortion against the engulfing noise.

'. . . As the facts of this case are outlined to you, ladies and gentlemen of the jury, one of the conclusions you may reach is that Gerald Lomax was a promiscuous womanizer,' Keflin-Brown was saying. 'While his first wife was still alive, Lomax was engaged in an extra-marital affair with Jennifer Stone, his brilliant, top-achieving trader . . .'

No! thought Jennifer, outraged. They were the facts but they weren't the facts at all. It hadn't been like that, as it was being made to sound, as if she and Gerald had been rutting animals. It wasn't sex: it was love. It was . . .

'*Yes!*' contradicted Jane. '*Exactly what you were, rutting, grunting animals. Pigs on heat. Fuck, fuck, honk honk.*'

'No!' protested Jennifer, forgetting where she was. She came up with a start. Hall remained looking forward but was hunched, almost as if he was trying to shield himself from her. Perry glared around and Keflin-Brown worsened the moment by halting in mid-sentence, turning his head from the jury to look enquiringly at her.

'Mr Hall!' said the judge, exasperated. 'I really will not allow this to continue, as you well know.'

'My Lord,' said Hall, rising. 'I apologize once more to the court for the behaviour of my client, which is in no way disrespectful—'

'But which is precisely how this court is minded to regard it,' stopped Jarvis, impatiently. 'I would remind you there are ways open to me to restrict such behaviour.'

'I am so reminded, my Lord, and I am obliged,' said Hall, meekly.

'. . . As I was saying,' restarted Keflin-Brown. 'Before their marriage, before the death of the first Mrs Lomax, Jennifer Stone and Gerald Lomax were lovers. After their marriage, the new Mrs Lomax gave up what had been a glittering career and chose to spend a considerable part of her time in the couple's country estate, in Hampshire. For part of every week, however, Gerald Lomax chose to remain and live in London, which was, after all, his place of work . . .' The slight, throat-clearing cough and the sip of water was as timed as everything else. '. . . At that place of work, the place where this terrible crime was committed and witnessed by no fewer than sixteen people, from all of whom you will hear, was employed another female trader, a fellow American named Rebecca Nicholls. You will hear, ladies and gentlemen, that for some years, maybe simultaneously with the affair he was conducting with the accused, Gerald Lomax was also engaged in a relationship with Miss Nicholls. Indeed, in New York which they had frequent occasion to visit and where Miss Nicholls retained an apartment, the couple lived virtually as husband and wife . . .'

'Doesn't that make pretty listening! That's your bastard of a husband he's talking about, Jennifer. This is Gerald who used to come across with all that shit about love and happiness and how much he adored you and would do anything for you. And Rebecca, your best friend. Listen up now. I don't want you to miss a single word.'

Keflin-Brown had turned, to look at Jennifer and by so doing brought most of the jury around with him. He said, 'After the hideous stabbing about which you will hear, Mrs Lomax did not make what amounted to a full statement to the police: did not explain herself. But it is the Crown's case that Mrs Lomax discovered the affair in which her husband was engaged with Miss Nicholls. That she decided to wreak the most terrible revenge imaginable upon the man, for his deceit and that in full and sound mind she set out just two months ago, entered her husband's office and in full view of the entire staff, stabbed, cut and slashed Gerald Lomax so savagely and so severely that he died on the spot . . . and that, ladies and gentlemen, is what I intend to prove to your satisfaction.'

'*And I shall make you insane. That's what I'll do, in the end, of course. Really destroy that mega-mind of yours. But slowly, so very slowly: I've got for ever, after all. So I want you to know how it's happening, when it's happening, every moment that it's happening: chip, chip, there it goes, every little chip of the way. And that's how I'll leave you in the end, Jennifer: a piss-soaked, mind-emptied imbecile, dribbling down her front without knowing it . . .*'

Jennifer was aware of Perry at the dock edge. 'For God's sake wipe your face! Spit is running all over you!'

'*. . . Just like that.*'

Chapter Twenty-one

The diminutive judge was the main target of Jane's attempted abuse, trying to get Jennifer to call him a dwarf and Santa's little helper and a short-ass, but she also tried with every formal witness with whom Keflin-Brown opened the prosecution. Almost every time Jennifer beat her, lips clamped against the outbursts. She did practically as well against any uncontrollable movement, arms rigid by her sides to hold the chair edge, her feet entwined around the seat legs. Had it not been secured to the floor to avoid its use as a weapon by a berserk prisoner, that unbalanced posture would have worked against her, bringing her crashing down entangled in the chair, when her body lurched violently sideways. As it was, the movement, the worst, stopped the court again. The motherly wardress who'd kept a handkerchief ready since the dribbling episode managed to snatch out, stopping Jennifer being thrown off, and Jarvis warned Jeremy Hall yet again. That was the occasion Jane tried to make her call the judge Santa's little helper at the same time as telling him to keep his rat-trap mouth shut.

Keflin-Brown, even more adept at ingratiating himself with a judge than he was with a jury, managed to create a very visible contrast between Jennifer's impromptu interruptions by the efficient quickness with which he called his technical witnesses.

A police photographer produced an extensive portfolio of pictures, individual copies of which were distributed to the jury and among the assembled lawyers. The man quickly itemized each print. Copies were not given to Jennifer but she could see some open in front of the lawyers that included Gerald's blood-soaked body and the gore-splattered office and the lip-clamped shuddering the sight caused her had nothing to do with Jane. The photographs were supplemented by the official plans of the Enco-Corps' office, which were sworn by the architect as those he'd drawn to rebuild the property after the IRA bombing but which had been additionally marked for the trial showing the positioning of Gerald Lomax's permanently visible office and its glass-sided approach corridor in relation to the open trading floor from which the murder had been witnessed by so many people.

It was Jennifer's own revulsion that again shook through her at the evidence of the Home Office pathologist Felix Hewitt, its awfulness worsened by the clinically unemotional way the man presented his post-mortem findings. He described the injuries as massive. The aorta artery and ventricle chamber had been penetrated – the aorta twice – and one knife wound had entered the brain through the left eye, inflicting huge damage to the frontal lobe and into the cortex. The carotid artery in the neck was also severed as well as the femoral artery in the groin, which was the worst of seven cuts and stabs to the genital area. The face was also extensively lacerated, the nose practically severed. In Hewitt's opinion six of a total of thirty-two severe stab and cut wounds would have been fatal. There were numerous others, less severe, to the arms and hands consistent with attempted self-defence. Death would have occurred in minutes, from a combination of the fatal stab wounds, extensive and immediate blood loss and shock.

'Tried to cut his cock off. Bastard deserved to lose it. Thought I'd managed it. He'd have felt it, though. Been in agony. Like that one in the eye: that would have hurt!'

By the time of the luncheon adjournment Jennifer felt totally exhausted, her arms and legs cramped from the way she'd forced herself to sit. The muscles in her arms and legs trembled and she needed the support of both wardresses either side to reach the downward steps and for them to be at her front and back to guide her down into the cell. The once crisp and pure white voile shirt was grey and limp from perspiration, sticking to her back and shoulders like another skin: sweat had soaked through into the suit, too, which was sagged with creases and damply uncomfortable. Her handkerchief was sodden with spittle, too wet for her to wipe herself dry any more. Her make-up would be totally destroyed, she realized. She shook her head against the motherly wardress' suggestion of food: nausea churned her stomach, bringing her close to vomiting.

She found it difficult even to look up at Jeremy Hall's entry from the table at which she was slumped. The solicitor was not with him.

'Are you all right?'

'Of course I'm not all right!'

'*She's insane. Everyone knows that!*'

'Shut up!' To Hall she said, 'She's saying I'm insane, like she always does.'

'Was it bad?'

'You saw how bad it was!'

'I meant how much did you manage to stop?'

'*Not enough!*'

'A lot. Nearly all the outbursts. A lot of the movement, too. But I know it wasn't enough. I've annoyed the judge, haven't I?'

'Do you want a doctor? An adjournment?'

'*No! You've got to go on suffering!*'

'What would that achieve?'

Hall made an uncertain movement. 'Tranquillizers might help.'

'*No! Say you don't want them.*'

Jennifer found herself clutching the underside of the cell chair. 'Are they permissible?'

'*No! Won't stop you being my puppet.*'

'I think so. I'll try to arrange something. It wouldn't be possible for Mason to hypnotize you. He's to be called as an expert defence witness.'

'You didn't question any of the witnesses this morning?' Jennifer challenged.

'There was nothing to ask them.'

'The women you so carefully got on the jury were appalled at the photographs. I saw their faces.'

'Don't try to anticipate reaction.'

'I didn't have to try.'

Hall shifted, discomfited. He'd come to the cells because he'd felt he had to but Perry had been right: there was nothing he could say or do. He hadn't expected to hope this soon that Jarvis would terminate the trial. 'Anything you want? Anything I can do?'

'The tranquillizers might help.'

'*Waste of time!*'

'I'll find the court doctor.'

'And can you let me have a handkerchief? This one's no good any more.'

* * *

Without her intending it to happen Jennifer's throat closed against the Librium the court doctor offered. She choked against regurgitating, coughing afresh at the water she gulped to help swallow them. She finally managed it, her eyes and nose running. She was still weak-kneed and unsteady on her feet, glad of the two women to help her back to the court: wanting to anticipate each and every problem, although do nothing to alert Jane in advance, she abruptly asked to use the toilet as they passed it, even though she hardly needed to when she entered. Almost at once her bladder collapsed and she only just managed to avoid wetting herself.

'*Difficult to keep up, isn't it Jennifer? But you can't relax, not for a moment. Not ever. Not until I've taken away so much of your mind that it doesn't matter any more.*'

Jennifer clutched apprehensively at the dock rail, her escorts tight on either side, for the judge's entry but no feeling was taken from her legs this time and she only had to remain standing for seconds. She grabbed at once for the seat as she sat, entwining her legs again. She felt desperately, achingly tired, tremors constantly flickering through her muscles. It all had to be from the strain of the morning: the tranquillizer would not have had time to work yet. She squeezed her eyes shut and then opened them wide, against the desire to close them altogether.

'*Tired, Jennifer? Want to sleep a little. Go on, close your eyes.*'

Jennifer stopped herself by continuously stretching and unstretching her face until she realized people were looking at her: two women jurors were shaking their heads, sadly. Abruptly she stopped. The pain of biting the inside of her lips helped fight off the tiredness as well as keep them closed, to stop herself being Jane's ventriloquist's dummy.

'Can't relax, not for a moment. Forgot again, didn't you?'

It was the prosecuting junior, Robert Morley, who took forensic scientist Anthony Billington through his evidence. Keflin-Brown sat relaxed beside the man, legs fully outstretched, head sunk on his chest as if he, too, was about to sleep.

Billington was a large, fat man who'd either put on a lot of weight since buying the over-stretched suit or been misled over its size. His deathly pale although heavily freckled face heightened the redness of his disordered hair.

As he began responding to the younger barrister's lead Jane said, *'This is what's going to convict you, so listen up, you hear? Don't want to miss a word of it.'*

The body of a man identified to him as Gerald Lomax had still been in situ although already dead upon his arrival, Billington agreed, to Morley's opening question. Mrs Lomax, whom he recognized in the dock, had also been there and identified to him. Both had suffered severe injuries, the man far more extensively than the woman. These injuries had caused widespread bloodstaining illustrated in the photographs, which Morley showed the man. Billington said he had taken numerous blood samples, which he had later identified. One, AB Rhesus Positive, was that of Gerald Lomax. The other sample was O Rhesus Negative. At Morley's urging the scientist isolated three pictures from the portfolio showing finger and palm prints in a splayed, arced pattern, where someone with blood-soaked hands had stood, supported on outstretched arms. At the scene was a German-made kitchen knife, heavily bloodstained on both blade and handle, which he again identified from the picture file. The fingerprints in the blood on the handle of the knife matched those on the window that overlooked the trading floor. Mrs Lomax had substantial cuts to her hand. The blood on the handle and the window was O Rhesus Negative. On the blade there was also a considerable amount of AB Rhesus Positive.

Jennifer had by now been lulled by the tranquillizer and Jane's absence for several minutes, so the sharp return almost caught her out. But oddly the slowing of her reaction at the same time gave her time virtually to hold it back, as well as to keep her lower lip tight between her teeth.

'Tell him Rhesus is a monkey and he's a fucking ape.'

Jennifer stopped the sentence halfway through and coughed to cover the words she did utter. The urge was to throw her arms wildly up in the air and make the animal grunting sounds echoing through her head but she fought the movement by hanging on to the chair and for once the permanently irate judge did not appear to notice. She thought some people in the court had detected it, like they'd seen her contorted face. There was a nudge from the friendly wardress, who offered Hall's handkerchief. Hurriedly Jennifer mopped her face, conscious that saliva speckled her suit front. She cleaned that off, too.

'Get you a bib. That's what we'll have to do. And some adult diapers for when you piss yourself.'

After his scene-of-crime examination Billington said he was later given samples of debris scraped from beneath the dead man's fingernails by the pathologist, Professor Hewitt. It included O Rhesus Negative blood and skin particles consistent with a self-defence struggle and with the extensive scratch marks on Mrs Lomax's arms and hands.

'*Couldn't stop me though, could he?*' demanded Jane, as Morley sat down.

For the moment he had to go through the motions of

presenting the defence demanded by his client, thought Jeremy Hall, rising for the first time.

'Did you take any further samples, for forensic examination?'

'Yes.'

'Which you haven't presented in court?' Hall asked the question half turned, accusingly, towards the prosecution.

'I was not asked about them,' reminded the scientist, defensively.

'Then I shall ask you now,' said Hall.

'If you must,' intruded Jarvis, wearily.

'He's going to be so pissed off at the end of all this it's going to be unbelievable!'

'Perhaps you would tell the court what other samples you took,' persisted Hall.

'There was considerable evidence of a struggle,' said the man. 'The desk was greatly pushed out of the position indicated by indented pressure marks upon the carpet and what had obviously been Mr Lomax's chair was overturned. Articles from the desk had been thrown to the floor and two decorative pots smashed. I examined several of these articles for fingerprints, to establish if anything had been used as a weapon—'

'Had anything been so used?' broke in Hall.

'There was some hair adhering in blood to one of the broken pots.'

'Whose hair?'

'Mr Lomax's.'

'Anything else?'

'There was other hair, which matched both Mr and Mrs Lomax, on the chair and against the window at which Mrs Lomax was slumped when I entered the office.'

'I'm sure the prosecution are greatly obliged for your assisting their case, Mr Hall,' broke in Jarvis.

'What about fingerprints?' continued Hall, determinedly.

'Widespread, throughout the office.'

'Of Mr and Mrs Lomax?'

'Yes.'

'But of no-one else?'

'Mr Hall!' said the judge, pained.

'*Shut the fuck up, you silly little bastard! Tell him!*'

Jennifer had the first word half-formed before she was able to stop herself, so the sound came out as a sibilant hiss.

Billington hesitated, unsure whether or not to answer. At an impatient nod from the judge, he said, 'There was a third set of fingerprints, which were found to be those of the cleaner.'

'Not of any other person, apart from the cleaner?'

'He's answered the question, Mr Hall!' said Jarvis.

'With respect, my Lord, I think it could be more fully responded to.'

This time the nod of permission was accompanied by a heavy sigh. Red patches of anger were picked out on Jarvis's cheeks.

Billington said, 'Apart from the cleaner's fingerprints, there was no forensic evidence whatsoever of anyone having been in the office other than Mr and Mrs Lomax.'

He'd made the pretence, thought Hall, gratefully sitting under the glare of the judge.

'I call Superintendent John Bentley, the arresting officer,' declared the younger prosecuting barrister and Jane said, '*I'm not going to be able to do anything here to make you sound more of a loony than you did yourself.*'

* * *

The detective entered the box only just short of a swagger and gave the smallest bow in the direction of Jarvis before looking towards the press gallery and smiling, to old friends. Jennifer saw several actually smile back.

Having allowed his junior the crumbs of establishing the technical, bottom-of-the-page evidence, it was Keflin-Brown who stood to take Bentley's account. The suave superintendent, flamboyantly immaculate in brown pin-striped suit complete with a deep red carnation, recited his rank and position and followed the older barrister's direction with accustomed ease, a well rehearsed double act. At precisely three-thirty on the afternoon of the 14th, he and Detective Inspector Malcolm Rodgers had responded to an emergency call to the City premises of Enco-Corps, off Leadenhall Street. In the third-floor office they found the heavily bloodstained body of a man subsequently identified as Gerald James Lomax, the managing director of the commodity trading company. He was already dead, from numerous wounds. Slumped against a floor-to-ceiling window overlooking the office's working area they saw Mrs Jennifer Lomax. She was alive although bleeding profusely from a number of injuries and appeared to be in a state of deep shock. Because of that, which was confirmed by an on-the-scene paramedic team, Mrs Lomax was conveyed to St Thomas's Hospital, for subsequent interview.

'Did you form an opinion of what had happened in that office?' demanded Keflin-Brown.

'I did, sir,' replied Bentley. 'From my observations and from interviewing witnesses at the scene I concluded there had been a violent altercation between Mr and Mrs Lomax, culminating in Mr Lomax's death.'

'Mr Lomax's murder,' clarified Keflin-Brown.

'Resulting in Mr Lomax's murder, yes, sir.'

Keflin-Brown allowed himself a tit-for-tat sideways look at Hall before asking, 'You came upon no evidence, nor did you form the opinion, that anyone else had been involved in this altercation?'

'No, sir.'

'What did you then do?'

'After ensuring that statements were being satisfactorily taken from the large number of witnesses to the incident I went with my inspector to the hospital, where Mrs Lomax was being treated for her injuries. I established from the doctor that she was sufficiently fit to be interviewed . . .'

'. . . There was no question of her fitness?' slowed the barrister, wanting what he was sure to be the following morning's headline delivered at the pace he intended.

'None, sir. In fact, the doctor decided that Mrs Lomax was not, after all, suffering from shock.'

'What then?'

Knowing his part in the publicity act, Bentley concentrated everyone's attention by laboriously taking a notebook from his pocket. 'The accused identified herself as Jennifer Lomax. I asked her if she knew why my inspector and I were there and she replied "Gerald"—'

'Nothing else, simply "Gerald"?' broke in Keflin-Brown again.

'That's all, sir. I then formally cautioned her and asked her if she had anything to say . . .' Bentley paused, expectantly.

'And what did she say?'

Bentley looked up from his notebook, directly towards the press. Quoting, he said, '"It wasn't me. It was Jane."'

There was an electric ripple throughout the journalists and a murmur from the public gallery above Jennifer. The jury exchanged frowned glances.

'"It wasn't me. It was Jane,"' echoed Keflin-Brown.

'That is correct, sir.'

'Help us if you will, Superintendent. Who is Jane?'

'The first wife of Gerald Lomax,' said Bentley, jolting the media with another electric charge.

'There you go, Jennifer. Off to the funny farm with the kind men in the white coats.'

It took the choleric Jarvis several minutes to bring the court to order. Throughout the delay Keflin-Brown retained a statue-like pose matched by that of Bentley, upright and expressionless in the witness-box. Every member of the jury and all the press were looking at Jennifer: the two artists were sketching even more rapidly.

There was a hurried gesture from the wardress with the handkerchief, which Jennifer snatched to clean her face. It meant she was only holding on to the chair with her left hand. She was lurched furiously sideways, to her left, dislodging her grip. She grabbed out frantically, at first missing the wardress's offered hand and briefly disappeared from sight beneath the court rail, as if trying to hide from the attention, before they righted her again. A fresh hubbub arose, which the agitated Jarvis once more shouted to control.

In Jennifer's head the voice chanted in rhyme: *'Peekaboo, peekaboo. Can't see me if I can't see you.'*

'I shall clear this court if this behaviour doesn't cease!' threatened Jarvis. 'Proceed, Mr Keflin-Brown. Let's stop this nonsense.'

'Were you subsequently able to discover from Mrs Lomax what she meant by that remark?'

'Not one that made any sense to me, no.'

'Did she decline to make a statement?' demanded

Keflin-Brown, eyes wide with feigned surprise.

'On the evening when I formally arrested her she refused to make a statement without the presence of her solicitor. I made another attempt, later, to interview Mrs Lomax at the hospital, prior to the taking of a formal statement. At that time her barrister, Mr Hall, and solicitor, Mr Perry, were present . . .'

'. . . You were pursuing your enquiries?'

'I was, sir. Yes.'

'A particular line of enquiry?'

'Yes, sir,' agreed Bentley, alert for Keflin-Brown's guidance on how far he was expected to go.

'This was in a police-guarded hospital ward?'

'But the attempted interview was to be taken in strict accordance with the required rules. By which I mean there was an audio recording.'

'What was Mrs Lomax's demeanour?'

'One of anger, mostly. She seemed upset that her legal advisors, their having apparently earlier told her to say nothing, had now agreed to our conducting the interview without prior consultation with her.'

'Was that all?'

'There were some remarks from Mrs Lomax which were disorientated.'

Hall rose to his feet, stopping the other barrister. 'I wonder, my Lord, if we are not endangering privilege here?'

'The witness has testified to having given Mrs Lomax an official caution. And you were present,' said Jarvis.

Hall ran his hand over the papers before him. 'There was no indication that this would be included, in the prosecution's disclosures.'

'I'm prepared to admit it,' ruled Jarvis.

'I'm obliged, my Lord,' said Keflin-Brown as Hall sat.

Then he said, 'Angry and disorientated? Anything else?'

'She demanded the presence of a doctor, to act as an independent witness.'

'So she was agreeing to be interviewed?'

'I believed that to be the case.'

'Why should Mrs Lomax have needed an independent witness with her lawyers being present?'

'It was never made clear, sir. She seemed to believe she would be cheated. At one stage she indicated she was dispensing with her legal representatives.'

'Cheated!' said Keflin-Brown, stressing artificial bewilderment. 'Cheated of what? By whom?'

'I never discovered that, sir.'

'Was there a particular line of enquiry you were pursuing at this time?'

It was coming, thought Jennifer, and Jane said, '*You bet your sweet ass it is.*'

'There was, sir.'

'Tell my Lord and the jury what that was.'

'I had discovered Mr Lomax's involvement with a member of staff and wanted to establish Mrs Lomax's awareness of it.'

'You mean a sexual involvement? An affair?'

'Yes, sir.'

There was a stir from both the jury and the press.

'What was Mrs Lomax's reaction?'

'She became hysterical. And collapsed.'

'Were you able to resume that interview at a later date?'

'No, sir. When I attempted to do so I was told by Mrs Lomax's legal advisors that she declined to speak to me further.'

'How long have you been in the police force, Superintendent?'

'Twenty-eight years, sir.'
'A man of considerable experience?'
'Yes, sir.'
'Including, regrettably, experience of murder cases?'
Speaking directly towards the jury again, Bentley said, 'A total of twelve. All of which have led to a conviction.'
'In that considerable experience, have people collapsed under questioning before?'
'Several times.'
'And in your opinion, based upon your considerable experience, was Mrs Lomax's collapse genuine? Or faked?'
'In my opinion, sir, it was faked.'
Keflin-Brown turned away from the detective, to face the jury again. 'As I told you at the beginning of this case, you must at all times be guided on the questions of law by my Lord. But I would advise you that it has been the law in this country, since 1994, that juries are allowed to draw inference of guilt or innocence from a defendant's insistence upon remaining silent.'

Jeremy Hall was annoyed but professionally so, still totally under control. Keflin-Brown had massaged the presentation to within a hair's-breadth of what was permissible and if he'd been the counsel to attempt it Mr-Justice-Bloody-Jarvis would have cut him off at the knees. But then it had been a very long time since anyone had seriously tried to advance a case that the law, any more than life, was fair.
'There is a lot more with which you can help the court, isn't there, Superintendent?' Hall spoke as he stood, a Keflin-Brown type mannerism.
'I'm not sure that I can.'
No 'sir', Hall noted. 'You were aware of something

else at the time of the attempted interview about which you've told the court, quite apart from any affair that Gerald Lomax might have been involved in, weren't you?'

'I am not sure,' repeated Bentley.

Trying to hold the knee-jerk temper, gauged Hall. 'That surprises me.'

'I am afraid I don't understand.'

'You're a police officer of twenty-eight years' experience? You've successfully solved twelve murders, a commendable record?'

'Is there a point here, Mr Hall?' demanded Jarvis.

It was an attempt to help the detective, but Hall saw at once how to use it to his advantage. 'Very much indeed, my Lord. I am seeking to establish the credibility of this witness.'

'Credibility?' queried Jarvis, still to Hall's benefit although not intending it to be.

'Very much so, my Lord.'

'How?'

Beside Hall, Keflin-Brown stirred, discomfited. In the witness-box the colour had begun to suffuse Bentley's face. Hall said, 'Upon the very essence of detection, I would have thought. His observation – about which Superintendent Bentley has already talked to this court – and of an incomplete record of an encounter at which, to the great benefit perhaps of my client, I was fortunate to be present.'

'*Watch him drop you right in the shit!*'

Jennifer tightened her slightly relaxed grip but there was no movement.

'Proceed,' allowed the judge, reluctantly.

Bentley's face was blazing and Hall was surprised it had been so easy. He said, 'Mrs Lomax's remark about

Jane didn't remain inexplicable to you, did it?'

Expectation surged through the press gallery.

'No.'

'Did you not make some comment about it, during the aggressive and unsuccessful interview with Mrs Lomax to which you've referred?'

'I may have done.'

The qualification was a mistake, which the man appeared to realize as soon as he spoke. At once the impatient Jarvis said, 'Well did you or didn't you, Superintendent? Yes or no?'

'I made reference to Mrs Lomax hearing voices in her head.'

'Be quiet!' snapped Jarvis, at the noise that rippled through the media.

Jane said, '*Jeremy's on my side, not yours! He's making it easy for me! I can relax!*'

Once more there was no impulse to move. Remembering, Jennifer looked enquiringly at the handkerchief-holding wardress, touching her mouth. The wardress shook her head.

'Voices?' pressed Hall. 'Or just one voice?'

'Just one voice.'

'Mrs Lomax's defence to this charge is that she is possessed, by the first wife of Gerald Lomax, isn't it?'

The reaction, which was varied but all noisy, was general throughout the court and the judge's fury wasn't specifically directed. It still took several minutes to subside. Eventually Bentley said, 'That is what I understand it to be.'

Hall felt very much in charge, enjoying himself. 'Do you believe in ghosts, Superintendent?'

The tight-faced man allowed himself a frigid smile. 'No.'

'Or spirit possession?'

'No.'

'*He's opening the door to the asylum for you!*'

'And you didn't believe Mrs Lomax's collapse was real, either?'

'No.'

'Despite the fact that a doctor – a doctor who will be called during this trial to testify – categorically assured you that it was, within a very short time of it occurring?'

'No.'

'You have medical training then?'

'No.'

'So you are prepared to argue a medical, clinical opinion with a qualified doctor?'

'In my professional opinion, it was a faked collapse,' persisted Bentley, temper completely lost. 'I'm certainly prepared to argue about ghosts and people being possessed!'

'You shall, Superintendent, you shall,' promised Hall, abruptly sitting.

Malcolm Rodgers, who followed Bentley into the witness-box, loyally supported his chief that the collapse was phoney and even agreed the apparent intention to fire her legal team could have been intended as a diversion, to avoid an interview. Conscious of looking remiss to a jury he intended to show he'd overlooked nothing, Keflin-Brown took the inspector in detail through every minute of every encounter with Jennifer Lomax. Who sat listening to Jane's mental reminders of how insane it made her sound, although not needing to be told because that was precisely how every accurately recounted word made her appear.

'Did you properly and completely carry out every part of a murder investigation, with the exception of a satisfactory interview or of obtaining a statement from the accused?' concluded Keflin-Brown.

'I did, sir,' agreed Rodgers.

'Absolutely?'

'Absolutely.'

Jeremy Hall had no questions, which Jarvis seized to end the day's proceedings. As they were tidying their files, the clerk hurried up to Perry with a folded note, from which the solicitor immediately looked up to Hall.

'Jarvis wants to see us in chambers before we start tomorrow.'

Overhearing, Keflin-Brown said, 'I'll still take the lesser plea, if she'll agree.'

Which Jennifer didn't, fifteen minutes later, when Hall reached her in the cell. He thought Jennifer looked more than simply drained: she appeared hollowed out, a shell of a person.

'I wasn't sure where your cross-examination of Bentley took us,' she said.

'*First stop the madhouse.*'

Hall wasn't, either. 'It dented his credibility.'

'For which Rodgers more than compensated.'

'It's a long list so there's no guarantee we'll reach her, but Rebecca Nicholls is listed as a witness tomorrow,' warned Hall.

'*This we've both got to hear!*'

'I think the tranquillizers helped today.'

'I'll see you have them again tomorrow.'

Jeremy Hall had a good note and an even better verbatim recall and went directly from court to chambers to compare what he considered relevant from the case notes with that day's evidence. It took him two hours and ended with a feeling of frustration he couldn't properly identify or even understand. 'What is it?' he demanded of himself, aloud and unembarrassed, in the solitude of his cramped back room. 'What the fuck am I missing?' Fuck wasn't a word he normally resorted to but it seemed in very common usage these days.

His room was so remote that it was served by narrow back stairs so there was no collision as they left but he emerged at practically the same time as Sir Richard Proudfoot, Humphrey Perry and Bert Feltham leaving from the main entrance with two men he didn't know. For several moments they remained looking at each other, startled. Then Proudfoot said, 'Working late?'

'Yes,' said Hall. Then, uncaring, 'You, too?'

'Something like that,' said the chamber head. 'Goodnight.'

'Goodnight.'

In Jennifer's one-person prison ward the matron said, 'There's the magic to make you sleep, my lovely. Now nursey will just rub you, very gently, so you'll relax.'

'Give me the cheque-book,' said Jennifer.

Chapter Twenty-two

So today she was going to face two enemies, one she would be able to see as well as listen to, the other only hear. Double torture, double humiliation: closing in, almost overwhelming despair that for the last thirty minutes she'd come near to giving in to. Quite apart – uncaring even – from Jane being aware of every mental reflection, Jennifer found it difficult to hold any thought. Which wasn't the chlordiazepoxide that Jane had again made her choke to the point of vomiting against taking. That hadn't had time to take effect. She was still thick-headed, that cotton-wool feeling, from the drug the matron had given her the previous night. Her pubic hair had still been slimed with whatever the woman had used for the game she'd played with her, after making her unconscious with the injection. But there'd been no soreness so Jennifer didn't think she'd been fingered or abused by anyone other than Beryl Harrison. Still more humiliation.

The warning of Rebecca Nicholls being the first witness to the actual murder had come from Jeremy Hall's cell visit, after her arrival from prison that morning. The barrister was still flushed from his pre-hearing encounter at which he'd told the judge of Jennifer's continued refusal to change her plea. Sir Ivan

Jarvis's alternative, to foreshorten what again he'd called a music-hall instead of a trial, had been to cut by half the number of trading-floor witnesses with virtually identical accounts of the killing.

The fast-footed, headline-conscious Simon Keflin-Brown had instantly agreed and nominated Rebecca to be the first, guaranteeing the continuation of coverage that had exceeded either his or John Bentley's expectations – and hopes – that morning. All the tabloids had led with the previous day's hearing – Murder by Possession was one slogan, Murder in Mind another – and almost every newspaper carried collected photographs of Jennifer, Jane and Rebecca. Inevitably, the captions had referred to eternal triangles. The motherly wardress ('It's Ann: Ann Wardle. I've got a son who's ill like you,') had shown her the *Daily Mirror* on their way from the prison. All three photographs had been taken in happier, laughing times: assured, confident women, women upon whom no misfortune could ever fall.

Despite the woolly-headed feeling – and not knowing then that she would be confronting Rebecca – Jennifer had tried as hard with her appearance as the previous day, although she accepted, bitterly, just how far short she was of how she'd looked in the pictures the newspapers had obtained.

She'd bribed her way into the bathroom again, carrying today's grey suit and black shirt which wouldn't so easily show her sweating or slobbering, and not just to prepare herself behind a locked door but to douche herself from whatever she'd been subjected to, by the matron. There was a sanitary pad dispenser and Jennifer took one and lined her pants, against Jane's threat to make her disgrace herself in the dock. She'd also brought several handkerchiefs, two of which Ann now carried escorting her along the corridor, towards the dock steps. The wardress also had the two Jeremy Hall had brought for her during their brief meeting.

'Just do your best,' he'd said, reaching across the battered cell table to squeeze her hands lightly in encouragement.

'I ache all over from yesterday. From trying to hold myself against what she might do.'

'Anything?' He was glad Perry wasn't in the cell, with his unnecessarily impatient sighs. There was no harm in humouring her: in trying to help her through. Jarvis had been furious at the refusal to alter her plea. He was going to be even more of a cantankerous bastard than he had the previous day.

'She's been humming, like she's pleased with herself.'

'*I am pleased with myself. Every reason to be. But what's all this hand-holding? Someone else trying to get inside your pants? Going to get crowded in there, isn't it?*'

'Just try your best,' repeated Hall, at a loss for anything else to say. 'That's all you can do.'

'I am making myself look a fool, aren't I?' That was at the brink of despair.

'I could go back to the judge, even now,' offered Hall, hopefully.

'No!' she'd determined, pulling back. 'No!'

And now she was walking towards the bear pit, to be taunted and prodded and reduced to a sniggering, pitiful joke. At the bottom of the dock steps Jennifer hesitated, momentarily refusing – frightened – to ascend.

'Up we go, love. Come on,' urged Ann.

'I don't want to.'

'You haven't got a choice. Come on.'

With leaden feet, at last beginning to feel the Librium,

Jennifer climbed, aware of the buzzed expectation as she got to the court level. As she became visible the noise grew, an excited, mob-like sound. Probably just like a bear-pit anticipation, she thought. Or maybe the entry into a Roman arena of a victim who didn't stand a chance of escape.

'*You don't. I keep telling you that. I don't think we'll make a fool of you just yet, not until Rebecca. Let's keep them in suspense.*'

Rebecca Nicholls looked sensational and Jane said, '*Holy shit, she's fantastic! And dressed to make you look a klutz.*'

Rebecca's hair, a darker, artificial blond against Jennifer's natural colour, was cut severely into her neck, around which there was just a single strand of plaited gold. The dress was black and figure-hugging, belted again by a gold strand. She took the oath with her left hand resting prominently on the edge of the witness-box, displaying on her engagement finger a diamond ring that was her only jewellery. Having returned the Bible to the usher she began playing with the ring with her other hand, drawing attention to it. She stood staring defiantly at Jennifer, the expression carefully balanced between haughtiness and contemptuous revulsion.

'*Great tits. Gerald always was a tit man, wasn't he? That and cunt-sucking. You think he did that with her? Sure he did. She probably gave him head, too. Nose to tail, like a couple of vacuum cleaners.*'

Jennifer held herself in her rigid pose, gripping the seat edge, legs entwined. The press concentration was entirely upon Rebecca, the same artists as the previous day sketching rapidly.

Keflin-Brown was on his feet, the consummate ring-master about to present his best act. The barrister took Rebecca smoothly through her Euro-Corps career, demanding suddenly: 'And now you're acknowledged its leading trader?'

The question seemed to surprise everyone as much as Rebecca. She said, 'I've achieved the highest commission over three successive years, yes.'

'As Mrs Lomax did, before her marriage?'

'I fail to see the relevance of that question,' protested Hall, quickly standing.

'A question of resentment, jealousy, at being replaced in every way?' suggested the older barrister.

'I see no problem with it . . .' began the judge and then 'Oh, Mr Hall, really!'

Ann thrust a handkerchief into Jennifer's hand. As she mopped her face she saw Rebecca look at her, lip curled in disgust. Now her make-up would be smeared, Jennifer thought.

'*Like a clown's*,' agreed Jane.

Jennifer felt her body being thrown to the left and tensed as hard as she could against it. Abruptly the sensation reversed and she went violently to the right, propelled by her own strength. Ann grabbed her. When Jennifer righted herself Rebecca was faintly smirking.

'So you replaced Mrs Lomax in more ways than one?' scored Keflin-Brown.

'I became the top trader,' said Rebecca, stiffly.

'*On top of the boss*.'

'You were, in fact, working on the trading floor on the day of Gerald Lomax's death?'

'Yes.' Some of the confidence went out of the woman.

'Describe it to us,' demanded Keflin-Brown.

'It was two-forty. We're very conscious of precise time:

that's how trades are recorded. There are clocks on the wall, directly beneath Gerry's office, showing the time variations in every major financial centre of the World . . .' began Rebecca, her presentation perfect.

'I bet she's rehearsed, in front of a mirror. Look at her, performing for the newspapers!'

It was exactly what the woman was doing, Jennifer saw. Rebecca was turned slightly away from the judge, more interested in addressing the scribbling gallery.

'. . . I wasn't aware of Mrs Lomax coming out of the elevator on the mezzanine floor above, but I was conscious of other traders looking up so I did and I saw her . . .'

'. . . Through the all-glass design of the office?'

'Yes.'

'You were able to see everything, in perfect and clear detail?'

'Yes. As she walked, Mrs Lomax was tapping her fingers against the corridor wall. That's what attracted the people who saw her first.'

'Which hand was she tapping with?'

'Her right. It had to be, because of the approach from the elevator.'

'Where was her left?'

'It appeared to be inside a large shoulder bag.'

'Did she look down at you?'

'Not then. She was staring straight ahead.'

'*My little robot.*'

'Go on.'

'I saw her walk into Gerald's office. He got up, to meet her . . .' Rebecca stopped, putting her hand to her face, shoulders heaving. There were no tears.

'*Worth a fucking Oscar.*'

'Are you all right?' enquired the barrister.

Rebecca nodded, without replying. After several moments she went on, quiet-voiced, 'It was awful. Terrible. She suddenly had a knife in her hand—'

'This knife?' interrupted Keflin-Brown, gesturing the court usher, who rose and offered the plastic-enveloped exhibit to the woman. There was still blood on the blade.

Rebecca physically recoiled. 'That looks like it.'

'What then?'

'I didn't see where it came from. It was just there, in her hand . . .' Rebecca's lip quivered. 'She began slashing and cutting him with it. Stabbing. Wouldn't stop . . .' She broke off again, both hands up against her mouth, the left hand on the outside with the ring visible. '. . . She just wouldn't stop! He tried to fight her but she'd stabbed him a lot. There was . . .' Another gulped break. '. . . blood everywhere. Spurting. Hitting the window . . .'

'*Say wonderful!*' shouted Jane.

Jennifer was totally engrossed in the horror, hand-hold even relaxed. 'Wonderf . . .' came out before she could prevent it, sufficient for everyone to decipher the bitten off word.

Perry swivelled, making waving-down gestures.

Jarvis said, 'Mr Hall! One more outburst and I will send your client down into the cells! And that's my last warning.'

'*Ah. Don't want that. You've got to stay up here, where everyone can see you. Santa's little helper's just saved you, Jennifer. What about that?*'

Perry was at the dock rail. 'I know it's difficult but please try to control yourself.' The stage whisper easily reached the tightly packed journalists.

Jennifer nodded. 'She doesn't want me out of court.'

'The accused said something, Mr Hall?' demanded Jarvis.

Perry bustled back, cupping his hand to Jeremy Hall's ear. The young barrister turned back to the judge and said, 'My client promises not to interrupt again, my Lord.'

'She doesn't have a choice,' said the small man, nodding to Keflin-Brown.

'Go on, if you can,' urged the barrister.

'. . . It was terrible. Obscene. Just stabbing and blood. Blood everywhere. Then Gerald stopped fighting. Stopped moving . . .'

'What was the next thing to happen?'

'She came and stood at the window, laughing. Just stared down at us and laughed and laughed . . .'

'*Christ, I enjoyed that. Looking down at the stupid fuckers.*'

'How, exactly, did she stand, Ms Nicholls?'

'With her hands outstretched, against the window. Supporting herself . . . People began running then. Roger . . . Roger Jones, the floor manager, began going upstairs. Someone had already rung the police.'

'What did you do?'

'Stayed where I was.'

'Why?'

'I didn't think there was anything I could do. Others were following Roger.'

'Was that the only reason you didn't go upstairs, Ms Nicholls?'

'I was frightened.'

'I'm sure everyone was frightened. Was there any particular reason for your being more frightened than anyone else?'

'*Doesn't your heart go out to her!*'

'Perhaps,' said Rebecca, hushed-voiced again.

'Last time I saw a performance like this it really did win an Oscar.'

'You were Gerald Lomax's lover, weren't you?' said Keflin-Brown, the tone almost as if he were confronting a hostile witness.

'Yes.'

'For how long?'

'Four years.'

'Not four and a half years?'

'Perhaps.'

'How long had you been aware that Mrs Lomax had learned of your relationship with her husband?'

'Objection, my Lord!' protested Hall. 'This court has had no evidence of Mrs Lomax knowing of an affair between her husband and Ms Nicholls.'

'Let's get things in their proper sequence, shall we, Mr Keflin-Brown?' sighed Jarvis.

'I beg the court's indulgence,' said the barrister. 'A regrettable oversight. Allow me to rephrase the question.'

'Too late for it not to have been heard and taken on board by every member of the jury.'

'Did you have any reason to believe Mrs Lomax knew of your affair with her husband?'

'Not positively.'

'Not positively?' echoed the lawyer. 'What then? How then?'

'We'd talked about it, Gerald and I.'

'Talked about what?'

'His telling her he wanted a divorce.'

No! thought Jennifer, anguished. Please no. Wasn't true. Couldn't be true. He wouldn't have abandoned her. Abandoned Emily. Already decided that. Decided it was impossible. Just sex. Nothing else. Sex.

'Just like it was with me: going to dump you just like

the two of you dumped me. What a shit! Think you'd have lived, Jennifer? Just think: I could have saved your life by killing him. He had to die though. Everything's working out exactly as I planned.'

In the well of the court Hall was studying Rebecca Nicholls' sworn statement to Superintendent Bentley.

'Did he?' asked Keflin-Brown.

'I don't know.'

'You're wearing a very beautiful ring. Diamonds, are they not, around a central stone?'

Jennifer closed her eyes, trying to shut out the sight of Rebecca and the ring and the court: shut out everything to curl up into the smallest ball that no-one could see and die. Why fight any more? No point. Give up. Plead however Jeremy Hall wanted her to plead and be sent somewhere as a sex toy, to be played with. Emily, she remembered. Had to survive – to fight – so there was someone to look after Emily. Jennifer waited for the taunt but Jane put no thoughts in her head.

'*You're doing fine, torturing yourself.*'

'Who bought that ring for you, Ms Nicholls?'

'Gerry.'

'Does it have a particular significance?'

'He bought it for me when we talked of getting married.'

'An engagement ring, in fact?'

'Yes.'

'What did you think, when you saw what Jennifer Lomax did to her husband that dreadful day in the office of Euro-Corps?'

'That he had told her.'

'And were you too frightened to go up to where your lover – your future husband – lay dying because you were afraid she'd try to kill you, too?'

'Yes.' Rebecca looked away from the press gallery, to stare directly and accusingly at Jennifer.

'There is a child, a daughter, from Mr Lomax's marriage to the accused, isn't there?'

'Emily,' confirmed the woman.

A fury, a hatred, boiled up within Jennifer. She began physically to shake, without encouragement from Jane.

'That's how I felt, Jennifer. Worse than you, even. That's why I killed Gerald and why I'm doing what I am to you. Balancing the score. An eye for an eye, a tooth for a tooth. Only fair, after what you did.'

'Steady,' hissed Ann, close beside her. 'Calm down.'

'You are, in fact, Emily's godmother, are you not?'

'Yes.'

'A child you love, like your own.'

'Yes.'

Jennifer's shaking worsened and she felt Ann's hand on her arm, restraining her.

'Was there any discussion between you and Mr Lomax about Emily?'

'He said whatever happened he couldn't give her up: that Emily was his life. And that he'd make Jennifer agree to his having Emily with us.'

Jennifer felt an emptiness, a void. He couldn't have been this cruel. He would have had to hate her to be this cruel: to have used her, like the matron and Emma and Fran and Harriet used her.

'That's it, Jennifer: that's what it was, all the time. Still think you're the luckiest woman in the world?'

'What was Mr Lomax's intention, as far as you were aware?'

Rebecca remained staring straight at the dock, the look of contempt on her face again. 'As far as I was aware

Gerald intended divorcing Jennifer and getting custody of Emily. And then we would marry.'

'Left with nothing! Tossed out, with the garbage.'

'And for the three of you to become a family?'

'Yes.' Rebecca's voice was soft again, trembling with the uncertainty of a happiness she'd now never achieve.

'Gerald would have told Mrs Lomax what he intended with the child, as well as wanting a divorce, wouldn't he?'

'Objection!' protested Hall. 'There is no way the witness can speculate about a conversation, if any, between Mr and Mrs Lomax.'

'Mr Keflin-Brown,' rebuked the judge, mildly.

'I beg the court's indulgence and of course withdraw the question . . .' apologized the older barrister.

'Too late. Motive all sorted and made perfectly clear. You're for the drop, Jennifer. Would have been if they still hanged murderers.'

'. . . and I have no further questions,' the man concluded, surrendering Rebecca Nicholls to cross-examination like a well-chewed bone upon which there was no meat left.

'You haven't the slightest idea – any way of knowing – if Gerald Lomax confessed his adultery to his wife, have you?' attacked Jeremy Hall, at once.

'We'd talked about his doing so.'

'But you don't know that he had done it?'

'No.'

Hall lifted Rebecca's statement from the mound of papers in front of him, hefting it as if testing its weight to attract the jury's interest. 'What you've told the court today is at considerable variance with what you told Superintendent Bentley, isn't it?'

'I don't remember.'

'You don't remember?'

'I had just seen the man I loved slaughtered, in front of my eyes! Seen his blood burst everywhere!'

'No, you hadn't! Your full statement was made to Superintendent Bentley several days after that.'

'I still don't remember.'

There was a tug at Jennifer's elbow, with the hand offering the handkerchief. Hurriedly she dried herself. Jane said, '*I'm not going to have you taken out of court but everyone's still got to think you're a drooling idiot.*'

'Then let me help you, Ms Nicholls,' offered Hall, beckoning the usher. 'I've marked a section, at the top of the third page: the page of a statement you've signed and agreed as an accurate account of your conversation with Superintendent Bentley. Doesn't that marked section say, and I quote, "But Jennifer never knew"?'

'Yes.'

'That's very different from what you're asking the jury to believe today, isn't it, Ms Nicholls?'

'I *was* still in shock. I've had time to think about it, since.'

'I quote again, from a paragraph marked just a little lower from that to which I've referred. Doesn't that say "She didn't kill Gerry because of me"?'

'Yes. But I told the police he'd promised me he would get a divorce.'

'But didn't you also say, in the third marked passage, that Gerald Lomax had *not* told his wife of your affair. Or asked for a divorce. And didn't you go on to say – and again, my Lord, I quote – "He said he'd tell me before he did. But he didn't say anything. So he didn't"?'

'I may have done.'

'Ms Nicholls, it's in a statement you signed as an

accurate account of your conversation with the superintendent.'

'I've told you, I was still shocked!'

'You'd been with Gerald Lomax the night before he was killed, hadn't you? Like you were every night when he remained in London?'

'Yes.'

'In his flat?'

'Yes.'

'Did you make love?'

'Mr Hall!' interrupted the judge, while Keflin-Brown was still only halfway to his feet. 'Is there a point to this line of questioning?'

'An extremely important one,' insisted Hall. He had no intention of considering it after the inevitable result of the trial, because it would not be in Jennifer Lomax's interest, but he was convinced that by now the transcript would already show sufficient unfair bias for an appeal to be lodged.

'Be very careful, Mr Hall. I shall be paying particular attention,' said Jarvis.

'You slept with Gerald Lomax the night before he died?' resumed Hall.

'Yes.' Rebecca was tiny-voiced again.

'You had no secrets from each other, did you?'

'No.'

'And he'd promised to tell you, before he asked Jennifer for a divorce?'

'Yes.'

'And he *did* want to marry you?'

'Absolutely.'

'To clear the way for you and he to marry, a divorce would have been the most important thing in Gerald Lomax's life at that moment, wouldn't it! He'd promised to tell you. You had no secrets from each other. Yet the night before he was murdered – by a woman it is being suggested was driven to kill by insane jealousy – in the intimate surroundings of the bedroom, he said nothing to you whatsoever about having confessed his adultery to his wife?'

'No.' There was very little defiance any more and practically no voice.

'So he hadn't told Jennifer Lomax what would have caused her to commit this terrible crime, had he? This whole—'

'My Lord,' broke in Keflin-Brown. 'How can this witness testify to what might or might not have taken place when she was not in Hampshire the previous weekend?'

'That was an inept question, Mr Hall,' criticized the judge.

'Questioning an inference that the jury have been asked to draw from uncorroborated testimony in Ms Nicholls' evidence-in-chief,' fought back Hall, refusing to be bullied. 'But let me try to find my answer from a different direction. To your knowledge, had Gerald Lomax ever deceived you?'

'*Wonder who else he was screwing. There would have had to be someone, wouldn't there?*'

'No.'

'*Doesn't know him like we do, does she?*'

'Held anything back from you?'

'No.'

'Broken a promise to you?'

'No.'

'He had promised to alert you, in advance, of his confessing everything to Mrs Lomax and demanding the divorce that would give him custody of Emily?'

'Yes.'

'But had not, at any time prior to the murder, told you that he had done so?'

'No.'

'That is a very beautiful ring. When did you buy it?'

'I told you, when we talked about getting married.'

'That wasn't the question. What was the date when you bought it?'

'I don't remember.'

'Ms Nicholls! You've told the court it's your engagement ring, the token of your intended marriage. Buying it was surely one of the most significant moments of your life?'

'We are meandering towards a point, aren't we, Mr Hall?' demanded the judge.

Bastard! thought Hall, curbing the frustrated anger the moment it came. 'Hopefully, my Lord.'

'An ambition shared by us both.'

'Then perhaps I can continue, my Lord?' Hall allowed himself, careless of the immediate tightening of Jarvis's face. 'Wasn't it a moment to remember, Ms Nicholls?'

'Yes.'

'So when was it?'

'Five or six months ago.'

'Still not sure,' said Hall. 'Was it a surprise, given to you over a candle-lit dinner? Or did you buy it together?'

'We bought it together.'

'And you've worn it ever since? For five or six months?'

'Yes.'

'So people you work with would have noticed it. It is, after all, a very distinctive piece of jewellery. They would probably be able to give an even more reliable timing than five or six months.'

'I can see where he's getting to, can't you? Clever bastard, isn't he? Pity there's nothing he can do to help you.'

'Maybe. You'll have to ask them.'

'I intend to, Ms Nicholls. Every one of them who's called to give evidence after you. You sure you can't give a more specific date?'

'No.'

'What shop did you buy it in?'

The woman began nipping her bottom lip between her teeth. 'Garrards.'

'Who will, of course, have a record of the sale. So we can establish a positive date by simply approaching them, can't we?'

'That's you fucked, Rebecca. He really is a clever bastard.'

'I suppose so.'

'Would it embarrass you if I did indeed obtain a sales receipt?'

'No.' There was no longer any defiance. Rebecca Nicholls was blinking a lot, constantly nibbling her lower lip, several times looking nervously towards the judge, who had stopped intervening.

'Wouldn't such a receipt show that your ring is a much more recent acquisition?'

'I said I can't be sure when I bought it.'

'*You* bought it!' pounced Hall. 'Remembering, before you answer, that you are on oath, Ms Nicholls, isn't a far more accurate story of the ring that you did indeed buy it yourself, not together with Gerald Lomax. That its purpose and purchase was to strengthen the motive of jealousy for the crime of which my client stands accused?'

'No.'

'Speak up, Ms Nicholls,' demanded Jarvis.

'No,' repeated Rebecca, only slightly louder.

'Could I place on record, my Lord, the possibility of my seeking to recall this witness after further enquiries are made?'

'He gave me the money!' shouted Rebecca, her voice snatched by a sob. Then the words rushed out. 'Gerald gave me the money and said it was for an engagement ring and when he died I bought it as he'd intended me to so I could keep it always, in his memory . . .'

'I don't think I need bother Garrards,' said Hall, sitting down.

He did, however, ask each trader subsequently called if they remembered the ring being worn by Rebecca Nicholls. None did. There was little else he chose to examine them upon. Their accounts of Gerald Lomax being murdered were identical, as were Jane's interventions which lessened anyway after a further warning from Jarvis to have Jennifer removed from the dock. The only variation was the evidence of Roger Jones, the trading-floor manager, who followed Rebecca into the witness-box. He testified that when he reached the office, Jennifer was cradling Gerald Lomax in her arms and said, 'Gerald's dead. Someone stabbed him.'

'"Gerald's dead. Someone stabbed him"?' echoed Hall. 'Not "I stabbed him, because he was deceiving me with Rebecca Nicholls" or some such words?'

'No.'

'Was Jennifer Lomax in any way threatening?'

'No.'

'You never feared she might attack you?'

'At first, when I got there. But not when I saw what she was like.'

'What was she like?'

'Bewildered, as if she didn't understand what had happened.'

Because their accounts of the killing were virtually the same and Jeremy Hall's cross-examination so minimal the evidence from the trading floor was completed by mid-afternoon. It was the prosecution who called the hospital doctor, Peter Lloyd, whom Hall had originally seen as a defence witness. Keflin-Jones did so to establish that when Jennifer Lomax was admitted she was not suffering from shock but appeared composed and aware of her surroundings.

Lloyd had volunteered a lengthier statement than even the prosecution needed, urged to do so by a hospital management anxious against any criticism to set out in minute medical detail every aspect of the treatment Jennifer had received.

The awareness – the abrupt recognition of the nagging doubt that he'd felt but been unable to resolve – exploded in Jeremy Hall's mind halfway through Lloyd's evidence, which Hall was following from the copy of the doctor's statement that had been made available under the rule of disclosure.

The significance was such that briefly the words fogged in front of Hall's eyes. He heard Lloyd say the words, exactly as they were written down, but then closed his senses to the rest of the man's evidence, sorting through the papers in front of him so hurriedly that Keflin-Brown paused, distracted, looking accusingly sideways. Perry leaned forward, nudging the younger man but Hall was oblivious to anything but the evidence they had already heard and the notes that he had made.

His concentration was such that he was not conscious of Keflin-Brown sitting, giving him the opportunity to cross-examine, until Jarvis said, 'Are you with us, Mr Hall?'

'Very much so, my Lord,' assured Hall. He rose slowly, checking the time as he did so, calculating he had fifteen minutes to fill before the adjournment of that day's hearing.

'You carried out every conceivable test and examination considered necessary upon Mrs Lomax, consistent with her medical condition when she was admitted?'

'Yes.'

'Some of which were repeated, according to clinical practice?'

'Yes.'

Still ten minutes to go. 'Physical conditions – illnesses – not immediately evident can be ascertained from certain pathological examinations?'

'Yes.'

'Faeces and urine, for example?'

'Yes.'

'I think this has already been well established, Mr Hall.'

'With the greatest of respect, my Lord, I think there is something of vital importance to this case that has not been established. And needs to be.'

'*What the fuck's he on about?*'

Hall welcomed the time the judge remained looking at him before nodding curtly. Five minutes, he saw. 'Spinal fluid?'

'Yes.'

'Temperature?'

'Yes.'

Three minutes. 'Pulse?'

'Yes.'

'Blood?'

'Yes.'

'How many times, doctor, were blood samples taken from Mrs Lomax?'

Lloyd went back to his medical reports. 'In total, five times.'

'Do you have many more questions for this witness, Mr Hall?' interrupted the judge.

'Possibly a very great many,' said Hall, satisfaction and anticipation surging through him.

'Then I think we will adjourn until tomorrow.'

Hall wheeled to Humphrey Perry before Jarvis was out of the court. 'Have Jennifer kept in the cells, below. I want an independent medical examiner. Our own forensic expert. And we'll need the prosecution's technical people who've already given evidence here again tomorrow. See they're called. Don't let Bentley or Rodgers leave the court today. And we'll need Jarvis's clerk . . .' Hall turned sideways, to Keflin-Brown. 'I'd like you to be present, too.' He stopped, trying to think of anything he'd overlooked. Urgently he said, 'Don't tell Jennifer Lomax what we're doing in advance of doing it. I don't want any warning given.'

Keflin-Brown was gazing at the other barrister in open-mouthed astonishment. 'What the hell are you on about?'

'I'm not sure,' admitted Hall. Suddenly he was chilled by fear, physically shivering.

Chapter Twenty-three

Sir Ivan Jarvis was incandescent with rage, the fury worsened by it being obvious to everyone in chambers – but to himself most of all – that he had no alternative. He was, nevertheless, still seeking one.

Jeremy Hall had endured the threats and gone through the music-hall accusations quite unworried: he'd already decided there were grounds for appeal upon the judge's court-recorded animosity. What had happened during the past twelve hours – with only God knowing what was likely to emerge in the coming twenty-four – guaranteed not just the legal overturning of everything if Jarvis didn't comply but ensured an ignominious end to the old man's lifelong career. Jarvis knew that, too.

'I made clear my attitude to tricks, Mr Hall!'

'And I've made clear, my Lord, that these matters only came to my notice at the conclusion of yesterday's hearing. This application is not based on trickery. It is based upon fact.' It was hard, in his excitement, not to appear overconfident: not too soon or too quickly to seek some personal satisfaction from how he'd been demeaned in open court.

'The facts were in a statement, for all to see and challenge!'

'One was, my Lord,' corrected Hall, not needing to

take the reminder further. Jarvis had prior access to Peter Lloyd's statement, as well as both prosecution and defence.

'My Lord,' intruded Keflin-Brown. 'My learned friend very properly provided me with every facility and access, after last night's conclusion. From what has come to light, overnight, I must support his application most strongly in every way.' There was his practised, mannered paused. 'In fact, subject to your Lordship's direction I intend suspending the prosecution until it has been resolved.'

Jarvis's mouth became an even tighter line. 'There could be an explanation for one of your disparities, regrettable though such a mistake might be.'

'But not for the other,' argued Hall, easily. 'Since last night I am in a position to prove from the prosecution's own witnesses, given your permission to recall, as well as from my own, that the second matter is incontrovertibly conclusive.'

'We heard yesterday from eight witnesses who saw your client murder her husband,' persisted the judge.

'We also heard, from those eight witnesses, how she stood hands outstretched against the window after appearing to have carried out that murder. Each account of which further supports my request this morning.' There had been a chance for him to sleep, after about 3 a.m., but the adrenalin had been Everest high and he hadn't even bothered to try. Instead, having found the key, he had forced himself yet again through Jennifer Lomax's entire file, sometimes consciously mouthing the words he read in his determination against missing anything else by being dulled by his familiarity with what he already knew. Now he was absolutely sure there were no more oversights.

To Keflin-Brown the resistant judge said, 'You have no objection to the introduction of a new defence witness?'

'None, my Lord,' said the older barrister, at once.

'What time is he due to land?' Jarvis asked.

'Just after midday,' responded Hall, prepared for every query. 'Arrangements have been made to convey him immediately to court.'

'With hearsay evidence?' challenged Jarvis, hopefully.

Another door he was going to enjoy slamming in the old bastard's face. It had been Humphrey Perry's suggestion to extend the enquiry. Which had produced the most dramatic – as well as perhaps the most inexplicable and frightening – evidence to support his application that morning. It was, Hall knew, what was unsettling everyone, something none of them understood and didn't want to think about. 'The court benefits from the time difference between this country and the United States of America: it was only 11 a.m. in Washington DC when your Lordship rose last night. The defence had already engaged an American lawyer, prior to the developments before your Lordship today. He was able to locate the doctor who took the original samples and have him swear an affidavit before an American judge in chambers that his findings were a true and accurate record. I would ask you to accept, my Lord, that it is therefore legally admissable and not hearsay evidence . . .' Closing the lid on the box, Hall finished, 'If that is not your view, then I will make arrangements to fly the doctor here, personally to appear before you.'

Jarvis shook his head, in defeated rejection. He looked intently and individually at the two barristers, then at Perry and Robert Morley behind. 'Have any of you thought of the implications of this?' he demanded, voicing the unspoken bewilderment of them all.

Keflin-Brown and Hall exchanged looks, each inviting the other to respond. Taking the responsibility, as the applicant, Hall said, 'I cannot explain what I believe I can prove.'

'Your application is granted, in full,' Jarvis surrendered. There was a pause. 'I'm minded to add God help us.'

No-one considered the remark an exaggeration or out of place. Perry was actually thinking the same thing himself.

It had been one of the most horrific times of the total horror, not as bad as having her mind taken over, or the murder itself or the lesbian rape but close behind. Jane had erupted against Jeremy Hall's refusal to explain what was happening, screaming so loudly and so long Jennifer had screamed herself, at the physical pain it caused. Twice, despite Jennifer's efforts to prevent it, she'd been thrown violently to the ground and had once been unable to stop herself suddenly striking out, catching the barrister a glancing blow on the side of the face. The fury had reached apoplexy at Hall's reaction to it all. He'd greeted every outrage as if he wanted it to occur – making no effort to avoid the slap – unnecessarily pointing the worst of her behaviour out to the people before whom she was paraded, very often like an exhibit. She recognized some, like the two detectives and the prosecuting barrister and court officials, but not others. They'd ignored her too when Jane had made her demand to know their names and what they were doing, snipping a sample of hair and fingerprinting her and taking yet another blood test. Jane had made her jerk her arm when the needle went in, breaking it off, so she had another sore wound in her arm: it had taken all her own effort as well as Hall physically holding her arm for the sample and the fingerprints to be taken. All that had been done by someone she didn't know, in her cell, although the prison doctor had attended as a witness. Hall and Perry and some other strangers were there, too, and so much official activity had obviously frightened the matron. Jennifer had used it further to scare the woman after everyone had gone, lying about an authority inquiry. There hadn't been any cream residue when she'd awoken that morning and Jennifer hadn't detected anything during the night, which she believed she might have done. Jane had maintained an unrelenting barrage of noise, penetrating even the sedative, so Jennifer had always had a vague awareness of her surroundings. It had been a pill, not an injection – further evidence the matron didn't intend drugging her beyond any awareness of what was happening to her – and Jane had succeeded in making her vomit the first one up before managing to swallow the second.

The tirade had continued that morning. Jennifer's hand had been jerked and pulled when she'd tried to make-up and dress her hair, so the effort was very much worse than at the beginning of the previous two days, although better than at their end, after Jane had made her drool. She'd chosen a dress today, dark blue again to minimize the inevitable staining and intended trying hard to remember to have more clothes brought up from Hampshire: both suits were too crumpled and sweat-and-saliva stained for a second wearing. She doubted if cleaning would help.

The threats had approached hysteria, on the way to court. There was: '*Find out what's going on! If you don't, I'm going to make you do things you can't even begin to imagine!*' And then: '*Forget the attack on Emily: Gerald even. You'll go out with the biggest bang ever.*'

Followed by: '*You find out or by tonight you're in the funny farm, for life.*' And then that most familiar of all: '*Don't fool yourself, Jennifer. You know you can't fight me – resist me – sufficiently.*' Before a return to the beginning: '*I want to know what's going on!*'

So did Jennifer. Desperately. From the fact that Keflin-Brown and his junior were involved, as well as the stone-faced Bentley and Rodgers and a lot of obvious specialists and experts it had to be important. Vital. Yet she'd been in court all the time, heard everything that was said. And there hadn't been anything: nothing, that is, that had meant anything to her. So what was it?

'*Find out: I keep telling you to find out!*'

Jennifer didn't have to talk. Thinking was enough. Really knocked you off your perch, hasn't it Jane? Really beating you this time. Said it would happen, didn't I? Not as clever as you thought you were. Panicking. Don't know what to do. Now you're lost, not me. Will lose. How's that feel? Lost and going to lose a lot more. Finished, Jane. Not just dead once. Dead twice.

'*Dream on, bitch! Enjoy, as long as you can. Which won't be long. That dock's really going to be your bear pit today. You're going to dance to every tune I want to play and I'm going to play the lot. Should have kissed sticky-fingered matron and your dyke friends goodbye. You won't be going back to them. Got a special place for you in the looney tune chorus. Here's a joke, just for you. A celebrity goes into an asylum, part of a compassion therapy experiment, and says to the first man he sees: "Hello. Do you know who I am?" and the man says: "No. But ask matron. She'll tell you."*'

Not good enough, Jane. Not even very funny. Panic. Not in control any more. Lost.

'*We'll see.*'

We will. Tough shit, Jane. You're fucked.

There was almost a phosphorous whiteness from the intensity of the window-reflected camera flashes at their arrival. Jennifer descended confidently from the van but the moment she reached the ground all support left her legs. Only the quick reflexes of Ann Wardle kept her from collapsing on to the ground: as it was she went down heavily to her left, where the second wardress failed to catch her, and hit her knee with sickening hardness against a kerb edge. Her tights tore and her knee began to bleed, all strength and sensation gone from the leg. Jennifer was virtually carried into the building, arms around the necks of both wardresses who in turn linked their arms around Jennifer's back to complete the bridge. The duty doctor was crouched in front of her, cleaning and dressing the darkly bruised cut, when Jeremy Hall entered the cell.

'*Ask him! Demand to know!*'

Instead Jennifer said: 'She made me fall. She's screaming to know what's happened.'

'I'm sure she is.'

'*What!*'

'She says she's going to make me do worse things than attack Emily. That I'll be in a mental hospital by tonight.' He was somehow different. Not frightened of her – he was one of the few who had never been frightened of her – but somehow holding back. He wasn't even leaning over the table towards her like he'd usually done, since the trial had begun.

The hesitation was obvious, too, before he said, 'I want her to do everything possible she can.'

Jennifer looked at the barrister, aghast. 'What?'

'The more ridiculous she makes you look – the more outrageous the actions or the words – the better it is for us. Don't fight against any of it, however bad it is. Do it and say it.'

'*WHAT?*'

'She's screaming! Hurting my head again.'

'Who or whatever is in your head is my defence witness now,' insisted Hall. 'Whatever she does or says is going to prove your total innocence. Do you hear that, Jennifer? I can prove you're not guilty! Not just that. Prove you're not mad, either.'

'*NOoooooooo!*'

The gossip of an impending although unidentified sensation inevitably came from the court officials and the anticipatory electricity was tangible when Jennifer entered the dock. The limp immediately became a cause for speculation, several journalists standing in the absence of the judge to crane over the dock rail in an effort to see the reason. Jennifer was tensed, nervous of an abrupt attack from Jane, but nothing came although she still had the tingling burn of Jane's presence, more uncomfortable than usual. Her knee throbbed and had swollen tightly against the dressing. She was ready when the judge entered the court, grabbing out for the rail and glad of the wardresses close behind but there was no weakness in her legs. Despite what Hall had said in the cells below it was instinctive for her to grip the underside of the chair. Ann had the first handkerchief ready, in her lap. At Jennifer's look the wardress shook her head, reassuringly.

Jarvis cleared his throat, staring fixedly at Jennifer for several moments before turning to his right. In his strangely sonorous voice he said, 'Ladies and gentlemen of the jury, since the adjournment of this trial yesterday, certain matters have most forcibly been brought to my attention . . .' He looked briefly down at Jeremy Hall, who was visibly hunched, like a runner eager to get off the blocks.

'. . . In the light of what has emerged, overnight, it is necessary, in my view, to allow these matters to be fully and properly examined, in your presence. And for that examination to be conducted at this stage of the trial, instead of waiting for the prosecution to conclude its case and for the defence to present theirs, which would be the normal course of events . . .'

The judge paused, to clear his throat again, and Jennifer was startled to see Perry turn and smile encouragingly at her. She was too surprised to respond.

'. . . To that end,' resumed Jarvis, 'certain witnesses who have already given evidence will today be recalled, for their evidence to be explored more fully than it was when they first appeared. I will do my best to ensure that this is done in a comprehensible manner, to prevent this extremely unusual course causing you any confusion . . .'

Briefly Jarvis's attention switched to Hall, as if in warning. '. . . If, however, something emerges that any of you do not understand, I require you at once to advise me, through the court officials. At which time it will be clarified. Is that quite clear to all of you . . . ?'

There were uncertain nods throughout the jury. The press beehive hummed.

'. . . We will pick up, however, with the witness who was giving evidence at the conclusion of yesterday's hearing,' announced Jarvis. 'Doctor Peter Lloyd . . .'

The hospital doctor re-entered the box, agreeing with a nod that he understood he was still bound by the oath he'd taken the previous day. Hall was already standing, waiting.

'Doctor Lloyd,' said Hall. 'Your answer to my final

question, yesterday, was that during the time she spent under your care a total of five separate blood tests were taken from the accused?'

'That is correct.'

'Taken by you?'

'Three were.'

'Did you take the first, upon her admission?'

'Yes.'

'That first test, upon her admission, would have been for a particular and specific purpose, would it not?'

'Yes.'

'What?'

'Mrs Lomax had quite severe injuries, to her arms and hand. She'd lost blood. It was necessary to give her a transfusion.'

'Before which you had to establish what?'

'Her blood group.'

'Why was it you who took that first sample?'

'I was the duty emergency doctor that day.'

'How long did it take pathology to identify Jennifer Lomax's blood group?'

Lloyd shrugged. 'Maybe thirty minutes. As I've said, it was considered an emergency: there's a fast-track system. By the time the wounds had been cleaned and Mrs Lomax prepared for surgery, we had the results.'

'Which were?'

'That Mrs Lomax's blood group is B Rhesus Positive.'

'Which was the blood you transfused?'

Lloyd appeared surprised by the question. 'Of course.'

'What effect would there have been upon Mrs Lomax if blood other than B Rhesus Positive had been transfused?'

The doctor appeared even more confused. 'An extremely severe reaction. Anything else would have been incompatible. She would have gone into shock: could even have died from renal failure.'

'But Mrs Lomax did not go into shock or suffer any adverse effects from your transfusion?'

Lloyd shook his head, bewildered. 'No.'

'During the pathological examination of blood samples subsequently taken from Mrs Lomax, would the group always be identified?'

'Yes. The check system requires it.'

'Do the medical records in front of you show the blood group of those four other separate tests?'

'Yes.'

'What are they?'

'The only group they could be, of course, B Rhesus Positive.'

'Thank you, doctor. I am extremely obliged,' said Hall, sitting. As he did so he turned invitingly to Keflin-Brown, who shook his head against any re-examination. After the constant groundswell of noise with which Jennifer had been surrounded on the previous two days, the court was now breathlessly silent as everyone tried to understand what was unfolding. The burn of Jane's presence was definitely hotter and Jennifer felt herself sweating again. She reached out herself for the ever-ready handkerchief, using it to dab her upper lip and forehead. There was an unintended jerk, a twitch of frustration, but Jennifer easily kept her hand steady.

'I call Professor Hewitt,' announced Hall. He was enjoying himself, savouring the reversal, refusing to be distracted by the underlying uncertainty. Jarvis was according him every consideration, no longer interrupting. And there had been nothing from Jennifer, in the dock. At the thought he turned to look at her, smiling slightly. This time Jennifer did smile back, although doubtfully.

The Home Office pathologist was a thin, bespectacled man with mousy, receding hair. He entered the witness-box briskly, a busy man irritated at being bothered a second time.

Discerning the man's mood, Hall said, 'There is only what you may regard as a small matter upon which I am going to ask you to assist the court, professor, but I must ask you to accept my word it is of vital importance. Gerald Lomax had been the victim of a violent and sustained attack, had he not?'

'Yes.'

'During which he had received wounds and injuries described by you during your earlier testimony as massive?'

'Yes.'

'As well as examining those massive wounds, about which you've already told us, and ascertaining that Gerald Lomax was not suffering any medical condition that might have contributed to his death, did you also take a sample of Gerald Lomax's blood?'

'Yes.'

'Did you have it pathologically analysed.'

'I did not do it personally. It was forensically analysed by Doctor Billington.'

'Quite so. He would have advised you of his findings, though, to complete your report?'

'Yes.'

'Can you tell the court the grouping?'

Hewitt flicked through the manila folder he had carried into the box. 'AB Rhesus Positive.'

'It is a customary forensic practice in such cases of violent attack and death for a pathologist to take samples of detritus that may be found beneath a victim's finger-nails, is it not?'

'Yes.'

'Help the court by telling us why that is done?'

'It is invariably instinctive for people to try to fight off their attackers: do something in self-defence. It is very common to find skin or blood particles or hair beneath a victim's fingernails.'

'Did you carry out such tests upon Gerald Lomax?'

'Yes.'

'And recover the evidence you sought?'

'Yes. Some skin particles and blood. There was no hair.'

An idea of what more he could do burst upon Jeremy Hall, so startling that for several moments he remained unspeaking, lost even to his surroundings. It would be absolutely conclusive and sensational – far more sensationally conclusive than he was already sure he could prove Jennifer's innocence – but he needed time and consultation to decide whether to go that far.

He was brought back to the present by a cough from the judge. Jarvis said, 'Mr Hall?' There was none of the irritability of before.

'I beg the court's pardon, my Lord,' apologized Hall. 'What did you do with these samples, professor?'

'Passed them on for forensic analysis.'

'Do you know the results of those analyses?'

'The blood was O Rhesus Negative. I do not know about skin comparison.'

There was a sound in Jennifer's head, like a sharp intake of breath, at the same time as a stir of growing, although still doubtful, realization from the press. Outwardly – audibly throughout the court – the disturbance was very brief, quickly shrouded in total silence.

'*Fuck!*' That was quiet, too. Not even addressed to Jennifer.

'In your expert opinion, professor, would those samples from beneath the fingernails of Gerald Lomax have come from his attacker, in his desperate attempt to fight that attacker off?'

'Unquestionably.'

'I want to challenge you upon that, professor. Unquestionably? Beyond any reasonable doubt, in your mind?'

'Unquestionably beyond any reasonable doubt.'

Again Keflin-Brown did not re-examine.

Anthony Billington came into the witness-box wearing the same taut, second-skin suit, his freckle-dotted face creased with curiosity at his recall. Because of its importance, Jeremy Hall began by taking the forensic expert through his qualifications and years of experience in his highly technical science.

'You head the Home Office forensic pathological investigation team?'

'Yes.' Billington's face coloured slightly, at the acknowledgement.

'I would like to explore more fully than I did earlier upon what you found when you entered Gerald Lomax's office, on the day of the murder. His body – and Mrs Lomax – were still in situ?'

'Yes.'

'You told us you took blood samples?'

'Yes.'

'How?'

'Both were – in the case of the man had been – bleeding profusely. I took slide provision.'

'Explain to us what slide provision means.'

'I quite simply took samples of blood, from both

people, later to transfer on to slides, for scientific examination.'

'Externally, from their weeping wounds. Not by intravenous extraction?'

'It was not necessary to draw blood off by needle.'

'Wouldn't that open the possibility of error? Picking up, for example, blood that might have splashed from another wounded person and not been that of the person to which you later ascribed it?'

'The circumstances of this case – of my scene-of-crime examination – were extremely unusual. The victim and his attacker were still there. No-one else had been involved. I lifted blood samples not from just one but from several open wounds of both people. By taking more than one sample and from separate sites, I ensured no splash error could contaminate my analysis.'

The silence Hall intruded now was intentional and very mannered: he was, he accepted, performing like Keflin-Brown. When it had stretched almost to break point, Hall echoed, '"The circumstances of this case were extremely unusual . . . no-one else was involved." Are you sure about that, Doctor?'

'Of course I'm sure about it!' said Billington, irritated by the doubt. 'I was there. Took the samples.'

'And I am extremely glad that you did,' placated Hall. 'How many blood groups did you identify from the scene of the crime?'

'Two.'

'What were they?'

'AB Rhesus Positive and O Rhesus Negative.'

The press gallery was in a tightly controlled frenzy and the burn on Jennifer's skin was so bad now she had surreptitiously to scratch her arms and her legs. Ann

Wardle was at once alert beside her. Jennifer whispered, 'It's all right.'

'Identify each to the persons from whom you obtained those samples, Dr Billington.'

'Gerald Lomax was AB Rhesus Positive. Mrs Lomax was O Rhesus Negative.'

In his satisfied excitement it was frustrating for Hall to hold back his presentation in the necessary, step-by-step order. 'You took blood samples other than from the wounds of Gerald and Jennifer Lomax, did you not?'

'Yes.'

'What about from the window, overlooking the trading floor?'

'Several samples.'

'There were some fingerprints, in blood, on that window, were there not?'

'Yes.'

'Did you take a sample from those bloodied fingerprints: where the blood might have run down the window.'

'Yes, I did.'

'But not in any way to affect the definition of the fingerprints.'

'Of course not!' said the scientist, affronted.

'Can you tell the court the group of the blood you took, running down from the fingerprints?'

'O Rhesus Negative.'

'You are absolutely sure of that?'

'There is no possible doubt.'

'O Rhesus Negative is an unusual blood group, is it not?'

'Yes.'

'One you would be unlikely to confuse or make a mistake over?'

'I do not *make* mistakes in my analyses.'

Jennifer couldn't properly recognize the noise in her head. It was a groaned, near wailing sound: despair almost. Jennifer didn't want to challenge at that moment – was still nervous of challenging – but she thought: Jane *has* lost. Not me that beat her. Jeremy Hall. But she's lost. And then she waited for a diatribe but nothing came. There was still a tingle but her skin was much cooler, no longer physically irritating or sensitive to the touch.

'I'm greatly obliged to you for establishing that in the court. You just didn't lift blood from the window: you lifted the fingerprints picked out in that blood, didn't you, doctor?'

'Yes.'

'Whose fingerprints?'

'Mrs Lomax's.'

'What proof did you have that they were Mrs Lomax's?'

'They couldn't have been anyone else's!'

'Why not?'

'That's where she'd stood, with her hands splayed against the window.'

'You'd seen her stand like that?'

'Don't be ridiculous!'

'How do you know that's how she'd stood?'

Less belligerently, Billington said, 'I was told, by the police.'

'By whom, of the police, exactly?'

'Detective Inspector Rodgers. He was there with Superintendent Bentley when I arrived.'

'And they pointed out to you Mrs Lomax's fingerprints on the window?'

'She was slumped directly beneath them.'

'That wasn't my question, Doctor,' said Hall, letting

nothing slip past. 'Did Superintendent Bentley and Inspector Rodgers identify fingerprints in blood upon the window as those of Mrs Lomax?'

'Yes.'

'Did they later provide officially taken fingerprints of Mrs Lomax, for you to make a scientific match?'

Billington hesitated, looking for guidance to Keflin-Brown, who remained unhelpfully with his head sunk against his chest. Finally Billington said, 'No.'

'So there was no proper scientific, forensic comparison between the bloodstained fingerprints upon Gerald Lomax's office window and fingerprints taken from Mrs Jennifer Lomax?'

Billington was no longer deathly pale. His face blazed, in odd contrast to his red hair. He looked hopefully again to the prosecuting barrister, who steadfastly refused to answer the plea. 'No.'

'That means, doesn't it, Doctor, that your evidence of the bloody fingerprints being those of Mrs Lomax has no forensic or scientific basis or value? The police told you whose they were and you accepted it, entirely upon their word!'

Billington didn't reply.

'Doctor Billington?' demanded Jarvis, all his waspishness transferred.

'Yes, it does,' finally admitted the forensic scientist.

'There were two types of blood upon the knife . . .' At Hall's gesture, the usher offered it to the perspiring witness. '. . . What were they?'

'AB Rhesus Positive and O Rhesus Negative.'

'And fingerprints?' persisted Hall, relentlessly.

'The same as those upon the window.'

'As the Home Office's first choice – its leader – in

forensic examination, would you consider yourself an expert in fingerprint comparison?'

'It is not my particular discipline but I am practised in it,' qualified the scientist.

'You have a chart of those bloody fingerprints, among the documents in front of you, do you not?'

'Yes.'

'I fully accept that these are not what you would consider proper scientific conditions, but would you compare these prints against the chart you claim to be Mrs Lomax's fingerprints?' asked Hall, gesturing again to the attentive usher to take the offered sheet to the scientist.

Billington spent several minutes studying the two sheets, side by side, at one stage taking a pocket magnifying glass from his strained suit. At last he looked up and pronounced, 'They do not match.'

'You mean they are the fingerprints of two different people?' persisted Hall.

'Yes.'

'Do you need to take them away to a laboratory, for more detailed examination?'

'I will of course do so if the court orders it. But I do not think it is necessary . . .' He waved with his pocket device like a flag of surrender. 'Even under this magnification the difference is obvious. One set is peaked, the other whorled. And the linear difference between the two is obvious, almost to the naked eye.'

'You also found – and eliminated – another set of finger-prints in Gerald Lomax's office: those of the cleaner?'

'Yes.'

'Would you compare what I have just handed you with those prints you lifted?'

It did not take the man as long this time. 'Again they are quite different.'

'You found some hair strands in Gerald Lomax's office, did you not?'

'Yes,' agreed Billington, cautiously.

'Whose were they?'

Billington's sigh filled the hesitation. 'I was told they were Mrs Lomax's. She's blond. So was the hair.'

'By whom were you told?'

'Superintendent Bentley.'

'Did you make comparison tests, from proven samples of Mrs Lomax's hair?' The earlier, half-formed idea was hardening in Hall's mind. He'd been demeaned, humiliated and shat upon by a pompous legal establishment and he wanted every ounce of revenge – and humbled recognition – that he was owed.

'None was made available to me.'

'Answer the question, Doctor Billington.'

'No, I did not make any comparison.'

'What about a B Rhesus Positive blood group?' demanded Hall, abruptly and intentionally going in yet another direction.

'I don't understand that question.'

'Did you, from anywhere in Gerald Lomax's office, lift blood subsequently identified as B Rhesus Positive?'

'No.'

'From the extensive sampling you took, do you believe you would have found B Rhesus Positive if there had been traces in Gerald Lomax's office?'

'Yes.'

'From your forensic examination of Gerald Lomax's office how many people were in it, at the time of his murder?'

'Two.'

'No-one else?'

'No. It isn't possible.'

'Doctor Billington, what explanation can you give the court when I tell you that the fingerprints I have just made available to you are those of Mrs Jennifer Lomax, taken last night in the presence of a number of witnesses, including the police? And that Mrs Lomax's blood group, again taken last night to confirm five different earlier samplings, is not O Rhesus Negative, but B Rhesus Positive? Or that the hair you early testified before this court to be that of Mrs Lomax is quite different, in colour, from that taken last night and which is, as we talk, being subjected to DNA analytical comparison.'

The scientist shook his head. 'That isn't possible.'

'It's more than possible, Doctor Billington. They are unarguable facts, witnessed among others last night by my learned friend for the prosecution, Mr Keflin-Brown.'

It was several minutes before Billington was able to reply. Then he said, 'I can't explain it . . . it's beyond explanation . . .' He looked apprehensively across the court at Jennifer. '. . . It's too frightening to explain . . .'

Everyone else in the court was looking at Jennifer at that moment. And there was very little noise.

There was a great deal, however, in the cells during the lunchtime adjournment. Twice the force of Jennifer's convulsions threw not just herself but both wardresses trying to support her off their feet. The harangue in Jennifer's head was so loud it made her scream with pain. She defecated and urinated at the same time but because her dress was up around her waist in a struggle with the wardresses it wasn't stained. Jennifer was too distraught – too possessed – to be embarrassed that it happened in front of Hall and Perry or that the corridor outside was crowded with onlookers. Everything Hall tried to say to her was drowned beneath obscene, shouted invective and so he stopped trying.

It ended as abruptly and dramatically as it began, with the arrival of the duty doctor and the Librium she'd refused earlier.

'*Don't want that. Not working things out properly.*'

'Please go,' pleaded Jennifer, to the two lawyers, wrinkling her nose at her own odour. 'This is disgusting! I'm all right.'

Nervous of the reaction it might cause, Hall nevertheless said, 'It's going well. Remember, don't worry about anything happening in the dock.'

'Jarvis wouldn't like *that* happening in the dock,' said Perry, as they both left the cell, Hall herding the bystanders away.

Neither man felt like eating. It was automatic to make their way to the canteen but having reached it they turned away, going back into the court corridors. Perry said, 'You believe it, don't you? That there's another person – Jane – in her head?'

'Don't you?' said Hall, avoiding the answer.

Perry ducked a response, too. 'Have you any idea what this could lead to? I mean there's only one direction Jarvis can order the jury now. And that's before he hears from Forest!' Ross Hamilton Forest II was the Washington lawyer at that moment airborne over the Atlantic.

'I worked all that out last night and early this morning,' said Hall. 'And all right, if you want me to say it, I will. I don't understand it and I'm not sure I want to and I'm frightened and I'm not sure what favours we're doing Jennifer Lomax.'

'I've had some messages,' said Perry, who had come to the cells after Hall and was reluctant to continue their present conversation. 'Forest's plane is on time. Geoffrey Johnson's meeting him personally. They should arrive here by the time the court resumes.'

'Perfect,' said Hall.

'And there was another from Bert Feltham. There's a conference tonight, with Sir Richard.'

'About Jennifer Lomax?' queried Hall. 'Or about whatever it is that made it so important for this case to be dumped upon me in the first place?'

Humphrey Perry didn't reply.

Chapter Twenty-four

Jennifer cleaned herself up but had to discard her already ruined underwear. Without which she felt naked, defenceless – revulsed by herself – and as she tried to restore her hair and repair her make-up the voice said, '*That's what you are, Jennifer, bare-assed, defenceless and revolting. You smell like a pig. And there's really no end to what I can make you do.*'

People are believing me now, she thought.

'*So what, you're still a freak.*'

But not a murderer.

'*The show ain't over till the fat lady sings.*'

People know it's you singing, not me.

'*Still a freak.*'

Jennifer made a positive effort to stop the mental conversation. She'd hit her leg, opening the wound, during the convulsion and when he'd re-dressed it the doctor had said it needed to be stitched but that it couldn't be done there. To the wardress Jennifer said, 'I hope I didn't hurt you.'

'We've had worse,' said Ann, speaking for both of them.

'*No you haven't, not yet.*'

Go away! thought Jennifer.

'Not until I've finished. And I've got a lot to do before I've finished.'

'It's pretty unusual up there? What's happening, I mean?' said Ann.

For the first time Jennifer was conscious of a change of attitude from the motherly woman who had befriended her and couldn't understand it. There was a caution, a distancing that hadn't been obvious before.

'Freak!'

'I didn't do it,' said Jennifer, replying to the wardress. 'We're proving I didn't do it.'

'Eerie!' said the second wardress, smiling uncertainly.

'Better get used to it!'

'I've been doing this for eighteen years,' said Ann. 'I've never seen anything like it.'

'It', isolated Jennifer. She was becoming an 'it', not a human being.

'That's what you are, honey: an "it".'

'Would you do something for me?' asked the second woman, tentatively.

'What?' asked Jennifer.

The woman offered a sheet from a notebook she took from the top pocket of her uniform. 'Sign an autograph? My name's Kathleen.' The accent was Irish.

'Hah!'

Jennifer flushed and Ann said to the other wardress: 'Don't be so bloody daft!'

'Of course,' said Jennifer, self-consciously taking the paper.

'There's a place for you in a carnival, along with the bearded lady and the fattest man in the world.'

'If you don't mind then . . . ?' smiled Ann, taking out her own pocket book.

Jennifer signed for the second time. Both women held the paper towards her at arm's length. 'Please stay close to me in court. In case anything happens.'

'They think you're contagious!'

'Sure,' said Kathleen, doubtfully.

'Do you know when it's going to happen: when you're going to be thrown about?' asked Ann.

'I know when she's with me.'

'Is she with you now?'

'Yes.'

Both women stared at her open-mouthed, dumb-struck.

'This is going to be the story of their lives! The only story of their lives.'

'How?' asked Kathleen, breathlessly.

'I don't want her to know.' Jennifer's face was burning and not from Jane's presence. She *did* feel a freak. What the hell was she doing, going along with this inane conversation, responding to their inane, stupid questions?

'You're the woman with two heads! That's the billing! Roll up, roll up, see the woman with two heads, one inside the other!'

Jennifer saw the two wardresses exchange awed looks. 'And I don't want to talk about it any more.'

'No, of course not,' accepted Ann, immediately deferential. 'It's time we were moving anyway.'

Jeremy Hall and Humphrey Perry were beside the dock when Jennifer re-entered, putting themselves between her and the press, who were noisier than ever before. Four journalists were outside the gallery, waiting for her to appear. When she did they surged forward, to be intercepted by police and a black-gowned court official. Perry moved to meet them. Each thrust pieces of paper at the solicitor, who accepted them.

'More autographs?' demanded Jennifer.

'What?' frowned Hall.

'What's all that about?' she demanded.

'Nothing for you to worry about. Is everything all right?'

'How do I know?' Jennifer was at once aware of the self-pity. 'Yes. I'm OK.'

'You're going to be fine.'

'Am I?' Hall wasn't standing as close to the dock edge as he could have done.

'*Not if I can prevent it.*'

From the bench there were demands for silence from the clerk. Hall hurried towards his place as Jarvis strutted into court, glowering towards the media. He remained looking in their direction when he sat. 'Your editors are already aware of my feelings about press intrusion. If your behaviour in this court offends me, then I shall conduct the remainder of this trial *in camera*, excluding you all. I want what I have said reported, verbatim, by whichever of you represent news agencies, so that all editors are aware of my feelings. I want that done now. I will not reconvene this court until it is done.'

Two men and a woman rose sheepishly from their places and hurried out. There were four court artists now, all sketching. Jennifer was conscious of every single person in the court staring at her. And that despite their undertaking, neither Ann nor Kathleen had their seats as close to her any longer.

'*Freak.*'

Not going to get me convicted of murder, thought Jennifer.

'*Never intended to, remember?*'

Jarvis had so subdued the court that the return of the news agency reporters was audible before they came into Jennifer's vision to regain their seats.

'Mr Hall?' invited the judge, with the briefest grimaced smile.

There was no swagger this time when Superintendent Bentley approached the witness-box. The suit, blue, was as immaculate as before but there was no buttonhole carnation.

'You headed the investigation into the murder of Gerald Lomax?'

'Yes, sir.'

'Sir', noted Hall. 'There are certain standard procedures in such investigations, are there not?'

'Yes, sir.'

'Is one of those standard procedures taking fingerprints from an accused, once that accused has been charged?'

'Yes, sir.' Bentley wasn't addressing the assembled journalists, nor smiling in their direction.

'Did you or one of your junior officers do that, in this case?'

'No, sir.'

'Why not?'

'Mrs Lomax declined to make a statement after I charged her,' tried the detective. 'That refusal was confirmed by her solicitor and by you.'

Hall stretched the pause as long as he felt able. Then, 'Superintendent, we are not discussing statements here, are we? We are talking of standard, operating procedures in murder investigations.'

'Yes, sir.'

'You ignored the standard, operating procedures you should have followed in the case of Mrs Lomax, didn't you?'

'She was too ill to be fingerprinted on the day of the murder,' Bentley fought, desperately. 'After that our enquiries were obstructed.'

'Obstructed?' seized Hall. 'Obstructed by whom?'

'My officers and I were denied the opportunity of interviewing or taking a statement from Mrs Lomax by yourself and by her solicitor.'

Hall wasn't perturbed the cross-examination was temporarily going sideways: the detective was damning himself with virtually every answer. 'Did you, at any time, approach myself or Mr Perry, my instructing solicitor, with a request to fingerprint Mrs Lomax?'

'No, sir,' admitted Hall, miserably, all the bombast gone.

'*Perry Mason shit. Who's impressed?*'

I am: you should be, thought Jennifer.

'*Guy's an amateur. Dumped on you.*'

'Did you instruct any of your junior officers to make such a request?'

'No, sir.'

'So no official police fingerprints were obtained of a person whom you had charged with murder?'

'No, sir.'

'That was a grave mistake, wasn't it, Superintendent? A clear failure to follow standard operating procedures?'

'Yes, sir,' conceded Bentley. His face was blazing.

'I didn't hear that,' protested Jarvis, glaring down.

'Yes, sir,' repeated Bentley.

'Yes, sir, to what?'

'It was a grave mistake for us not to have taken fingerprints.' Bentley practically choked on the words.

'In your evidence-in-chief you were obviously proud of your conviction record. Twelve, was it not?'

'Yes, sir.'

'Do you consider yourself an expert in murder investigations, Superintendent?'

Bentley did not immediately reply, fervently seeking an

answer that couldn't be turned against him. In the end, hoping formality would save him, he said, 'I have brought to a successful conclusion twelve murder investigations.'

'An enviable record,' agreed Hall. 'So murders are a crime you have wide and long experience of investigating?'

'Yes, sir.'

'After the conclusion of yesterday's hearing, you were present with myself and others when the fingerprints of the accused – fingerprints you had failed to obtain – were finally taken?'

Bentley squirmed. 'Yes.'

He could be forgiven for finally omitting the 'sir' but for nothing else, Hall decided. 'Were you given the opportunity last night to compare Mrs Lomax's fingerprints with those lifted from the glass wall of Gerald Lomax's office?'

'I was.'

'And were you in court this morning to hear the evidence of the prosecution's forensic scientist, Doctor Billington?'

'I was.'

'They don't match, do they?'

'No.'

'You also heard Doctor Billington's evidence about blood type and grouping?'

'Yes.'

'Mrs Lomax's blood does not match any of that found in Gerald Lomax's office, does it?'

'No, sir.'

'Superintendent,' said Hall, allowing the patronizing tone. 'As an expert in murder investigations – a man who has successfully brought twelve murderers to rightful justice – would you have charged Mrs Lomax with murder if you'd properly carried out the investigation you should have done, from which you would have realized the fingerprints upon the bloodstained murder weapon were not those of Mrs Lomax?'

'Sixteen people witnessed her do it!' protested Bentley, writhing.

'Her fingerprints are not on the knife, are they?' persisted Hall.

'No.'

'Her blood isn't at the scene, is it?'

'No.'

'So answer my question. Would you have charged her with murder?'

'I would have referred it to higher authority,' said the detective.

'Superintendent, who, in your expert opinion and now with the benefit of the forensic evidence you did not earlier have, do you believe murdered Gerald Lomax?'

Bentley looked desperately around the court, as if seeking inspiration. As with Billington, earlier, Keflin-Brown steadfastly refused any rescue because no rescue was possible.

'Answer the question, Superintendent!' demanded Jarvis, a bully with a new target.

'I don't know, sir,' Bentley finally capitulated.

'You do not know who killed Gerald Lomax?' echoed Hall, triumphantly.

'No.'

'I am grateful, finally, for your honesty,' said Hall to Keflin-Brown's headshake against the offer to re-examine. As Malcolm Rodgers was summoned, the older barrister leaned sideways and said quietly, 'You're not taking prisoners, are you?'

'Not as readily as everyone else was prepared to do,' said Hall. He'd made his decision upon that morning's idea. Perry would probably argue against it. So, most definitely, would the heavy breathing, unctuous Feltham along with Sir Richard Proudfoot. So they wouldn't get the opportunity: they'd be presented with a *fait accompli*.

Inspector Malcolm Rodgers was an ambitious career policeman who'd hitched his wagon to Superintendent Bentley's unstoppable express but who now detected the vibrations of an impending fatal crash. And who had decided, the previous night and then again listening in court so far that day, that it was time to disconnect the coupling. He studiously avoided the staccato and truculent answers that Bentley had given, repeating again and again that he'd gone through every stage of the investigation under the command of a superior officer. He regretted that superior officer had not insisted upon Mrs Lomax's fingerprints being taken. And would obviously have himself ordered it done by a junior officer – or done it himself – had he not automatically assumed the order for such basic routine had been given while he was otherwise engaged. He could offer no explanation or suggestion for the disparity between the fingerprints and the blood. Certainly, from none of the sixteen eyewitnesses was there evidence of anyone other than Gerald and Jennifer Lomax being in the totally visible room at the time of Gerald Lomax's death.

'Who then, in your opinion, killed the man?' demanded Hall.

'I do not know, sir,' dutifully replied the responsibility-avoiding detective.

Which brought Jeremy Hall to Ross Hamilton Forest II, senior partner in the Washington DC law firm of

Forest, Pilton and Camperstone, a white-haired, cultivated man with practised, courtly manners and a clipped, New England accent. Forest had reached the court fifteen minutes before the afternoon resumption, giving Hall ample time to read and discuss the documentation the man carried. It was, in fact, that documentation that finally decided Hall upon the application he intended making. But which now – while Forest was being formally sworn and thanked by Sir Ivan Jarvis for his Atlantic dash ('an act of unprecedented legal cooperation between our two countries and our two legal systems,') to Forest's repeated assurance that it was nothing, nothing at all, sir – Jeremy Hall had stomach-hollowing second thoughts.

He had sufficient to create reasonable doubt, the corner-stone of defence. To seek more – which he could – would turn what the following day's newspapers and television would build into a legal and public phenomenon, for which there wasn't an adjective extravagant enough to describe. And for whom would he be doing it, by going further? For Jennifer, whose categoric instructions had been to prove her not guilty of murder? Or for his impatient, ambitious self, cynically grabbing the opportunity to pole-vault ten, maybe fifteen mundane, ladder-climbing years with one mighty leap to the Sir Richard Proudfoot ice-capped echelon? Yet more questions for which he couldn't find an answer. Maybe never would.

After the pleasantries from on high, Hall went through the ritual at his level, tempering the sycophancy by coupling it with the establishment of Ross Hamilton Forest's legal qualifications.

That done, Hall said, 'At the request of my instructing solicitor, Mr Perry, did you some time ago establish in the United States of America the marriage of Gerald James Lomax to Jane Mary Herbetson?'

In Jennifer's head there was again the sound of sharply indrawn breath. '*I don't want to hear this.*'

You don't have a choice: isn't that what you're always telling me? thought Jennifer.

'*Shut up!*'

Tables turned!

'I did, sir,' beamed Forest. He had the tanned face of a man who conducted a lot of business on a golf course or from a yacht on the Potomac.

'Jane Mary Herbetson was Gerald Lomax's first wife?'

'She was indeed, sir.'

'The daughter of one of the most respected families in Virginia?'

'Proud history going back over two hundred years, according to my enquiries: one of the founding fathers of our great and good country,' said the American lawyer, proudly. 'Her father was the Episcopalian bishop: there's a bust in his cathedral, commemorating the work and the impact he made within his diocese. Mrs Herbetson was an extremely rich woman and throughout their lives together – and after her unfortunate death – the bishop was an extremely generous benefactor. He personally paid for two schools and a clinic for the disadvantaged. In his will he left a substantial bequest in trust to benefit the poor.'

'What do you mean by Mrs Herbetson's "unfortunate" death?'

'The poor lady drowned, in a boating accident when Jane was just fifteen years old.'

'*Pompous legal prick. Probably first generation descent from some Irish shit-kicker!*'

'As I understand it, Mr Forest, there is a certain

statutory health requirement in your country – certainly in the State of Virginia – prior to marriage?'

'There most certainly is, sir.'

'*Bastard! Bastard! Bastard!*'

'Of particular importance in view of a condition from which Jane Mary Herbetson suffered from birth?'

'The poor child was a diabetic.'

'*Poor child, my ass!*'

'Quite so, as this court has already heard. What is the requirement we're talking about?'

'Blood tests, sir. To ensure compatibility: a protection for offspring. And for any hereditary disease.'

'Such tests were conducted upon Gerald Lomax and Jane Mary Herbetson?'

Despite the judge's earlier warning there was a growing murmur of anticipation from the media coral. Jarvis looked sharply towards it: the noise lessened only very slightly.

'They were, sir.'

'And are retained, on file?'

'For a statutory period.'

'You were able to gain access to those records and have an affidavit from the doctor who compiled them sworn before a judge in Washington DC yesterday? And which you produce to my Lord and to this court today?'

On cue the American took an impressively bound folder from his briefcase and handed it to the waiting usher.

'Would you tell the court the blood group registered as that of Gerald James Lomax?'

'AB Rhesus Positive.'

Here we go, thought Hall, the moment of no-turning-back commitment: saving Jennifer from one fate without any idea of what other she might be thrust into by what he was going to say and do. 'And would you tell the court the blood group registered as that of Jane Mary Herbetson?'

'O Rhesus Negative.'

The court exploded, beyond any control. The predominant reaction was, predictably, from the media in a virtual mass exodus from the room. But there was a lot of noise, discernible gasps, from the jury. An aviary of sound descended from above from the public gallery.

The time it took to restore order gave Jeremy Hall the opportunity finally to make up his mind. His primary duty, always, was to Jennifer. And the only course open to Sir Ivan Jarvis was now a positive direction that to proceed upon the newly available evidence would be unsafe, in law. Which fell short of a verdict of not guilty. So, Hall convinced himself, he had to press on. He turned, to smile at the strained-faced Jennifer, aware as he did so of several of the returning journalists bunched around Humphrey Perry, who was making rapid, dismissive hand gestures.

There was still some noise when Jarvis hurried Hall on, but it ended abruptly when Hall turned back to the American, no-one wanting to miss a single word of the exchange.

'Those findings are written ones, the result of pathological examination carried out prior to the marriage?' Hall resumed. 'The actual samples themselves no longer exist.'

'No, sir. Storage would be an impossible task.'

'Mr Forest, you have travelled an extremely long way for what may seem a very short period of time to give evidence in this court. But, in thanking you, I assure you your help and your evidence has been invaluable.'

Once again Keflin-Brown declined to examine and

there was a hiatus of several minutes while Jarvis effusively thanked the American lawyer, who, equally effusive, insisted it had been a pleasure.

'Mr Keflin-Brown?' invited the judge, after Forest stood down.

'As I made clear to you in chambers this morning, my Lord, I am subject to your direction.'

'I am minded, Mr Hall, to make a certain recommendation to the jury. Is there anything further upon which you feel it necessary to address me, before I do that?'

'There is, my Lord. But with the greatest respect, anticipating your Lordship's possible feelings, I wonder if my submission might be made in the absence of the jury . . . ?'

'*What's the sneaky little bastard up to now?*'

Something else to screw you.

'*He's just building up penalty points against you. You'll be sorry.*'

Hall was aware of Keflin-Brown's sharp look and of Jarvis's face closing against him. The judge said, 'I trust you can infer the way my mind is directed. And I have allowed you considerable leniency, Mr Hall.'

'Which I must assure your Lordship I have not – nor will – abuse.'

'You are insisting?'

'I am humbly requesting.'

'Members of the jury,' said Jarvis, turning towards them. 'You will be taken to a room assigned for your deliberations while I hear a submission from learned counsel. You are not being excluded. Indeed, if I so decide, I will fully acquaint you upon your return with what Mr Hall has said. The purpose of asking you temporarily to leave is to prevent anything wrongly said during legal exchanges adversely to affect your final deliberations. I hope it possible to recall you very shortly.'

As the jury filed away Hall felt a tug at his gown and leaned back towards Humphrey Perry. 'What are you going to do?' demanded the solicitor. 'It was obvious he was going to rule the prosecution unsafe. We've won.'

'I'm going to prove her totally innocent . . .' said Hall. He hesitated, guessing from how close and attentive Keflin-Brown was holding himself that the man could probably hear. '. . . and identify the real murderer.'

Jarvis held up his hand against Hall speaking, going again to the media. 'You should all of you be aware of the restrictions when a jury is out of court. But I will once again remind you. Not one single word of what is said in their absence can be reported. I will have my clerk and other court officers read every newspaper, listen to every radio transmission and watch every television broadcast. If I recognize one word from what is about to be discussed, the provider of that report and his or her editor will be jailed for contempt . . .' He turned back to the barristers. 'Mr Hall?'

'It is my submission, my Lord, that upon the evidence I have brought before you today, it would be legally unsafe to continue the prosecution for murder against my client—'

'Which it was unnecessary to send the jury out to make,' broke in the judge. 'And precisely the guidance I intend to make to the jury.'

'I'm obliged for that advice, my Lord. But it will not constitute a verdict of not guilty for my client.'

'Of course it will in everything but pronouncement, Mr Hall. You're nitpicking.'

'With respect, my Lord, there is something more that could be done publicly and totally to exonerate my client of any guilt for the crime upon which she has been arraigned.'

Jarvis's face was furrowed into a frown that made him appear more wizened than ever.

'*What the fuck now!*'

'What is that, Mr Hall?'

'As your Lordship has already heard, the shank of hair recovered from Gerald Lomax's office is a different colour from that of Mrs Lomax. Last night, with Mrs Lomax's agreement, samples were taken of her hair. Both are at this moment being subjected to DNA analysis and comparison, not just by Doctor Billington but by a separate forensic expert engaged by the defence. I am hopeful of a result within the next twenty-four hours. Some of the O Rhesus Negative blood is also being subjected to DNA matching . . .'

'. . . Your submission, Mr Hall, your submission!'

'The grave of Mrs Jane Lomax is in Mortlake cemetery. I am applying to you, my Lord, for an exhumation order for that grave to be opened for DNA tests upon the hair and bone that the coffin will still contain. And for the findings of those tests to be compared with the DNA found in the blood and hair currently being examined by defence and prosecution forensic specialists—'

'*NO!*' Jennifer stopped herself echoing the deafening scream but couldn't prevent being hurled bodily across the dock so violently that she crashed into its side. Her breath was knocked completely from her and the duty doctor who examined her in the dock guessed at two cracked ribs. When the doctor insisted upon X-rays – which later confirmed three – Hall immediately applied for bail, with a condition of residency in hospital. Within an hour she was back in the same private ward at St Thomas's to which she'd been admitted after the murder.

Completing the coincidence, she was put under the care of Dr Peter Lloyd, who travelled from the court with her in the ambulance.

With difficulty, wincing against the pain, Jennifer said, 'I'm glad it's you. There's something I need to know.' She wasn't going back to prison to be used as a sex toy, she realized.

Jarvis continued in Jennifer's absence. The fully co-operative Keflin-Brown hurriedly supported Hall's application – totally aware of the incredible events and inevitable publicity in the wake of which he was being borne along – and the judge issued the exhumation order with a further injunction against press intrusion, warning that he was extending the precincts of the court for a radius of five hundred yards around the grave of the first Mrs Lomax.

When he arrived at St Thomas's, Hall realized he'd made an error in not anticipating what would be happening there and by failing to ask the judge for an additional precincts order. The hospital authorities had already complained and adding to the irony of Jennifer's return Superintendent Hopkins was again in charge of the police unit confronting the press siege. There was none of the officious belligerence he'd shown towards Hall for Emily's disastrous visit. They were doing their best to prevent any media person entering the premises, he reported formally, and there were uniformed officers in the corridor outside Jennifer's ward, intercepting anyone who approached. Four journalists and two photographers had already been arrested and charged with behaviour likely to cause a breach of the peace: one, an Italian, had been wearing a white coat and insisted he was a doctor.

'Is it a fact that she's genuinely possessed by the first wife?' demanded the policeman, incredulous.

'I think so.'

'What's going to happen to her?'

'I don't know.' He wished he did, thought Hall, moving through the hospital. His responsibility towards Jennifer Lomax ended with the conclusion of the trial, extending beyond that only to any outstanding legal formalities. But the end of the trial was hardly going to be the end of her problems. But they weren't legal, he warned himself. They were personal: medically – or perhaps more accurately psychiatrically – personal. Not his consideration then.

He was challenged twice at the level of Jennifer's ward, once directly outside the elevator and again at the police barrier outside the individual room. There it needed Dr Lloyd's intervention to persuade the suspicious policeman he really was Jennifer's lawyer.

She smiled wanly up at him as he entered the room. 'Here we are again.' She plucked at the hospital-issue nightdress. 'And the fashion hasn't changed.'

'*And I'm still here, too.*'

'How are you?' asked Hall.

'It hurts, when I breathe.' He'd moved the chair away from the bed, not closer, when he sat.

'*Frightened of you. Frightened of me. Cowardy, cowardy custard, his balls are made of mustard.*'

'The judge granted the order.'

Jennifer was ready, gripping the side of the bed. The movement vibrated though her and the voice screamed, '*Mother-fucker. I'd get you too, if I could.*'

'She called you a mother-fucker.'

'She's got a dirty mouth,' taunted Hall.

'Will I have to go back to the prison hospital?'

Hall shook his head. 'I got Jarvis to agree to bail, on condition you resided here.'

'*Well aren't you the smarty pants!*'

'Never?' demanded Jennifer, intensely.

'Whatever the result of the exhumation, Jarvis is going to direct the jury that it's unsafe to convict.'

Jennifer closed her eyes. 'Thank God for that!'

'*Doesn't matter a damn.*'

'She says it doesn't matter a damn.'

'Why's she so hysterical then?'

'*Kiss my ass, cocksucker.*'

'You believed me from the beginning, didn't you?' said Jennifer. 'No-one else believed me but you.'

'Yes,' lied Hall. He did now, he accepted, finally confronting the phenomenon. He was talking to a woman inside of whose head there was another woman, a woman he knew all about, a murderer. Believed it so much he was talking to Jane as if she existed: was a real person, in the same room. He shivered, visibly.

'What's the matter?' frowned Jennifer.

'*Scared shitless, that's what's the matter.*'

'Someone walked over my grave,' Hall said, inadequately.

'*Leave mine alone!*'

Jennifer held his eyes for several moments. Then, nodding to the corridor outside, she said, 'There's more police than before.'

Hall shifted, further discomfited. 'The hospital is virtually under media siege. The police outside are to keep them away from you. There's a lot more downstairs.'

'*Freak.*'

'I hadn't thought of that.'

'Neither had I, not until now. Everything's happened very quickly.'

There was another wan smile. 'You did what I asked you. Proved me not guilty. Thank you.' She reached out her hand, towards him.

Hall hesitated, then took it.

'*Where's the fucking violins and pink doves?*'

'I was testing you,' confessed Jennifer.

'Testing me?'

'To see if you'd take my hand. To see if you were frightened of me. She says you are.'

Hall retained her hand. 'Then she's wrong about that, too, isn't she?' It wasn't a lie. He wasn't scared. He was . . . He didn't know what he was but it wasn't fear. Disbelief, perhaps? No, it couldn't be that. He'd already decided he did believe. It was, he supposed, how someone would feel confronting a creature from outer space, although the analogy offended him, because Jennifer Lomax wasn't an alien creature. Despite what she'd gone through – was still going through – she was a very beautiful and physically attractive woman. He released her hand. Not that he felt any physical attraction. To have allowed that would have been unprofessional: he had to behave like a doctor in that respect.

'*I'm not wrong! He's scared. Everyone's going to be scared. You're going to be a pariah for the rest of your life. We'll get you a drum. That's what it means, you know. A drummer because that's what Hindu pariahs do, beat a drum as a warning for people to get out of the way when they're coming.*'

'I've got to think of Emily, haven't I?'

'You haven't ever stopped.'

'I mean about getting back with her. Properly.'

'I've told you, Annabelle says she's virtually forgotten what happened here.'

'She'll remember, when I go home.'

'You don't know that.'

'I'm frightened that's how it will be.'

'You'll have to take it a step at a time,' said Hall, hating the cliché.

'How long, before it's all finished with the court?'

'Depends how long the DNA takes. Just days.'

'It's been a lifetime.'

'*And it's only just beginning!*'

'Now it's over.'

'I won't have to go back to prison to get my things?'

Hall shook his head again. 'I'll have them collected and taken back to Hampshire. Or to the flat here, if you'd prefer.'

Now Jennifer shook her head, but much more positively. 'That's where he went with Rebecca. In our bed. *My* bed. I don't want to go there again. Not ever. I'll sell it. In fact . . .' She paused. 'I'll certainly be here all day tomorrow?'

'Yes.'

'Ask Geoffrey Johnson to come. He can make arrangements to put it on the market immediately.'

'I'll fix it,' undertook the barrister. It all sounded very normal, so very ordinary. Would it ever be possible for Jennifer Lomax to know normality – to *be* normal – again.

Jennifer looked abruptly to the bedside cabinet and what was on top of it. 'And I can use the telephone, whenever I like, can't I?'

'Yes,' agreed Hall, guessing the point of the question.

'So I could telephone Emily?'

'If you want to.'

'I want to,' said Jennifer, hesitantly. There was a pause. Then she said, 'But I don't know what to say to her.' There was a further silence before she added, 'And there's something else . . .'

Hall waited for Jennifer to finish but she didn't.

Jeremy Hall wasn't conscious of being followed from the hospital until he parked along the Embankment and was immediately surrounded by people who leapt from three separate cars which screeched to a haphazard halt behind him. There were seven reporters, three women among them. They all began talking and shouting at once, drowning each other out, and for several moments Hall was totally bewildered.

'Who are you? What . . . ?'

The names of the newspapers were the first thing that positively registered. He didn't bother to match the identification with the representatives.

'Is she all right?'

'What's she say?'

'What's Jane telling her?'

'Can Jane make her do whatever she wants?'

'She's a Frankenstein, isn't she?'

'Will she always have to be locked up, as a danger?'

Hall used his bulk to shoulder his way through, shaking his head but saying nothing. Envelopes were thrust at him and instinctively he took them.

'That's not final.'

'We'll negotiate.'

'Call us first, before anyone else.'

'We'll be sympathetic, put Jennifer's side of the story.'

The cordon was much bigger around his chambers. When the crowd saw him approaching there was the blinding whiteness of cameras and television lights and

Hall actually stumbled into people he could not see. It was impossible to distinguish anything from the shouted, screaming questions. More envelopes were thrust towards him, which he let fall to the ground. It wasn't until after he bulldozed his way through and was admitted through the briefly unbolted door by the uniformed porter that Hall realized he was still clutching those that had first been forced upon him.

Everyone was already assembled in Proudfoot's room. The QC and Bert Feltham were in shirt-sleeves: Mickey Mouse figures were propelled up and down Feltham's braces by the heaviness of his breathing. Humphrey Perry looked mournful.

Proudfoot said, 'What the hell have we opened up here?'

'Pandora's Box?' suggested Hall. After the previous night entirely without sleep he was suddenly extremely tired.

'I've never known anything like it. It's incredible. We've called the police, to clear them,' said Proudfoot.

Choosing partly to misunderstand, Hall said, 'There's never *been* anything like this. That's why they're here. It's as bad at the hospital. I was followed back.' He looked uncertainly at the envelopes in his hand and thrust them towards Perry.

'It'll be more offers,' predicted the solicitor, holding up a sheaf of already opened letters. '*The Sunday Times* heads the list at the moment. Quarter of a million. They all say they're prepared to negotiate. And that they'll be sympathetic, whatever that means.'

Proudfoot indicated the open cocktail cabinet and said to the younger barrister, 'Help yourself.'

Hall wasn't a drinker but he poured whisky, deciding that night he not only needed but deserved it. He wondered if there would be any congratulations for representing a client as he had. He said, 'I hadn't thought this far ahead. Anticipated the reaction.'

'I don't want it to continue,' declared Proudfoot, accusingly. 'I'm wondering what the Bar Council attitude will be.'

'Disappointment among its members that they're not involved,' guessed Hall, cynically. 'And I don't see how I could have avoided it.'

'Applying for exhumation was unnecessary,' insisted Proudfoot.

'If the DNA is the same as that at the scene, Jennifer Lomax will be officially and fully declared not guilty instead of the trial closing because the evidence is unsafe.'

'Which means Gerald Lomax was murdered by a ghost,' said Proudfoot, contemptuously.

'Yes,' said Hall, with flat simplicity. 'The court has already accepted evidence that proves that.'

A heavy silence encompassed the room. It was broken by the wheezing Bert Feltham. 'I've gone through the transcript of today's evidence. That's exactly what it proves.'

'Precisely a Pandora's Box,' said Perry, distantly.

Hall helped himself to more whisky, uninvited. 'We can only go on a day at a time,' he said, remembering it was the cliché he'd used at the hospital because he couldn't think of anything.

Proudfoot smiled, in sudden affability. 'Thought I might sit in, at the resumption.'

Wigged, gowned and ready for recognition inside and out of the court, guessed Hall, bitterly. 'I'm sure Mr Justice Jarvis would welcome someone rumoured to be his successor.' He was tired and fed up and didn't care.

'It might not be a good idea, for that and other reasons,' cautioned Feltham.

'Reasons that might affect my case?' demanded Hall, considering the impertinence justified if it did, although he couldn't imagine how. He slightly stressed 'my'.

Proudfoot looked sharply at his Chief Clerk, who flushed in unaccustomed and rare embarrassment, dragging an inhaler from his pocket. Proudfoot said, 'It's of no consequence. I don't think I will attend.'

'It is of consequence if it is in any way connected with my client,' insisted Hall, curious at the obvious feeling between the two men.

Proudfoot sighed, heightening Feltham's colour with another look. The older barrister said, 'We have accepted the brief to represent Enco-Corps in a civil matter. Some derivatives dealing in copper, predominantly on the Far East market.'

'And?' persisted Hall, dissatisfied.

Now Proudfoot looked at Humphrey Perry. 'We understood at the outset there was no question of culpability on the part of Enco-Corps: that they were acting in genuine good faith for Asian dealers. It would seem, however, that there might be some doubt . . .'

Hall waited.

'Gerald Lomax was inflating prices on offer to Hong Kong and Singapore,' finally admitted Proudfoot. 'Manipulating the buy-in prices. It created a snowball effect, artificially heating both exchanges. Dealers panicked, continuing to buy high to cover their losses.'

'Will it become public?' demanded Hall. The deal, he recognized at once. His uncle had allowed the Jennifer Lomax murder to be dumped on to the chambers – and personally on to him, whose career was still too new to be of any importance – to gain a civil brief that would take months to prepare and months to litigate, all at a fee of £1,000 a day.

'In my opinion any British prosecution will have died with Gerald Lomax himself,' said Proudfoot. 'Rebecca Nicholls' name is on some of the sell orders but she says she was acting on Lomax's instructions: there's nothing criminally to link her.'

And with Gerald Lomax's death went the hope of all that money, thought Hall, satisfaction warming through him. 'Thank you, for advising me.'

'I would have done so, had I considered it had any relevance,' insisted Proudfoot. Now it was he who coloured.

'I have no doubt whatsoever that you would have done,' said Hall, maintaining the sarcasm.

'What shall we do with all these offers,' Perry hurried in to the rescue, waving the letters in his hand like a flag.

'We're Mrs Lomax's agent,' reminded Hall. 'We're required to pass on any correspondence.' He paused. 'I doubt she'll be interested. Money's the one thing she isn't in need of.'

At the hospital Peter Lloyd said, 'There was something you needed to know?'

'I was lesbian raped in prison. They used something: an artificial penis. If it had been used on someone else, someone with AIDs, could I have been infected?'

Lloyd swallowed, swamped with pity. 'I doubt it.'

'But you're not one hundred per cent sure?'

'Would you like to be HIV tested?'

'Yes.'

'*Now here's a whole new ball game!*'

'Are there really ghosts?'

'Of course not,' said Annabelle.

'Margaret Roberts says there are.'

'Well there aren't.'

'Margaret Roberts say's Mummy is a ghost.'

'How can your mummy be a ghost? She's your mummy.'

'She's not here though, is she?'

'She will be, soon.'

Chapter Twenty-five

Conducting the exhumation in the traditional early hours, just before dawn, to minimize public awareness and offence was totally pointless. There needed to be practically a shoulder-to-shoulder cordon of police to enforce the judge's five-hundred-yard radius order around Jane Lomax's grave and beyond that barrier night was transformed into day by the permanently switched-on film and television lights. It was made even brighter by the constant flicker of flashes for cameras that looked more like field guns from the length of their zoom and magnifying lenses, and the noise was almost at battleground level, too. The screens were totally inadequate, diaphanous and far too low, and concealed practically nothing.

It was equally crowded around the burial plot. Two gravediggers toiled under arc lights swarmed by insects, carefully shovelling earth on to canvas protecting the surrounding interments. A black-cassocked vicar stood at the gravestone ('Jane Lomax, much loved and missed wife of Gerald. Always in my heart'), his lips moving in silent prayer. Felix Hewitt and Anthony Billington were encased in sterile white plastic scene-of-crime tunics, complete with fully enclosing head cowls and over-shoes. So were the forensic experts whom Jeremy Hall had engaged, a slim and unexpectedly young woman named Phylis Shipley and beside her a man to whom he had only just been introduced. Harold Carter looked old enough to be the girl's father but visibly deferred to her. There were two uniformed police superintendents, one standing permanently with the exhumation group, the other acting as liaison with the outer police cordon. Hall wasn't sure the liaison officer needed to go back and forth as often as he did but at every approach to the media there was a flashlight explosion, which Hall supposed provided the reason. Standing slightly apart from the superintendents was a police photographer, at the moment the only such operator in the cemetery with an unused camera. Hall had been unsure how to dress and settled for cords and heavy-weather anorak, which was a mistake because it was too hot under the arc lights. Now he stood with it open as wide as possible. He hadn't expected Keflin-Brown but understood the other barrister's presence the moment he saw the size of the press invasion. The older man wore a gaitered plus-four shooting suit, with highly polished brogues and topped off by a peakless cap. Humphrey Perry was dressed for court.

Keflin-Brown said, 'I've got the newspapers in the car: found a shop open early. Astonishing. Absolutely astonishing. You'll be beating clients off with sticks from now on.'

'I'm not sure I want to make a reputation this way.'

'It's happened, whether you like it or not. You're made, old boy. Famous.'

Hall's flat had been surrounded when he'd finally arrived home the previous night. Among the inevitable envelopes in his pigeon hole had been three invitations to television chat shows: £100,000 had been the highest bid for his personal story but all the other offers, nine in all, had insisted they were open to negotiation. Among a lot of messages on his machine from newspapers and publishers there'd been a message from Patricia asking him to ring her. He hadn't. Two cars had followed him when he'd left an hour earlier, to drive to the cemetery. He hadn't opened their envelopes yet and wasn't sure if he'd bother. Pointedly Hall said, 'Mrs Lomax broke three ribs.'

'Oh, yes, of course,' said Keflin-Brown, reminded. 'Painful things, broken ribs.'

'To go with all her other problems.'

'But you've solved her biggest one.'

'Have I?' asked Hall, seriously, looking at the milling scene beyond the police line. 'I'm not sure we even know the full extent of her problems. How many there are, even.'

'You know the rules, old boy. Do your best in wig and gown but say goodbye at the court door.'

'You forgot to mention the fee,' said Hall, sarcastically.

'Never, dear boy. Never forget the fee. And yours should take care of the rent for a year or two.'

There were some muted calls from the grave and almost at once an instinctive move forward. The cleric immediately halted it, indicating a cleared area of canvas to be left for the coffin. One of the diggers lowered himself gently into the grave to thread lifting straps beneath the casket. After several grunted minutes he re-emerged to call for help. The second gravedigger eased himself into the hole and the vicar said, 'Be careful! Do be careful! It's probably very rotten by now.'

For the first time Hall became aware of a smell he'd never experienced before, an odd combination of sour mustiness which was at the same time sweet: at first it was almost pleasant, an unusual perfume but very quickly it became overwhelmingly sickening and Hall's stomach began to churn at the very moment everyone around the grave, with the exception of the two men inside and the vicar, pulled back. Hall saw Phylis Shipley and Hewitt put on nose clips.

'Ready,' declared one of the diggers, clambering out of the grave. Two other cemetery workers who had been standing apart came forward, hefting the lifting straps. The vicar was bowed-headed again, praying aloud now. The count of 'one, two, three,' clashed irreverently. Every camera light came on at the emergence of the coffin as it swung on to the waiting canvas. The police photographer at last had something to do.

Hall became aware of the sound of one and then another helicopter overhead. The graveside police superintendent immediately glanced up, then began talking urgently and loudly into his radio. Hall over-heard 'licence revoked' and 'bugger off.' To the waiting forensic teams, he said, 'Is it going to interfere?'

'Not at the height they are at the moment,' said Hewitt.

'But it'll blow everything about if they come much lower,' added Phylis Shipley.

The officer went back to his radio, talking and listening. He said, 'We've got their registrations from their flight plans. They've been warned.'

'Warn them also that if there's the slightest interference from their down-draught with what we're doing here I'll sue them in a civil court,' said Hall. 'And I'll also ask Mr Justice Jarvis to include them in his precincts ruling, for whoever they represent to be jailed.'

There were several more minutes of muttered

exchanges and then a perceptible lessening in the overhead noise, as the helicopters gained height.

The distraction of the helicopters momentarily took all their attention from the contents of the grave. There was bewildered astonishment when they looked back. It was Keflin-Brown who spoke, the exclamation without any religious connotation: 'Jesus Christ!'

The coffin was pristine. No earth attached to it. The pale oak glistened, as it must have done on the day of the burial. The brass fittings dazzled the reflected light from all around.

'I don't think Jesus Christ has anything to do with this,' said Hall.

The two men who had re-dug the grave had recoiled from its smell, hands at their faces.

Urgently Keflin-Brown said, 'It shouldn't be opened! That's what we're supposed to understand. That we shouldn't open it.' He stepped back.

The vicar had launched into a confused, jumbled litany. Hall recognized 'forgiveness' and 'mercy' and a lot of references to 'evil.' The permeating sick, sweet, cloying miasma enveloped everything and everyone, wrapping around them like an embalming shroud, layer after layer, lingering from the open grave but seepingly far more overpoweringly from the still closed coffin. Someone retched and there was the raucous sound of vomiting. Everyone groped handkerchiefs from their pockets: Billington and Carter finally but very hurriedly attached their nose-clips.

'The judge's order says the coffin has to be opened,' insisted the superintendent, voice muffled through his handkerchief but making no effort to perform the duty with which he was officially entrusted. Unnecessarily he said, 'But I don't think I can do it.'

'We're certainly not going to,' said the first grave digger.

The vicar mumbled on, standing well back.

'Here!' demanded Hall, reaching out for the screwdriver being offered to the unresponsive police officer.

There seemed a solid although invisible wall of fetid, putrid stink against him. Having gone forward he was at once forced back, bile stinging his throat. Hall inhaled as deeply as he could, then held his breath to approach again. The wood gleamed at him, the brass glittering. There was almost a physical sensation of something – the smell – being wound around him, again and again and again. It stung his eyes, making him squeeze them almost shut, so it was hard to connect with the real lid screws beneath their artificial, decorative caps. Hall was alone now, isolated and oblivious in his total concentration. Three times, like a boxer pulling back from a punch – actually feeling dizzy, on the very edge of unconsciousness – Hall had momentarily to retreat, to breathe out and inhale less stinking air.

The bolts unscrewed with the smooth newness of the rest of the container. Just before he was driven back, gasping, for the fourth time, Hall managed to push against the lid, skewing it to provide easy-lifting handholds.

From beyond the barrier there were camera flash fireworks. And from the helicopters above, startling them all, two separate, piercing spotlights stabbed into the scene.

'I can't lift the lid by myself,' croaked Hall.

No-one around him spoke. No-one moved.

'Help me get the lid off!'

Still no-one spoke. Or moved.

'You!' said Hall, demanding finger towards the police

superintendent. 'You have by law to enforce the judge's order!'

The policeman didn't think to hold his breath, as Hall was doing. The retching caught the man's breath, became a spasm and finally he began to hyperventilate.

In one, panicked heave, they lifted the lid free. The superintendent staggered back, gasping.

The overhead fluttering of the helicopters and the rumble beyond the police line totally hid the audible reaction from the graveside group, although a lot of their horrified facial reactions were caught on film. The police photographer was frozen. The noise was a whimpering mix of gasps and groans and even some barely held-back screams, all of incredulous terror. The agonized vicar fell to his knees, hands cupped before his face, and audibly said, 'Oh dear Lord, protect us from this evil and from mysteries we do not understand,' and began reciting the Lord's prayer, head bent, refusing after the first instant to look inside. Unhesitatingly the cemetery workers followed, loudly joining the invocation with their hands clasped before them: two crumpled to kneel to pray. They all averted their eyes from the coffin.

Once more Hall inhaled as deeply as he could before biting into his handkerchief and pinching his nose beneath it to lean forward better to focus. Perry did the same, but Keflin-Brown still held back, making choking, gagging sounds.

Hall didn't have any anticipation. At most he'd expected a properly defined skeleton, all the bones in their normally accepted and physically proper place. None was so in the coffin, apart from the fleshless, grinning skull. Adorning that, appearing freshly combed and dressed and very full, was abundant hair, still visibly blond despite the artificial discolouring caused by so much light.

Nothing else was intact. Instead, running the entire length of the coffin – still lined in perfectly preserved and plush vivid red velvet – FUCK YOU was spelled out, straight bones like the tibia and fibula and femur and humerus and radius and ulna and larger fingers forming the upright letters, the curved but individually separated ribs fashioned into the Us and the C and the O. There had been sufficient, even, for the rejection to be finished off, as if forming an exclamation mark, with what was clearly a stiffly upright middle finger.

'That's not . . .' began Keflin-Brown, from behind, but Hall impatiently closed him down. 'For God's sake stop telling me what is or what is not possible! You're seeing it with your own eyes!'

'I wish I hadn't.'

'So do we all,' said Hall. Abruptly he realized that the stink had completely disappeared.

The meeting was already scheduled but Jeremy Hall had not originally intended it to be anything more than an apology for their psychiatric analyses no longer being necessary, coupled with the assurance of their being paid, in full, despite their not having been called. The seemingly uncontrollable, but now understandable, media hysteria – by the time he returned to the Temple that morning there were four book publishing offers, one from America opening at $1,000,000 – and the unavoidable revelation of the coffin's contents made him change his mind. They could, after all, work for their fee.

The Temple Inn yard is a public day-time thoroughfare and although there was a police guard directly outside the Proudfoot chambers there were pockets of loitering media representatives, circling in ambush like medieval skirmishers and Julian Mason, the first psychiatrist to arrive, entered shaking his head in bemusement.

'I didn't imagine it would be like this, despite what I've read and seen on television.'

'No-one did. It is unimaginable.' Flexing his newly developed muscle Hall had told – not asked – Bert Feltham that he needed the main conference room. Which he'd got, without question. In addition to which Feltham had politely asked – not autocratically decreed – if he could attend. Despite Keflin-Brown's cemetery opinion of his unstoppable future career – which he had anyway already assessed for himself – Hall realistically acknowledged Feltham's unique position and influence within chambers and went as far as saying he'd welcome the man's presence. He was, at Mason's arrival, already by the window overlooking the Thames in head-together conversation with Humphrey Perry. At that moment Johnson was on the telephone, Hall presumed arranging the collection of Jennifer's belongings from jail.

'I heard on the radio coming in that there was a sensational discovery at the cemetery, although they didn't know what it was?'

'Let's wait for the others,' suggested Hall.

The American, Milton Smith, whom Hall had intended calling as an authority on Multiple Personality Disorder, was the next to arrive. Hall was in the process of introducing him to Feltham when Steven Denning and Walter Elliott, his other two psychiatrists, entered together.

The introductions completed and the already prepared coffee served Hall quickly disposed with the original purpose of the gathering, asking each to submit their bills to Feltham.

'There's no doubt about the outcome of the trial?' queried Denning, a heavily tweeded and bearded bear of a man. It had been Denning who'd used the truth drug, scopolamine, during one of his sessions with Jennifer and been totally satisfied with the honesty of her answers.

'Not after this morning,' said Hall. The four psychiatrists listened without any exaggerated reaction to his account of the exhumation. Neither Feltham nor Johnson, already briefed by Perry, showed any surprise.

'Have you realized yet that you've made history?' demanded Walter Elliott. Like Mason, he was a laid-back exponent. He wore open sandals, jeans and a roll-necked sweater: the sweater had a heavy darn in the left elbow.

'It's being thrust upon me,' said Hall, making a general arm movement in the direction of the outside yard. 'But that's not what I want to talk about, not directly. After what we found in the grave the DNA comparison is largely academic. I'm going to make history by having an English court of law rule that Jennifer Lomax is physically possessed by a ghost. And that it was the ghost of Jane Lomax that murdered her husband—'

'Jesus!' intruded Denning.

'Where the hell's that going to take you?' demanded Mason.

Hall shook his head against answer. Instead he went on '. . . That disposes of the charge against Jennifer. She's not guilty of murder . . .' He paused, looking around the assembled group. 'But she's still possessed . . .'

'. . . By a homicidal maniac, whom she can't always control,' completed Elliott.

'So,' demanded Hall, 'you're the experts. How do we get rid of Jane?'

He asked the question looking at Milton Smith. So did everyone else.

'Woa!' cautioned Smith, an angularly featured, sparse-bodied man. 'It's becoming accepted – legally recognized in some states in America – that a person's mind can consist of two or more, sometimes many more, separate personalities. And that each personality, each different person if you like, can at any one time control the body it's in: *be* the person. There's medically and clinically recorded and analysed cases. But we're not talking Multiple Personality here. There's an alien presence inside Jennifer Lomax. She's been invaded . . .' He returned the attention being concentrated upon him by the other three psychiatrists. 'OK, you guys. I've never heard of anything like it before, encountered anything like it before and quite honestly I wouldn't know how to begin helping or treating this lady. Any of you got a contribution?'

One by one the three men shook their heads. Denning said, 'I asked to speak to Jane.'

'Did you?' said Hall.

'For what it was worth. It was just foul mouthed.'

'That's what it is, most of the time,' said Perry.

Mason sniggered, despite himself. 'I talked to her, too. How many people have been told to go fuck themselves by a ghost?'

No-one laughed. Briefly, into Hall's mind, came Keflin-Brown's cut-off-at-the-court-door cynicism earlier that day. He said, 'How can we – any of you working separately or all together, as a group if necessary – rid Jennifer of her ghost?'

'I don't even . . .' began Elliott, '. . . didn't, until now,' he corrected, '. . . believe in ghosts.'

'I don't think any of us did,' said Hall. 'Now we do. So let's try to answer the question.'

'I've already told you I can't,' said the American. 'I

don't know how to. If anyone's got any idea I'll go along with it.'

Again, one after another, the other three psychiatrists said the same.

'You can't say that,' protested Hall.

'There's nothing else for us *to* say,' insisted Mason, in return. 'We're psychiatrists, not exorcists.'

'We suggested exorcism,' reminded Perry.

'She refused,' Hall told the other men. 'She said she didn't believe in God.'

'I said I didn't believe in ghosts,' repeated Elliott. 'I think exorcism's worth trying, whether she believes or not.'

'Anything's worth trying, the jam she's in,' said Smith. He paused. 'But I'd like to spend a lot more time with her . . .' He looked vaguely embarrassed.

'Like a culture under a microscope,' accused Hall.

'Think of what she is! We can't begin to imagine her clinical value, to psychiatry. Psychology. Every science of the brain!' urged the American.

'I'm not going to think of her as an experiment,' refused Hall. In sudden realization, he said, 'But she's sane, isn't she?'

'That's what we were all going to tell the court,' agreed Mason.

'So there couldn't be a committal order for her own protection?'

The psychiatrists considered the question. Elliott said, 'She could admit herself.'

'That's what she told me Jane was trying to do, get her declared insane and locked up in an asylum,' remembered Denning.

'Me, too,' said Mason. 'So Jane could win after all.'

Hall felt a frustrating surge of impotence. 'I just can't

leave her,' he said, a remark more to himself than to anyone else.

'Your legal responsibility ends with her acquittal,' said Perry.

'I know what my legal boundaries are,' said Hall, sharply. 'But I haven't practised law long enough yet to lose my moral or humane responsibilities.'

Perry flushed. 'Don't we have to face the fact that there's nothing we can do to help her?'

'You know where to find me, if you think there's anything I can do,' offered Mason. 'Exorcism's the only thing I can think of.'

'I agree,' said Elliott. 'And I'll help, if anyone comes up with an idea.'

'I'll talk to some guys back home: see if they've got any thoughts,' offered Smith. 'But I'm not holding out any hope.' There was another pause. 'If she were to agree to a period under analysis I'd appreciate being involved. You never know. It might produce something . . .'

'Like a Nobel prize?' said Hall, bitterly.

Geoffrey Johnson waited until the psychiatrists had filed out before saying, 'And there's another problem . . .' He nodded towards the telephone by the window. '. . . I spoke to Annabelle. The foreign press don't consider themselves bound by any order Jarvis has made. The place is under siege, too. The police are doing what they can but she says Emily's terrified.'

'We'll move her,' decided Hall, at once.

'And get her involved in the sort of car chase we had before?' challenged Johnson.

The memory of that morning came to Hall. 'Helicopter,' he decided. 'The grounds are big enough. Tell Annabelle to get everything prepared, so they're ready to move the moment it lands. The press won't be able to catch up . . .' That morning's memory remained. '. . . But don't let it land where you're going to hide her. They'll trace her from the flight plan. Have it put down somewhere where you're waiting. *Then* you go on by road. But not in that Bentley: it's too identifiable . . .'

Johnson blinked at the flurry of instructions. Perry said, 'Where the hell's it all going to end?'

'I don't think it is going to,' said Hall.

At the hospital Jane said, '*They were terrified when they opened my grave. You know what we've done! We've made everybody believe in ghosts.*'

Chapter Twenty-six

Jennifer was surprised – annoyed even, as she had been throughout the previous day by his lack of contact – at Jeremy Hall arranging for her to travel to court in a police van and under front and rear police escort. Her uncertainty lasted only until they attempted to leave the hospital. The Embankment outside, in both directions, seethed with people – more public than press – through whom it was practically impossible to move. It took thirty minutes to move as many yards, the outside of the van constantly banged and hit, her name shouted again and again, in an echoing, chanted demand for her to put herself at the narrow window. From which, in fact, she recoiled.

It was far worse at the approach to the court. The solid block of a baying, gawking mob began to form a quarter of a mile away, jamming every street they tried, and they only reached it, finally, edging along in the middle of a linked-arm guard of walking policemen, with others forming an outer barrier physically forcing a path. Jennifer finally closed her eyes altogether against the camera lights, careless of how she'd look in any picture that might be snatched.

It was clearly impossible for her to use the public access, which she was entitled to do on bail. Instead she entered as she had on all the previous days, through the gated-off rear doors.

Hall was already there, waiting. Jennifer was shaking, frightened, and said, 'This is incredible. Awful. Do something!'

Before Hall could reply Jane said, '*This is how it's going to be!*'

Hall began walking with her along the corridor, hand cupping her elbow, careful not to come into contact with her strapped side. 'I spent yesterday trying to think of something. We'll sort it out.'

'Believe that and you'll believe anything!'

'Where's Emily? I phoned home, yesterday afternoon. Mrs Jenkins said Annabelle had taken her away. By helicopter! What the hell . . . ?'

'For the same reason you had to be brought here by the police. We had to get Emily away. Annabelle's with her, of course. Johnson, too. Emily thinks she's on holiday.'

Jennifer shuddered, flinching at the pain from her ribs. 'I want it to end. For everyone to go away.'

'It's just beginning! I keep telling you!'

'Let's get today over.'

'I saw what was inside the coffin,' declared Jennifer. The contents had been photographed from both helicopters, by television as well as still cameras, and in the majority of cases published without the obscenity being air-brushed or blanked out. It had first been shown on the previous evening's television news.

'Today's really just a formality.'

'But there's a lot of surprises still left.'

The two regular wardresses were waiting at the bottom of the court steps, reminding her. 'You've got everything from the prison?'

'Johnson has.' To the wardress, Hall said, 'Keep close to her.'

'Tell him not to worry. I've got a different surprise today. One you're really going to like.'

'She says she's got another surprise.'

Ann Wardle visibly stood back. As the Irish-accented Kathleen did the same she said, 'What?'

'Surprises are surprises!'

Jennifer shook her head against the question.

Hall said: 'There's nothing that can go against you in court. You're provably innocent.'

'We've been beyond that for the last two days, haven't we?' demanded Jennifer, objectively. She didn't have to stress the weariness. Her injured ribs and knee ached and Peter Lloyd had told her that morning that the result of the HIV blood test might take longer than he'd first thought, although he'd made it a priority request. Jane had been noisily in the background throughout her sedated half-sleep and she'd had her first real experience of how mobs would react (*'Told you you'd be a freak, from now on: didn't listen, did you?'* to that reflection) and Jennifer at that moment wasn't sure how much longer she could go on fighting: didn't know – wouldn't know – after today what she *had* to fight. The court, the murder charge, had been a reality, an actuality she could confront: understand. And she'd had someone believing her, supporting her. She wasn't faced with any reality from now on. And her defender wouldn't be around to help her. She wouldn't be in any court and so Jeremy wouldn't be there to rely on. He hadn't tried to distance himself from her today: actually held her arm, helped her along the corridor and been careful he didn't jar into her side, to hurt her. She didn't want to lose him: be without him. Didn't want to be alone, apart from her tormentor.

'But I'm all you've got, honey. Think of it like a marriage; the worst marriage in your worst nightmare. Then double it.'

'Here it is,' announced Hall. 'The last time you're going to have to stand in a dock.'

'Ready, steady go!'

Yet again Jennifer had to force one foot in front of the other to ascend into the dock. The approaching noise was practically deafening – louder than it had ever been – but at her appearance it died, into an awed silence that was even more disconcerting. Police were shoulder to shoulder around the dock but today there was no darted media approach. For her own satisfaction Jennifer stood at the dock rail, for the first time not trying to withdraw from the incredulous fascination but gazing defiantly, challengingly, back at her onlookers. Briefly she was tempted to say something, anything, (*'Go on! Go on!'*) to see how frightened the reaction would be but she didn't. (*'Lots of time, later,'*). Jeremy Hall turned and smiled and she smiled back.

Even Jarvis's expression was less gargoyle-like when he entered and he extended it in the direction of the media and, Jennifer thought, everyone desperate to ensure their little place in the history of the supernatural bizarre. How many other people would want her autograph, like the wardresses who sat behind her now with what they regarded a safe distance between them?

'Why not sign for both of us? We could do double-sided photographs, Jane and Jennifer!'

'Jennifer and Jane,' said Jennifer, softly but aloud, watching the shocked reaction – the awareness that she was talking to the ghost inside her – from around the court. Not funny, she corrected herself, at once: playing games, stupid, insane games.

'That's it, insane! And that's how I'll do it: take your mind away. And you won't even notice it until it's too late.'

Oddly, or perhaps befitting the complete unnaturalness of the moment – the moment a staid, undemonstrative, unhysterical British court of law legally established and recognized the existence of the supernatural – there was a strange anti-climax about the conclusion of the trial.

The scientists contributed with the formality of their findings, which they presented in microscopic detail. Anthony Billington even insisted, throughout his evidence, upon referring to DNA by its full name, deoxyribonucleic acid and, following his lead, Phylis Shipley did the same. Although there was no possibility of prosecution challenge or appeal, upon technicality, Hall allowed both to introduce charts and diagrams showing the formation and relationships between double-stranded molecules and nuclei and chromosomes, which they illustrated in hugely enlarged detail. And asked each virtually identical questions when they came to the end of their esoteric explanations.

In Jennifer's head Jane hummed: Jennifer thought she recognized snatches of 'Small Town Girl'.

'*Wrong. How about "I've Got You Under My Skin"?*'

'Describe, in laymen's language, what deoxyribonucleic acid provides for you,' Hall demanded, from the prosecution expert.

'A unique and individual genetic picture,' responded Billington.

'A body fingerprint,' suggested Phylis Shipley, when she followed into the witness-box.

'Each different from any other?'

'The same only in identical twins,' qualified Billington.

'Have you prepared photographs of the DNA you

extracted from the blond hair and O Rhesus Negative blood samples found in Gerald Lomax's office?'

Billington said, 'Yes.' Phylis Shipley offered sufficient individual folders for the entire jury.

In Jennifer's head echoed the sound of a protracted yawn.

'Did you successfully extract comparison DNA from the hair and bones in the coffin of Jane Lomax?'

'*Ruined the spelling!*'

'I did,' said Billington.

'What was that comparison?'

Although it was already obvious, there was a loud and disbelieving intake of communal breath when Billington indicated his photographic charts and said, 'There is absolutely no doubt the hair and O Rhesus Negative blood from Gerald Lomax's office contains deoxyribonucleic acid identical to that I found in the bodily remains in the grave of Jane Lomax.' The sound echoed around the court again when Phylis Shipley repeated the finding.

Hall remained standing, as the woman scientist left the witness-box. He said, 'My Lord, is it your wish that I make a submission?'

'That will not be necessary,' refused Jarvis. It took him only minutes to direct the jury formally to return a verdict of not guilty, to the background of rising noise throughout the court. It quietened only slightly when Jennifer was called to rise.

Jarvis said, 'Jennifer Lomax, you leave this court having been found not guilty of the charge of murder brought against you, it having been admirably, legally and scientifically proved by your learned counsel that the crime was perpetrated not by yourself but by the spirit of Jane Lomax, who possesses your body and your mind. You are, Jennifer Lomax, a woman to be greatly pitied and in need of help that none of us can begin to understand. There was, in a certain period of British legal history, a phrase utilized at the conclusion of some murder trials that seems to me to be very fitting today . . . May God have mercy upon your soul.'

'*You know what you're going to do, now that this is all over, don't you?*' said Jane. '*You're going to be reunited with Emily. And one day, when I feel like it, I'm going to make you kill her. Won't that be fun?*'

Jennifer emitted an anguished, strangled scream. Ann Wardle only half-caught her so Jennifer still hit the dock floor hard but she had fainted too deeply into unconsciousness to feel the fresh pain in her ribs.

Geoffrey Johnson was waiting for Annabelle in the bar of the Wiltshire theme park when she came down from the room she was sharing with Emily. Annabelle accepted the waiting glass of wine and said, 'She's asleep. But I'll need to keep checking her. She's started wetting the bed.'

'Kids of that age do. Mine did.'

'Geoffrey!' Annabelle erupted. 'She hasn't seen her father for months and doesn't know what's happened to him! Her mother tried to kill her! She thinks the bad men who invaded Hampshire wanted to take her away and to escape them she had to leave in a helicopter. And at four, helicopters aren't exciting. They're bloody frightening. Emily wetting the bed isn't a thing that kids do. She's developing psychological problems.'

'Jennifer's not guilty. She's free. So she'll be back with Emily in a day or two.'

'Is that how long she's going to stay in hospital?'

'They don't know yet. They're not sure why she fainted, apart from the obvious relief.' Johnson poured more wine. 'I spoke to Humphrey while you were upstairs. And I've booked in. They've asked me to stay: make sure you're not found. Apparently the scenes in London were incredible. Humphrey said it had to be like the hysteria of a medieval execution when people were hanged, drawn and quartered.'

'I've unplugged the television. I didn't want Emily waking up and putting it on, just in case . . .' She sipped her drink. 'It's not going to be as easy here as it was at home keeping newspapers from her. I know she can't read but she can see the pictures. There were a couple of bad situations at home.'

'Jeremy asked me to thank you, for what you've done. And are doing.'

Annabelle looked seriously at the solicitor. 'I'm not sure for how much longer.'

'You can't quit now!' protested the man.

'You think I've enjoyed it?'

'Of course you haven't. None of us have. But it's all over now.'

'She's still possessed, isn't she? And you told me the psychiatrists couldn't help.'

'Jeremy's trying to think of something.'

'I don't want to live in a house with a woman who's got a ghost in her head. And I don't think we can allow Emily to after what happened at the hospital.'

'Let's wait until we know why she collapsed,' pleaded Johnson.

Chapter Twenty-seven

Jeremy Hall didn't want a celebration – found it difficult at that precise moment to believe he had anything *to* celebrate – but as he had in allowing Bert Feltham into the conference with the psychiatrists he considered his future in the chambers and accepted the pre-lunch invitation to Sir Richard Proudfoot's rooms. The decision was made easier by Peter Lloyd, who during their prior telephone conversation told him Jennifer was still heavily sedated and wouldn't be able to respond properly to visitors until that afternoon at the earliest. Lloyd admitted still not knowing the cause of the collapse and agreed to Julian Mason coming as well. Mason immediately agreed to mid-afternoon after asking, with professional jealousy, if the other psychiatrists were also to be involved to the obvious satisfaction of being told they weren't.

It was Feltham who organized the chambers gathering. Humphrey Perry was included and Hall was briefly curious that all eight senior members were able to attend, at such short notice. From none was there the resentment he'd known previously at the nepotism of his joining his uncle's firm, not even from Sir Patrick Piltbeam – whose chambers they would become upon Proudfoot's elevation to the bench – or Jonathan Cappell: both, he knew, had voted against his penniless admission.

Now everything changed. His acceptance went far beyond being effusive to be cloying to the point of sycophancy. There was the artificiality of individual handshakes and back-slapping congratulations, and the embarrassment of a eulogizing speech from Proudfoot. There was a lot about his potential being recognized from the start and of the fame he'd brought to the chambers as well as to himself. There seemed a contest among the QCs to be the first to take him to lunch and Cappell, who until now had barely acknowledged his existence, suggested proposing him for membership of the Garrick or the Reform or both. It was, decided Hall, like being the dog to win the supreme championship at Crufts: everyone wanted to take him for a walk to show off.

It was Henry Kerslake, another junior, who asked the question. 'What's she *like*?'

'A frightened woman,' said Hall, unhelpfully.

'I mean does it show, physically?'

'She doesn't look any different from any other woman: just one head.' Immediately despising the cynicism, which sounded as if it were directed at Jennifer and not Kerslake, he added, 'The only physical evidence is when she can't resist being forced to do something.'

'Good Lord!' said Kerslake, as if he'd had a revelation. 'She looks beautiful in the newspaper pictures.'

'She is. I told you, there's no outward manifestation.'

'You frightened of her?'

It was like a courtroom cross-examination, Hall thought. 'There was a frightening episode in the hospital.'

'When she attacked the child?' prompted Piltbeam.

Hall looked accusingly between Perry and Feltham, supposing it was inevitable. 'Yes.'

'What an experience,' enthused Kerslake. 'Actually being close to someone like that. Incredible!'

'Actually it's very sad.'

'When does the lecture tour start?' demanded Piltbeam, half joking to lighten the moment.

'As a matter of fact there was an approach from an agent this morning,' admitted Hall. It had been one of the five new offers in the pigeon-hole of his still beleaguered apartment. Patricia had called again, as well as five newspapers all of which increased their initial offers for interviews and personalized stories.

'And I've got four briefs specifically asking for you by name, Mr Hall,' disclosed Feltham. 'I haven't made any commitment yet: wanted to discuss them with you first.'

'More consideration than you show us, Bert,' complained Cappell.

'The offers to Mrs Lomax herself are astonishing,' came in Perry. 'An American publisher is offering the equivalent of £3,000,000 for a book.'

'Jennifer Lomax could become an industry!' said Cappell, in another attempted joke.

'She won't,' Hall said, positively. Why did they think it was so amusing?

'Still no trouble with the fees, though?' suggested Hugh Norton. He was the oldest QC in chambers, a passed-over lawyer who never appeared in criminal court and only took sufficient civil litigation to support the middle of each day at his regular ground-floor corner table of El Vino.

'Unlikely in the first place, quite apart from our being awarded costs,' assured Perry. 'I had Johnson anticipate the verdict: make an assessment. Mrs Lomax was already wealthy in her own right and Lomax's Will makes her a millionairess. And having been found not guilty she qualifies for all the insurance policies, company as well as private. And they're worth a fortune. He's still working it out.'

Hall shifted, uncomfortable with the bone-stripping dissection. 'Aren't we being premature?'

'Practical, old boy,' defined Cappell. 'You pulled off a brilliant defence. Earned your fee. Everyone should be well and truly satisfied.'

He wasn't, Hall abruptly realized. He supposed they were right, although their attitude offended him. He'd fulfilled his function and owed Jennifer Lomax nothing more: if anything her debt was to him. But he wasn't going to leave it: leave her. He'd chosen the four psychiatrists because of their expertise – and wanted Mason with him later for the same reason – but it had only been four: there were others he could consult until he found how to free Jennifer. The answer might even come from Milton Smith when he talked to people in America who might be able to help. And exorcism. He definitely had to discuss that with Jennifer, irrespective of any initial reluctance.

'We're certainly more than satisfied,' said Proudfoot, as the other barristers began drifting from the room.

Looking more towards the solicitor than anyone else, Feltham said, 'I suppose we should start on the paper-work then?'

'Don't see why not,' agreed Perry, cheerfully.

'I do,' stopped Hall. 'I don't want any bills submitted until I say so . . .' He was, he acknowledged, directly challenging Feltham on the man's own territory, a cardinal offence. Quickly he added, 'I don't consider the case is finished yet. So as I said, it would be premature.'

'Not too long, though Jeremy,' urged Proudfoot. Misquoting, he said, 'Time and tide in the affairs of men and all that sort of thing. Bert's got an orderly queue waiting for your services, by the sound of it.'

'What do you want me to do about them, Mr Hall?'

'Mr Hall' from the in-chamber legend, 'sir' from an arrogant police superintendent, recognized Hall. Things had very clearly changed. 'Ask them to wait, Bert, if you would. Anything that couldn't be held for a few days?'

'I don't think so, Mr Hall.'

'I'll leave it to your judgement . . .' He smiled, aware of his own hypocrisy. 'That's what everyone else does here, isn't it?'

Feltham smile back. 'Leave it to me, sir.'

Hall declined all the immediate lunch offers and was glad because he was in his rooms to receive both panicked calls. Superintendent Hopkins he already knew. Peter Lloyd initiated the second approach, verbally to introduce the hospital administrator Hector Beringer.

Hopkins complained that the crowd around the hospital had become so bad that twice already that day they'd had to close Westminster and Lambeth bridges and seal off the westerly approach to Waterloo station to maintain the barest minimum of a totally interrupted rail service.

'I stopped counting after we'd issued three hundred breach of the peace and obstruction summonses,' said Hopkins. 'There's been assaults upon my officers: people just won't leave, even after they're officially charged more than once. And I've suspended actual arrests to prevent a riot . . .' The man paused, for breath.

'... There's actually a group of about forty who say they belong to the Resurrection of Life church, trying to set up a bivouac encampment alongside Lambeth Palace: they're claiming Jane's ghost has summoned them. Over a hundred extra officers have had to be seconded in—'

'What's your point, Superintendent?' Hall cut in.

'I would have thought that was obvious, sir. It's becoming difficult for us to cope, even with mounted assistance. We're on the verge of losing control.'

'Your responsibility is to maintain order,' reminded Hall.

'I don't need to be told what my responsibilities are, sir. I'm trying to get some idea how much longer this nonsense is going to continue . . .' He paused, imagining the nearest he could come to a threat. 'And also to find out to whom officially to address a formal notification that I am going to suggest to my Watch Committee that we attempt to recover from Mrs Lomax the money all this is costing.'

'I haven't an answer to your first question. Address your letter about costs to my instructing solicitor, Humphrey Perry. It will, of course, be strenuously resisted.'

Hopkins sighed, defeated. 'Haven't you any idea when Mrs Lomax might be discharged?'

At that time Hall had not been contacted by the hospital administrator. 'Not yet. I might get an indication this afternoon.'

He got it, in fact, just five minutes later. Hall listened patiently to Hector Beringer's description of the chaos outside the hospital, guessing he'd rehearsed the protest and needed to vent the obvious anger. 'It's become impossible effectively to run the hospital. Emergencies can't get through: every ambulance is surrounded by mobs who believe she's inside. One was almost turned over an hour ago.'

'I understood this morning from Doctor Lloyd that she is still seriously unwell.'

'In the opinion of consultants senior to Doctor Lloyd she is not too ill to be moved. I'm responsible for the care of a great many people, not just one. And the health of a lot of them is being endangered. I have to ask you to take Mrs Lomax to a private hospital when you come here this afternoon, which I understand from Doctor Lloyd you intend to do.'

'With a psychiatrist,' agreed Hall. 'And when I'm independently satisfied that Mrs Lomax *is* fit enough to be moved then I will make arrangements. But not before.'

'Mr Hall, I don't want there to be any misunderstanding about this. You don't have a choice.'

'I don't want any misunderstanding either, Mr Beringer. And I do have a choice. I have the choice of going before a judge to ask for Mrs Lomax to be placed under a court's protection against being ejected from your hospital into the sort of uncontrolled mob you've just spent fifteen minutes describing to me.'

'That's ridiculous!'

'It would be, if you attempted to do it. I sympathize with the stress you're under. And what's happening at your hospital. But threats aren't the way to resolve it. I'll expect to see you there this afternoon.'

It was worse than Hall imagined: worse, even, than the scenes that completely dominated the lunch-time television news bulletins that he watched before he left. He decided to walk, disregarding the entourage of bobbing, questioning and envelope-thrusting media who ignored his demands to be left alone, encountering the build-up as soon as he crossed Blackfriars Bridge to the south side of the river. Stamford Street was lined either side by barriers in an attempt to keep the road open but they'd been pushed forward by the crush of people, reducing the thoroughfare to a single line that was being controlled in a stop-and-go system by police radio cars at either end. It took Hall almost fifteen minutes to find a sergeant and to identify himself, to be escorted along the road on the outside of the barriers. By that time the protesting media pack, forbidden to follow and held behind a police block, had drawn sufficient attention for Hall to be recognized. His name became an immediate, meaningless chant. He ignored the outstretched hands, not knowing what they were reaching for, but was abruptly pulled sideways by someone managing to snag his pocket, which ripped. At once he was overwhelmed by a flurry of hands, grabbing and pulling at him: his tie tightened, garrotting him. It snapped when he desperately yanked it loose and it disappeared into the crowd. One of the two policemen wrenched him free, taking him into the middle of the slow-moving line of traffic, beyond the tendril wave of snatching hands. Twice people – the first a girl, then an immediately encouraged boy inexplicably stripped to the waist – tried to leap the barrier at him. Both were simply knocked roughly back into the crowd by his escorts.

Alerted by radio, Superintendent Hopkins was waiting for him at Waterloo station. 'Believe me now?' the man demanded.

'I didn't disbelieve you before. I just couldn't imagine it.'

'They're bringing soldiers in from Wellington barracks.'

York Road could not be cleared sufficiently for cars. Policemen were positioned every ten yards desperately trying to keep in place the metal fencing to maintain a passage barely wide enough for Hall and Hopkins to walk between a tight, linked-arm encirclement of more riot-uniformed officers. Despite that protection there were still snatched attempts to touch him. A snowdrift of paper thrust at him to sign built up on the ground when he refused to take it. Two mounted policemen joined the phalanx at the Addington Street junction for what became a final dash into the hospital forecourt. They didn't stop, running faster without obstruction into the final safety of the hospital reception.

Hall became aware that he was shaking and wasn't able to prevent it and realized, surprised, that it was his first experience of real fear. He couldn't remember how the top pocket had been torn almost out of his jacket, to match the early rip in Stamford Street. Both cuff-links had vanished and his cuffs now hung clear of his sleeves, covering his hands.

He started back when Lloyd came very close, to examine his face. The doctor said, 'You've got a couple of scratches but they're only superficial. Here.'

Hall took the offered antiseptic wipe and after rubbing his face used it to clean what looked like spit off his right sleeve.

As Lloyd introduced him to the hospital administrator Hall said to both the police controller and Beringer, 'I don't need to be told again that it's unacceptable. Of course it is. Totally . . .' He concentrated upon the hospital official. 'Like it would be to think of discharging Mrs Lomax out into it.'

'I never suggested that and you know it,' rejected Beringer. 'I want it solved. Today.'

'Is Mason here?'

Lloyd nodded. 'He was lucky. He didn't get to court to

be photographed and recognized. It still took him an hour to get through. He's already with her.'

'How is she?' Hall asked, as they went to the elevators.

Lloyd hesitated, looking towards Beringer before saying, 'I'd like her to be a lot better. The sedation hasn't totally worn off. But I don't think it's physical: thank God she didn't do any more damage to her ribs when she fell.'

'What's she said?'

'Virtually nothing other than keep asking for you.'

Hall frowned. Conscious of the immediate apprehension from Beringer at the question – but not embarrassed at asking it – he said, 'What about Jane?'

'She's saying something, over and over again but Jennifer won't say what it is.'

'Why not?'

'That's what Mason is trying to find out now.' The doctor paused, when they reached the level of the private ward. 'I really don't think she'll be able to hold on to her sanity much longer. Neither does Mason.'

'But this is a medical, not a psychiatric hospital,' warned Beringer, from behind.

Jennifer was lying in bed, the covers drawn up to her chin as if she was trying to hide. She was very pale – there was no make-up and her hair was unkempt – and her eyes, dulled from medication, were black-ringed again. She didn't smile at Hall's entry but there was some slight animation in her face. At once she brought a hand from beneath the sheet and held it out to him. He took it, sitting as he did so on the chair Mason pushed towards him. The action was to draw Hall's attention. The psychiatrist shook his head against having learned anything.

'How are you feeling?' he asked, inadequately.

'You've got to do some things. Legal things.' Her voice was drug slurred but urgent.

'Like what?'

'Keep Emily safe.'

'What is it, Jennifer? What's happened?'

'Tell him! Tell them all!'

'She's going to make me kill Emily. That's what she said in court. What she's been saying ever since . . .'

There was a stir from Lloyd and the administrator. Hall didn't bother to look, beyond any surprise. How in God's name was he going to help her? The vague, unformed idea that came was mad but they were in a totally mad, unreal, unknown situation.

'. . . You've got to have her legally taken away from me,' Jennifer stumbled on, weak-voiced. 'I can never know where she is. See her again. I know that. Just do it. Don't tell me about it. Just do it.'

'Don't be a spoil-sport!'

'I'll do something.' His hand hurt from the tightness with which she was gripping it, physically needing to hold on to force herself to abandon her baby.

'Not something! Do what I ask you. Get her taken away from me, please. She'll never be safe, if you don't . . .' She swallowed, heavily, unable to go on for several moments. 'Then it can be all over.'

'No,' refused Hall, fearing he understood the final remark. 'It's not going to be all over.'

There were five of them in Beringer's office but when the proposal to get Jennifer out began to take shape Hall kept a telephone line open to Perry because it was easier for the solicitor to make their part of the arrangements from his end. Hopkins used another extension to co-ordinate the police participation and Mason a third. It took three hours and they spent a further hour objectively criticizing each other's contribution in the hope of exposing unforeseen flaws.

'You sure about the security?' Hall asked the psychiatrist.

'That's what you pay for and how they can afford me as a consultant,' assured Mason. 'They've treated a cabinet minister and two pop stars in the last six months and not a word leaked out . . .' He made a vague gesture through the window overlooking the chaos outside. 'What you're seeing there is mass hysteria: strangely, something like a mass *religious* hysteria. There's already the cult camped outside Lambeth Palace. It'll grow far beyond any police or army control unless we get her away. For hundreds of people – hundreds who are going to become thousands – Jennifer Lomax is the equivalent of someone from outer space. Or the second Messiah.'

'I wish we could use a helicopter again,' Hall said, to Hopkins.

'So do I. But we can't. The crowd should get smaller, after midnight. And we've kept the sightseeing ferries and boats away all day.'

'Let's hope it stays that way.'

Only Mason and Lloyd accompanied him when Hall returned to the small ward to explain to Jennifer what was going to happen. She listened blank-eyed, disinterested, shrugging when Lloyd asked her if she physically felt up to it. She said, 'I suppose so. It hardly matters, does it?'

Lloyd remained in the ward, insisting upon personally restrapping Jennifer's ribs and making a final medical examination.

As Hall and Mason walked back towards the administrator's office, which was to act as the control room, Hall said, 'What do you think Jennifer meant by saying it would all be over when I got a protection order for Emily?'

'That she intends killing herself, of course,' said the psychiatrist, without any hesitation. 'Are you going to take Emily away, legally?'

'It's not necessary at the moment. There's no way Jennifer can get to her.'

'What are you going to do then?'

'Take Jane on,' said Hall, simply. Insane ideas for insane situations, he thought again.

Back in Jennifer's ward Lloyd said, 'I've got something you're going to want to hear. The blood test is absolutely negative. Not a trace of HIV.'

'I was hoping there would be,' said Jennifer.

'*It would have imposed a time limit on what I'm going to do but it would have been a wonderful way to see you finally die, wouldn't it?*'

Chapter Twenty-eight

It worked.

When the moment came no-one truly believed that it would, because too many uncertainties were compounded at the outset. Despite the examination and re-examination of what they were going to attempt they hadn't allowed for equipment failure or interference: the police radio linking Hall's group to everyone else wouldn't work from the below-basement boiler room, isolating them completely.

'We can't go back,' decided Hall, at once. 'Everyone else will already be moving. Just keep trying.'

There were five of them. Hall and Mason, like the two escorting policemen, wore hospital maintenance overalls. As additional disguise the barrister wore a yellow hard-hat. Jennifer wore a nurse's cloak, over a regulation uniform: the shoes pinched. The headscarf was ready, for when they emerged through the heating service door. Jennifer was shuffling along automatically, engulfed in apathy, moved by Hall and Mason either side.

'Two o'clock was start time,' agreed Mason. 'It's five past.'

Three floors up, at ground level, it had started although not from the hospital itself. A route for vehicles had been forced through by the army reinforcements, particularly across Westminster Bridge because it was visible from the Albert Embankment. Across it, promptly on time, streamed a cavalcade of motor-cycle outriders, lights on, sirens blaring. The three police vans and two Range Rovers burned their siren-connected lights, too. Police and soldiers, shoulder to shoulder, pushed back against a crowd smaller than during the day but still large enough to block the entrance, reacting to the prearranged signal of an ambulance emerging from the hospital garage to park directly outside the main entrance. Following it from the garage came a squad of soldiers at the double to form another shoulder to shoulder wall between the vehicle and the crowd. 'Jennifer, Jennifer,' was an isolated shout at first but at once was taken up to become a repetitive howl. A lot of people tried to kneel in prayer but almost at once started screaming when they were trampled on. Everything was in fact made ghostly white by camera lights. Again, from circling helicopters, lights stabbed down.

The noise was so loud that it reached them, close to the boiler-room door, although the radio remained dead. Hall gently touched Jennifer's arm as if to rouse her, to confront the problem they had recognized but couldn't anticipate. 'What's she saying?'

'Nothing.'

'Is she there?'

'No.'

'What about the sedation?'

'I feel all right. Quite clear. My chest still hurts.'

The two policemen edged back, despite their personal selection by Hopkins: one was a sergeant, the other an inspector. 'My best,' Hopkins had called them.

'Try to give me a warning,' Hall told her. 'If it works at all the diversion won't last long.'

'She'll do something. She has to.'

'*Hah!*'

'She's back!' It had been abrupt, the numbness practically at the same time as the triumphant exclamation.

'Tell me what she says,' demanded Hall, urgently, trying to maintain a timetable for which he'd attempted to make allowances for Jane's inevitable interference, although not able to judge how long they'd need. If Jennifer erupted in attention-attracting convulsions the intention was to retreat, back into the hospital. And everything would have been a waste of time. 'Every word, as she says it.'

'*Throw you to the wolves! How about that! They'd tear you apart, like a pack: frightened of the unknown.*'

'And you're frightened too, aren't you?' demanded Hall, addressing Jane.

'*Cocky little scumbag! You talking to me?*'

'Yes. And you *are* frightened: not sure of yourself any more. Not sure what you can make Jennifer do.'

'*You want me to show you what I can make her do?*'

Three minutes, estimated Hall, unable to check the timing. And still unable to discover any setbacks above. 'What would that prove?'

'*That I still call the shots. Which I do.*'

'I disgraced you in court: disgraced the memory of your father. Exposed you as a murderess and destroyed the Herbetson family name.' He'd discarded the destroyed jacket but wore the boiler-suit over the rest of his clothes. He was saturated by sweat. It had to be five minutes by now.

'*Who gives a fuck?*'

'You should. You fouled your family name. Didn't prove anyone murdered you. Jennifer's free. Couldn't keep a husband when you had one. You failed all the way down the line, didn't you?' Jennifer had both arms clutched around her, holding her sides. Mason was intently forward, determined against missing anything of the exchange. The two policemen were pebble-eyed, in astonished bewilderment. It had to have been going on for eight minutes by now.

'*What the fuck are you saying?*'

'That I can defeat you, whenever I want. And that you're too scared to admit it. So you're going to make a scene when we get outside, like a spoilt child . . .' He looked to the policemen, shrugging. 'Let's go back. It's a waste of time . . .'

He'd been sure of Julian Mason but not of the other two men, so they hadn't been rehearsed. But the psychiatrist had, although he hadn't thought this dialogue remotely possible: it was, of them all, the greatest uncertainty.

Mason matched the barrister's shrug and set off back along the metalled walkway, pausing after a few steps to turn back. 'Aren't you coming?' he asked the uncertain policemen.

'*Bullshit and bluff. How you going to get her out?*'

'From the emergency helicopter pad on the roof,' lied Hall. 'Whenever we choose, any time later today when it's light.'

'*What the fuck's all this about in the first place then?*'

'You've seen the television pictures of what's happening outside,' said Hall, knowing from Lloyd that Jennifer had watched. 'The police wanted to end the chaos as soon as they could. Now they're going to have to wait.' He took Jennifer's arm and began to follow the psychiatrist. He *had* lost, he admitted to himself. The fifteen minutes he'd built into the timing had to have expired by now.

'*What do you think you can do?*'

'It's not important now.'

'*Tell me now!*' Jennifer jerked her arms up, to cover her ears at the shouted demand, crying out at the pain it caused but still gasping out the reply.

'Fuck off, Jane. Another failure! How about that?'

'*Now!*'

Hall continued walking Jennifer back into the hospital, behind Julian Mason. There was the clatter of footsteps on metal, as the policemen followed. He didn't reply.

'*I mean let's go. Now!*'

'No, you don't,' said Hall, not pausing.

Jennifer was brought to a halt, stopping him. '*You want a fight?*'

'You're not up to it.'

'*You want a fight?*' Jennifer whimpered at the pain of trying physically to close her ears off again.

'Yes. I want to fight.'

'*Then let's go, asshole.*'

Far above, the assembled waggon train was also ready to go. The final trigger that brought the 'Jennifer' howl to a throbbing crescendo was the sight of a blanket-embalmed figure – the nurse whose uniform Jennifer was wearing far below – being stretchered between attentive hospital staff into the ambulance. It only just negotiated the left-hand turn back on to the attention-drawing Westminster Bridge before the police and soldier line burst, under the irresistible pressure of frenetically mind-robbed people. But by then the procession was already halfway over the bridge, quickly turning south west past the Houses of Parliament on to Millbank in an obvious direction: back to Hampshire.

It had already crossed and was out of sight when one of the St Thomas's overalled policemen cautiously eased through the gully-submerged oil delivery opening and even more cautiously climbed the steps to look around, his hand raised in readiness for the down-wave that would tell his colleague, who had finally established radio contact at ground level, to slam shut the scarcely open door. Already the crowd on the river-bordering Albert Embankment was thinning and they – and those that remained – still all gazed and crushed towards the bridge over which they appeared to expect the autocade to return. Others strained to follow the identifying searchlight beams of the helicopters, pursuing along the other side of the river. There was still a loud 'Jennifer' wail. The prepared door slamming gesture turned into an urgent beckoning.

They came out together, Mason and Hall either side of Jennifer, the remaining policeman close behind, all three ignoring her scarf-muffled pleas to slow because she was hurting.

'The launch is there: we're all right,' reported the radio-man, at the top of the stairway but without pausing, anxious now for them to get into the concealing ebb-and-flow of people.

The two hundred metres to Lambeth Pier was a barefoot walk on glowing coals. Only Hall could sensibly remain as close as might be necessary to Jennifer: the others had to become gawking sensation-seekers although within a second's leap. Mason actually joined in the still-existing excitement, pointing up like others were needlessly doing, tracing the distant progress of the convoy from the helicopters' search-light fingers. They were constantly jostled because the majority of people were going in the opposite direction, still towards Westminster Bridge, but the apologies, when there were any, were invariably automatic, made without looking.

Several times Jennifer groaned from the sudden pain of a collision.

With fifty yards still to go Jennifer said, desperately: 'She's taking my legs away: I can't walk much further.'

'*Can't run back and hide now. Too far away.*'

'So she couldn't risk a fight, after all!' said Hall, even more desperately. The bitch! But he should have guessed.

'*Just testing: flexing muscles.*'

'It's all right,' said Jennifer. 'It's better.'

The boarding was another potential and anticipated flash point. The launch that Perry had hired but which was crewed by casually dressed river police had been unobtrusively moored at the bottom of the steps for two hours, in total darkness and apparently battened down. An obvious and official police boat, one of four that throughout the day had kept the river between the hospital and Parliament clear of a would-be armada of water-borne sightseers, burbled about ten yards offshore like a growling guard dog, just holding itself in position against the tide. The look-out policeman reached the chained-off steps first, seeming to loiter and then expansively stretched. At the signal there was shadowed movement from below, the faintest footscrape. At the moment the rest of them drew level, on the embankment, a figure rose from the river steps to release the chain.

'Careful. The steps are slippery.'

They were in and descending within seconds, Hall groping down backwards to reach up with both hands against Jennifer's shoulders, Mason trying to balance her from behind. Twice Hall slipped, the second time grating his shin against the edge of the step. The surprised exclamation came when they were half way down, then a shout. They were at the pontoon, Jennifer handed in first and unseen, before people appeared above. At once there was a blinding, obscuring beam from the police launch as it swept in under sudden power. The subterfuge was brilliant, a rehearsed performance they hadn't been told about. With Jennifer, Hall, Mason and the two escorting policeman huddled unseen in the cabin there was a shouted argument between the uniformed and plain-clothes river police, quickly concluded with an even louder shouted announcement that the boat was under arrest. By the time the civilian boat moved off obediently in the wake of the launch, the Embankment level embarkation stage had cleared of people.

Jennifer had burrowed into Hall's shoulder, shivering. Quietly she said, 'Hold me. Please hold me.'

As he did so Jane echoed, in a small-child voice: '*Hold me. Please hold me.*'

Humphrey Perry was waiting at the designated berth at Richmond, which Hall had chosen because he rowed from there, although not from that specific boat club. They finally parted from their police escorts with whispered, hurried thanks, anxious to get on the road before their arrival was seen: already the sky was lightening. Coffee had been waiting, once they had got underway, and just before they arrived Jennifer had managed without any choking, rejecting difficulty the painkilling pills Lloyd had provided. Within minutes of the car beginning to move she was lolled against Hall's shoulder, occasionally moving, fitfully, but most of the time snoring. Mason made an exaggerated, lifted-eyebrow expression but didn't speak. Hall answered the look but didn't say anything either.

It was completely light by the time they reached the private psychiatric clinic at Hertfordshire, although the only people, apart from the nightstaff, were the medical doctor and two nurses whom Mason alerted from the car phone just before they arrived.

There was a wheelchair for the half-asleep Jennifer but the efficient smoothness of her immediately being swept into her private suite was broken by her abruptly twisting, seeking Hall who for once had retreated into the background.

The imploring hand came out again. 'You're not leaving me?'

'No.'

'I don't want you to.'

'I told you I'm not.'

'*I'm not leaving you, either.*'

There was still too much adrenalin for either of them even to consider sleep. Hall sat through the formal admission procedures, which Mason completed with the resident doctor, Charles Cox. He was a pipe-smoking, slow-talking man who showed neither surprise nor awe at Jennifer's presence.

'What about you three?' he asked, in a strangely high-pitched voice.

'I'd like my usual room,' accepted Mason, at once.

'I haven't thought about it,' admitted Hall.

'From what I've seen on television you're going to need somewhere to hide, too.'

'I suppose I am,' accepted Hall. 'Thanks.'

'You looked bloody scared among all those people yesterday.'

'I was.' He hadn't been aware of any television cameras.

'I won't be staying,' refused Perry, hurriedly.

'No,' agreed Hall, just as quickly. 'I'm going to want you back in London.'

'Am I still professionally engaged?' demanded the solicitor.

'Yes,' sighed Hall.

'Upon whose instructions?'

'Mine. Which will be confirmed by Mrs Lomax tomorrow. Or rather later today, when she wakes up.'

'What is there legally left to do?'

'At the moment I'm not sure. But it could be a lot.'

After Perry left with the doctor, Mason said, 'You really think you can drive Jane out? Make her leave Jennifer?'

Hall felt a flicker of embarrassment. 'We're not talking reality here. So it's as sensible in a nonsensical situation as anything else.'

'I still think you should try exorcism. There's a chapel here. A priest.'

'I'm willing to try anything.'

'What about me?'

'I don't understand?'

'Am I being professionally retained again?'

'You told me there was nothing you could do, psychiatrically.'

'That was to get rid of Jane. Jennifer's now in a depressed suicidal state. That *is* treatable. And should be treated, shouldn't it?'

'Of course. But can it be, despite Jane?'

'I don't know,' admitted the psychiatrist. 'We've obviously got to try.'

'Then I'd like you to be the one to do it. To organize the exorcism, as well.'

'*Attempted* exorcism,' warned the psychiatrist. He didn't immediately continue, although it was obvious he wanted to. Finally he said, outright, 'I'd like her permission and authorization to do a Paper.'

Another vulture, picking at the carcase, thought Hall. Except that Jennifer wasn't a carcase – yet – and it was unfair to criticize Mason as a vulture. What was he going to do when it came around to considering all the media and book offers? Not a question needing an immediate answer. There were a lot of others to be settled first. He said, 'I'll talk to her about it. We both can, in fact.'

'I can give you one early diagnosis.'

'What?'

'One of the commonest treatment methods for mental illness is for a psychiatrist to gain the utter reliance of his patient.'

'So?'

'It's going to be hard for me to do that with Jennifer. She's already transferred her total dependence on to you.'

In her adjoining room, through the drug haze and exhaustion and despair, Jennifer was distantly aware of Jane singing, to her own tune and adjusted words, 'Three Little Piggies Went to Market'.

'*One little piggy went to the slaughter.*
Another little piggy makes two.
A third little piggy is waiting by the door
Who can we find to make four?'

Chapter Twenty-nine

They did finally sleep but only for two or three hours and then fitfully. Hall was glad Jennifer was still asleep. Henot House, he discovered, was not specifically a psychiatric hospital – although it had a dedicated and fully staffed wing – but a drug and alcohol dependency clinic for the ultra rich and very famous, set in wooded grounds at least three times as big as those in which the Hampshire mansion was set, these complete with an eighteen hole golf course. He took particular note of the helicopter pad.

Within the building there was a shopping mall. He charged a designer track suit, trousers and shirt, underwear and shaving gear to an account he already found opened for him, although against his suite number, not his name. He checked at once with Charles Cox, reassured it was all part of the £500-a-day system and that Jennifer's identity was similarly protected.

While he waited for Humphrey Perry to get into his office, Hall watched breakfast television. It was almost totally occupied, as it had been for the past five days, by Jennifer. Hector Beringer repeated in a live interview, with Superintendent Hopkins in insistent support beside him, that Jennifer was no longer at the hospital. Every channel had its own reporter who'd taken part in the previous night's chase talking over the helicopter film of the decoy ambulance driving as far as Basingstoke before returning, without stopping, for the nurse dressed in Jennifer's clothes very publicly to get out and actually pose for photographs at the hospital entrance. There was ground footage of her doing that and a lot of that morning's film of a disbelieving crowd build-up which already looked as large as it had been the previous day. Soldiers were still there. Every station featured their resident psychiatrists, two of whom thought Jennifer could be freed of Jane's possession by treatment they offered to provide against three who insisted Jennifer would be possessed for life. The latter view appeared to be the opinion of newspaper contributing psychiatrists, whose views were also discussed in detail. One tabloid held up to the camera had the headline Twinned for Life to a Murderer. There was a lot of psychiatric references to religious hysteria that had attracted the crowds and footage of the cult squatters by Lambeth Palace. There was on every channel discussion about the book and media offers as if they were being seriously considered by Jennifer and her legal advisors. On a commercial station, the last to which Hall turned, a pop group performed a Country and Western style *Ode to Jennifer* with a prediction from a disc jockey that it would be in the charts by the end of the week. The repeated chorus was that Jennifer was doomed for life.

Despite having had little sleep himself, Humphrey Perry was in his office promptly at nine, waiting for Hall's call. It took the solicitor fifteen minutes to take down Hall's instructions, which included having collected from Geoffrey Johnson and delivered the clothes and belongings he'd collected from the prison. When Hall told the solicitor what he wanted from both the defence and prosecution sections of the murder file, Perry said, 'That absolutely—'

'Don't even bother to say it!' stopped Hall.

'We actually know Bentley, a trained murder squad detective, looked into it,' still protested the man.

'The same detective who didn't properly carry out the investigation at the scene of the crime,' rejected Hall. 'It was all too obvious. They laid back.'

'Leave it to the priests and the psychiatrists.'

'Just have what I want sent down. But not by courier: someone you can trust from your office who won't be recognized and followed.'

Mason and the clinic doctor were in deep conversation when Hall emerged for the second time.

'I've managed a preliminary medical examination,' said the squeaky-voiced doctor. 'I don't like all the medication she's been having. What St Thomas's administered was fine but God knows what was pumped into her in prison. I'm going to put her on detox, to clean her out.'

Hall flinched at the brutality of the doctor's expression. In daylight Cox was an unusual looking man: Hall guessed the hooded eyes were normal but weren't helped by the man waiting up for their arrival. 'You consider she's medically unwell?'

'She's not in good physical shape,' said Cox. 'I don't think she's eaten properly for weeks. The knife wounds have barely healed. The cut on her leg is still open. And I'm going to take X-rays later to see how the ribs are knitting.'

'And that's before I get involved or we think about exorcism,' said Mason. 'We're wondering just how much more, at the moment, Jennifer Lomax can take, physically and mentally.'

'Surely it's a measure of how strong Jennifer is, mentally, that she's been able to withstand it?' said Hall.

'There's a limit,' warned the psychiatrist. 'I think she might be close to reaching it. Which is why I'd like to know what you think you can do?'

Before Hall was halfway through explaining Mason and Cox were exchanging looks. The moment Hall finished Mason said flatly, 'I don't like it. You've no basis for believing that it would work. And it'll put a hell of a strain on her.'

'Any greater strain than she's already under?'

'Additional.'

'I outmanoeuvred Jane to get us away from the hospital.'

'You're talking of more than outmanoeuvring her now.'

'Are you telling me, on medical or mental health grounds, not to try it?'

Both doctors were momentarily silent. Cox said, 'I'd want to detox her, first. And after that give her some time to rest.'

Mason said, 'And I'd like to start treating her for the depression.'

'I wouldn't be able to do anything for some time . . .' Hall paused, forcing the admission. 'Perhaps never.'

'What if both of you fail?' demanded an unimpressed Cox.

It was the psychiatrist who answered. 'Then she'll probably kill herself. Which maybe she should be allowed to do before Jane makes her kill someone else even if she isn't allowed to get near Emily.'

Jennifer was wearing a track suit, too, grey against Hall's deep blue. Her hair was combed but her face was devoid of make-up, shiny and sallow. There was a hollowness to her cheeks Hall hadn't noticed before and her eyes, still black-ringed, were red-rimmed, too: incredibly, startling him, it actually made Jennifer look ghost-like. She looked up disinterestedly through glassy eyes at their entrance. The animation was brief, with her first demand. 'Is Emily safe? Hidden?'

'Absolutely,' promised Hall. 'No-one can get to her.'

'*Wanna bet.*'

It seemed an instinctive movement for Jennifer to reach out for Hall's hand. Unquestioningly – almost just as instinctively – he took it. Her skin was clammy but at the same time cold, feverish. She said, 'I saw what was happening at the hospital.'

Hall located the television, close to the window, louvred doors enclosing the screen. It was a huge suite, by comparison to the wards she had been in. The furniture was predominantly comfortable, appeal-to-everyone modern, with a few pieces – a side-table and a bureau – that could have been antique and from the cost of the clinic probably were. There was a profusion of flowers, mostly roses and lilies, in the sitting-room in which they were and more in what he was able to see through the open door of the bedroom. 'You're out of it now.'

'When we were getting out Jane said they would have torn me apart if they'd got to me,' reminded Jennifer. 'Would they have, really?'

'*You betcha!*'

'It didn't happen,' said Mason, placating. 'They didn't get the chance and you don't need to think about what didn't happen.'

'*What's going to happen from now on?*'

'But would they have done?' insisted Jennifer.

'It was an uncontrollable mob,' said Mason. 'They might have tried to hurt you. Others would have wanted to worship you.'

'*Don't I always tell you the truth! Remember the slogan: you heard it here first!*'

Hall frowned at the psychiatrist's directness and at the fear that shuddered through Jennifer, making her hand tremble. Forcefully he said, 'The past is just that, past.

We're planning a future now. We've got a lot to talk about.'

'*Let's hear it, big boy!*'

'She's talking to me all the time. Mocking, as usual.'

'And I want to talk to her. Like I did last night. But not immediately . . .' He indicated the psychiatrist. 'Dr Mason wants to try to help get rid of Jane—'

'*Don't waste your time! What's lover boy want with me?*'

'She says don't waste your time,' said Jennifer, stopping short of repeating the entire remark.

Hall ignored the interruption. 'I know we talked about it and you don't believe in any God, but he wants you to try exorcism . . .'

'. . . There's a chapel here. A visiting priest: rather high Church of England. He'll try to help,' picked up Mason. 'It doesn't matter that you don't believe. And I want us to spend a lot of time together, on other things. You're giving up. You mustn't give up. I want to stop you thinking like that . . .'

'I don't know how to think any more. Too tired.'

'*I won! I'm in charge.*'

'No, you're not too tired. Not really. Just for the moment. We're going to get you better.'

'*I've never felt better.*'

'How can I be got better?'

'By letting me help you. By letting us all help you,' insisted the psychiatrist. He looked pointedly towards the lawyer.

'Dr Mason has helped us a lot already,' responded Hall. 'Not just last night. Before. He wants to treat you – help rid you of Jane – but he also wants to write a clinical report on it. A technical paper that other psychiatrists and psychologists can read and learn from . . .'

'Freaky, freaky, freaky!'

Jennifer gave a weary sigh. 'There was a discussion about books on television.'

'This isn't – won't be – a book,' stressed Mason, urgently. 'It will be a technical account of everything that's happened. Not sensational at all.'

Jennifer gave another sigh. 'Why not?'

In his urgency Mason had been leaning forward, elbows on his knees. Now he eased back, smiling.

'*And he's got his piece of flesh. You're going to make a lot of people rich, Jennifer.*'

'There's another reason you don't feel well,' said Cox, involving himself. 'Your body's full of chemicals. I'm going to wash them all out. Make your body clean as well as fit again.'

Hall was glad it was better expressed than before. Breathing in, preparing himself, he said, 'And now it's time to talk to Jane again. Like I did last night. Just me and Jane, her words coming out of your mouth, exactly as she says them.'

'*Got you by the balls, scumbag, before you start!*'

'You can't read my mind, just Jennifer's. So how do you know what I'm going to do?'

'*Don't need to know what you're going to do.*'

'Oh, you do. Otherwise you'll never prove a lot of things.'

'*Don't need to prove a lot of things!*'

'Didn't prove that anyone murdered you, did you?'

'*So what? I'm getting my revenge. He's dead. She's a freak.*'

'You saw the television this morning?' demanded Hall, as the recollection – and the opening it offered – came to him.

'*What about it?*'

'Hear what they were calling you: what the papers were saying? Homicidal maniac, on the channel I watched. That true Jane? You a maniac . . . a *homicidal* maniac? People can understand a wife driven to despair by a cheating husband: sympathize, even. But not someone who kills for fun. That's what they're calling you. A maniac who kills for fun . . .'

Jane's rage began shaking through Jennifer and her hand slipped from Hall's. She snatched out for it again.

'*Not mad! Jennifer's going to be mad but not me. The bastard deserved to die. Murdered me so he had to die: eye for an eye, tooth for a tooth. That's the rule.*'

'You don't know that,' challenged Hall. 'You know he was cheating on you, with Jennifer. Like he was cheating on Jennifer with Rebecca. But you can't prove he murdered you . . .'

'*He doubled – trebled – my insulin! I'd been self-administering since I was a kid old enough to hold a syringe. I knew my dosages. I never, never, never over-dosed.*'

Mason was sitting back, familiar with the scene although professionally intent on every word, but Cox was open mouthed, the hooded eyes appearing wider than normal. There was an unlit pipe cupped between his hands, like a comfort symbol or a talisman. It didn't have a decorative bowl, like those Johnson preferred.

'"He doubled – trebled – my insulin,"' echoed Hall.

'*What?*'

'That's what you said. He. Gerald. Not he and Jennifer. Where's the proof she had anything to do with your death?'

'*She had the motive! To get married to him!*'

'A motive isn't proof. Where is the proof – the proof that

was overlooked or missed at the inquest – that she had anything whatsoever to do with killing you, if indeed you were killed.' He'd read the inquest material that the efficient Perry had provided but only as part of the general background, not as something essential to the main defence and his recollection was hazy. Perhaps he should have waited until he'd read the duplicate he'd asked Perry for that morning.

'*I was there, remember! I witnessed my own death! He lied, at the inquest. Over and over again. And no-one challenged him because it was all too cleverly done. And people were frightened of him: respected him because he was rich. He killed me with what Jennifer provided.*'

'I didn't provide anything,' said Jennifer, weakly.

'If everything is so easily proved, I can't see why you are so frightened for me to go into it. Unless, of course, the TV and newspapers are right about your sanity.' There was a desperation that didn't show in his voice. He had no argument left in reserve. Everything depended upon Jane's response.

Hall's initial thought was that Jennifer's finger-tightening was the beginning of another uncontrollable fit, but nothing came and he realized it was Jennifer tensing, as he was tensed, against a physical and verbal tirade that would overwhelm them. But there was nothing.

When they came the words were even, measured, with no anger or hysteria. '*I am getting justice for myself. Justice I was denied.*'

Momentarily Hall took his hand away, not believing he could prevent the tremble of excitement at her reaction and the argument it made possible. 'Just as you are denying justice to Jennifer. I wonder how your father would have felt about that.'

'*She had a proper trial!*'

'And was found not guilty. Not guilty of killing Gerald Lomax. She hasn't faced trial for killing you.'

'*How can she be?*'

'By letting me re-examine the inquest evidence. But not as it was examined at the inquest. As it would have been examined in a court of law if Jennifer Lomax had been on trial for your murder. And present it to you like a trial, here . . .' He briefly swept his hand out. '. . . in front of the doctors, if you like.'

'*Who decides guilt or innocence?*'

'The weight of evidence.'

'*You could cheat.*'

'And you'd know if I did. You've just said you witnessed your own murder. And Jennifer would know if I tried to cheat. And she can't think anything without your being aware of it, can she?'

There was another protracted silence. '*And if there's no evidence you expect me to leave: give up my possession?*'

'Yes.'

'*What if there is evidence?*'

Now the long silence was Hall's. For several moments he held Jennifer's eyes before saying, 'Then it becomes a police matter, to be properly prosecuted in court, as she was properly prosecuted for the murder of Gerald. Wouldn't that be better revenge, for her to be re-arraigned on a provable murder charge in a public court?'

'*Brilliant! Oh yes, absolutely brilliant! I'll go along with that!*'

Hall still held Jennifer's eyes. 'Are you prepared to accept it, too?'

'*Trapped her there, haven't you?*'

Jennifer relayed Jane's words but didn't answer Hall's question.

'Jennifer?' he prompted.

'You're separating things: making it sound like Gerald might have done it by himself.'

'She's scared!'

'I'm not scared!' protested Jennifer, answering an accusation she hadn't mouthed verbatim. 'I didn't murder her. Neither did Gerald.'

'Then agree to my doing what I want.'

There was still a hesitation before Jennifer said, 'All right. Do it.'

'I should have prevented it,' insisted Mason, after Cox had taken Jennifer to begin the complete medical examination before her first meeting with the priest. 'You're putting her through what amounts to a second trial. It'll be intolerable.'

'Not if it gets rid of Jane.'

'There's no guarantee it will! No guarantee Jane would leave her alone, even if you did prove Jennifer innocent.'

'It's a gamble,' conceded Hall.

'With a sick person's sanity,' protested the psychiatrist.

'It gives you time to do what you can for her professionally. And for the exorcism to be attempted.'

Mason shook his head, unpersuaded. 'Would you really tell the police if you thought there had been a murder conspiracy between Jennifer and Lomax?'

'I believe she's totally innocent. I wouldn't have started any of this if I hadn't been totally convinced of that.'

'That isn't an answer to my question.'

'Would you?'

'I'm not sure, after what she's gone through. But it still isn't an answer.'

'I'm not sure, either.'

'Why's Mummy's picture in the newspaper?'

Annabelle and Johnson, either side of the child at the

luncheon table, each looked expectantly at the other, neither wanting to reply.

'Sure it was her?' asked Johnson, falling back on well practised legal avoidance of ducking a question by asking another.

'Course it was her!' said Emily, indignantly. 'There was a man by the pool this morning reading about her. There was another picture of lots of people. And there was an M word but it wasn't mouse. I can read mouse.'

'It might have been about people being happy that she's getting better,' suggested Annabelle, floundering.

Emily looked doubtfully between the two adults. 'Will she be coming home soon then?'

'If she gets better.'

'Will she be nasty to me again?'

'No,' said the girl.

'I don't want her to be nasty any more. I didn't like it.'

'I told you it only happened because she was very ill. Now she's getting better it can't happen again.'

'Good,' said Emily, brightly. 'Then everything's all right. I want to go to the pool again this afternoon.'

While she and Johnson were watching an arm-banded Emily thrash in the shallow end Annabelle said, 'I've just broken a cardinal rule. I've told a child a lie that's bound to be found out.'

Chapter Thirty

The inquest had returned an open verdict, the only one possible from the evidence. And it was unclear from local Hampshire newspaper reports, the only public record available, how much of that evidence had been considered by the coroner, solicitor James Davies, against the prepared statements of witnesses.

Hall read the newspaper reports first, for a general understanding of how deeply Jane's death had been examined. Gerald Lomax had been the main witness and his evidence made up the major proportion of each account. His wife had suffered diabetes from birth and had always needed to take insulin. She injected herself, usually without any problems, although on two previous occasions, before their move from America to England, there had been two serious overdose incidents. Fortunately there had been people with her on both occasions and doctors had been quickly summoned: on the second she had been admitted to hospital to be stabilized.

In the *Hampshire Chronicle*, which carried the longest account, the report had been broken here by a series of questions and answers, between the coroner and Lomax.

'Was your wife careless about her injections?' the coroner had asked.

'Sometimes,' Lomax had replied. 'She also ate too irregularly for her condition.'

'What about alcohol, which I understand can contribute to an imbalance?'

'That had greatly reduced, since our move from America.'

'You mean she drank immoderately?'

'Rarely, since our transfer to this country.'

'But before?'

'Sometimes.'

'Would you say your wife was careless of her condition?'

'I would say she had grown too familiar with it.'

'Familiarity breeding contempt?' clichéd the coroner.

'That is so.'

'Was your wife in any way suicidal because of her condition?'

'Absolutely not! She loved life.'

'Did your wife take sleeping pills?'

'No.'

'You are aware that some were found. And that traces were found in your wife's body?'

'I can't account for that. The pills were mine. An old prescription. They should have been thrown away.'

It was his working practice usually to spend at least three days a week in London. On the day of her death, a Friday, he had arrived home in mid-afternoon. The house had appeared to be empty, which had surprised him because he had telephoned the previous evening to give her his time of arrival. He had assumed Jane was out, shopping or with friends. He'd actually telephoned a particular acquaintance, the wife of an American on an exchange secondment from IBM, to see if she was there. It was not until an hour after his return that he'd gone upstairs to find his wife in bed, in a coma. He called her doctor at the same time as the ambulance and travelled in it to hospital with her. She'd died an hour after admission.

Police Constable Harry Elroyd testified to being automatically called to the mansion by the ambulance alarm. Mrs Lomax had been in bed, still wearing her nightdress: that and the bedding was soiled, where her bladder had apparently collapsed. On a bedside table he found an insulin pack with four ampoules missing. Two, both empty, were on the table. He'd found the other two, also empty, in the bathroom waste bin. In the bathroom cabinet he had found a half-filled bottle of temazepam sleeping tablets. On the bedside table was a syringe, with a needle still attached. Close to it was a goblet still containing sufficient brandy to be identified by its smell. He'd found a two-thirds-filled bottle of brandy on the downstairs kitchen table, together with the uncleared remains of an evening meal, for one person. There was the residue of red wine in a glass and in the kitchen waste bin an empty Margaux bottle. He had located no note to indicate Mrs Lomax had intended to take her own life.

Dr Allan Greenaway said he had been Mrs Lomax's physician since her arrival in Hampshire. Considering her diabetes she was a woman in reasonably good health, although she had consulted him about stomach pains. He had prescribed mebeverine hydrochloride, for irritable bowel syndrome, but had feared she might be developing stomach ulcers, not uncommon in her condition. For that he issued repeat prescriptions for the insulin he identified from the pack shown to him. Because of her long history of diabetes he had never thought it necessary to warn her against heavy indulgence in alcohol. It was a precaution of which she would have been permanently aware.

Pathologist Michael Bailey described Jane Lomax as a woman in general good health, apart from some pancreatic atrophy consistent with the history from childhood of her diabetes. His autopsy had also disclosed the evidence of impending ulceration suspected by Dr Greenaway, which again resulted from her condition. Her blood sugar level was radically out of balance which would have inevitably caused shock, not just to the virtually inoperative pancreas but to the liver and heart. Forensically that imbalance was caused by an excess of insulin, compounded by alcohol and the lactose and sucrose ingredients of the specific meberevine hydrochloride tablets that had been prescribed. It had been impossible for him to calculate with any accuracy the excess of insulin that had proved fatal. He understood her daily dosage to be twenty units, twice a day. The discarded ampoules represented twice that amount and should not, additionally, have been present during what had evidently been a night-time period. He had found substantial traces of temazepam in Mrs Lomax's body and agreed with the coroner that a dangerous but common side effect of sleeping pills was for someone to awaken, forget they had already taken some and ingest more.

'In your opinion, could this have happened in this case and further disorientated Mrs Lomax so that she self-administered a totally unnecessary and lethal injection of insulin?' the coroner had asked.

'I consider that the most likely explanation for what happened,' replied the pathologist. His phrase – a fatal cocktail – had provided the headline in two separate newspapers.

It had also been used – and justified the headline – by James Davies in his summing up, although not part of the quote that appeared.

> There are many facets of this tragedy for which I cannot find a satisfactory explanation – because of which I feel I am prevented from anything other than an open verdict – but all the evidence before me indicates an unfortunately afflicted woman neglecting, through familiarity, the medical condition with which she had been born. Mr Lomax is a new but already respected member of the local community and to him I express my sympathy in his sad loss.

Jeremy Hall was swamped with pointless, unresolvable frustration. At once – objectively, reminding himself of what he was trying to achieve – he suppressed the distraction, as he would have suppressed a flicker of anger in a court. The coroner's remarks had done more than sum up the inquest: indeed, the concluding words had thrown up in neon-bright clarity the entire formularized direction of the inquest. Sadly bereaved – there were three photographs of a darkly-bespectacled, black-suited, head-bent Lomax hurrying from court – charity supporting pillar of the local community robbed of an adored, medically afflicted wife through a combination of small but fatal misjudgements by a past-his-prime country doctor who himself had died six months later and an occasionally wilfully-challenging woman prone to disregarding her illness. All the statements read and filleted beforehand. A verdict determined ('Sorry, Gerry: accidental or misadventure just wouldn't have been right,') in advance to get the legally required but painful official business over and out of the way in the shortest acceptable time.

In his eagerness he was making the mistake of examining the inquest evidence as he would have done in a far more rigidly structured Court of Law. But the inquest hadn't done that. Inquests rarely did. Nine times out of ten – maybe slightly less – they were occasions of commiseration. Which is what Jane Lomax's had been. Her death had been investigated and decided upon in the familiar, non-adversarial surroundings of a village hall, with flower show and horticultural exhibition flyers on a tattered notice board and fold-away chairs stacked at the back amidst smells of paraffin and dust and chalk.

He had to come from the totally opposite direction, the criminally minded, suspicious, believe-nothing direction. The way of John Bentley and Malcolm Rodgers, thinking the worst of everybody and every situation until proven wrong: sometimes not even then.

Jeremy Hall determined upon a middle course, refusing the easy criticism of a country inquest but rejecting, too, a guilty-until-proven innocent approach. As he picked his way with methodical care through the written statements he had consciously to keep that determination in mind, so easy would it have been to veer wildly across both self-imposed guidelines. When he finished he had seven closely handwritten pages of reminders, believed anomalies, seeming contradictions and outright inconsistencies. It had taken most of the day and occupied a further hour separating his own uncertainties into a list of positive requests to Humphrey Perry. They still occupied four pages and after telephoning to ensure the man would be at the receiving end, preventing anyone else identifying the source, Hall faxed them for convenience and to ensure there was no verbal misunderstanding between himself and the solicitor.

Hall allowed a further hour for Perry to read everything before he telephoned London for the second time.

'You sure you want all this?' demanded the solicitor, at once.

'I wouldn't have asked if I hadn't been.'

'I've read the same file, as closely as you have. It was a scarcely adequate inquest but then a lot of inquests are scarcely adequate. None of the statements – not even of witnesses who weren't called – incriminate Lomax in any way whatsoever. And it doesn't take you one step further to what you're trying to prove: Jennifer isn't involved at all.'

'That's what I'm trying to prove?'

'That wasn't what I meant and you know it,' said Perry, irritably.

'There were a lot of questions that should have been asked but weren't.'

'Six years ago!'

'That's when Jane died. The time we're talking about.'

'The time you're talking about.'

'I'd like the answers as soon as possible.'

'Bert called me. He wants to know where you are.'

'Did you tell him?'

'I promised you'd call.'

'I will,' agreed Hall.

'I've got five more offers, all for books. Three are repeats, upping their first offers.'

'Hold them.'

'Have you discussed any with her yet?'

'That's way down the list.'

'We've got a bill for police time. And for damage to equipment. Twenty-three thousand.'

'Ignore it. If they issue a writ, file a necessity defence under the Public Order Act. Anything else?'

'You tell me.'

'Not for the moment.'

Colin Dawson perfectly suited the opulence and ambience of his surroundings, a white-haired, pink-faced avuncular gentleman priest of independent means who had never believed his genuine religious piety needed to be reinforced by secular hardship. He rode to hounds on one of his two hunters, favoured burgundy over claret in a wine cellar the envy of the county and donated his entire church salary to Save the Children. His cassocks were tailored.

He came curiously but sincerely concerned into Jennifer's suite, made totally unafraid of encountering a woman possessed by a murderous ghost not just by his belief in the protection of God but by never having known a life without a financial armour through which no harm or ill had ever penetrated.

'*The Jesus jockey,*' Jane greeted.

The man had been well briefed by Julian Mason. He said, 'It doesn't matter what she makes you do or say. She can't frighten or shock me. I'm stronger than she is, because I have God and she is evil, the Devil incarnate. Let her fight me. I'll fight her back and I will win.'

'*The fuck he will.*'

Jennifer had found it easier – a relief even – simply to be the conduit between Jane and Jeremy Hall and she did it now with Dawson, too exhausted, too apathetic, any longer to censor the words.

Dawson laughed at the obscenity. 'And St Matthew said "The blasphemy against the Holy Ghost shall not be forgiven unto men".'

'*And Exodus teaches "Life for life. Eye for eye, tooth for tooth, hand for hand, foot for foot, burning for burning, wound for wound, stripe for stripe."*'

He laughed again. 'And the Prayers say "Keep thy tongue from evil: and thy lips, that they speak no guile. Eschew evil and do good: seek peace and ensure it."

Which is what I'll do, if you help me, Jennifer. I'll eschew the evil that possesses you and give you peace.'

'If only you could,' said Jennifer.

'*Verse 8. Romans.*'

'Ah!' said the priest. 'Interesting!'

'*Forgotten it?*'

The man shook his head. '"Let us do evil, that good may come." So you know your Bible, Jane? Therefore you must believe? Or did believe, once. Philippians, 26?'

'*Be ye angry and sin not: let not the sun go down upon your wrath,*' Jane recognized, immediately.

'All right,' accepted Dawson. 'So I have a formidable adversary.'

'*You'd better believe it. I can out-argue you creed for creed, ritual for ritual.*'

'When did you lose your way, Jane?'

'*When I lost my fucking life!*'

'Become a catechumen again, Jane,' said the priest, urgently. 'Be my pupil. Learn to believe again. To love again. And leave this child whose mind you occupy and whom you want to destroy.'

'*This "child" conspired to kill me! Took part in it . . .*'

'Then hers will be the punishment on the terrible day of judgement.' He was sweating, his face pinker than usual.

'*No way, pops. I'd rather do it myself. My way.*'

The psychiatrist's briefing had been total. Dawson said, 'You've chosen judgement without proof.'

'*Been talking to people, haven't you?*'

'Will you listen to me?'

'*Until I get bored.*'

'Will you listen to the lawyer who's trying to prove you wrong?'

'*He won't.*'

'Will you go, leave her, if he does?'

'That's the deal. Easy one for me to make.'

'Maybe I'll persuade you to leave first.'

'Then again, maybe you won't.'

'Jennifer, could you learn to believe in God? Love God?'

'I don't think so.'

'Will you go through the services with me? Pray with me? Try?'

'Yes.'

'Hypocrite.'

'"Though ye believe not me, believe the works",' retorted the man.

'OK pops. Show us the works.'

'I will,' said Dawson, sincerely. 'I'll make you believe again, even if I can't make Jennifer.'

'Nah!'

'"Rejoiceth not in iniquity, but rejoiceth in the truth",' said the priest, quoting again.

'Corinthians,' identified Jane, as quickly as before.

'I can guide you back.'

'Let's make it a challenge, like it is with Jeremy Hall!'

It was in the lawyer's rooms, thirty minutes later, that Dawson, who could find his way around the establishment's wine list with the sure-footedness of a tightrope walker crossing Niagara Falls, selected the Roederer Crystal ('the Krug they've got is too buttery,') and announced, 'I've found the weakness.'

'What?' demanded Mason and Hall, almost in unison.

'Jane believes in God. Or did, very devoutly.'

'Her father was an Episcopalian bishop,' remembered Hall.

'Ah!' exclaimed the man, a mystery solved. 'This might not be as difficult as we thought it was going to be.'

'You think you can do it?' demanded the lawyer.

'I'm more confident now than I was an hour ago.'

'Which only leaves me to do what I have to do,' accepted Mason.

Dawson nodded. 'And Jennifer will be saved.'

Chapter Thirty-one

The well established and practised discretion of the clinic extended to a pool of cars registered to Henot House, which avoided Jeremy Hall having to hire one in his own name and risk disclosing their whereabouts. He had to identify himself by telephone, though, to get the meetings he wanted and from the quickness with which people – even the police – agreed he decided the danger of being publicly recognized was outweighed by the speed with which every door opened to him. And he was in a great hurry.

Despite the psychiatrist's warning of Jennifer's dependence upon him, he'd been confused by the strength of her reaction to his leaving. He only bothered to tell her at all at Julian Mason's urging and was glad the psychiatrist was with him when he did. She at once came close to tears – which he realized for the first time she'd rarely done during a lot of the horror she'd suffered – and needed the hand-holding assurance repeated several times that he was not abandoning her but would return immediately from talking to people it was imperative he see.

'Today. Tonight,' she'd insisted.

'It should be tonight. Everything's arranged.'

'You're not sure?'

'If I don't manage to see everyone I'll come back and go again tomorrow.'

'Don't leave me!'

'I told you I'm not leaving you: and where and why I'm going. Which you know I've got to.'

Hall had been disconcerted but Mason had called it valuable. 'Think what she's gone through, without breaking. That showed me just how deep the depression is.'

'Can you lift her out of it?'

The psychiatrist pulled an uncertain face. 'I've probably got a more difficult job than either you or the priest.'

The incident delayed him but he still arrived in good time for his first appointment, uncomfortable in the jacket he'd had to buy from the clinic outfitters which didn't stock clothes in his chest size. He was unhappy, too, that Michael Bailey had decreed somewhere as public as Winchester hospital, although the nearby railway station car park was convenient to hide the hire car against its number being noted at the hospital and traced to the Hertfordshire clinic. He walked the intervening distance and grew unhappier at the obvious attention from the suddenly busy corridors, with their open-doored offices, along which he had to pass to get to the pathology department. There was a lot of activity there, too. It had been wise to abandon the car.

Bailey was a tall, gangling man with a stutter, which worsened with the intensity with which he leaned forward to get the blocked words out. Jeremy Hall went through the quadrille of thanking the pathologist for seeing him so promptly and being told in return it was in no way inconvenient: Bailey patted the dossier in front of him and said he had recovered his original statement from the archives at Humphrey Perry's pre-trial request and of course he'd followed the sensational events.

It took longer agreeing the case of Jennifer Lomax was absolutely incredible – 'earth shattering' was the phrase it took the pathologist three attempts to say – threatened the very foundations of conventional imagination and even religious belief. Hall went through the routine recognizing that it was indeed every one and more of those things but that, perhaps most incredible of all, he'd become so closely involved that he'd ceased thinking so and was now accepting the totally abnormal as the totally normal. He invoked professional confidentiality to avoid talking about Jennifer personally, supposing this encounter to be a rehearsal for those to follow.

'You want to reopen the inquest?' anticipated Bailey.

'I don't know that would be possible. Or whether any useful purpose would be served.'

'What then?'

'It is, as you say, an astonishing case,' said Hall, the lie carefully prepared. 'Everything about it has to be compiled and assessed for legal and academic study. And that includes any reassessment that might be necessary of what happened in the past.'

'I understand,' assured Bailey, getting stuck halfway through the word.

'All I've been able to do is compare newspaper reports with written statements. It's not clear to me how much of those written statements were actually introduced as evidence or how much the coroner took as read, from access to the statements beforehand.'

'The usual way,' smiled the pathologist, uncertainly. 'He just picked the relevant points to put to me, from my statement.'

Everything decided in advance, Hall thought again. 'In your report you refer to aspects of the puncture wounds, where Mrs Lomax injected herself. Was that finding examined or taken as read?'

'Actually I discussed it with Mr Davies before the inquest began,' admitted the pathologist. 'He felt it would be distressing for Mr Lomax for us to go too deeply into it at the hearing itself.'

Hall swallowed the sigh. 'Go through it with me, if you would.'

'The puncture mark in the left arm was larger than the others on the body and was dangerously close to the vein. The other three were much smaller and properly injected subcutaneously.'

'What did you think about that?'

'The largest puncture mark would have been the last injection she self-administered. By then, I believe, she would have already overdosed on insulin. And additionally have taken one lot of temazepam after another. She would have been extremely unsteady.'

'The majority of the injections were to the right of the body: two to the right arm, one in the right thigh?'

'That's right.'

'You referred to skin hardening, because of the length of time Mrs Lomax had been injecting?'

'Yes. It happens to diabetics, particularly those who take soluble insulin, which she did.'

'In which side of the body was that hardening most prevalent, the right or the left?' Into his mind, abruptly, came a fact that could have greatly contributed to Jennifer's innocence at the trial, if the other evidence hadn't been so overwhelming.

Bailey frowned, needing for the first time to go back to the file on his desk. It was several moments before he looked up, smiling. 'Not a great deal in it, really. But on balance the right.'

'What about the left arm. What was the extent of the hardening there?'

The pathologist went back to his file, although more briefly this time. 'Very little. The softness of the skin was a contributory factor, I decided, to the puncture wound being larger than the others.'

'Something else not in the newspaper reports but mentioned in your statement, was how long Mrs Lomax had been unconscious.'

Bailey breathed in sharply and the irritation made it even more difficult for him initially to respond. 'Mr Davies was furious with the policeman, for talking about the bladder collapse. That was most unnecessary. Most distasteful.'

'How long?' repeated Hall.

'A considerable time: the bladder collapse was an early indication of organ deterioration.'

'Working back from the time she was found – three-twenty in the afternoon, according to Gerald Lomax – what time the previous night would she have become deeply unconscious?'

'Twelve hours, at least. The evening meal had been steak: very little had been digested. The blood alcohol content was also extremely high.'

'There was no mention whatsoever in any report I read but in your written statement you talked of an abrasion inside Mrs Lomax's upper lip?'

Bailey nodded. 'Something else that didn't need to be brought out to cause Mr Lomax any further distress. In my opinion it resulted from Mrs Lomax, in a very unsteady condition, accidently striking her lip between the glass and her teeth, when she attempted to drink from the brandy goblet that was found on the bedside table.'

'As a medical expert, what's your opinion of Mrs Lomax being prescribed meberevine hydrochloride?'

Bailey gave the impression of considering the question. 'As you know, a diabetic makes excess glucose. Some proprietary brands of meberevine hydrochloride have lactose and sucrose added to them. I don't think it's an ideal preparation for a diabetic but the two, by themselves and with the instructions being strictly followed, wouldn't be overly dangerous. But with an excess of alcohol and insulin it is, as I said at the time, a lethal cocktail.'

He smiled, expectantly, but Hall didn't respond. Instead, tightly, he said, 'Thank you,' and stood up. How many deaths crying out for a proper investigation, as this had been, were dismissed by platitudes, quick chats between fellow members of the local golf club and preconceived, unsubstantiated opinions?

Bailey frowned. 'But I haven't told you anything.'

'Enough,' assured Hall.

Hall considered recovering the car but decided against it, instead taking a taxi from the station. The recognition took longer than he expected and was encouragingly disinterested.

'You're the lawyer, aren't you?'

'Yes.'

'She coming home.'

'Maybe.'

'Lots of stuff on television.'

'I saw some of it.'

'Lot of people believe in ghosts, you know. My Doris does.'

'So do a lot of other people now.'

'Suppose you're right, considering.'

Hall was relieved to get to the one-constable police house at Four Marks, which was the closest to the Lomax mansion. He was early but Harry Elroyd was already waiting in a front parlour with chintz loose covers on the furniture and long ago photographs of the man stiffly upright in army sergeant's uniform. Elroyd sat nervously with a tattered, yellowing notebook on his knee. With him was Paul Hughes, the police inspector whom Hall had confronted over the press intrusion and who had been called before Mr Justice Jarvis. A third, narrow-faced man very formally offered a card attesting that Derek Peterson was a solicitor at law.

'Protecting the interests of the Constabulary,' declared the man.

'Do they need protecting?'

'We've no indication of the purpose of this meeting.'

The personal curiosity went far beyond the professional but there wasn't the awe of the hospital and Hall was glad. He recited the same explanation he'd given the pathologist and at once Peterson said, 'Are you alleging professional negligence or incompetence?'

'No. I simply want to talk to Constable Elroyd to understand a few things more clearly.'

'Whom do you represent?' asked the solicitor. 'I can't let this proceed unless I am sure you are representing someone.'

'Mrs Jennifer Lomax, who is the unencumbered heir to the estate of Gerald James Lomax,' said Hall, matching the formality.

Peterson nodded, the reluctance obvious. Mrs Elroyd came hesitantly in with coffee and biscuits on a tray. She was so intent upon Hall that she jarred the tray against the table edge, spilling the coffee, and hurried out muttering apologies. She was a lot fatter now than she'd been in the wedding photographs on the sideboard.

The irritation at the solicitor's attitude was fleeting. If there were oversights in the investigation into Jane Lomax's death – and Hall was becoming increasingly convinced there had been – then this man was responsible. Was there anything after so long to learn from a portly, rubicund country policeman who could probably spot an illegally shot pheasant through thick canvas but miss an inconsistency that might have led to a murder charge? 'Did you know Mrs Lomax, before you went to the house that afternoon?'

'Knew who she was,' said the man, the voice blurred by his local accent. 'She and the mister. They'd made themselves well enough known since moving in . . .' He looked uncertainly at the senior officer. 'Not, perhaps, as much as the new Mrs Lomax, though. I hope she's going to be all right.'

'So do we all,' said Hall. 'But let's stay with the first Mrs Lomax. What sort of things did you see her at?'

'Village show. She was high church so she worshipped in Alton but she gave a lot of money, over £1,000, to the church roof appeal here in the village. Even attended services there sometimes.'

'So she was well liked?'

'Oh yes.'

'What about the pub?'

'Pub?'

'There is a local pub, isn't there? Did she ever go there?'

'No. They never did things like that.'

'You hear a lot in a village like this, a man in your position?'

Elroyd smiled, proudly. 'Keep my ear to the ground. Eyes open.'

If only, thought Hall. 'Did you ever hear that Mrs Lomax drank?'

'I never did. That's what surprised me that day, all that drink around.'

'Not enough to mention it to anyone? A senior officer, maybe?'

Peterson stirred.

'I didn't know she had an illness: that she shouldn't,' protested the man. 'What people do in their own house is their business, as long as it's not breaking the law, isn't it?'

'That sounds perfectly satisfactory to me,' said Hughes, in quick support.

It did, conceded Hall. 'I know what you found in the kitchen and in the bedroom but what about the rest of the house? Was it tidy or untidy?'

'Very tidy. Mrs Simpson was the housekeeper then. She's a very neat person. Her cottage is a picture.'

'Mrs Lomax was in her nightdress, in bed, when you entered the bedroom?'

'Dr Greenaway and the ambulance people were trying to revive her.'

'This is all in Constable Elroyd's statement,' reminded Peterson.

Hall ignored the interruption. 'What about the clothes Mrs Lomax had been wearing, before she changed into her nightdress. Was there any sign of them around the bedroom?'

Elroyd shifted, uncomfortably, squinting down into the ancient book. Looking up doubtfully he said, 'I haven't made a note here of any day clothes.'

'Would you have done?' asked the inspector, irritatingly ahead of Hall.

'I think so, sir. I was very careful that day. I realized how important it was.'

No you didn't, thought Hall. 'So what's the answer, Constable?'

'There couldn't have been any visible in the bedroom.'

'So Mrs Lomax must have put them away before getting into bed?'

'Presumably,' said the policeman, even more doubtfully.

'Is there any importance in whether or not Mrs Lomax left her day clothes lying around?' said Peterson.

Again Hall ignored the solicitor. To Elroyd he said, 'What about underclothes?'

The constable visibly blushed. 'I've no note of any, sir.'

'And you would have done, if you had seen any?'

'I took a careful note of everything.'

'Like the sleeping pills, the temazepam, in the bathroom medicine cabinet?'

'Yes, sir,' said the constable, brightening.

'Did you take a note of the chemist who dispensed the sleeping pills?' He felt a quiver of excitement at something that occurred to him from Gerald Lomax's written statement and wondered if he was interpreting it correctly: if he were, this could be the most vital question of the day. It could also be, he realized, the most damning for Jennifer.

'Hemels, Bury Street, EC3,' read out the man, triumphantly. 'And the date of dispensing. June thirteenth.'

'Thank you,' said Hall, sincerely. 'That was most helpful. And there was the empty wine bottle in the kitchen wastebin? You even recorded what wine it was, Margaux?'

The plump man checked his notes. 'That's right, sir. Margaux.' He mispronounced it, stressing the X.

'Apart from the Margaux bottle having been put in the bin, would you describe the rest of the kitchen as messy?'

'Only the table. There were even food scraps on the table. But everything else was in its proper place.'

'Do you intend trying to reopen the inquest, upon some new evidence?' demanded Peterson.

'I'm not sure there would be sufficient. Certainly not now that Mr Lomax is dead,' said Hall. 'I don't even intend seeing the coroner.'

'What, then, is the point of all this?'

Hall hesitated. 'I'm not sure yet whether Mrs Lomax shared the housekeeper's love of tidiness: I intend to ask her. But I don't understand why Mrs Lomax would have discarded an empty wine bottle in a wastebin but left the rest of the dinner – even food scraps – uncleared on the table. Or why she went to the trouble when she got upstairs – still, it would seem, with a glass of brandy in her hand – presumably to hang up her clothes. Or why some insulin ampoules were properly thrown away in the bathroom – where the temazepam was neatly in a medicine cabinet – but others on a bedside table—'

'. . . From my reading of the inquest evidence Mrs Lomax was clearly drunk,' broke in Hughes. 'Drunken people do inconsistent things.'

Which was unarguably true, Hall cautioned himself. He still wasn't sure if there was the remotest chance of his achieving anything with what he was doing – insane idea for an insane situation echoed in his head – but he had to be careful against turning discrepancies into incontestable facts. 'Had you been involved, inspector, wouldn't those inconsistencies have prompted you to question Gerald Lomax a little more closely than he was?'

'No,' said Hughes, at once. 'Mr Lomax wasn't *there*. How could he have helped us beyond telling us how he found his wife?'

'Is that all?' demanded Peterson.

Hall was reluctant to be dismissed – could imagine the solicitor's "and-I-took-no-nonsense" dinner-table anecdotes that night – but there wasn't anything else about which he wanted to satisfy himself. 'I'm sure you'll help me further if something else comes up that I want clarifying.'

'Are you going to the house?' asked Hughes.

Hall shook his head. 'I didn't intend to.'

'We're still having to keep officers there all the time. And it's not just all the media people who're hanging around for Mrs Lomax to come back. There's a lot of souvenir hunters now. The house nameplate has gone and we caught a family three days ago digging up plants, to take home and put in their own garden. We've charged them. The gardener says he's lost some tools.'

'What is it you want, Inspector?'

'A private security firm. We'll perform a police function but we'd like the general protection taken over by someone else.'

'I'll arrange it,' promised Hall.

Elspeth Simpson lived just two miles along the same road as the village policeman, who hadn't exaggerated the woman's house-proudness. Even the garden flowers were in order of colour and in regimented lines and inside everything looked as if it were arranged soon to be packed away for safekeeping. The tiny, bird-like woman was as neatly packed as her belongings, her white hair tightly netted, the white collar of her uncreased paisley-patterned dress hard with starch. She appeared relieved that Hall refused tea but looked anxiously at a man of his size occupying one of her best-room chairs. He did his best not to ruffle the protective loose covers on the arms.

For the first time that day he discerned no attitude at all towards him. Elspeth chattered like a bird and he let her, eager for the gossip of which he quickly guessed she was the self-appointed village archivist. Jane Lomax's death had been a tragedy, awful. Poor Mr Lomax had been very brave. They'd been devoted. There was a sniff at how quickly he had married again and at Jennifer's name but it wasn't for her to criticize. The second Mrs Lomax had fitted every bit as well into the village and local life, apart from the church, although she supported its events and had put money towards the new organ. She didn't understand how the murder ('that awful thing,') could have happened but thought everything in court had been all wrong ('no disrespect to you, of course, sir,') because ghosts weren't natural (said without a suggestion of a smile) and it wasn't God's way. There was only one ghost, the Holy Ghost. Perhaps it wouldn't have occurred if the second Mrs Lomax had gone to church, not that she was criticizing, of course.

'Why didn't you stay on as housekeeper to the second Mrs Lomax?'

'George, my late. He was ill, before they got married. I had to leave to look after him all the time. Emphysema. Mr Lomax was very good to me. Gave me £1,000 when I left and £500 for the funeral. And the second Mrs Lomax used to call by sometimes to see if I was all right. By then Alice – that's Mrs Jenkins – had been engaged so there wasn't any cause for me to go back.'

'You made a statement after the first Mrs Lomax's

death but you didn't give evidence at the inquest?'

'I went but the policeman – not Harry Elroyd, the one who organized it all – said the coroner didn't want me because I hadn't been there that day.'

'Why was that?'

'It was my day off, a Friday. Mr Lomax always came home early on a Friday, so Mrs Lomax wasn't too long alone.'

'Because of her diabetes.'

'Yes. And they were devoted, like I said.'

Lomax must have been a consummate actor. 'You knew she was a diabetic?'

'Of course. That's why I couldn't understand a lot of what was said at the inquest.'

Hall breathed, deeply. 'What exactly didn't you understand, Mrs Simpson?'

'Mr Lomax saying she was careless with her treatment. She never was, as far as I was concerned. She'd always done it, you see. It was automatic, like washing her hands.' As if in reminder the woman checked her own to ensure they were clean.

'Didn't you tell anyone at the time?'

'Harry Elroyd. He said I couldn't really know, which I suppose was right. I mean she never did it in front of me. Always in the bathroom attached to the bedroom. But she always said something when she went to do it. She had to do it twice a day, you see. Morning and night.'

'Said something like what?'

'"Pin-cushion time." That's what she called it.'

'None of this was in your statement. I've read it.'

'I wasn't asked.'

And if you don't ask you don't get, thought Hall. 'What about something else Mr Lomax said at the inquest, about Mrs Lomax's drinking?'

'I didn't understand that, either,' the elderly woman chirped at once.

'Tell me why,' encouraged Hall.

'I'd never seen her drink, hardly at all. There used to be church council meetings at the house . . . did you know she was on the church council . . . ?'

'No.'

'She was. And used to let there be meetings at the house midweek, on the nights Mr Lomax was in London . . .' There was a pause. '. . . I thought sometimes she was lonely, in that big house all by herself.'

'Tell me about the meetings.'

'I was on the church council myself then. Mrs Lomax was very generous: they both were. She used to serve drinks, before the meeting started. All sorts of drinks, anything you wanted. She always had sherry, as if she was joining in, but usually I'd see she never finished it.'

'Never finish one glass?'

The woman nodded. 'I asked her about it. She said it wasn't good for her to drink.'

'You used to stay behind on church council nights?'

'Always. George wasn't so bad then.'

'But on the other days what time would you come back here?'

'Five usually. Certainly in the week when Mrs Lomax was by herself although I used to stay later when the mister was home and they had people in. I thought that was only fair for the way they let me go early other times, because of George.'

Hall patiently let her finish. 'I don't want to talk about the nights when people were in: not even when the church council met. After a night when Mrs Lomax had been by herself and you arrived the following morning, did you ever find empty wine bottles like the one Harry

Elroyd discovered, after Mrs Lomax was found in a coma?'

She shook her head. 'Not that I can recall.' Her small, sharp-featured face creased into a frown. 'Is there something wrong? About what happened, I mean?'

'No,' said Hall, quickly. 'It's just that everything is so unusual. It's got to be gone into more thoroughly than usual. You understand that, of course?'

'Of course,' agreed the woman, invited into a confidence.

Hall looked around the polished-for-approval room in obvious admiration. 'You've got a very nice house, Mrs Simpson. Perfectly kept.'

'Thank you, sir.'

'You kept Mrs Lomax's house like this?'

'Of course!'

'What about Mrs Lomax?'

'I don't understand.'

'As far as you were concerned she wasn't careless about her medication. Did she rely upon you to keep her house like this . . .' Hall swept his hand admiringly around the room. 'Or was she messy?'

'Never!'

'How often did you arrive in the morning to find the remains of a dinner like the one described at the inquest?'

'Never. Not even when there'd been a party. They always brought in caterers, so nothing was ever *left*. Sometimes things were put away wrongly in the kitchen. Mrs Lomax would tell me about it the following day. How she'd had to put it in the right place.'

'In the right place,' echoed Hall, letting his thoughts coalesce. 'Did you come into the house on the Saturday, the day after the tragedy?'

'Not the day after. The same day. Mr Lomax came to

the house the night it happened. Asked me to come in to clear up. Actually drove me there in his car.'

Momentarily Hall closed his eyes in despair. 'That would have been what time.'

'Just before seven. George and I were settling down to listen to *The Archers* on the radio. It hadn't started.'

'Four hours after he'd found Mrs Lomax unconscious and she'd been taken to hospital?'

'I can't tell you how shocked I was. It was terrible.'

'The bed was soiled?'

'Poor love.'

'You changed it?'

'Of course I did,' said Elspeth, with a trace of indignation. 'Mr Lomax didn't intend to sleep there, of course. He slept in another room.'

'What else had to be done, to Mrs Lomax's bedroom, to tidy it up?'

'There were things all over the cabinet. A syringe and ampoules. I knew what they were, of course.'

'But you'd never seen them before, not scattered about like that?'

'No.'

Another idea came abruptly to Hall. 'Tell me about the bed itself. Was it a double, in which they slept together? Or two singles?'

The woman pursed her lips, as if she was reluctant to disclose an intimacy, which he was sure she'd never been. 'Double.'

'Which you made, every day?'

'Yes.'

'On what side did Mrs Lomax sleep, left or right?'

She frowned. 'Left.'

'So it would have been with her left hand that she reached out for anything on the bedside cabinet?'

'I suppose so.'

'What about the clothes Mrs Lomax had worn . . . it would have been the Thursday, the day you were there, wouldn't it?'

'A grey dress with a very faint yellow pattern,' remembered the housekeeper. 'Doesn't sound like it but it was beautiful. It was hung up in the closet.'

'She always hung her clothes up?'

'I told you, she liked things neat and tidy almost as much as I do.'

'What about underclothes?'

'Where they always were, in the laundry basket in the bathroom.'

'Put away?'

She frowned. 'That's what you do with dirty underclothes: put it away to be washed.'

'Did you see much of Mr Lomax, when you were back at the house that night?'

'He was lost. Devastated. He just wandered about, from room to room, not knowing what to do.'

'How did you see a lot of him if he wandered about from room to room and you were working in two specific places: the bedroom and the kitchen?'

The question surprised the woman. 'Because he was always where I was, I suppose. I hadn't thought about it.'

'How long were you back at the house?'

'Not very long. There really wasn't much to do but obviously he didn't want to do it himself. No more than an hour, I suppose.'

'Mr Lomax had taken you there. Did he drive you home?'

She shook her head. 'He was too upset. He got a taxi for me. Fred Knowland. Works out of Alton. He was the man Mr Lomax always called: took people to the station at Winchester or Alton, things like that. All the way to London sometimes.'

Briefly, believing he could indulge himself, Hall tried to imagine what the carnation button-holed Superintendent John Bentley, the hitherto successful investigator of every murder, would have done now.

Elspeth, the gossip to whom any verbal silence was torture, said, 'It was funny, about Fred.'

'What was?' said Hall.

'He collects cars. Knows about them. He's got an old open-topped bus he restored and hires out for weddings. It's ever so popular. He saw the mister's car, when he picked me up – it was one of those big American ones then – and said it was unusual for him to be home so much during the week and that he'd seen him arriving the previous night.'

Hall looked steadily at the woman. 'The previous night? You mean the Thursday?'

'That's what he said. He was working a contract, picking up someone from Winchester station, and he'd seen the mister's car turning off the M3.'

'What did you say?'

'That he had to be mistaken. That the mister had been in London that night, like always – Mrs Lomax told me he was going to be, before I left – and that he never came home on the M3 anyway. He always said the A3 was quicker and there weren't so many cars.'

'Did you tell anyone this? Harry Elroyd?'

'Why should I have done? It wasn't right because I knew the mister was in London. It was daft.'

That's how Knowland described it – 'bloody daft: had to be, didn't it?' – when he responded to Elspeth Simpson's call. The man's recognition was instant – the reaction bright-eyed greed – and Hall immediately guessed Fred Knowland had profited hugely from the press invasion of the area and imagined even greater financial benefit from this encounter. The man, fat from sitting permanently in a driving seat, sparse-haired and quick to smile, asked as many questions as he answered and Hall didn't doubt he would alert the press posse before he'd had time to get back to Winchester station. Elspeth was visibly distressed at having another chair seat dented, picking up and moving ornaments and picture frames and then putting them back in their original place.

'It was exactly that, a mistake,' she said, more than once, trying to hurry things on so she could polish and tidy away their intrusion.

'What car was it?' Hall persisted.

'Cadillac de Ville,' said Knowland. 'Beautiful car. Had one once. Sorry I got rid of it.'

'What colour?'

'Mr Lomax's? Black.'

'You must have known the number?'

'The system's funny. The filter off the M3 is from a roundabout on to the road to get into Winchester. I was actually going in the opposite direction, on to the roundabout, as this car came off. I was never in a position to see a number. It was dark – it was past ten: I was going to pick up a contract customer – and it was raining. I just recognized the shape of the car: knew it immediately.'

'As Mr Lomax's?'

'Why is it important?'

'I'm clearing up the estate: there's some dispute about whether it was a company car or personally owned,' lied Hall, improvising.

'No,' responded Knowland, answering the question. 'I recognized it as a de Ville.'

'How many people were in it?'

'What's that got to do with whether it was a company car or not?'

'Mr Lomax would have been alone, wouldn't he? If there were several people it couldn't have been his.'

'It was by me in a second. But one person, I think.'

'You must know most of the unusual cars around here, driving all the time as you do? And having the interest?'

The man smiled. 'Not many I don't see.'

'So around the time we're talking about how many other Cadillac de Villes were there in the area?'

The smile went. 'None, as far as I know. That's why I thought at first it had to be Mr Lomax. Until I talked to Elspeth.'

'I think you're right,' agreed Hall. 'I've been wasting my time.' Knowland would obviously lead the media horde to Elspeth Simpson, who was looking visibly confused at his questions about the car. It was going to be a confused story.

'Far to go?' asked Knowland.

'London.'

'I could drive you back. Drove people around a lot for Mr Lomax. I could tell you a few stories.'

All of which had already been told and re-told and embellished, Hall was sure. 'I've got a return ticket.'

'Winchester station taxi?' said Knowland, showing off his local knowledge and nodding to the retained vehicle outside. 'He'd understand if you paid him off. It's more comfortable by car. Give you a company rate, like I used to give Mr Lomax.'

'No. But thanks.'

'You got a number I can call you on, if anything else occurs to me?'

'Sure,' agreed Hall at once, offering a card with the chamber's number.

Knowland's hand snatched out and enclosed it like a lizard's tongue capturing an insect. 'Will you be down again?'

'Maybe.'

The man's hand was shaking with excitement as he offered his own card. 'You need a car, just give me a ring. I'll meet you anywhere. Come to collect you if you like.'

'I'll remember that,' said Hall, accepting it.

A relieved Elspeth hurried them to the door and said she hoped Mrs Lomax would soon be back in the village and Knowland quickly said the same. He drove out on to the main road ahead of them, risking a barely sufficient gap in front of an approaching lorry, to a blast of protest.

'What's she like?' demanded the driver, taking up the earlier conversation as if it had never been interrupted.

'Who?'

'The ghost.'

'There's nothing to see.'

'Can you talk to her.'

'I can't,' avoided Hall, unwilling to spend the entire journey under interrogation. 'She talks to Mrs Lomax.'

'She's going to have to be locked up for the rest of her life, isn't she? In an asylum?'

'She'll be going abroad soon,' said Hall, the font of all false rumours. 'To a special place in the sun.'

'I suppose she can afford it with her money,' agreed the driver, miserably.

They reached the station ahead of any pursuit. Hall had the fare ready, thrusting it into the driver's hand and, avoiding the main ticket office, cutting into the underground tunnel to reach the London-bound platform. The train already there hid him from the main entrance opposite. He didn't go on to the platform but to his right, out into the car park. He drove without direction away from the city, not bothering to look at a map until he reached Stockbridge and was sure there was no pursuit.

Only then did he begin to review his day, trying to get it into perspective. The circumstantial evidence begged for a proper investigation that could never be carried out now that Gerald Lomax was dead. But Jennifer couldn't have been involved: he was sure she couldn't. Or could she, he wondered, remembering a particular phrase in Gerald Lomax's statement.

'Eleven to one, one to eleven, eleven to one, one to eleven . . .' incanted Mason, his voice measured, even, soporific. He held the watch in front of Jennifer, as he had the first time he'd hypnotized her. 'Eleven to one, one to eleven . . . !'

'*Why not go along with it? Humour the idiot? Can't hurt me, after all. Can't make me go anywhere.*'

'Can you hear me, Jennifer?'

'Yes.'

'And Jane?'

'Yes. She's not trying to stop me this time.'

'*Help anyway I can, honey.*'

'Do you believe we can get rid of Jane?'

'No.'

'*Right!*'

'So you're not going to try any more?'

'No point.'

'You told me the last time how strong your mind was. Always better than anyone else.'

'Not any more,'

'*Right again!*'

'Do you want to die?'

'Yes.'

'Do you want to kill yourself?'

'Yes.'

'You haven't lost your strong mind, Jennifer.'

'Jane's there.'

'So you're giving your mind over to her? Letting her have it?'

'She already has it.'

'Not if you don't abandon it to her.'

'Too tired.'

'No you're not. You fought, in court. Made Jeremy fight. You beat Jane, because you stayed strong-minded. You can beat her again, rid yourself of her, but you must stay strong.'

'*What a load of crap!*'

'I can't get rid of her. Ever.'

'Do you want Emily?'

'Can't have her.'

'Won't you fight to have her?'

'*Don't listen!*'

'Yes.'

'But you're not fighting. You're letting Jane take over.'

'She wants to hurt Emily.'

'She can't. Emily's safe. Nothing can happen to her. If Jane wants to hurt Emily, throw Jane out.'

'Don't know how.'

'Could you believe Mr Dawson?'

'Not really.'

'Jane could believe him, couldn't she?'

'*Shut up!*'

When Jennifer didn't reply the psychiatrist repeated: 'Couldn't she?'

'*Don't bother to listen. It's crap.*'

'She doesn't want to listen.'

'Because she's afraid.'

'*Shut up!*'

'She's getting angry.'

'No, Jennifer. She's getting scared.'

Mason was excited, at the animation that was emerging through the hypnotic trance. 'Try with Dawson, Jennifer. Try as hard as you can.'

'It's not just that.'

'What then, Jennifer?'

'I don't want to talk about it.'

'You've got to talk about it, if I'm to help you.'

'Too awful.'

'*Oh go on! Shock him.*'

'Was it something that happened in prison?' Mason guessed.

'Don't want to talk about it.'

'Were you attacked in prison, sexually?'

'Horrible.' She physically shuddered.

'You're not in prison any longer. Never will be, again. What happened can't hurt you.'

'Jeremy wouldn't want me if he knew, would he?'

Hall didn't try to establish any contact, hurrying directly to his rooms at the clinic to telephone Humphrey Perry before the solicitor left for the day. 'You've got the name? Hemels, Bury Street.'

'There'll never be a record, after all this time,' protested Perry.

'We won't know, until we try to find one. And take a photograph of Jennifer with you.'

'What could it prove, anyway?'

'We don't know that, either. Anything from America?'

'If there had been I would have told you.'

'You've got to admit it was an inadequate inquiry.'

'All right,' conceded the solicitor, reluctantly. Falling back on his most frequent complaint, he said, 'But you're still clutching at straws.'

'And as I keep telling you, that's what we've been doing from the beginning.'

Hall bumped into the psychiatrist almost immediately outside his door. 'I was coming to see if you were back,' said Mason.

'I was just going to see Jennifer.'

'I think you should.'

'I've been on all the rides,' said Emily. 'Lots of times. And been in the pool every day.'

'What would you like to do now?' asked Annabelle.

'Go home to Mummy and Daddy. And go to school with my friends.'

Chapter Thirty-two

'Is she there?'

'No.' Jennifer knelt in the chapel, as Dawson told her and bowed her head under the pressure of his hand. The chapel smelled heavily of the incense smouldering in the burners. Despite the softness of the well-padded hassock her knee hurt, where she'd cut it.

'I want to speak to you, Jane,' declared the priest. When there was nothing he said, 'Don't be afraid. You know you don't have to be afraid of God.'

When there was still no response he began the exorcism ritual with oil and holy water and salt and said, 'Hear me, oh Lord, not in the name of this supplicant but in the name of the spirit that possesses her, a spirit in need of release and of your succour . . .'

'*Stop!*' Jennifer relayed the word, according to the previous arrangement. Ennui embalmed her.

'Pray with me, Jane.'

'*I don't want to pray with you.*'

'You do. You want to pray for forgiveness for the sins you have committed. To release yourself from the terrible torment of Hell.'

'*I'm not in torment.*'

'You're in terrible torment, to be saying what you are. Behaving and threatening as you do.'

'Not true. Won't listen.'

Dawson sprinkled holy water and intoned, 'And in Philippians it says, "Work out your own salvation with fear and trembling".' The priest hesitated. 'God exacts his vengeance, Jane. Not mortals.'

'I'm not mortal,' she scored. *'I'm dead. Killed. Without the chance of salvation.'*

'I could save you, if you'd pray with me. Give you absolution.'

There was nothing for several moments. Jennifer's knee was throbbing, rhythmically, like a heartbeat.

'Not for what I've done.'

'Yes, Jane!' said the priest, almost too urgently. The beginning of the Apostles' Creed was too hurried as well. '"I believe in God, the Father Almighty . . ."'

'I don't want to hear it!'

The ache wasn't any longer confined to Jennifer's injured leg. It was suffusing her entire body, as if she was straining to oppose the man.

'". . . who was conceived by the Holy Ghost . . ."' Dawson pressed on.

'Stop! I won't listen!'

As well as pain Jennifer felt frightened, although strangely not for herself. She couldn't – wouldn't – think it was for Jane.

Dawson ignored the interruptions, '". . . From thence he shall come to judge the quick and the dead . . ."'

It was a discordant, moaning chant, a rhythmless noise to drown out any other sound.

'". . . I believe in the Holy Ghost; the Holy Catholic Church; the Communion of Saints; the Forgiveness of sin; the Resurrection of the body and the life everlasting . . ."' The priest's face ran with sweat, like his hand against Jennifer's head. 'God can forgive the most terrible sin:

any sin . . .' He hesitated again, remembering Jeremy Hall's account of the Hampshire visit. 'You know that, Jane. You don't believe in one creed, one denomination. You believe in God: the total love of God—'

'*No!*'

'Yes! Pray with me, Jane. "Our Father, which art in Heaven, Hallowed be thy name . . ."'

The moaning chant started again.

'". . . Thy kingdom come. Thy will be done . . ."'

The closing-out sound in Jennifer's head wavered.

'". . . as it is in Heaven. Give us this day our daily bread . . ."'

'*And forgive us our trespasses, as we forgive them who trespass against us. And lead us not into temptation, but deliver us from evil. For thine is the kingdom and the power and the glory, for ever . . .*'

'We can do it, Jane!' said the priest, exultant but physically as close to the exhaustion that Jennifer now felt. He was crying. 'We'll pray together. Worship together. And find your way back.'

'*I'm frightened*,' confessed Jane, the voice distant, like somebody hiding.

So quickly – and at times so confusingly – did events unfold that day that even for someone with a trained lawyer's mind it was difficult for Jeremy Hall to differentiate explicable inconsistency from outright contradiction. And before he reached that comparable analysis there was the first telephone call from Humphrey Perry, which began with an apology for questioning the check Hall had asked for the previous day.

'It's not important,' dismissed the barrister. 'It's what you found that matters.'

'And I think it matters a great deal,' said Perry.

'You've got the doctor's name?' demanded Hall, the moment the solicitor finished telling him.

'Ian Halliday.'

'I can be there . . .'

'. . . You don't need to be,' stopped Perry. 'I spoke to Halliday an hour ago. Harley Street, naturally.'

'What did he say?'

'Lomax had always been a private patient. He was an American, remember. Didn't qualify for National Health, even if he'd wanted it.'

'The prescription was filled on the same day as the temazepam?'

'And collected by the same person,' confirmed Perry. 'It should have been obvious to me but it wasn't. Hemels is an independent chemist, not part of a chain. Been there for more than fifty years. And they still keep their records on the premises: part of their history.'

Hall paused, curious at the strange hollowness in his stomach.

'Who collected it?'

'I didn't need the photograph of Jennifer. It was Elizabeth McIntyre. And I've got a photostat of her signature, from the ledger. She's . . .'

'. . . I know who she is,' said Hall, as impatient as the other man. 'She was one of the ones never called.'

'You're assuming it's the basis for Jane's accusation.'

'You've read everything I have. Did you find another?'

'No.'

Hall accepted Perry's insistence it was impossible for them properly to discuss the latest responses from Washington DC from Ross Hamilton Forest II without having a transcript in front of him. He had the solicitor fax it personally to the clinic to prevent its location becoming known throughout the solicitor's office. That morning's media coverage maintained the hysteria – and the pursuit – at fever pitch: he'd succeeded in causing some confusion by the different stories he'd given but the consensus was that the death of Jane Lomax was being reopened as a murder inquiry, although the police and the coroner denied it. Pathologist Michael Bailey had been traced, as well as Inspector Hughes and PC Elroyd. Everyone was photographed and extensively quoted. Hall felt sorry for the avalanche that would have engulfed Elspeth Simpson. Fred Knowland appeared on all five breakfast television channels.

Forest's report from America ran to twenty-five A4 pages, including two signed affidavits, and took the barrister two hours to digest as fully as he wanted.

When they spoke again Perry, who had monitored the media as closely as Hall, said, 'We probably could get an investigation reopened on the strength of what we've found out. I'd take a bet on a posthumous murder verdict.'

'That's not what we're trying to prove,' reminded Hall.

'What do you want me to say if there's an official approach from Hampshire?'

'Let's hear what it is, first. We wouldn't be legally bound to hand our evidence over but I don't see any reason why we shouldn't. Jennifer wouldn't be involved any more.'

'They might try to involve her. Don't forget the motive of an affair.'

'Let's wait for an approach.'

'You think you're ready?'

'As ready as I'll ever be.'

'You thought what life's going to be like when it's all over?'

'No,' admitted Hall, honestly. 'Sometimes I can't

imagine that it ever will be.' Or, he mentally added in a thought that surprised him, that he particularly wanted it to be. He was certainly anxious to get rid of Jane, but not Jennifer.

Dr Cox confirmed the priest's insistence that Jennifer was too exhausted by being Jane's conduit to face what amounted to a quasi-trial and Mason deferred to their opinion and also abandoned any analysis that day. They used Hall's room to talk through what he intended and Cox said he'd wait until tomorrow before deciding whether Jennifer would even then be able to stand the strain.

'It's an attempt to persuade Jane to go, after all,' the doctor reminded, unnecessarily. 'The most important thing in her life. She'll be wound up tighter than a spring.'

'I couldn't be more encouraged by how she's responding,' enthused Dawson. 'I *know* I can exorcize Jane, if this doesn't work.'

'It's not important which of us does it, as long as it's done,' said Hall.

'Jane prayed with me,' said the priest. 'And there's no obscenity, not any more.'

'I wonder if it'll be any different when she's talking to me?' said Hall.

'Gerald Lomax was quite a bastard, wasn't he?' said Cox.

Mason sniggered, cynically. 'I think he had more of a Multiple Personality Disorder than some people suspected Jennifer of suffering.'

Chapter Thirty-three

That evening they walked together in the grounds, the first time Jennifer had ventured outside the clinic: her first unguarded outing, in fact, since the murder. It was her suggestion, seized by the psychiatrist, whom she pointedly told she didn't want to come with her. Just Hall: just the two of them. Jennifer held his right hand tightly in her left and reached across herself to clutch at his arm with the other, so that he was always close, their bodies touching. There was still a faint shimmer from the heat of the day encouraging insect clouds: encouraging, too, other patients out into the grounds. Hall started out carefully to avoid getting recognizably close to anyone before realizing Jennifer was being just as cautious, always keeping anyone else at a distance. He noticed, too, that in whichever direction they went she always kept the buildings in sight, needing their reassuring nearness.

'Jane isn't here.'

'No reason to think about her then: nor talk about her.' It had been a prompt from Julian Mason, before they'd set out. There had been others. He felt her shrug, beside him.

'Do you know what this is?'

'What?'

'Being normal. Ordinary.' It was blissful, almost as if she was floating. She tried to hold the sensation, her own special drug blocking out the reality of the unreal.

He squeezed the hand holding his arm against his body, rehearsing what he was going to say, not wanting to break her mood with the wrong word. 'It's a good feeling. I'd forgotten it.'

She squeezed back. 'Were you angry at me?'

'When?'

'At the beginning, when I said I didn't want you: that I wanted a QC.'

'No. That was professional: your choice.'

'Can you always be impartial, like that?'

'It's an essential of the job.'

'Are you impartial now?' She looked intently sideways at him.

He wasn't sure how to answer: wasn't sure what she even meant by the question. 'I'm not going to abandon you: leave you by yourself.'

She looked away and walked without speaking for several moments. 'Thank you, for what you did then. At the trial I mean. I haven't thanked you before, have I?'

'You haven't seen my fee yet,' he said, trying for lightness.

'Did you always believe me?'

Truth or lie? Truth, Mason had dictated: no other way, blunt truth in fact. 'Of course not, not at first. It was too absurd.'

'What did you think was going to happen?'

Keep to the truth. 'That the judge would stop the trial. Order the jury to return a verdict on mental incapacity.'

'Which would have achieved what you wanted all along?'

'Yes.'

'Sneaky bastard!'

She actually laughed, the first time he'd ever seen her do that – the first time since they'd met that she'd ever had the slightest cause, he supposed – and Hall came close to faltering. 'I thought it was the best outcome. The only outcome.' And still might be, he thought, worriedly.

'The television is saying that you're famous now. In demand.' She veered off the path, on to the grass, to avoid a rapidly approaching track-suited jogger.

'We'll see.' Bert Feltham hadn't been happy at his continuing to delay a response to the offered briefs: the total, as of the previous evening, stood at twelve.

They walked unspeaking again, in the general direction of a display of oaks, bowed and gnarled by age.

'They were there hundreds of years before we were born and they'll be there after we die,' she said.

The remark unsettled him. He said, 'But in between we have a life,' and at once regretted the remark.

'Do we?' She turned away from the tree-line, towards the clinic. To have gone around the coppice the other way would have taken the refuge out of sight. 'Do you know what I thought, on the day it happened? *Before* it happened: before Jane? I remember thinking that I was the happiest, luckiest, most contented woman in the world . . .' She snorted an empty laugh. '. . . Can you believe that?'

'Yes.'

'Did you believe Rebecca in court? That he was going to divorce me and take Emily away?'

'I thought we were trying to forget things, just for a moment.'

'We can't, can we?'

Honesty, he reminded himself. 'Not for very long.'

'So what's the answer?'

'She was performing: wanting the jury to make a comparison. She couldn't be challenged.'

'Still not an answer.'

'I can't give you one. If I'd had anything to challenge her with, I would have done.'

He followed her lead again, accepting they were returning to the clinic. He waited for her to lead the conversation, too.

'Did Gerald do it?' she demanded, abruptly.

Gently to warn her might lessen the shock, according to the psychiatrist. 'There are a lot of things that don't add up: things the police would have investigated, if they'd known.'

'Do you believe I wasn't involved.'

'Yes.'

'Can you prove it to her?'

'If it's based on the remark I think it is, yes.'

'What if it isn't?'

'Then at least I'll know where to go on looking.'

'Why is she letting me alone, now?'

'Because of what happened in the chapel?' he suggested.

'Wouldn't it be . . . ?' Jennifer began, then stopped.

'Yes,' he agreed, not needing her to finish.

Jane wasn't there the following morning. Of all the setbacks and reversals Jeremy Hall attempted to anticipate – accepting as he tried to forearm himself there were too many unknowns possibly to insure against – he'd never imagined that when he came to argue Jane's possession with legal objectivity she wouldn't be there to argue back.

Cox had declared Jennifer fit for the ordeal and all of

them – Hall, Dawson and Julian Mason – were startled by the visibly obvious recovery. It was not so much physical although her face, still free of make-up, had for the first time in weeks a glow about it and her freshly washed hair still hung with the flow of expensive, if long past, attention. It was more in Jennifer's demeanour. The apathy had lessened – lessened, not gone completely – to give way to something Hall held back from identifying as an eagerness for the confrontation.

Jeremy Hall was frightened, far more apprehensive than he had been entering the Old Bailey that first day to argue ghostly possession as a murder defence to a hostile, God-fearing judge. The desperation of the whole idea, which had seemed reasonable, even logical, in those adrenalin-exploding first hours of their anything's-possible escape from hospital now seemed preposterously absurd.

Jennifer's words the previous night – normal, ordinary – echoed in his mind. Which Hall acknowledged to be his difficulty. For two days – three because to begin with night had merged into new day and new day into night – he'd been normal and ordinary, a lawyer immersed in the normal and ordinary defence of a client. So immersed, inconceivable though it now was for him to concede, that he'd dismissed from conscious thought who that client was and the circumstances and to whom he would be presenting her defence. He'd lapsed – relaxed – into *becoming* ordinarily normal. Which nothing was. Or could be. He had to step back into the supernatural, into the unknown and the unpredictable, unable to judge anything by the safe and logically enshrined rules and process of law.

And now he was being off-balanced before he'd started.

'I reached her,' argued Dawson, hopefully. 'She prayed. Renounced evil.'

'She didn't come afterwards. Not at all during the night,' agreed Jennifer, just as hopefully, eager for omens.

'She was devout, before she died,' accepted Hall, although less convinced. 'Incredibly so. But I can't imagine it could have been this easy.'

'You hadn't tried God before,' reminded the priest, critically.

'We hardly had the opportunity!' protested the barrister. 'We were arguing a murder charge.'

'What do we do?' demanded Mason, delighted at Jennifer's very obvious mental recovery although secretly disappointed there wouldn't be more to take to its exaggerated limit his participation and the honour-awarding thesis that would come from it.

'We wait,' decided Hall.

'For how long?' asked the priest.

'As long as it takes.'

Mason was about to protest the glib near-cliché but stopped at the thought of how it might sound to Jennifer. Instead he said, 'Yes. We wait.'

Which they did. Every day Jennifer attended services in the chapel and underwent analysis, sometimes under hypnosis, with Julian Mason, who even – dangerously – invited Jane to join them. Jeremy Hall read and re-read everything he'd assembled, actually glad of the opportunity the delay gave him to search for something that incriminated Jennifer that he might have missed. And found nothing.

His solitary walks with Jennifer in the clinic grounds, each evening, grew longer – the building not needing to be in view any more – and afterwards the four of them ate together, sometimes joined by Cox. And Jennifer did eat, hungrily, and the priest boasted his knowledge of the wine list, showing off in front of a beautiful woman.

On the second day Hall had Bert Feltham send him the outlines of the four most urgent briefs, simply by posting them care of Dr Cox. He instructed Geoffrey Johnson to arrange the private security protection for the Hampshire mansion. He didn't even consider telling Jennifer of the problems with Emily or of Annabelle's growing reluctance to continue the role of surrogate mother.

All five of them were at dinner on the sixth night, as usual in Jennifer's suite. It was Dawson who ordered the Roederer Crystal with the promise to pay for it himself, declaring a celebration for the complete return of Jennifer's physical health that had just been announced by Dr Cox.

Jennifer insisted upon joining in her own toast. 'Here's to Jane's departure. I know she's left me.'

'*I haven't*,' said the familiar American voice. '*I've had a lot to think about.*'

Depression swamped them. Jennifer was devastated although she didn't fall back into immediate apathy. Legally it was a recognized ploy, acknowledged Hall: protract a case to unsettle its participants and then spring the surprise of a hearing.

'*I've been looking forward to this.*' It was virtually automatic for Jennifer to mouth the words, as Jane's puppet.

'So have we,' said Hall.

'*I'm right, aren't I? I was murdered.*'

Jennifer sat with her head slightly bowed, both hands gripping the table edge. If Jane threw Jennifer into a fit she'd probably upend the table over all of them, Hall calculated. How they would stage this was something else he hadn't anticipated: as they were, encircling a table, actually made it look like a seance. Or what he imagined a seance to be like, although he thought people were supposed to link hands. 'I'm not sure. I haven't heard your argument.'

'*You first.*'

'Prosecution before defence.'

'*My rules, not yours.*'

'Making me the prosecutor as well as the defender?'

'*With me as the judge. The way it always had to be.*'

Dawson's head was more bowed than Jennifer's. He had his hands clasped before him and his eyes tightly shut, his lips moving in silent prayer. Julian Mason was tensed forward, eyes bright with excitement. Cox appeared frozen, transfixed.

'Your death wasn't properly investigated,' conceded Hall.

'*It was murder!*'

'There wasn't a proper investigation,' repeated the barrister, reluctant to concede anything.

'*Do you think you've conducted one?*'

'Better than that carried out at the time.'

'*So tell them! I want everyone to hear it! I want my trial. Not the trial there should have been but for the truth to come out at last.*' Jennifer was panting, short-breathed from gabbling Jane's insistence. The words that followed were measured, a threat the barrister didn't need to hear. '*And I do hope you've got it right. Found it all out. I shall be very angry if you haven't.*'

He didn't have any of the carefully listed notes, the points enumerated: any of the inquest statements or the replies from the American lawyer to the specific queries he'd raised. Everything was back in his own rooms, at the far end of the corridor. 'I have to collect some papers.'

'*What?*'

'The evidence you need.'

'*I don't think you've got evidence?*'

Could he risk the courtroom ploy of engendering anger? 'Or don't you want to hear and see evidence to prove you wrong?'

'*Careful!*'

'The real truth? Or the truth according to Jane Lomax, not interested in hearing any story other than that she wants to believe?'

'*I told you to be careful!*'

'"Not the trial there should have been but for the truth to come out,"' Hall quoted, throwing Jane's words back at her.

'*Hurry. Be very quick before I lose my patience.*'

Hall indicated the cluttered table to Julian Mason as he rose, conscious of Jennifer's pleading eyes upon him. He walked normally to his own suite, refusing to be panicked. It was all prepared, waiting. For a few moments, just seconds, he remained there, composing himself. Or delaying? he demanded. Positively he strode out of the room and back along the corridor. The table was cleared except for water, the dinner debris piled carelessly on to the coffee table by the television. The priest still prayed. Jennifer looked up at his entry, imploringly. Hall poured water first for her, then for himself.

'*You planning any more delays?*'

'None. Are you?'

Jennifer looked up at him again, shaking her head.

'*She doesn't think you can save her.*'

'We need an undertaking, don't we?'

'*What undertaking?*'

'If I make the case, you'll free Jennifer?' pressed the

barrister. He'd left normality and the ordinary behind again, he accepted. He wished he knew where that put him now.

'*Make your case.*'

It wasn't the commitment he'd wanted but it would have to do. Hall breathed in deeply again, readying himself. He sipped some water. 'Let me make yours, instead. I think you were murdered.'

'*Hah!*'

A gasp came from Jennifer, too. Her look towards him now wasn't any longer imploring. It was accusing and at the same time bewildered, the expression of someone who had been deceived and couldn't understand why. Almost, in fact, one of guilt. The other three men were regarding him with varying degrees of astonishment: he'd discussed some but not all of the inquest disparities with them but said nothing about Humphrey Perry's findings.

If he was to be the prosecutor, Jane had to be his witness. The realization – the full, incredible awareness – momentarily held him speechless: he was about to cross-examine the victim about her own murder. 'He did come home that night, didn't he? The night before you died?' he forced himself to ask.

'*Hey, what's this?*'

'The way it has to be, if you want the priest and Cox and Mason to hear your story: hear the truth. And the only way you'll be able to judge whether I am going to get to the truth or not. So, Gerald came home that night?'

'*Yes.*'

'After ten?'

'*About ten-thirty.*'

'Were you in bed?'

'*Just going.*'

'What did he say?'

'We'd spoken on the phone, earlier. I told him I had one of my bad headaches. I got them sometimes: Greenaway's treatment for the stomach pains could have been contributing. Gerald said he'd driven all the way home to make sure I was all right.'

'You'd already eaten supper?'

'Steak.'

'And cleared away?'

'I don't like leaving a mess.'

'But you got something for him?' Hall pushed her water closer to Jennifer. She ignored it.

'Steak. There was a lot left over, in the refrigerator.'

'And wine? Margaux?'

'Gerald opened it. He liked wine.'

'Did you sit with him, while he ate?'

'The commission earnings had been calculated that week. He said . . .' There was a break. *'. . . He said Jennifer Stone had come out on top again, even though she'd been away from the office . . .'*

Jennifer began to cry, soundlessly, tears edging down her face. She grabbed for the water at last, gulping it.

'You shared the wine, while you talked?'

'I only had one glass: didn't drink all of that. The headache had begun to go.'

'Gerald drank the rest?'

'He enjoyed wine. Drink didn't affect him.'

'And he had a brandy, afterwards?'

'Yes.'

'Did you go to bed straight away?'

'I started to clear up, put the wine bottle in the bin, but he told me he'd finish doing it. That he wanted to go to bed . . .' There was another break. *'. . . It was obvious he wanted to make love . . .'*

Jennifer squeezed her eyes shut, still crying. The other

three men were locked on to Jennifer, speaking for Jane. Cox's mouth hung open.

'So you went up ahead of him? Put your clothes away, like you usually did?'

'*Yes.*'

'And put your underwear in the laundry basket?'

'*Yes.*'

'And took some insulin?'

'*I'd had problems since Dr Greenaway prescribed the stomach pills, as I told you. Nausea as well as headaches sometimes. I thought there might be a slight imbalance – I'd told Gerald, downstairs – and decided I could correct it. It was quite safe. After so long I knew exactly what I could and couldn't do.*'

'How much did you inject?'

'*Twenty units.*'

'Two ampoules, each of ten units?'

'*Yes.*'

'What did you do with the ampoules?'

'*Put them into the disposal basket.*'

'And then got into bed?'

'*Yes.*'

'You didn't take the syringe into the bedroom with you and put it on the side table?'

'*Of course not!*'

'Or any ampoules?'

'*No.*'

'Or a glass of brandy?'

'*No.*'

'Tell us what happened when you got into bed.'

'*I shouldn't have drunk what little wine I did: the headache came back. I told Gerald when he came up: I didn't want to disappoint him, after he'd come all the way from London.*'

He had to crush every feeling, Hall decided: stick always to the truth, according to the psychiatrist. 'Disappoint him about making love, you mean?'

'*Yes.*'

Jennifer's shoulders were heaving but still she wasn't making any sound. She drank again.

'What happened?' Hall drank, too.

'*He got me something from the bathroom.*'

'Something for the headache?'

'*Yes.*'

'What was it?'

'*Gerald didn't bring a bottle back. Just some pills, in his hand.*'

'Did he say what they were?'

'*Paracetamol. I could safely take that.*'

'You saw they were paracetamol?'

'*The headache had got bad again. I was keeping my eyes closed against the light, although it wasn't very bright.*'

'So he gave you pills and you took them without looking to see what they were?'

'*Yes.*'

'What then?'

'*He said it didn't matter. About making love. He just held me.*'

'He got into bed to hold you?'

'*No, not then. He sat on the side of the bed.*'

'Not then. What about later.'

'*I don't remember later. I went to sleep.*'

'Don't you remember anything about later?'

'*Vaguely that there was something against my face, hurting me. And a smell, of something strong . . . and then of choking.*'

'Was it brandy you smelled?'

'I don't drink any spirit. Never have. I told you, it was only vague. It could have been brandy. It must have been, from what was said at the inquest.'

Hall paused at the next question, held this time by the inanity of it, telling himself that nothing could be inane. 'You were at your own inquest?'

Only Cox showed any reaction, shaking his head. There was no facial reaction.

'I wanted to know! But it was all lies!'

'I know some of them,' promised Hall. 'You're left handed, aren't you? All the stab wounds to Gerald's body were from a left-handed person and Jennifer is right handed.'

'Yes. I'm left handed.'

'Could you inject, with your right hand?'

'It wasn't easy.'

'Did Gerald ever inject you?'

'I didn't like him doing it: I always thought it was a private thing. And he didn't like doing it.'

'But he could, in an emergency?'

'I'd taught him how. But he was clumsy. It hurt.'

'That night you injected yourself in your right thigh?'

'Yes.'

'Twice?'

'Yes.'

'Not three times?'

'That was a lie, at the inquest! I didn't administer the third, the most obvious one.'

'What about the even more obvious one, the big puncture mark in your left arm?'

'No! I've never ever injected myself in my left arm. I couldn't, obviously.'

'Did Gerald do it?'

'He must have done. I was asleep. Unconscious.'

Hall pushed across in front of Jennifer the copies of the American enquiries that Humphrey Perry had faxed him. 'There's your American medical records. And another affidavit from your family doctor, up until you moved to England. You were never hospitalized, for an insulin overdose, were you? You've never ever overdosed?'

'*Never! It was another lie!*'

'And you never had a drink problem, in America?'

'*How could I have had, with diabetes as severe as mine?*'

Jennifer was slumping lower and lower over the table, pressed down again by exhaustion. Hall was drained, too, but wouldn't stop. There was a momentum he didn't want to lose. He was doing more than follow the basic legal precept of never asking a question to which he didn't already know the answer. He was intently listening, too, gauging his knowledge against Jane's. He was sure he was ahead. Now he was about to go beyond the established precept: to grope out for answers he didn't already know and needed to guess precisely the right questions to ask.

'It's all guesswork, though, isn't it? You can't prove Gerald killed you? It's what the police would consider circumstantial.'

'*More than circumstantial! Everything at the inquest was lies! The police would have investigated, if they'd known.*'

'Of course they would,' agreed Hall. 'And I believe they would have found enough for a murder charge, like I believe I have.'

'*So where's your argument?*'

'Where's yours, to prove Jennifer was part of it?'

'*His mistake! What he said in his statement.*'

It was too soon for any satisfaction. 'Where, precisely, in his statement?'

'*About the temazepam, which I know now he gave me instead of paracetamol: drugged me to make everything else possible. Read it! It says "I had it collected." Not "I collected it." Had it collected, by her. By Jennifer Stone.*'

He was there! thought Hall, euphorically. He'd guessed correctly – had Humphrey Perry agree with him – and now he had his defence. '"I had it collected",' Hall repeated yet again, returning the quote. 'Not "I had it collected by Jennifer Stone." You don't know *who* collected it, do you?'

'*Had to be her. She had the motive, the reason.*'

'You didn't know about the affair with Jennifer Stone when you were alive, did you?'

'*No.*'

'You went to bed that night wanting to make love to him. Thinking he loved you.'

'*He did. Always did.*'

The denial of the cheated wives isolated Hall, sadness mingling with the satisfaction: Jane refusing to admit losing to Jennifer and Jennifer refusing to admit losing to Rebecca. How many other lives of other women would Gerald Lomax have shattered if he hadn't died? 'And you hate Jennifer, don't you? Hate her not because you think she had anything to do with your death but because she stole your husband from you.'

'*Yes.*' For the first time there was a discernible emotion, the word hissing out in snake-like loathing.

'Who's Ian Halliday?' demanded Hall, abruptly.

There wasn't an immediate answer. Then, '*Gerald's doctor.*'

'Never yours?'

'I spent most of my time in the country. I needed a local doctor.'

'Halliday never treated you?'

'*No.*'

'Never prescribed for you?'

'*No.*'

'Did you ever meet him?'

'*No.*'

Hall went to a paper in front of him, lifting it. 'This is a signed statement, made to Humphrey Perry eight days ago by Doctor Ian Halliday, of Harley Street, London. It sets out the history of his medical association with Gerald Lomax. Part of it reads, "Two months before the death of his first wife – the actual date of the consultation was June 12 – Gerald Lomax—'

'I wasn't there!' Jennifer's interruption croaked out, the sound so strained and unexpected that everyone jumped. She gulped from her glass again, spilling some water down her chin. She didn't bother to wipe it. 'I wasn't there!' she repeated, stronger voice. 'In June of the year Jane died . . . in fact throughout May *and* June and part of July . . . I was on secondment to New York . . .' She sniggered, disbelievingly. 'It was there, that time, that I met Rebecca. Isn't that ironic . . . ? There'll be proof . . .'

'I have it,' promised Hall, not wanting to lose control. He went back to Halliday's statement. 'It goes on, "Gerald Lomax complained of having difficulty in sleeping: blamed the pressure of work and asked for sleeping pills. I prescribed temazepam . . .' Hall slowed, unnecessarily building up the moment. '. . . At the same time he said he was worried about his wife, who was a diabetic although not a patient of mine. He told me she was extremely careless about her medication: sometimes even forgot to bring it with her when she came up to their apartment in London . . ."'

It was impossible to tell whether the sound, a whimpering, groaning noise, was initiated by Jane or Jennifer.

Hall waited for the sound to become an identifiable word. When it didn't he went back to the statement. Quoting again he said, '"She'd done it the previous week and they'd had to cancel everything and go back to Hampshire. He asked if I could issue a script for emergencies: something that he could keep in London if it happened again. I gave him a prescription for a month's supply of ten-unit strength soluble insulin, the type he told me his wife used."'

All three men were looking at Hall now, the awareness registering. Only Mason spoke. He said, 'Good God!' and then looked apologetically at the priest.

'He did it! I knew he did it.'

'I haven't finished yet,' said the barrister, determined to maintain the pace. 'Jennifer was in New York, all that time. And you knew it. You've told us that Gerald said she was away when he talked of her commission. The Enco-Corps records, which are part of this pile, prove it, in black and white: Jennifer Stone didn't get back to England until July 9, just two weeks before your death. The prescription, for the temazepam and the insulin, was made up on June 13 by an independent chemist in Bury Street, in the City of London, named Hemels. Who still have the dispensing record, signed by the person who collected it . . .' He slid a photocopy across the table. 'The person who collected it was Elizabeth McIntyre, Gerald Lomax's secretary . . .' Hall stopped, dry-throated, all the water gone, desperately searching his mind for something – anything – he'd overlooked. Just the final accusation, he decided. '. . . You never thought Jennifer conspired in your murder . . . you wanted to kill her because she stole Gerald from you . . . that's the truth, isn't it Jane? The truth you didn't want to admit!'

Jennifer said, 'She's crying. That's the sound in my head. Crying.'

'She didn't go.' Jeremy Hall was slouched over the table, drained, his arms and legs too heavy for his body, his head lolling. The heaviest weight was the feeling of defeat.

'She didn't swear, not once. Get angry or make Jennifer do anything. And in the end she cried,' said Mason, enumerating points for his own benefit. He looked across at the lawyer. 'And you did what you promised you'd do.'

'But she still didn't go,' repeated the barrister.

Dawson was the only other man still in the room with them. Having weaned Jennifer completely from drugs during Jane's absence, Dr Cox had decided that night she needed a tranquillizer and was still in the adjoining bedroom: it had needed Hall as well as the doctor virtually to carry Jennifer away from the table. They hadn't been sure whether it was her own or Jane's tears she was shedding.

'There is nothing more I can do,' admitted the barrister.

'Which only leaves me,' accepted the priest. 'Dear God, please help me: please help us both.'

Chapter Thirty-four

'Your father taught you to love God?'

'*Yes.*'

'And you do love Him, don't you?'

'*I did.*'

'And you still do, Jane.' As always Dawson stood with his hand on Jennifer's head, his eyes tightly shut, his whole will concentrated upon the woman kneeling before him, a woman who would be for ever damned by another if he failed. Feeling he, too, would be damned if he failed.

He'd not slept at all. He'd spent the whole night prostrate, outstretched before the altar in prayer, pleading for guidance and for a miracle and for Jennifer to be released from a living purgatory.

Two hours before he'd anointed her with oil and marked the cross upon her in holy water and spread the salt and gone through the exorcism ritual until there were no prayers left to be said as part of it.

Jennifer hadn't slept, either. And not because Jane had filled her mind: she hadn't needed to. Jennifer knew this was the last chance, the last hope. Now she prayed, too, eyes as fervently shut as the man above her, her desperation even greater, not caring that Jane would know the agony of her fear: that she was giving Jane a target to attack. Despite her daily periods with the priest Jennifer still couldn't believe, although she wanted to: told herself she had to and mouthed the litany to the priest's dictation and made her own childlike vow – if You grant me this one thing I will worship, I truly will . . .

'*I'm frightened.*'

'God can help you! Save you!'

'*No-one can help me.*'

'God can forgive all things: all sin.' Why were the words so empty, so trite?

'*He could not forgive me. I'll be for ever in Purgatory . . . in Hell . . . I know the teaching . . .*'

'You don't want to cause any more suffering, do you?'

'*No.*'

'Then you must leave this woman.'

'*I have sinned too much.*'

'To stay would be the greater sin.' Not enough. Never enough. There had to be more to say, a way to convince someone who had once believed, as Jane had believed.

'*I am beyond forgiveness.*'

Please, prayed Jennifer. Make her go away. Leave me alone. I'm sorry, so very sorry I can't believe in You. But please make her leave me alone.

Dawson held back from the forgiveness of the Lord's Prayer. Instead he said, '"Her sins, which are many, are forgiven; for she loved much."'

'*Saint Luke wasn't talking of murder. And I wanted to send Jennifer mad, for taking Gerald . . . Said I'd kill the child . . . I can't be forgiven for that . . . None of it . . .*'

'"I am not come to call the righteous, but sinners to repentance,"' preached the man, hands shaking with emotion. 'Repent Jane! Truly repent! You'll descend into Hell, which you know we all must, but then you'll rise again, into Heaven. You *know* that's true. The way.'

I will kill myself, decided Jennifer. No other way. Don't

want to live. Not living. A body for someone else. Destroy the body, destroy the horror.

'I have done such terrible things. Now I am so very, very frightened.'

'Do you love God, Jane?'

'I abandoned Him, for evil.'

'Do you want to love him again?'

'Yes.'

'So you want a way back?'

'There can't be a way back, not for me.'

'Do you truly repent, Jane?'

There was no immediate reply. Finally, *'Yes.'*

'Then trust God. You know you can. You always did in life. How better can you show your true repentance than by freeing Jennifer? To remain is to go on sinning: to continue evil and deserve an eternity in the fires of Hell . . .'

There was no response. The only sound was their breathing, the priest's heavy from his effort. 'Jane?'

'She deserved to suffer, for taking Gerald.'

'Don't you think she has?'

'I'll only ask for God's forgiveness: for God's mercy. Not her.'

'It's only God we have to ask.' He could pray for his own forgiveness for that later.

There was another long silence. Nothing left, thought Jennifer: no way to stop it. Die then. Pills. Pills wouldn't hurt and she didn't want to be hurt. Not hurt any more. Just—

'. . . I repent. Oh dear, merciful Lord, forgive me . . .'

A fraying thread of excitement held Jennifer and the priest from total collapse. Cox had worriedly taken both their pulses and Dawson's blood pressure. He still wore his vestments, even his shawl: he sat holding it, running it through his fingers as he talked, which he did haltingly, in short bursts, with not enough breath for what he wanted to say.

'She's gone, hasn't she, Jennifer? Definitely gone?' He'd asked the same question a lot, since helping her from the chapel, a reassurance they all needed.

Jennifer nodded. At first she'd spoken, agreeing, but now she just moved her head, as if to repeat herself would risk bringing Jane cackling back.

'It was God,' insisted Dawson, another repetition. 'God's work. God's mercy.'

'She disappeared before,' reminded Hall, cautiously. He wanted it to be true as much as any of them – was as anxious as any of them for it to be true – but couldn't accept it this soon, this easily.

The priest made an angry gesture of denial. 'It's over now. All over.'

Hall found the possibility of that the most difficult of all to believe. It was too quick, too sudden. But how else could it have been? Exorcise meant to cut out, to remove evil. Which was what the priest was insisting had happened. There was no process, apart from the service. No prolonged treatment and after that a period of recuperation. Or wouldn't there be? Not the recuperation after an illness, although what Jennifer had suffered was as bad as the worst imaginable illness. An adjustment then. A time – who knew how much time? – to become normal, ordinary. Would it be possible for Jennifer ever again to become normal and ordinary? For the rest of them, perhaps. For Dawson it was a religious miracle that proved the power of God and would sustain him for the rest of his life. For Charles Cox and Julian Mason it was the most incredible clinical experience of their lives: Mason would become world famous from his thesis. And Hall supposed he would in time accommodate the curiosity and notoriety.

But how could life ever again become normal and ordinary for a woman who'd been possessed – physically occupied even – by the spirit of someone else and been used as a vehicle for murder? Perhaps this was where the prolonged treatment began, the counselling and the guidance.

Not over at all, in fact, for Julian Mason and Jennifer. But over for him, if Jane had definitely gone. At once came the objective balance. Over for him even if Jane *hadn't* gone. There was nothing more he could do. There were still some things to tidy up, perhaps: two or three weeks' work, maybe a month. And after that . . . After that, what?

His difficulty, he at last realized, wasn't that it was all over. It was at the thought that after that time, after a month at most, he wouldn't be seeing Jennifer again. Have any reason to see Jennifer again. Too soon to think like that. Despite the conviction of the priest and of Jennifer, none of them yet knew – were convinced, beyond doubt – that Jane *had* gone. And there was still a lot to do, if she had. He'd let things take their own course, at their own pace. There wasn't any hurry. He smiled across at Jennifer at the thought and she smiled hesitantly back.

'It's so wonderful,' she said, faint-voiced. 'I'm so . . .' She shook her head, unable to finish, too tired for the words to form.

'We all want it to have happened,' warned the psychiatrist, joining Hall's caution. 'But we don't know for sure, not yet.'

'What do we have to do now?' frowned Cox.

'What we'd already decided,' said Mason. 'We go on waiting.'

Chapter Thirty-five

Which they did. Nervously. With Jennifer in those early days the most nervous of all, the convinced priest the least. Jennifer very much needed his conviction to sustain her own hope, after the immediate elation of the exorcism. But as those days passed it became easier for her, the confidence growing imperceptible layer by imperceptible layer.

She kept her vow and maintained her religious instruction under Dawson, eager to pray – although unsure to whom – for the freedom to be permanent. She continued her treatment under Julian Mason, too, surer that she'd come through the horrific mental ordeal with her sanity intact but realistically accepting she needed that agreed and confirmed by a trained psychiatrist – a mind doctor – just as much as she needed to be guaranteed physically to have recovered by Charles Cox. Least perceptible of all was the gradual preparation each provided, unconsciously at first and each in their own specialized way, to equip Jennifer for her return to the closest she'd ever come to life among ordinary people who would never consider her anything but abnormal, apparently free of Jane or not.

Mason identified Jennifer's unprompted acceptance that she needed him as one of the most important indicators of her mental health. 'She *has* come through it,' he told Jeremy Hall. 'She could still be damaged, wrecked even, if Jane comes back: that's the key, which it's always been. But basically she's as solid as a rock. What we're seeing – what I'm seeing – is the determination always to win, to be the best, that we'd heard about but never properly been able to see, until now.'

'Isn't that a pretty quick prognosis?' queried Hall.

'What are you talking about?' demanded the psychiatrist. 'I've been with her, night and day, for weeks, remember! She's been my *only* patient. And she never had a mental problem: she had Jane, inside her head, trying to give her one. And it didn't work.'

'What about thinking of killing herself?'

'Thinking of doing it is very different from actually doing it. Wouldn't you have considered suicide, if you'd been the victim?'

Wanting to make his practical contribution to Jennifer's rehabilitation – secretly disconcerted that he wasn't doing as much as the other three men – Hall said, 'There's been quite a few things left in limbo. Is it too soon to involve her in making decisions?'

'It can't be soon enough. One thing that's got to be restored is her total confidence, the arrogance if you like, that she had before. People become confident making decisions for themselves.'

'It's about confidence that I'm concerned. I need to go back to London: get a lot of things on course. We talked about it last night, out walking. She asked me not to go. Got upset at the thought.'

Mason nodded, 'That dependency is something we've got to deal with.'

'So do I just go?' It was a clinical question, his only concern to do nothing to cause Jennifer any setback. He still couldn't imagine everything coming to an end: that there was a finite point and that it was fast approaching.

'No,' decided Mason. 'She's making giant strides but at her speed, not ours. She's still in a cocoon here. She's got to be eased off her dependency upon you and me and upon Mr Dawson. Not have anything snatched away.'

'What needs to be settled is still largely about her. How about bringing people here? Involving her that way?'

'Good,' nodded Mason. 'A very good idea.'

Jennifer thought it was, too. Guided by the psychiatrist Hall gave her two days' warning and hopefully briefed everyone else just as thoroughly against anything she wasn't prepared for. Bert Feltham was to be the only stranger and Jennifer said she was quite happy with his inclusion, too.

'My first single-minded contact with someone from the outside world!' she said. Mason was as pleased with the joke against herself, as he was with everything else Jennifer was doing and saying. But not as pleased as Jennifer. She felt alive, vibrant, a sensation she could scarcely remember. It was going to be all right. Everything. All right best of all – most of all – with her and Emily. Jennifer abruptly stopped the reflection, refusing it.

The chamber's chief clerk, unaccustomably subdued in dark grey, arrived with Humphrey Perry. Well briefed – perhaps too well briefed was Hall's initial thought – by the solicitor, Feltham tried overly hard to behave as if there had been nothing whatsoever unusual about Jennifer. But couldn't quite carry it off at the moment of introduction, offering and then withdrawing his hand.

Jennifer laughed openly at the man and said, 'I don't bite any more: and I no longer have an alter ego that does it, either.'

Geoffrey Johnson got to the clinic fifteen minutes later, burdened by briefcases and files. Inevitably the plump family lawyer was smoking one of his carved-bowled pipes. He paused by the Bentley to knock out the dottle before coming into the clinic.

Although she had already agreed Hall again queried Feltham's presence at the meeting and again Jennifer insisted she had no objection.

'Let's get as much done as soon as we can. There must be a lot to catch up with: things to do,' said Jennifer, eagerly. Back in control of herself, she thought: in control, in charge, of everything concerning her. Jennifer Lomax was Jennifer Lomax again. What she wanted – what she decided – these men would do. Follow her instructions and her wishes. From today she'd go forward. Pick up the pieces: rebuild a life. Shouldn't be frightened to be by herself, Julian Mason had told her at their last session, the previous day. More than strong enough to cope. And she was: she was sure she was. Jane had gone. Wasn't coming back. Ever. That's what Dawson said. The man she had to believe because he'd driven Jane away. And God: God too. It was still easier to believe the priest. So there *was* a lot to do. There was the rest of her life – her life and Emily's life – to work out. Make safe and secure and never endanger again. She hadn't talked about Emily to Peter yet. Hadn't talked to anyone, not even Dawson. Or Jeremy. Had to, soon. The big decision. The biggest. Talk about it and then plan the reunion. Not reunion: pompous word. Mother's didn't have reunions with baby daughters. The meeting then. Plan the meeting. But not yet, not today. Formalities was how Jeremy had described the purpose of this gathering: settling the formalities. She looked expectantly at the barrister, who took the cue.

Hall said, 'A lot of today is going to be taken up with money. This isn't the way this is normally done – certainly not between barrister and client – so it's going to be an exception to the rule . . .' Encouraged by Jennifer's self-mockery he said, '. . . But then everything has been an exception to every rule.' He looked to the family solicitor. '. . . Which sets the stage for you, Geoffrey . . . ?'

Johnson cleared his throat, a smoker's cough, as he unloaded his briefcases. Hall was glad he'd had a larger conference table moved into his suite.

Johnson said to Jennifer, 'With your power of attorney I've had to expend rather a lot of money. I'm anxious you should see the accounting and approve it . . .' He smiled, briefly. 'It's not an essential decision today, providing you're satisfied with my discharge of my duties, but you also might like to decide whether you wish me to continue with power of attorney, now that you're . . .' The man stumbled to a halt.

'. . . Now that Jane's gone?' finished Jennifer, helpfully.

'I'm very glad you're better,' said Johnson, still awkwardly.

'You and me both, Geoffrey. You and me both,' said Jennifer, with bright glibness. She was actually enjoying herself, amused at the apprehension everyone apart from Jeremy was finding it so difficult to hide. She was seized by the urge suddenly to say, 'Boo!' to see what they'd do.

The solicitor burrowed protectively into his bank of paper, isolating separate sheets like a bombardier laying out his ammunition. The financial outlay had necessarily been extremely high, Johnson warned, firing his first salvo. The Regent's Park apartment had sold within days of being put on the market for its full asking price –

instead of stating the price, the man slid the first of his prepared papers across to Jennifer – but completion had only just been concluded. Until five days earlier the estate had been responsible, as it was for the Hampshire mansion, the running of which cost considerably more. Another account sheet followed the first across the table towards Jennifer. Against that maintainence had also been put the cost of removing Emily and Annabelle by helicopter and their accommodation since. Here Johnson hesitated, looking to Hall who shook his head, unsure if Jennifer saw the gesture: she'd been gazing down at the figures. Also included were the costs of the private security firm now necessary to protect the Hampshire house and all the costs being incurred at the clinic: more invoices slid across the table.

'And then there are very considerable legal expenses,' said Johnson. 'And why Mr Feltham is here. Those expenses have, officially, to be submitted to my firm, of which Mr Perry is a partner and which, in turn, represents Mr Hall. I can't obviously approve payment from your estate to a firm of which I am also a partner: it constitutes a conflict of interest. It is necessary for you, personally, to authorize that.'

As if rehearsed, Feltham pushed the account sideways to Johnson, who passed it, unread, directly to Jennifer. She sniggered and said, 'Surely it's not too heavy to pick up.' She lifted it, looking at the amount. '. . . But then again!'

Hall was embarrassed and thought the other three men were as well.

'Seems to me like everything adds up to around £1,200,000?' said Jennifer, furthering all their discomfort and knowing it. 'You guys do even better than I as a trader and I thought I was good . . .'

'There is no difficulty,' said Johnson, hurriedly. 'You are extremely well provided for . . .'

'Geoffrey, you're tying yourself in knots trying to be discrete!' interrupted Jennifer. 'Why don't we talk figures: make it easier for you? I don't give a shit . . .' She looked quickly at Hall. 'That was me swearing, not Jane!'

Hall grinned back at her, very much liking a Jennifer Lomax he hadn't known before.

Johnson pushed doggedly on. 'The legal fees have not yet been put against any account. They will be more than covered from the sale of the London apartment: there was no outstanding mortgage and the sale price was £650,000. There is a Swiss deposit account, in yen, amounting to £400,000. I transferred £75,000 from deposit to current here, so all the other bills have been settled, as of today. That still leaves you with £20,000 in your joint current account, with £50,000 on deposit. Your personal account, which I have not touched, is in credit for £30,000. There are share portfolios which, on yesterday's stock market quotations, amount to £1,500,000. And there are company and private insurance policies totalling £3,000,000: I have applied both to the private companies and to Enco-Corps for the discharge of those policies in your favour. Your late husband's will still has to be admitted to probate but there is a £500,000 trust fund in Emily's name, with yourself and myself as trustees. It becomes operable when Emily reaches the age of eighteen . . .' He straggled to a halt. 'Those are the main items which I want immediately to bring to your attention . . .'

'At least I'm financially secure,' agreed Jennifer.

Hall wondered if anyone else noticed the suggestion of uncertainty in Jennifer's voice at the remark and wished he hadn't. Johnson had covered everything they had discussed by telephone under general headings, although the solicitor had not itemised the financial outlay until that day. Hall said, 'I don't think it's anything that needs an instant decision but there are a lot of offers outstanding that legally we should put to you.'

'Offers?' frowned Jennifer.

'For books, original screenplays, magazine and newspaper serialization,' listed Perry. 'We've had twenty: the highest, from an American publisher, is for $8,000,000.'

'We've had five in chambers, in the last two days that I haven't yet passed on,' said Feltham. 'And I've heard two British publishers are bringing out "books of the trial".'

Jennifer laughed, nervously. 'What do they want?'

He should have given her better warning, decided Hall. 'What it was like, for you,' he said, lamely.

'It was horrific for me.'

'Which is what people want to know about,' suggested Perry.

'That's . . . that's ghoulish . . . voyeurism . . .' She stopped, blinking rapidly. 'It's what Jane said she'd do. That she'd make me into a freak . . .'

Damn! damn! damn! thought Hall. 'It's nothing we need to talk further about, not now. Like I said, just something we had to tell you about, as your legal agents . . .'

'. . . I don't know . . . I don't think . . .' said Jennifer, haltingly. Her attitude in the beginning, something close to ebullience, was slipping away. That's all people wanted to do, look at her and laugh at her, like people used to go on family outings to laugh at the unfortunates in Victorian mental asylums.

'We'll leave it,' determined Hall, positively. It had been his mistake and he was angry at himself. He wanted to finish it all quickly now, to try to recover. He looked briskly around the room. 'There's nothing else is there?'

'Yes,' said Johnson, back among his papers and missing the look that Hall gave him. 'The bank, quite rightly, have raised a query about your personal account, Mrs Lomax . . .' He smiled up, having found what he wanted. Attached to the letter were a number of cheques. 'These, in all, total £1,000. All, from the dates, while you were in prison. Obviously you had difficulty in writing, because of your injuries, but four are quite obviously forgeries: the bank have refused to pay out on them. Who's Beryl Harrison?'

No! No! No! 'I don't want it taken any further!'

'It's a police . . .' began Johnson but Jennifer talked over him. 'Only if I choose to make a complaint. Which I don't. I don't want any more discussion about it. It's ended.' Had to get away: get away and hide.

The men in the room sat regarding her in varying degrees of surprise at an attitude that had run the gamut from recovered confidence through brief uncertainty to seemingly forceful, angry authority.

Jennifer shuffled through the papers, finding the legal invoices. She extended her hand towards Johnson and said peremptorily: 'Give me a pen, please. Let me sign a cheque for this. Everything will be paid up to date then, right?'

'Right,' agreed Johnson, chastened but not knowing why.

Jennifer quickly scrawled her signature, beginning to stand as she finished. 'Thank you all for coming. And for everything each and every one of you have done for me. I greatly and very sincerely appreciate it. Now you must excuse me. I have another appointment . . .' Quickly, while she could still hang on.

None of them were fully to their feet before she swept out of the room.

'What the hell . . .!' exclaimed Perry.

'We tried to cover too much,' said Hall. He knew Jennifer did have an appointment, another instruction session with Dawson, but that it wasn't for another two hours.

'But we achieved a lot, very satisfactorily,' said Feltham, picking up and looking at the cheque that Jennifer had signed in full settlement of the legal fees to date. He went directly to the barrister. 'I charged you at £1,000 an hour, Mr Hall. With refreshers, of course. That's what I'm quoting from now on, with no assurance that we'll accept the brief . . .' He smiled sideways, at Perry. 'You might keep that in mind, Humphrey.' He came back to Hall. 'As of today you're officially finished here, sir. Although of course I don't know what your personal plans are. But I thought I might as well bring some work down, for you to consider. A hospital negligence on behalf of a child damaged by oxygen deprivation: insurance company need their wrists slapped. Heroin possession by the youngest son of an earl: says it was planted on him because his elder brother's a registered addict. Dodgy, but I think it could be true: there've been two police complaint investigations in the division in the past three years, for stitching people up. And a grievous bodily harm. Black kid says he was defending himself against a racist gang: four against one and he gets charged!'

Back to normality, thought Hall. 'I hope to be in the office in a few days. I'll look at them before then. Let you know.'

'It'll be good to see you there, sir.'

'What's it like? The siege, I mean.'

'Still pretty bad,' said Feltham. 'And I suppose it'll get worse when the word gets around that you're back. Surprised you got away so easily when you went to Hampshire.'

'So was I,' admitted Hall.

'I didn't need the reminder frown not to mention Emily,' complained Johnson.

'Where is she?'

Johnson shrugged. 'They've gone to Disney, in Paris. And she's wetting the bed all the time now. Annabelle is genuinely worried.'

'Have you told Annabelle what's happened here?'

'She said she's glad it's all over. She thinks it would be best for Emily if they went back to Hampshire, after France. That living under a security screen would be better for the child than wandering about from theme park to theme park.'

'Any more talk of her quitting?'

'At least that's stopped,' said Johnson. 'But solicitors for the Metropolitan police have offered a compromise over their policing claim for the hospital. They're suggesting an independent assessment, by a fee draughtsman.'

'Rubbish!' rejected Hall. 'That's presupposing an acceptance of responsibility on our part. Which there isn't. Draughtsmen don't come into it: someone's playing with legal words they don't understand. Tell them we don't consider there's anything to negotiate.'

'It's going to seem strange, getting back to other work,' mused Perry. 'I'm sure you can hardly wait.'

'It's certainly going to feel different,' conceded Hall.

'It might have been a lot at one session,' conceded Julian Mason. 'It's not a setback.'

'You don't seem surprised,' challenged Hall, curiously.
'Maybe I'm not.'
'So you know what it's about?'
'I think I probably do.'
'And I can probably guess.'
'Jennifer said it was closed, didn't she?'
'Something like that. Are you going to tell me?'
'Of course not. And you should know better even to think I would.'
'I'm concerned for her, that's all: want to guard against a repeat of what happened today.'
'You can do that by forgetting about it.'
'She was upset by the idea of a book, too.'
'I can understand that as an initial reaction. But I think it could be thought about more fully.'
'It would make her into the freak Jane threatened. What she's terrified of.'
'Come on!' said the psychiatrist, brutally. 'She's always going to be that. It's something she's going to have to learn to live with and don't ask me how, because I haven't got a clue.'
'Have you told her that yet?'
'She doesn't have to be told. But she won't admit it. That's why it might help to write about it.'
'How?'
'If she committed herself to one publisher or one outlet, whatever, the others might eventually go away. But more important than anything, the very act of writing about it would be a catharsis.'
'Actually benefit her, you mean?'
'Probably more than I'm going to be able to.'
'Should I talk to her about it?'
'It's all part of encouraging her back into the real world, isn't it? The real world she hasn't been in for a

long time.' The psychiatrist looked very directly at the other man. 'But Jennifer is always going to be a freak.'

'I ran away.' She wasn't telling him anything he didn't already know. She didn't want to tell him the reason: risk everything.

'Your choice,' said Hall.

She wished he hadn't sounded so disinterested. 'You sound like Julian. Have you discussed it with him?'

Always honesty, he remembered. 'Yes.'

'What did he say?'

'He didn't tell me why, obviously. Just that it was a matter for you.' It was their evening walk, to the outer perimeter now although she was still careful to avoid close contact with anyone else. Hall didn't think Jennifer being there was a secret any more, obviously not among the staff, and was glad that Julian Mason's assurance about money buying silence had proved true. The danger, then, had always been other patients.

'I don't want to tell you.'

'Then don't.'

'I still shouldn't have run. I panicked.' She felt so safe on these walks: enjoyed the warmth of his hand, feeling his closeness.

'It was your first time in a group like that.'

'It wouldn't have happened once.' She hoped she wasn't sounding self-pitying.

'You've got to learn again.'

They walked on in silence. Jennifer said, 'Could you help me learn?'

'I'm not sure that would be helping you.' The silence lasted longer. This time he broke it. 'Would a book be such a bad idea?'

'I wouldn't know how to begin,' she protested.

'You don't have to study or pass exams to do it, do you? There'd be editors, people like that, to shape it for you. You'd probably get a lot of guidance before you even got started.'

'It would be like letting people stare at me.'

He searched for the right reply. 'Or stop them doing it.'

'I know that's going to be a problem,' she admitted.

You don't, thought Hall: you haven't any conception. 'I think you should think about it quite seriously.'

'I hardly need the money.'

'I'm not thinking about the money. It would get the whole thing out of your memory.'

'I don't imagine anything could ever do that,' Jennifer said, soberly.

'I wasn't talking about forgetting. I was talking about adjusting.'

'That's something else I know I've got to learn: how to adjust.'

It was time he himself adjusted, Hall decided. Past time. So he had to stop putting it off.

Chapter Thirty-six

His going burst her bubble. No-one knew, of course. Not even Julian Mason, with whom she had always been totally open and honest. She supposed being one hundred per cent better which was what Mason and Cox, with Dawson smiling beside them, had just declared her to be – meant she could successfully lie now without anyone guessing. Like Dawson hadn't guessed about her conversion. That wasn't so much an outright lie, any more than her not telling the psychiatrist the aching loss – the feeling that something had literally burst – she felt at Jeremy leaving. It was more retaining some privacy, which everyone did. In fact she was probably more honest than most people. Always had been. She did believe in something because when everything else had failed she'd been set free by a miracle, with a priest's hand on her head. So there had to be some higher authority, some Supreme Being. And if Dawson represented it, then it was to his God she had to be eternally grateful. So she would be. It was the most sincere promise she'd ever made and she'd keep it. She'd probably need to.

There was a huge difference between talking to Dawson and Julian Mason but talking was the operative word. Jeremy's departure had signalled the beginning of the end. Now Mason and Cox had told her there was nothing more they could do, so their contact was virtually over as well. So she needed the church as much – maybe even more – than people who insisted they didn't have the doubts. Which wasn't badly dishonest, either. More a compromise, which again everybody did about a lot of things, religion most of all. The important thing was keeping her promise.

She wished it was as easy to rationalize her feelings towards Jeremy Hall. Julian had done his best to prepare her – not about Jeremy alone but about all of them, himself and Dawson and Dr Cox – and she'd recognized at once that her dependence upon them had to be broken. But it wasn't the same with Jeremy. It wasn't dependence. What then? It couldn't be love. That was ludicrous. Their close-together walks had been kindness, nothing more, just his helping her get better. And she didn't think love – any sort of relationship – had a place in her life any more. She was still unsure what did, apart from Emily. And that remained the biggest, still-avoided uncertainty of all.

She wasn't sure, either, whether his daily telephone calls weren't adding to whatever it was that was troubling her. They weren't specifically to her, she reminded herself. He always spoke to the two doctors, sometimes even the priest, and there was always a practical reason for their conversations. She'd needed to confirm she still wanted Geoffrey Johnson to retain her power of attorney, for instance. And it had seemed important for him to tell her the Metropolitan authority had dropped their claim for the cost of policing St Thomas's Hospital and to remind her she still hadn't made a decision about the media and publishing offers.

Did her uncertainty – the pricked-bubble feeling – really have so much to do with Jeremy Hall? Or was she transferring on to him – lying to herself – the true reason for it? Wasn't it, quite simply, the terror of going back into the outside world: of being alone, with no-one to rely on? None of them – Mason or Cox or Dawson – would have made the decision if they hadn't been totally convinced, individually and collectively, that she was ready for it. It was Jennifer herself who wasn't convinced. So she had to convince herself about her readiness, as she had to convince herself about a God.

There was no cause to be ashamed – embarrassed – by how she felt: nor try unnecessarily – unfairly – to involve Jeremy. It wasn't even the unknown terror of what awaited her. Jennifer was terrified about only one person she was going to meet. And from whom, because of what Mason had just told her, she no longer had to be parted.

Jennifer jumped at the telephone, momentarily hesitating before picking it up.

'I've already spoken to Julian,' announced Hall. 'Excited?'

'Frightened.'

'I'd be surprised if you weren't.'

'I can leave whenever I want.' Stop avoiding it! she told herself.

'I know.' There was a long pause. 'Jennifer?'

'I can go back with Emily. Be her mother again.' The words sounded odd: artificial.

'Yes.'

'Where is she?'

'Hampshire. She arrived back last week, from Paris.'

'Is it safe for her to be there?'

'We're employing a lot more security people. Annabelle thinks it's best.'

'Does she know I'm better?'

'I've only just heard myself.'

'It's going to take me a day or two to get ready.'

'Is it?' Hall asked, pointedly.

'Emily will have to get used to the idea, as well as me. Just a day or two.'

'I'll probably need that, to set things up.'

Jennifer felt a jump of excitement, through the apprehension. 'You're going to fix things for me?'

'Would you like me to?'

'Yes, please!' she said, hurriedly.

'And come with you?'

'Yes. I'd like that very much.'

'Welcome back!' he said.

'Yes,' she said, doubtfully.

Jeremy Hall had discerned her mood and understood it, with more practical cause to be apprehensive than Jennifer could yet imagine. The circus had begun again the very moment he'd arrived back at his neglected, mailbox-overflowing apartment. A media ambush still awaited him and he literally ran the envelope gauntlet. There were more letters inside. There were also two from his bank, which coincidentally he opened in the right order. In the first the manager assured him he had no cause whatsoever to worry at being overdrawn because the man fully understood the preoccupying circumstances and cordially invited him to lunch. The second thanked him for the cash infusion so substantial that the lunch would be a good opportunity to discuss investments. The tape on his answering machine was exhausted with messages, some from people he hadn't heard of since university, others from girls claiming to have met him at functions and parties he couldn't remembering attending. There were three calls from Patricia Boxall.

The chambers were besieged the following morning

and one by one the forgotten luncheon invitations from Proudfoot's celebration party were pressed upon him during the morning. Experimentally he accepted Sir Richard's. They had to force their way out of the building and led a pursuing road race to Pall Mall. He was asked three times for his autograph in the Reform Club, which Proudfoot insisted he'd never known before and promised to complain to the membership committee. When he returned to chambers, Hall had his home telephone number changed and made ex-directory.

He took all three briefs Bert Feltham had offered at the clinic. A police line had to be formed to get him into court to defend the earl's son on the heroin charge, which he won in a single day's sitting which ended with the case being dismissed and the magistrate referring the evidence of a drug squad officer to the Metropolitan Police Commissioner with a suggested internal enquiry. The hospital insurers had doubled their original out-of-court settlement offer, which Hall considered satisfactory, but the parents of the child urged him to take it to court. 'It's not as if you can lose, is it, Mr Hall?' said the father, who wouldn't be persuaded otherwise.

His rowing club had been discovered in his absence and he was followed there the first Saturday anyway. He was hopelessly out of condition and the pursuing press launches created waves and wash that engulfed him. He watched himself on television that night paddling waist deep and water-logged back to the pontoon, glad the cameras unmistakably caught him calling the photographers bastards and telling them to fuck off.

And he missed Jennifer. He told himself in the beginning that it was unavoidable, his having been thrust into such close proximity with her for so long and for such a reason. But gradually he changed his mind. It wasn't the situation he missed it was Jennifer herself. He felt responsible for her, worried about her. He appreciated the guidance he got during his daily calls to Mason and Cox and even the priest – calls he always routed through them, so there would apparently be a reason for his later speaking to her – but he wasn't entirely satisfied Jennifer was yet ready to leave the safety of the clinic.

Which today they'd insisted she was. So the final moment had come and he'd consciously – intentionally – intruded himself into it. Right that he should. Seeing a case through to its proper conclusion: earning the exorbitant fee demanded by Bert Feltham.

He had Geoffrey Johnson alert the security company greatly to increase the manpower at the mansion and ordered the helicopter to fly her from the clinic directly into the grounds of her home. He telephoned Annabelle several times after she got back from Paris with Emily, initially disappointed but then accepting the nanny's subdued reaction.

'She's been medically and psychiatrically declared totally recovered,' he insisted.

'It can't be a moment too soon for Emily.'

'Have you told her?'

'Of course I have! She needs as much preparation as Mrs Lomax. More maybe.'

Hall wasn't interested in debating the greater need. 'How's she reacting to all the security?'

'I've tried to make it into a game. Told her they are her soldiers and a lot of them are nice enough to go along with it. It's not brilliant but it's the best I could think of . . . I'm running out of things to think of.'

'Is she excited?'

There was a pause before Annabelle responded. 'She says she doesn't want her mummy to be nasty again.'

Hall briefly considered driving to Hertfordshire to fly down with Jennifer but decided against it for the sake of the clinic: it would have been poor recompense for the way they'd protected Jennifer's anonymity to lead the media of the world to whoever else was seeking privacy.

It was a wise decision. By the time he came off the M3 towards Alton – ironically following, he realized, the same route Gerald Lomax had taken on the night he'd murdered Jane – he headed a line of at least fifteen identifiable press and television vehicles. Most, during the journey, pulled out of the convoy to draw level to photograph and attempt to talk to him through their open window. Worryingly, by the time he did turn off, there were two helicopters fluttering overhead.

He was glad he'd had the forethought personally to speak to Inspector Hughes before setting out that morning. The scene outside the mansion was reminiscent of the road-blocked approach to St Thomas's Hospital. It required a police Range Rover front and back and walking policemen either side for him to cover the last hundred yards to the mansion entrance and a squad of security men had to come out to complete the wedge in the middle of which he was finally able to get inside.

Annabelle was waiting for him, at the entrance. Emily was beside her, curly hair loose, in jeans and Mickey Mouse sweater, a forlorn attempt by Annabelle to make it seem an ordinary day. The child held Annabelle's hand and stood with one foot awkwardly on top of the other, twisting precariously.

'Listen!' demanded Annabelle, as he got out of the car.

There was an audible roaring hum from the road, like bees or maybe even the distant sound of approaching hooves. It was worsened by the hovering helicopters.

'And the road's more than a mile away,' completed the girl.

'Like the zoo,' suggested Emily, with childlike prescience. 'You were at the hospital with my mummy!'

'Yes.'

'She's coming home! She's better!'

'I know.'

'I don't know about Daddy, do you?'

'No.'

'Maybe he'll come, too.'

'Maybe.' He looked helplessly at Annabelle who looked expressionlessly back, offering no help.

'There's another one!' said the child, pointing up. 'I've been in a helicopter.' She pronounced it 'elcopter'.

It fluttered down, far enough away for them not to be buffeted by the downdraught, but it didn't save its passengers from that of the pursuing media machine. They came in low and their cameramen had ample time to picture Jennifer, who was hurried towards the house by Colin Dawson. By the time they reached it Annabelle had already carried the suddenly frightened Emily inside, away from the noise and the artificial gale.

Every effort Jennifer had made for the homecoming was totally wrecked. Her dress and jacket were in disarray, her hair churned into a bird's-nest and her nose as well as her eye was running from the dust that had blown in, streaking her make-up: before she could even speak the priest had to pick out a piece of grit with a handkerchief tip. It did mean, though, that Jennifer had the perfect excuse for the real tears that started the moment she was able properly to look at Emily.

'Hello darling,' Jennifer said. 'Mummy's home.'

'But not Daddy?' said Emily.

'No,' said Jennifer. 'Not Daddy.'

* * *

It was the unexpected presence of the wealthy priest, perfectly accustomed to such opulence and sincerely believing himself chosen to be God's vehicle for miracle, who saved the situation.

No-one else knew what to do or say. Emily had instinctively started back when Jennifer moved as if to kiss and hug her – so she'd stopped – and Annabelle ran out of words after saying it was nice to see Jennifer back. Hall couldn't think of any contribution at all. So Dawson sipped the Earl Grey and ate the triangle sandwiches served by Alice Jenkins as if afternoon tea there was a regular ritual and talked to Emily, who seemed to welcome the relief as much as the rest of them, playing up to it even.

'Does your collar hurt like that?'

'No.'

'Daddy doesn't have a shirt like that.'

'This is because I am a priest.'

'What's that mean?'

'I work for God.'

'Not for my daddy?'

'No.'

'Do you know God?' she demanded, seemingly genuinely curious.

'Yes.'

'Does he really have a beard? He's got a beard in the picture on Miss Singleton's wall: she's my teacher. G stands for God.'

'The picture's of his son.'

'Do you know him, too?'

'I know of him.'

'But you haven't met him?'

'Not like I'm meeting you now.'

'You're very clever to know what G stands for,' ventured Jennifer, as the tension eased.

'I know all my letters now. Annabelle taught me while we were away. We've been away, while you've been ill. I saw Mickey Mouse . . .' She plucked at her sweater. To Dawson she said, seriously, 'He's real, you know?'

'No, I didn't,' said the priest.

'He is. I met him. And Goofy and Pluto and Minnie. I met them all.' She looked back to Jennifer. 'But I'm glad I'm home now.'

'I'm glad, too,' said Jennifer, hopefully. 'And I'm glad most of all to be home with you. Are you glad that I'm home?'

Hall saw the fleeting frown cross Annabelle's face.

Emily remained serious for what seemed a very long time. Finally she said, 'I *think* so. But I wish Daddy was here too.'

Jennifer's face began to crumple more but she managed to stop it. 'I've missed you,' she blurted.

Emily didn't say anything.

'It's getting late, darling,' said Jennifer. 'While everyone else is having their tea here why don't we go and have ours in the kitchen? And after that I can give you your bath and then read you a story and you can show me all the letters you know, on the page?'

Emily looked between her mother and the nanny. 'I want Annabelle to give me my tea and bath. And read to me.'

'But with Mummy as well,' said Annabelle.

'All right,' agreed the child, uncertainly.

The excuse of grit in her eye had almost gone by the time Jennifer asked Hall and the priest to stay as she followed Annabelle and Emily out of the room.

Hall said, 'Not at all what she expected, I wouldn't think.'

'She said she'd tried not to imagine anything.'

'It'll take some getting over,' suggested Hall.

'Hardly, with her resilience,' said the priest. 'It could have been better, but only just. They've got a lot of catching up to do.'

'Are you here to help?' queried Hall.

Dawson's shoulders lifted and fell. 'She asked me to come with her at the last minute. Said she wanted moral support . . .' He smiled. 'I've never been in a helicopter before.'

'Easier than getting here by road.'

'We saw what it was like when we came in. Incredible.'

'I think I might get a lift back with you. Come back and get the car later.' Purely for the immediate convenience, he told himself. It was ridiculous even to think of trying to drive through that mêlée again.

Dawson made another vague gesture through the lounge window in the direction of the distant road: inside it wasn't possible to hear the animal roar. 'They're not going to be able to live like this. No-one could. Not for long.'

Hall was still trying to think of a reply when Jennifer came back into the room. She didn't try to hide the fresh tears. 'She was frightened of me being too close to her in the bathroom so I came away.' She paused. 'I saw what I looked like in the bathroom mirrors. A mad woman.'

None of them wanted to eat. Hall and the priest drank whisky. Jennifer didn't drink anything and neither did Annabelle when she came down to say Emily had gone to sleep. They were all too anxious to reassure Jennifer it was always going to be difficult at the very beginning:

each insisted, again too eagerly, that it had in fact gone far better than they'd anticipated. None of it helped.

Jennifer agreed at once to Hall leaving in the clinic's helicopter and said, 'There's something we could discuss in detail when you come back for your car, although I might as well tell you now.'

'What?'

'I've decided to write the book. And I want you to negotiate the contracts for me.'

'I'm not a literary agent,' Hall protested, weakly.

'Literary agents arrange deals. We're having deals shovelled at us. I need a lawyer to pick the best and negotiate the best . . .' She smiled through the sadness. 'And you, Jeremy Hall, are the very best lawyer I've ever met in my life.' And by acting for me, she thought, you're staying in my life.

Jeremy Hall was thinking the same. 'I'd be pleased to,' he said.

Chapter Thirty-seven

Jeremy Hall didn't collect the car on his first return, nor on the second and when he tried on the third the battery was flat and it had to be jump-started from the gardener's Land-Rover. He learned to enjoy helicopter travel and tolerate the unremitting curiosity and media hounding. Unthinkingly on his part the routine became his spending the week in London before coming down to Hampshire on a Friday, although there were telephone calls in between. It was Emily who said it was what her father did, briefly creating an awkwardness that Jennifer handled better than Hall did.

By then the relationship between Jennifer and Emily had almost completely reverted to what it had been before. Emily stopped bed-wetting the second week and by the fourth she had practically lost any attention-seeking precocity. It was during the fourth week – the week when Hall finally persuaded the parents of the brain-damaged boy to accept the hospital insurer's newly increased out-of-court offer – that Jennifer suggested he stay for the weekend instead of flying back the same day, which was what he'd always done until then.

'I might need support,' she said. 'And I've started to write it. I'd like you to see what I've done so far.'

Jennifer recognized the risk on several levels and was

nervous of each – nervous one would collapse and destroy the still secret hope of the others – and still wasn't sure if she would positively force the issue, although she wanted to. Wasn't sure, even, if she was correctly reading the signs because there'd scarcely been any. He always came laden with papers and faxes and letters from publishers and newspapers and they always spent part of his visit, sometimes the majority, comparing the advantages of one contract against another but she didn't think he'd needed personally to come so often. Unless he'd wanted to. Her satisfaction that he did went beyond the unspoken hopes. She had figures and percentages and subsidiary profits to think about and calculate and it was like a door opening on to a dusty room in her mind, although the dust quickly blew away. She was far better at the financial assessments than Hall, who said so openly when they'd pared the approaches down to a final three.

'You don't really need me,' he complained.

'We're not negotiating yet: we're necessary together as a team,' said Jennifer, intentionally ambiguous.

'Let's see,' said Hall, which didn't help her.

It was the fourth, full weekend visit. As usual he came heavy with briefcases, although by then they both knew the figures from the three favoured publishers, all American.

'I've been thinking about that,' she announced, consciously boasting her financial acumen because she wanted him to be impressed. 'These three are all for world rights. One upfront payment, the highest at the moment $8,000,000. Each contract gives them the right to sell individually to other countries. But we've got offers of £1,500,000 from England and $5,000,000 from Japan and approaches from all those other countries in

Europe. Which the Americans will pick up if we sell outright. They're not spending *anything*: they're into profit before they start. Why don't we sell just the American rights to the Americans and negotiate ourselves and separately with each of the other countries? That way we make the profit.'

Emily had long since been put to bed and Annabelle was in her separate annexe. They'd eaten dinner – duck – in the kitchen and carried the remainder of the wine through into the lounge. He'd shaken his head against brandy, uncomfortably aware of the similarity with the night of Jane Lomax's death. Jennifer didn't appear aware of it. He smiled at her and said, 'I didn't think you needed the money.'

'I don't!' she said, coming forward in her facing chair. 'It's never the money! It's the *deal*: shaving a point, gaining a percentage.'

'Like the old days?' he suggested, seriously.

'Close enough.'

'It'll involve our having to discuss a lot more, after we close the American contract,' he said, looking directly at her.

'I know,' said Jennifer, holding his eyes. Meet me halfway, she thought.

'I'd like that.'

Far enough! Still room to retreat. 'I hoped you would. I would, too.'

He was as relieved as she was, almost too eager. 'We could create a lot of new problems for ourselves.'

There was no misunderstanding that! 'You want to see my CV? There's a whole page listed under problems.'

'Your terms. If you decide . . .'

'. . . I don't want ground rules!' she stopped. 'Just for once, for the first time since I can't remember when, I want something to happen as it happens. OK?'

'OK.'

'But there *are* things to get out of the way.' It wasn't an immediate contradiction. She had to tell him. It would be her barrier if she didn't: she had to risk it becoming his.

'I don't think you do,' he said, cautiously.

'It's for me,' she admitted.

'OK,' he said again, although more doubtfully this time.

Jennifer had tried to rehearse it, to take away the vileness, but there were no words that could. She talked staring intently at him, seeking the twitch of revulsion that would tell her she'd lost before it began. His face remained blank. She almost wished it hadn't: for there to have been something, whatever it was. 'Doctor Lloyd made the tests, at the hospital. I'm not . . . it's all right. I'm all right.'

Hall nodded but didn't speak.

'I wanted you to know.' Say something! Please say something!

'And now I do.'

Not enough. Still blank faced: non-committal. 'And?'

'I can understand it being your problem. It's not mine.'

There was a flood of relief. The smile was still hesitant. She had to get everything out of the way: a fresh start or whatever cliché it was. 'And we haven't talked about Gerald.'

'Do we need to?'

'I don't want to begin with any . . .' She stumbled to a halt, sniggering nervously.

'. . . Ghosts?' he suggested, smiling back.

'I can't imagine I was going to say that!'

'Julian Mason would probably think it was good that you were.'

Jennifer became serious again, her emotions on a switch-back. 'I don't feel anything. I supposed I should . . . wish almost that I did because it's not right to feel nothing . . . but that's what it is. Nothing. Not hate or sadness or regret. Nothing. It's as if he never happened. Never existed . . . Does that make me strange . . . ?' She managed another faint smile. '. . . Stranger than I have been . . . ?'

'That *is* a question for Julian Mason.'

'I'm asking you.'

'You were married to a man you never knew: whom no-one knew. How can you feel something for someone you never knew?'

Jennifer's smile broadened. 'Thank you. That makes some kind of sense . . . as much as anything does.'

'Is that the end of the ground rules that never were?'

'Yes.' I don't expect another miracle, God, but make this work: please make this work.

'Do you want any more wine?'

'No.'

'Neither do I.'

'Your room. Emily's taken to coming in to mine, if she wakes up.'

It didn't work. Jennifer was tense, rigid, and Hall couldn't relax, either, and was too relaxed because of it.

'It's my fault,' he apologized.

'Mine.'

'It's no-one's fault. It'll be all right.'

'It will be, won't it?' she said, anxiously. 'You're not frightened of . . . you know. . . ?'

'I'm not frightened of anything. I'm very excited,

which is the problem and I love you and everything is going to be wonderful.'

'There's one more thing we haven't talked about.'

'What?'

'I think it's time Emily knew about Gerald.'

Hall felt an intruder when Jennifer discussed it with Annabelle, trying to decide a good time and concluding between them there wasn't one, and even more awkward when Jennifer pulled the child on to her lap and said she had something important to tell her.

'It's about Daddy,' Jennifer said. Would she feel anything about Gerald now? Not about Gerald, she thought. For Emily, about Gerald, perhaps.

'When's he coming home!' demanded the child, pulling away from Jennifer and grinning up at her.

'That's what I've got to tell you. He won't be coming home, darling.'

'Not till when?'

'Not ever.'

'Not ever, *ever*?'

'No.'

'He's got to!'

'You know when I came home, with the man who told you he knew God?' began Jennifer, anxiously.

Emily sat with her lip between her teeth, tiny face creased in uncertainty. She nodded.

'And you told him about Miss Singleton and the picture of Him on the wall?' It was becoming too long! Too convoluted!

Emily nodded again.

'Has Miss Singleton told you about Heaven.'

'It's where God lives.'

'That's right,' encouraged Jennifer. 'And that's where

Daddy is now. God needed someone to help him and asked Daddy to go. So he has.'

'That's not fair!' protested Emily, eyes brimming. 'I want him! I want him to come back.'

'He can't, darling.'

'Tell the man who knows God to make Him send Daddy back.'

The tears started and Jennifer had to swallow, against her own. 'He can't do that.'

'I want Daddy!' demanded Emily, through the tears, slapping out rudely at Jennifer.

'Daddy has gone,' said Jennifer, as firm-voiced as she could manage. 'He's not coming back because he can't.'

'I want him!'

'It's just going to be the two of us now, you and me,' said Jennifer, looking solemnly over Emily's head to Jeremy Hall.

Emily pulled away from her mother again, looking in the same direction. 'You're not going to be my Daddy!'

'I know,' said Hall.

That night Emily wet the bed. Jennifer and Hall still didn't manage to make love properly.

Until that week Jennifer had not maintained her promise in a church: instead a priest in Alton, an anxious young man named Tomkins, had twice a week braved the outside multitude to come to her and with inadvertent naivety provided three days of tabloid headlines the worst of which had been 'God to the Rescue'.

That Sunday Jennifer decided to go to him and to his church for the first time.

Considering himself a hardened expert, Hall warned Inspector Hughes – suspecting as he did so that police leaks resulted in the very media invasion he was seeking protection against – and there was a familiar cordon around the church when they arrived after battling through the throng immediately outside the house. In the pew Emily positioned herself very positively and suspiciously away from Jeremy Hall, between Annabelle and her mother. The row behind them remained empty. Only two people stayed in the one in front, crushed together at the far end. Tomkins took his sermon from the Book of Proverbs and quoted, 'Let us solace ourselves with love, for the good man is not at home, he has gone on a long journey,' which Hall thought appropriate for their reluctant acceptance by the congregation. He expected her to take communion but she didn't. Seeming aware of his surprise she said on the chaotic ride back, 'I'm not ready yet. My baptism and confirmation will be my acceptance.'

Before he got into the helicopter that came that night to collect him Hall said, 'It's been quite a weekend.'

Jennifer said, 'I'd wanted it to be better.'

'There'll be a lot more that are.'

Chapter Thirty-eight

Jeremy Hall did not consider himself a literary judge but he was impressed by what Jennifer had written when he got back to London that night. She wasn't hurrying it: hadn't, in the first seventy-five pages he'd brought back with him, yet reached the moment of Jane's possession. Jennifer was being brutally, scathingly honest about herself and her affair with Lomax – a casual adventure to begin with, growing guiltily into love – and Hall accepted how fully her confidence had returned for her to want him to read it now that their affair had begun, if not yet been properly consummated.

He amused himself with the impression of the President of the American publishing company trying to crawl down the telephone to get to him when he called to finalize the $8,000,000 contract. As it was the man insisted on catching an evening flight to London, despite Hall's warning that he wouldn't be available the following day because of a court appearance that might occupy him for the remainder of the week.

In the event it didn't. Humphrey Perry was again the instructing solicitor and had obtained copies of the National Front membership cards of two of the four white youths upon whom his black client was accused of inflicting grievous bodily harm. Hall broke one of the youths in cross-examination to admit setting out to ambush the boy, who in blind panic had stabbed one of his attackers with his own wrestled-away knife. A typical caption under his newspaper photograph the following day called him 'Jeremy the Unbeatable'. He told Bert Feltham he didn't really want to increase his fees to £2,000 a day so soon. They compromised by reserving the figure for lengthy cases to which he had to devote his entire time. Hall promised to tell the chief clerk by the end of the week whether he would defend a murder charge as mercy killing.

Wilbur Blake reminded Hall of the American lawyer who'd provided so much valuable background defence material about Jane Lomax. Like Ross Hamilton Forest II, the patrician-like publisher wore his pure white hair long and had the same clipped, New England accent. The lawyer with him, Craig Beaumont, was an immaculately dressed and comparatively young black man whom Hall guessed from his height to have been a college basketball player.

Blake put up only a token resistance against abandoning his demand for world rights – Hall surrendered the English-speaking provinces of Canada and South Africa but retained Australia – and Hall suspected he wouldn't have attempted to reduce the $8,000,000 if Beaumont hadn't prompted him. They ping-ponged figures across the table and settled at $7,250,000. Hall had been prepared to drop the further $250,000 and wished Jennifer had been there to witness the negotiation, particularly when he specifically excluded any film, television or video-recording rights. It had been Jennifer's suggestion, to lessen the tax liability, for the money to be assigned, in tranches, to an acculumation and maintenance trust in Emily's name. Hall allowed it to appear the American's bargaining success.

While Hall went legally, line by line, through the American contract he let Blake read Jennifer's first seventy-five pages, occasionally distracted by the American's very visible excitement.

It was Beaumont who insisted Jennifer, not anyone with power of attorney, sign such a large contract and they flew down the following day. Blake was courtly and congratulatory about what he'd already read ('It's hardly going to need any editing at all,') and the practical Beaumont worked hard to include a clause in their agreement guaranteeing Jennifer undertaking a countrywide promotional visit to the United States tied in with a lecture tour just prior to her book's publication. It was left to Jennifer's final decision, nearer the time.

Neither American regarded or treated Jennifer as an oddity. Nor did the individual publishers who followed them in succeeding weeks, although the Japanese publisher wanted several photographs of himself with her.

On the day of the American signing Hall issued a public statement detailing the deal, although withholding the figure. He repeated it with every contract in every country that followed and by the end of the first month had managed to divert the offers and the mob-like attention away from Jennifer and himself to the organizations with reproduction rights. A hard core of paparazzi remained but the siege was virtually lifted in London and Hampshire.

Emily was even able to go back to Miss Singleton's playschool, although driven by Annabelle and initially escorted by security men. Jennifer was no longer ostracized in church on Sunday. Her first public outing with Jeremy Hall in London – to a restaurant in Chelsea Harbour – was a mixed ordeal of curiosity, distancing apprehension and autograph demands but Jennifer confronted it then and every time afterwards until the intrusion became bearable.

They adjusted to the need for permanent bodyguards. Inevitably, because Hall was always photographed with her, newspapers and magazines linked them romantically. They refused to deny or confirm it. He went with her to the plastic surgeon who advised that she wait another three months for cosmetic surgery to her arms.

Hall's plea of mitigation gained a suspended sentence for the mercy killing mother. He was almost glad to lose a case – a fraud charge against a company chairman whose lies he didn't learn about until they were in court – and those that followed but on average he won more than he lost and the newspaper eulogies, and the briefs, continued unabated. Jennifer's manuscript grew and grew.

'It's not perfect but out of ten I'll score life at the moment at nine,' said Jennifer.

She made the remark on a Saturday, just the two of them at dinner but in the dining room because they were celebrating the completion of her manuscript. She'd refused to let him read any more than those first seventy-five pages. 'It's still rough. Needs polishing.'

'You'll have to let it go eventually.' She'd already revised it once. The writing had consumed her – which was hardly surprising – but he suspected she was having second thoughts about the initial honesty. 'Any particular problem?'

'I've got two endings,' she admitted.

'Two?'

'One, where Jane finally goes. The other with us. And we're kind of in limbo, aren't we?' They'd become lovers, although still with difficulty, the weekend after the American visit. Now the sex was perfect every time but they still bed-hopped because of Emily's nocturnal wandering.

Hall recognized an awkward apology. 'What makes you think I want to marry you anyway?' he said, trying to lift the seriouness.

Jennifer made the effort to respond. 'I don't give a damn about you. I want to marry you. And I'm going to.'

'Let's give her more time,' he said, seriously. 'She's coming around, gradually: seeing me as part of the furniture.'

'I want you to be more than that to her.'

'I want that, too. But it's got to be at her pace, not ours. We've got all the time in the world, haven't we?'

She smiled. 'I hope so.'

'You know so.'

'I want to have a party!' Jennifer announced excitedly, smiling at him eagerly. 'I'm being baptized in two Sundays' time. I've asked Dawson to do it: Tomkins understands. And I want Julian Mason and Dr Cox and Lloyd, too. Everyone who helped me as much as they did. And Humphrey and Geoffrey as well, I suppose. The house is big enough for everyone. How's that sound!' I'll be keeping my promise, she thought: debt paid. To everyone.

'Wonderful, if that's what you want.'

'You're not keen?'

'It'll be another media bun fight if it leaks out when I ask the police for additional protection.'

'I don't see why it should be. And if it does I don't give a damn about that, either.'

It didn't leak.

The adhesive paparazzi were alerted by the sudden influx of helicopters and then the emerging convoy of cars but they'd resigned themselves to some media pursuit. At the church, with Dawson's agreement, Jennifer actually invited three in to photograph the ceremony. Emily wore a new party dress and the laid-back Mason had made a supreme effort by wearing a suit. The pews were filled, all around them, and quite a few people came up to Jennifer afterwards to congratulate her. Some even shook hands.

Emily was allowed to stay up for the start of the dinner and showed off, although not irritatingly so. The only dip was when she asked Dawson to tell God to send her Daddy back but Jennifer refused to be depressed even by that, agreeing when it was time for Emily to go to bed that as it was a special occasion Emily could sleep in her bed. Jennifer only just managed to avoid looking at Jeremy Hall as she did so. When she finally caught his eye Jennifer grinned and he grinned back and she didn't care if anyone around the table saw the exchange or not. It had given her an idea.

Hall perfectly performed the role of host but it was Jennifer who proposed the toast, with Roederer Crystal for Dawson's benefit and enjoyment. She acknowledged each of the men around the table by name and reserved calling her recovery a miracle until she got to the urbane priest. Annabelle had been included in the dinner and Jennifer embraced her in the gratitude.

'That's all over now,' she declared. 'And because of you all I have a future. A future that I am looking forward to more than I can properly express in words, although I've tried to express everything else in words over these last few months . . .' She hesitated, looking directly at Jeremy Hall. '. . . It's a future I am going to share with the brilliant lawyer who, can you believe, I once told I didn't want in my life. And now without whom I couldn't live. So I am very glad I won't have to . . .' She raised her glass. 'I've just drunk to you all so now I invite all of you to drink to Jeremy and I. And to our future together . . .'

There was a babble of congratulation and Dawson demanded to perform the wedding ceremony and they agreed at once. There were more toasts, to the success of the book, and it was gone midnight when the two doctors helped the unsteady priest to bed. Before he went upstairs Hall managed to separate himself sufficiently from those who remained downstairs to say he wouldn't expect her that night. Jennifer, who was slightly and happily drunk, retorted that she wouldn't be denied anything on her official engagement night and would come if she thought Emily was sleeping soundly enough.

She'd had caterers in for the evening and spent some time seeing them off the premises, finally checking the kitchen before going upstairs herself.

Emily still slept with a low night-light, which Annabelle had moved into Jennifer's bedroom when she'd settled the child down. Emily was sprawled sideways across the bed and stirred and muttered something from her growing-up dream when Jennifer lifted her back to one side so that she could get into the other.

Having done so Jennifer remained propped up on one arm, looking down. Emily's hair was curled out, on the pillow, and she'd put her thumb in her mouth and was sucking, noisily. Jennifer felt an engulfing, overwhelming rush of love. So perfect, she thought: so perfect and beautiful and wonderful.

'Emily,' she whispered, softly. 'My Emily. I love you, my darling.'

Her arm began to numb, from the way she was supporting herself, so she lay back to take her weight off it. And then the numbness seized her, paralysing her.

'*Hello Jennifer*,' said Jane.

Chapter Thirty-nine

'Jesus, I've been bored! Almost couldn't wait, several times. Glad I did though. This is perfect: everyone I want, all in the same place at the same time. Here, where it happened the first time . . .

'There have been a few bright moments, but not a lot: difficult not to have hysterics at all that exorcism shit from the priest . . .' The voice deepened, mockingly. '. . . *"This, my child, is a miracle. Proof that God loves us." And what a hypocritical cow you turned out to be, pretending you believed it. I know what believing is and you sure as Hell haven't got it. It was fun, conning the old motherfucker, though. Conning you all. Remember how clever I was! How I stopped swearing and pretended to be contrite, repentant . . . !'* There was another voice change, deep again. '"*Pray with me, my child: seek God's forgiveness . . .*"' Then high, childlike. '*Oh, yes please! Forgive me, God, for I have sinned!*

'And don't I know about sin. I'm a practising expert. Learned it all from dear Daddy, beloved Bishop, the man of God. Taught me all the lines, all the bullshit, and was like every other man. Preached from a pulpit on Sunday and fucked every woman he could lay his hands on every other day of the week while he spent Mummy's money impressing everybody what a good guy he was. Mummy

didn't die in a boating accident. She committed suicide – drowned herself – for what she couldn't tolerate: not the fucking of every other woman. When she saw him hit on me. He never fucked me but he wanted to: was panting for it. So I set the whole thing up. Asked them both, but separately, to see my confirmation dress on the day of the ceremony: asked him to come to my room first. I was waiting for him, naked. Let him feel, so he'd be doing it when Mummy came. I wanted her to divorce the bastard: cut him off without a penny, so he couldn't buy his respect any more. But she killed herself instead. For the rest of his life I kept him never knowing if I'd tell anyone. And at home I always walked about naked, taunting him with what he couldn't have. Drove him mad. And I loved it. Loved torturing the dirty, lying, cheating bastard. A cheating bastard of God.

'That's when I decided the Devil was more fun, all those years ago. That's how I amused myself, when I got here. Used to pretend to all the Jesus jockeys and kneel among them and when they prayed to their God I prayed to mine for my father to burn in Hell in more agony than anyone else. Imagine that: I became a bigger, better hypocrite than Bishop Daddy, which is what he made me call him.

'Think what I've done, Jennifer. Dawson was right. I really am the Devil incarnate. I left my blood and fingerprints and hair for DNA on purpose. I really did! I planned it. I've legally proved in a court of law that ghosts exist. I've fucked religion. When I've finished tonight there are going to be Devil cults all over the world, praying to me.

'That's the most brilliant part of everything I've done but it was fun torturing you like I tortured Bishop Daddy. You really believed you'd worked out the

numbness, to tell you when I was with you, all by yourself, didn't you! I did it on purpose, shit-for-brains: all of it. Made you numb when I wanted to, didn't bother when I intended you and the idiots with you to imagine you were free. You've never been free. There hasn't been a moment when I haven't been there, knowing everything that's been going on. Never will be. Christ I can't believe how stupid you all were!'

Jennifer struggled to move but couldn't. Her mouth was frozen half open but no sound came when she tried to scream: she couldn't even move her tongue.

'. . . *Don't tire yourself, honey. You're not going to do or say anything for yourself any more. Just for me. What I want to do.*

'Your boyfriend's not much good in the fuck stakes, is he? I've seen bigger dicks on newborn babies. Hardly knows how to use it, either. You did a good job, faking orgasms, Jennifer. Best supporting role in our own very special Oscar nominations, how about that! Not a bad lawyer, though. I was frightened no-one was going to pick up on the clues I'd left behind: thought I was going to have to have you do it. Wasn't that phoney trial a scream! Another time I could hardly stop myself laughing. Interesting, what he found out though. Would have put Gerald in the gas chamber, where he belonged . . . And he got it right about why I'm doing this to you: nothing at all about my murder. Always knew you weren't involved in that . . .'

Emily stirred, turning in her sleep and throwing an arm out as she did so. Jennifer could feel the warmth from the little hand.

'. . . *That book you've spent so much time on – not bad, by the way – is going to round it all off very nicely, isn't it? I'm going to be the one to provide the ending you could not make up your mind about. One you never thought of . . . my very own Bible, for all my waiting worshippers . . .*

'Now here's what we're going to do, Jennifer. We're going to kill Emily first. And then Jeremy: he's expecting you, after all. After that we'll just take them out as they come, simply wander down the corridor, helping ourselves: the priest and Cox and Lloyd and the psychiatrist. And those other fucking lawyers. Might as well include Annabelle while we're about it. How many's that? Eight and the brat. That'll do.

'And don't think you'll be able to stop me. Oh, and don't think I'll let you commit suicide, either. I'll stop you ever doing that. You're going to suffer until you're a very old lady for taking Gerald away from me. That really was your crime, taking him from me. Mine was believing he was any different from all the other men. But then that was yours, too, wasn't it?

'Now just so you'll understand everything you're going to be able to move your head. Just your head, sideways, but not speak. See it! That's a kitchen knife, just like the one you used on Gerald. You carried it up here tonight and you didn't even know I'd made you, did you? Here we go then. I'm taking over now, Jennifer: taking over until I want you to realize what I've made you do . . . Emily's got to know before you do it, of course . . . Hate her mother for the last few seconds of her life . . .

'Emily, wake up Emily . . .'

THE END